AN I-TEAM NOVEL

STRIKING DISTANCE

"Packed with action and
raw sexual tension...fans
have come to expect from
this talented author."
—Cindy Ge███████████
Times best██████████████

PQV085738

PAMELA CLARE

NATIONAL BESTSELLING AUTHOR OF *BREAKING POINT*

ISBN 978-0-425-25735-7

5 0 7 9 9

continued . . .

"Will grip your senses . . . You'll love this series and enjoy an afternoon immersing yourself in a culture that is fascinating."
—*Romance Reviews Today*

UNLAWFUL CONTACT

"Powerful, sexy, and unforgettable, *Unlawful Contact* is the kind of story I love to read. Pamela Clare is a dazzling talent."
—Lori Foster, *New York Times* bestselling author

"A spellbinding, gut-wrenching page-turner with a gripping plot. This story is unique and creative with an imperfect hero you can't help getting sweaty palms over . . . Pamela Clare is a remarkable storyteller."
—*Fresh Fiction*

"This is an exciting, fast-paced romantic suspense thriller . . . Action-packed."
—*Midwest Book Review*

"A romantic suspense that has it all: gritty realism, edge-of-your-seat action, dynamic characterizations, surprising plot twists, and a scorching romance between two leads you won't soon forget."
—*BookLoons*

"A gripping and emotional story . . . An engaging tale that will have readers on the edge of their seats."
—*Romance Reviews Today*

"A thrilling, captivating suspense novel . . . It has great characters, a wonderful story line with different connecting plots, and a happy ending for a couple that has many obstacles that they must surmount together."
—*Romance Reader at Heart*

"Clare's impressive novel is rife with gripping suspense, secrets masterfully revealed, and characters in whom readers can become emotionally invested. The sexual tension between the protagonists is deliciously steamy, and the skillful plotting makes this thrilling book one readers won't be able to close until the final page."
—*RT Book Reviews* (4½ stars)

HARD EVIDENCE

"A page-turner, a pulse-pounding thriller . . . Whether she is writing her incredible historicals or these great contemporaries, Ms. Clare proves, once again, she is one of the best storytellers today . . . It is a thriller, it is a treasure, and it is tremendous."

—*Fresh Fiction*

"Superb romantic suspense . . . Fans will appreciate this strong thriller." —*Midwest Book Review*

"I cannot recommend this book highly enough. Pamela Clare's *Hard Evidence* is a powerful and, dare I say, flawless book, in my opinion. For those who love a good suspense or even just a good, satisfying read, it's a 'don't miss.'"

—*Romance Reader at Heart*

"This was a hard-to-put-down book with an exciting story line."

—*MyShelf.com*

EXTREME EXPOSURE

"Investigative reporter turned author Clare brings a gritty realism to this intense and intricate romantic thriller. *Extreme Exposure* is the launch book for a sizzling new suspense series that promises to generate lots of intrigue, action, and romance. An author to keep an eye on!" —*RT Book Reviews*

"A gem, *Extreme Exposure* has all the elements of great romance and is an entertaining summer read."

—*Romance Reviews Today* (Perfect 10)

"I really loved this book because it was so realistic. The characters were people I would love to know. Obviously, Ms. Clare knows this world and the nuances of investigative reporting. She communicates this in a terrific love story that grabs you and will not let you go. Believe me, I lost some sleep reading this book. I predict that Ms. Clare is an author to watch for the future and readers of romantic suspense are sure to love this excellent, well-written novel, one of the best I've read this year." —*The Romance Readers Connection*

Berkley Sensation books by Pamela Clare

The I-Team series

EXTREME EXPOSURE
HARD EVIDENCE
UNLAWFUL CONTACT
NAKED EDGE
BREAKING POINT
STRIKING DISTANCE

The MacKinnon's Rangers series

SURRENDER
UNTAMED
DEFIANT

STRIKING DISTANCE

PAMELA CLARE

BERKLEY SENSATION, NEW YORK

THE BERKLEY PUBLISHING GROUP
Published by the Penguin Group
Penguin Group (USA) LLC
375 Hudson Street, New York, New York 10014

USA • Canada • UK • Ireland • Australia • New Zealand • India • South Africa • China

penguin.com

A Penguin Random House Company

STRIKING DISTANCE

A Berkley Sensation Book / published by arrangement with the author

Berkley Sensation Books are published by The Berkley Publishing Group.
BERKLEY SENSATION® is a registered trademark of Penguin Group (USA) LLC.
The "B" design is a trademark of Penguin Group (USA) LLC.

For information, address: The Berkley Publishing Group,
a division of Penguin Group (USA) LLC,
375 Hudson Street, New York, New York 10014.

ISBN: 978-0-425-25735-7

PUBLISHING HISTORY
Berkley Sensation mass-market edition / November 2013

PRINTED IN THE UNITED STATES OF AMERICA

10 9 8 7 6 5 4 3 2 1

Cover photography by Claudio Marinesco.
Cover design by Rita Frangie.

This book is dedicated to M.O., whose service and courage are an inspiration.

ACKNOWLEDGMENTS

Special thanks to Officer Bryan Bartnes of the Loveland Police Department for his help in understanding explosives, the work of EOD teams, and the way authorities investigate bombings. Sitting at tables in coffee shops and discussing how to blow things up certainly does draw curious glances.

Deep personal gratitude to my sister, Michelle, and my son Benjamin, who once again went above and beyond, offering a sounding board and emotional support for me for thirteen long months as I wrote this story.

Thanks, too, to Arlene and Beatrice Ríos and Wilson Cruz for their help with the Puerto Rican Spanish in this story, and for helping with elements of *Boricua* culture. When they swear in their native tongue, they will forever think of me. ¡*Wepa!*

Additional thanks to my editor, Cindy Hwang, for her patience and understanding; to Natasha Kern, my agent, for more than a decade of support and friendship; and to Diane Grimaldi Whiting for walking me through the Dark Side, that is, the world of broadcast journalism.

Love and thanks to dear friends, old and new, for their amazing support and encouragement: Julie James, Libby Murphy, Julieanne Reeves, Norah Wilson, Jenn LeBlanc, Joyce Lamb, Kaleo and Kristine Griffith, Kristi Ross, Sue Zimmerman, Stephanie Desprez, Ruth Salisbury, Ronlyn Howe, Joyce Lamb, Bonnie Vanak, Jan Zimlich, Alice Duncan, Alice Gaines, and Mimi Riser.

And a heart full of thanks to the I-Team Facebook group, whose members gave me the best birthday present ever—weeks of home-delivered organic meals that kept me out of the kitchen so that I could write! I am so lucky to know you all.

As always, thanks to my sons Alec and Benjamin, whom I love beyond all things, and to my parents, Robert and Mary White, who see far less of me than they'd like to because I spend all my time with fictional people.

PROLOGUE

February 11, 2011
Near Parachinar, Pakistan
15 clicks west of the Afghan border
22,000 feet altitude

Socs Javier "Cobra" Corbray sat in the dimly lit belly of the modified C-130J "Super" Hercules, waiting with the other operators of Delta Platoon for the signal to start their oxygen. Banter had given way to silence as the men turned their minds to the night's mission. They'd trained for months for this one, the predeployment workup one of the most grueling Javier could remember in his twelve years as a SEAL. Endless fast-roping drills. Night jumps, rock climbing, and uphill PT runs in full night combat gear. Close-quarters combat practice. Mock raids on a scale model of the compound.

The stakes were high tonight—both for the U.S. and for Javier personally.

Then again, the stakes had been high on every deployment since 9/11.

Abu Nayef Al-Nassar, a Saudi national, had been high on Uncle Sam's list of most-wanted assholes for five long years. The leader of an al Qaeda splinter group operating out of northwestern Pakistan, he had masterminded simultaneous bombings in Hamburg, Paris, and Amsterdam that had killed hundreds, not to mention orchestrating attacks against U.S.

citizens in the Middle East and Shia Muslim villages around Pakistan. Al-Nassar was also the sugar daddy for a network of AQ groups, turning heroin profits into cash for weapons, travel, forged documents. If Delta Platoon managed to bring him in alive, along with his computers and cell phones, they would strike a major blow against AQ—and give the alphabet soup intel agencies a crack at uncovering his operation both abroad and in the homeland.

That was Javier's duty and goal as a SEAL. His goal as a man was simpler.

Vengeance.

"Hey, senior chief!" Rick Krasinski had been with the Teams for about a year now. He'd been nicknamed "Crazy K" for his love of rough water. There was no one more at home pounding surf than Krasinski. "This asshole—he's the one who kidnapped and killed the Baghdad Babe, isn't he?"

The Baghdad Babe.

U.S. troops had given her that nickname back in 2007 during the Surge, when they'd crowded around mess hall televisions to watch her nightly live broadcasts from Baghdad. She'd earned the respect of U.S. troops when she'd gone after the Pentagon for failing to provide adequate gear for service members. Then she'd turned around and exposed a group of soldiers for looting and running a shakedown racket on Iraqi civilians. She was tough, but fair, they'd agreed. And she was hot.

Tall with pale blond hair, big ice-blue eyes, and sweet curves, she'd fueled the fantasies of every man in uniform, though not Javier's. Oh, she'd been one sexy *mami*, but her Nordic good looks and on-camera reserve had been a bit too cold for a man with a Puerto Rican mother and a Scots-Cherokee father. He'd take a woman with the heat of the island in her blood over a Valkyrie like Laura Nilsson any day.

Or so he'd thought until the night he'd met her.

He'd been touring Dubai City on his way home after a long deployment. She'd walked into a hotel bar where he was having a steak and a beer and had sat at a table nearby. He'd recognized her instantly. When two big Russian men had wandered over and started hassling her, he had intervened. It had pissed her off—but it had also gotten her attention.

What had followed was a weekend of the most amazing sex

Javier had ever experienced. She might have seemed cool and reserved on the outside, but beneath her skin Laura Nilsson had been pure fire, igniting Javier's blood, sending him into a kind of sexual meltdown, the two of them risking not only their careers, but also a flogging and prison time to be together. Unmarried sex was illegal in Dubai, even for foreigners.

If he closed his eyes, he could still taste her, still feel the softness of her skin, still hear the breathy sound of her cries as she came. She'd been a fantasy come true, more woman than Javier had ever hoped to hold in his arms. He was nothing more than a kid from the South Bronx who'd enlisted in the navy to give some meaning to his life, a simple man who drank beer and played guitar when he wasn't deployed. She'd been classy, refined, and sexy, all silk and sophistication.

She had blown his mind.

The only thing that had kept Javier from calling her and trying to see her again was their agreement that the weekend came with no strings. Laura had told him flat out that she wasn't interested in marriage or motherhood. That had been fine with Javier. He already had one divorce under his belt—a hazard of being a frogman—and didn't want another. Still, he'd flown back to the U.S. hoping they could get together again.

Two months later, she'd been gone.

Her last broadcast had come from a women's safe house in Islamabad where she'd been reporting on the ongoing epidemic of fatal burnings in Pakistan—hundreds of young women burned alive every year by husbands and in-laws, their excruciating deaths blamed on "stove accidents" and never investigated. One moment she'd been interviewing a young burn victim, and the next the room around her had exploded with AK fire. Her security detail, her cameraman, and the safe house director had all been killed. She'd been dragged fighting and screaming from the building while the abandoned camera continued to broadcast from its tripod.

That had been the summer of 2009.

Javier had been at home in Coronado Beach when it happened. He'd seen the live broadcast, had found himself on his feet, helpless and thousands of miles away. Her screams had ripped him apart. They haunted him still. When Al-Nassar's group had claimed responsibility for the attack and bragged that they'd decapitated her, there hadn't been a U.S. serviceman anywhere in the world who hadn't wanted to send Al-Nassar straight to hell—and that included Javier.

Now Delta Platoon was going to hit that target.

Javier had pushed hard to get his guns into this fight, had done everything he could to make sure Delta Platoon got tasked with this job. To this day, no one knew about his weekend with Laura, and he couldn't tell them or they would question his ability to handle this operation. Did he want to bring Al-Nassar down? Hell, yeah, he did. For his country *and* for Laura. And that made him the *right* man for the job as far as he was concerned.

Canto hijo e la gran puta.

Dirty son of a whore.

"Yeah, he killed her." Javier met Krasinski's gaze. "But she had a name, and it wasn't Baghdad Babe. It was Laura Nilsson. Show her some respect, man."

She'd been one hell of a journalist, an incredible lover, a smart and beautiful woman. She deserved that much.

Krasinski's expression was hidden by shadows and by black-and-green face camouflage, but there was regret in his voice. "You got it, senior chief."

A voice came over the speaker. "Forty-five minutes till drop."

"Masks on!" Boss, known to the rest of the world as Lt. Morgan O'Connell, shouted out the order, making the motion with his hand.

JG—Lt. Junior Grade Ben Alexander—repeated it, as did Javier, before fastening his O_2 mask in place.

The men breathed normally, inhaling one hundred percent oxygen to eliminate the nitrogen from their bloodstreams so that no one would die from the dramatic increase in atmospheric pressure on the way down. This was a HAHO jump—high altitude, high opening. The mountains were too full of insurgents for them to risk the noise of parachutes opening close to the ground.

As the minutes ticked by, Javier ran through the details of the mission in his mind. Al-Nassar knew how to hole up—that much was for damned sure. His lair was built on a plateau with a fifty-foot cliff at its back, elevation giving him a clear one-eighty view of the landscape below. Caves at the base of the cliff provided Al-Nassar a handy place to stash weapons, ammo, explosives, heroin—and men. They also gave him a place to hide should he see anyone headed his way.

That was why Delta Platoon wasn't going to drive up and ring the doorbell.

They were being dropped over a mountain valley west of Parachinar about 3.5 clicks from Al-Nassar's hideout. They would hike their way from the DZ to the cliffs. There, the Boss's squad would divide into two elements. He, Howe, Force, and Murphy, the platoon sniper, would remain atop the cliffs with suppressed Mk12s, an FN M249 Para for suppressive fire, and a M72A2 LAW grenade launcher to watch the men's six, while the rest of the platoon would fast-rope down to the compound. JG would take the caves with LeBlanc, Johnson, and Grimshaw, setting charges to demolish any ordnance they found, while Javier infiltrated the compound with his squad—Krasinski, Ross, Zimmerman, Salisbury, Wilson, Reeves, Desprez. When Al-Nassar was in custody and the compound was secure, three modified CH-47D Chinook helos would swoop in for extract. As they lifted off, JG would blow the caves to hell.

Of course, they weren't being sent up against a high-value target like this without backup firepower and air support. They'd be in touch with their tactical operations center, or TOC, throughout the night. A drone with thermal/infrared capability would patrol the sky above the job site, giving them a bird's-eye view of the action. If things got messy, two Marine Special Operations Teams—MSOTs—would arrive in Black Hawks to make them messier.

Provided nothing went wrong, it would be a piece of cake.

Forty minutes later, a voice came over the speaker. "Two minutes to drop!"

The men switched from the prebreathers to their bottled O$_2$, careful not to inhale in the transition. Then both squads got to their feet, boots thudding dully against the steel plating, each of them carrying more than a hundred pounds of gear on his back. With an efficiency born of constant training, each checked his own gear and that of the man in front of him. They'd already passed a jumpmaster inspection, but in their line of work there was no such thing as being too prepared, too careful.

"Ramp!"

The ramp and door began to open, and icy, thin air rushed in. The two sticks of SEALs moved toward the yawning exit, waiting for the signal to jump. Javier touched a gloved hand to the chest pocket that held the photograph of his brother Yadiel that he carried with him on every mission.

The light flashed green.

The men moved together, tumbling almost as one into the slipstream, Javier leading his squad out of the Hercules and into the black night.

SHE KNELT ON the carpet facing Mecca, going through the motions of the first Rak'ah, doing her best to say each word of the Sura Al-Fatiha correctly so that no one would find fault with her.

Inshallah. God willing.

She kept her voice quiet, barely a whisper. This morning while praying *Fajr*, she had failed to do so, and Zainab had claimed that Abu Nayef's guests, who were not family—not *mahram*—had heard her. Zainab had struck her, making her lip bleed.

But then Zainab always struck her.

"You will never learn, Hanan!" Zainab had shouted in her face. "You are as stupid as you are ugly!"

"I am sorry, Umm Faisal." She never dared to call Zainab or any of the other women by their given names, for they would deem it disrespectful and beat her. "You must help me to do better, sister."

She'd called Abu Nayef's wives her sisters, but only Angeza, who'd been given to Abu Nayef by her Pashtun father in payment of a debt when she was only fourteen, had ever treated her with kindness. Angeza had sneaked her food, helped her study the Suras, even protected her from Zainab and Abu Nayef. Still, she was the least of all the women here, and that was why she prayed at the back of the room, behind all of the other women and girls. And yet Zainab still seemed to see every mistake she made.

The women bowed, and she bowed with them, standing up straight once more before performing *Sujood*, prostrating herself, her nose, hands, knees, and feet touching the carpet, her belly pressed against her thighs as was proper for a woman, the odors of sweat and dust rank in her nostrils. She rose, caught a glimpse of the mirror across the room, but could not see her own reflection. She prostrated herself again, the prayers and motions flowing together in a rhythm that was familiar, even comforting, as they finished the first Rak'ah and moved without pause into the second.

But as they began the third Rak'ah and prayed at last in silence, her heart began to pound. It was time for her nightly rebellion. She clenched her hands to hide their trembling, afraid that Zainab, Nibaal, Safiya, or one of the other women would notice her nervousness and guess what she was doing. If they knew what she was thinking, they would surely denounce her to Abu Nayef.

Then he would do what he'd always promised to do and cut off her head.

Pulse racing, she reached secretly for her Swedish and English, words she didn't dare to speak aloud burning in her mind like a fever.

Mitt namn är . . .
My name is . . .
My name is Laura Nilsson.

SHE LAY IN the dark in the corner of the small back room that was hers, her bed an old blanket, her head pillowed on her neatly folded burka. Her mind ached for sleep, but sleep wouldn't come, chased off by the knot of dread in her stomach. It was the same dread she felt every night until she was certain everyone was in bed asleep.

In the next room, Safiya's baby girl cried.

She would have offered to help. She *wanted* to help. Safiya was only twenty-four and already had six children. But Safiya wouldn't let her near the baby. No one would. They all believed her unfit.

A creaking door. A man's deep voice. Footsteps.

She held her breath, listening until the footsteps faded away.

Would he come tonight?

She'd seen him take Nibaal to his room. Surely, Nibaal would be enough for him and he would leave her alone.

Inshallah.

She squeezed her eyes shut, hoping with everything inside her that he would stay away. Angeza had once told her that Zainab struck her only because Abu Nayef came to her bed so often. But she would gladly have traded places with Zainab. If only she could! She cared nothing at all for Abu Nayef. In truth, she hated him.

She hated the feel of his old man's hands on her. She hated the sour odor of his skin, his breath, the coarseness of his beard. He was always rough with her, even when she lay still and didn't fight.

Stay away. Stay away. Stay away.

She drifted off, only to jerk awake at the sound of a man's voice.

His door opened, closed, soft footfalls sounding in the hallway as Nibaal made her way back to the room she shared with her four children.

She exhaled, certain she'd been spared for the night, her body relaxing, sleep stealing over her at last.

Screams.

She sat bolt upright on a rush of adrenaline and grabbed her burka, drawing it over her head just as the door to her room crashed open.

A dark shape filled the doorway.

A man with a weapon.

He aimed it at her, a red dot dancing over her chest.

Too terrified even to scream, she shrank back against the wall, her heart hammering, her mouth dry, fear making her mind go blank.

A light blinded her.

He aimed his weapon at the corners as if he expected someone to be hiding in the room, then shouted in heavily accented Arabic. "Come with me!"

She *wanted* to do as he'd asked. She didn't want to be shot and killed. But fear kept her grounded to the spot, her breath coming in terrified pants.

"Clear! All clear! Got another female here, senior chief."

He crossed the room in two big strides. "Bring her to the courtyard. Roger that."

The sound of his American English made her breath catch.

"Come." The man spoke more softly this time, motioning for her to get to her feet and come with him.

As if in a dream, she rose, her heart beating erratically in her chest, his uniform and his American accent awakening something nameless and terrifying inside her.

He nudged her ahead of him, his weapon still raised. "Go!"

Her legs seemed to be made of water as she walked down the stairs, across the main room, and out into the frigid night, where the other women stood in their veils huddled together with their children, all of them crying, some praying aloud.

"Hanan!" One of them reached for her, called to her in Arabic. *Zainab.* "Hanan, sister, come here to us!"

She felt a rush of warmth to hear Zainab call her "sister," something comforting in Zainab's concern for her. The older woman's fingers dug into her arms as she drew her roughly into the cluster of women, pushing her to the center, where other hands reached out, grabbed her, held her.

And then she saw.

There, in the center of the courtyard, lay Abu Nayef.

All but naked, he lay facedown in the dirt, his wrists bound together behind his back, a tall uniformed man standing guard over him.

A dead man lay on his side not far from Abu Nayef, his eyes open, part of his head missing, a spray of blood and brains on the wall behind him.

Her stomach seemed to fall to the ground, vague memories of another day, images of blood and dead men flashing through her mind. She looked away and swallowed hard, fighting to keep down her supper.

"They are going to kill us all!" Nibaal sobbed.

"Is this true?" Angeza whispered in frightened Pashtun.

She shook her head, whispered back. "They won't hurt us."

She couldn't say why she was so sure about this, but she was.

Armed men in heavy uniforms seemed to be everywhere— on the rooftop, in the courtyard, inside the house. Their faces were covered in black paint, making them look like shadows in the darkness. They seemed to be searching for something.

"Where are your tears, Hanan?" Zainab pinched her. "Do you see what has become of our husband? Do you see what these Americans have done to him?"

Americans.

The nameless terror inside her grew stronger.

But she couldn't bring herself to weep, not for Abu Nayef. She loathed him. Instead, she listened to every word the men in uniform said to one another.

"Hey, JG, we've got a dozen terrified women and kids here. Are they going to be safe when you blow those caves?" asked the tall one standing over Abu Nayef, speaking into a slender mic near his painted lips. "Roger that."

"Hey, senior chief, we got nine hard drives, four cell phones, a handful of flash drives, and a box full of CDs, along with some files."

"Bag 'em," the tall one said. "Boss, we're good to begin our exfil. Yo, boys, it's time to go!"

Americans.

Chills shivered up her spine.

"What is that? Do you hear that?" Zainab looked up.

It was the thrum and whir of distant helicopters.

She looked up through the mesh of her burka at the starless sky, saw nothing, the night having taken on an air of unreality.

One of the women—Safiya—started to sob, clutching the crying baby to her chest. "They're taking him away! What will become of us?"

Out of the dark sky appeared three helicopters, black against the black night, each with one rotor in back, another in front. One lowered itself to perch against the cliffs above, men in black uniforms rising like ghosts from the ground and climbing aboard, weapons in their hands. Another landed at the base of the cliffs. Still another landed inside the compound, its giant rotors blowing dust everywhere.

The house had been surrounded, and they hadn't even known it.

One of the men began shouting to the women in bad Arabic, telling them to take shelter inside the house for their own protection, warning them that the caves in the cliffs had been set with explosives and were going to blow up.

She found herself caught up in a panicked tide of blue and

black as women clad in burkas and abayas pushed her toward the house, Zainab's fingers holding fast to her arm, digging deep into her flesh. She looked over her shoulder to see the tall one standing guard while two of his men lifted Abu Nayef by his elbows and dragged him toward the waiting helicopter and up its rear ramp.

They were leaving.

The Americans were leaving.

There was a buzzing in her brain, her pulse pounding so hard it all but drowned out the sound of the helicopters, that nameless fear gathering momentum, rushing against her like a wave, the terror in her mind coalescing into a single, heartstopping thought.

Ana amrekiah.

I'm an American, too.

"Ana amrekiah." She didn't realize she'd stopped walking or spoken aloud until Zainab jerked her arm.

"Shut your mouth, or I will cut out your tongue!"

Strong hands shoved her toward the house, making her stumble. She looked back, saw the tall man watching them, and she realized he was waiting to board the helicopter until the others were safely back inside. Then he, too, would disappear up that ramp.

As the women reached the door, he took two steps back, then turned away from them, speaking words she couldn't hear into his microphone.

The Americans were leaving—without her.

Dizzy with terror, she jerked away from the other women. "Wait! I'm an American, too!"

But her words were blown away by the roar of the helicopter's rotors.

WAIT! I'M AN American, too!

Javier caught the words over the drone of the helos, but it took them a moment to register. Had that come from beneath one of the burkas?

"Senior chief, watch out! You got one running up behind you!" Ross ran down the ramp, dropped to one knee, aimed his weapon.

Javier pivoted, weapon ready, and saw the tallest of the women running toward him, the red dot from Ross's laser sight dancing on her covered forehead.

"Hold your fire!" Javier aimed his M4 at her. "Stop! Get down!"

But she had already fallen to her knees, turquoise blue cloth billowing around her, her breath coming in terrified sobs. She cried out again, her accent American. "H-help me! I'm . . . I'm an American, too!"

He started toward her, just as one of the other women broke out of the group, this one holding a knife in her hand. She shouted something in Arabic and ran not toward Javier, but toward the woman on the ground, her intent clear.

Without hesitation, Javier raised his M4 and dropped her with a double tap, her knife falling to the dirt.

The other women, now clustered together in the doorway, screamed.

JG's voice sounded in his ear. "Senior chief, what the hell's going on?"

"I think we've got a hostage." He strode quickly to the terrified woman, grabbed a fistful of blue burka, and ripped it aside, exposing her completely.

For a moment all he could do was stare, his gaze taking in the tears and bruises on her cheeks, her swollen lip and thin face, her threadbare nightgown, the shock and terror in her eyes.

Laura!

And then his training kicked in. "This is now an AMCIT recovery. I say again: This is now an AMCIT recovery. Do you copy?"

Ross and Zimmerman ran down the helo's ramp and took up defensive positions, ready to take out anyone who threatened Javier or Laura.

"We hear you lima charlie, senior chief," the Boss answered from the third helo several hundred feet in the air above them. "Get her, and let's go. We've got enemy QRF pushing our position from the east. You need to get airborne *now*!"

The second Chinook was already nosing its way downwind. Slow and cumbersome at liftoff, the helos made great targets for the Soviet-era RPGs that AQ combatants loved to fire at them. If the pilots couldn't get them in the air and up to speed before the enemy got within firing range . . .

"Roger that." Knowing the others were covering for him, Javier clipped his M4 into his tactical sling, lifted Laura into his arms, and turned toward the last helo, covering the ground in long, fast strides. Without a glance back, he ran up the ramp and settled Laura into his jump seat, Ross and Zimmerman pounding up the ramp behind him.

"All boots on board!" Zimmerman shouted.

"Ramp!"

"Ramp!" The shout was repeated as the cargo ramp was raised.

The helo rotors accelerated, seconds ticking by like hours as the big bird slowly left the ground, heading into the wind, the pilot fighting for translational lift. Javier listened as the pilot relayed their altitude, enemy QRF drawing ever closer.

A shell exploded not far from the helo's tail, its blast wave making the helo lurch and drawing a gasp from Laura. Javier put a gloved hand on her shoulder, hoping to reassure her. "Sit tight."

Too damned close.

The seconds ticked by, punctuated by two more explosions, each of them more distant than the last as the helo gained speed. Then came the deep rumble as JG detonated the explosives in the caves.

"We did it, senior chief!" Krasinski pointed at Javier. "Cobra strikes again!"

"We're not done with the mission till we get back to home plate, Krasinski." Heart beating hard, Javier leaned back against the webbing that lined the helo, grabbed it for balance, catching his breath, ratcheting down on the adrenaline, taking stock of his men, of the situation. Reeves had caught a round in the shoulder. Wilson, the platoon medic, had already treated it. Reeves would need surgery and PT, but he'd be fine. Apart from a few bruises and scrapes, no one else was wounded. Al-Nassar was battered but alive, his laptops, cell phones, disks, and drives bagged and tagged.

Delta Platoon had done what they'd been tasked to do on this mission—and they'd come away with something extra.

He let his gaze drop to Laura, felt a tangled rush of relief and rage. Clearly in shock, she sat there shivering in a white cotton nightgown that left little to the imagination, her face downcast, her long hair tangled. She was rail thin and pale, as if she had recently been ill or hadn't eaten a good meal in months. There were fresh bruises on her face and her arms, proof that the other women had tried to restrain her.

All this time—eighteen goddamned months—she'd been here *alive*.

¡Carajo!

Al-Nassar's group had claimed they'd executed her. They'd lied. Why?

He glanced at Al-Nassar, whose gaze was fixed on her, hatred mingling with something predatory in his eyes.

Lust.

The asshole had wanted her, had used her, had hurt her.

¡Mamabicho!

Cocksucker.

Like some trapped wild thing, Laura looked around at the helo full of men, her vulnerability tearing at Javier. He drew a blanket out of the webbing and wrapped it around her shoulders.

She hugged the blanket tightly around herself and looked up at him as if she weren't quite certain he was real. "Th-thank you."

"You're welcome." He'd never told her he was a SEAL, and he was certain she didn't recognize him beneath the uniform and camo face paint.

One by one, Javier's men acknowledged her with polite nods.

"Ma'am."

"We're happy to have you on board, ma'am."

"Welcome back, Ms. Nilsson."

Then Al-Nassar began to speak, muttering something to her. Her pale face went a shade whiter, fear in her wide eyes.

And something inside Javier snapped.

He smashed his fist into the bastard's face—once, twice—the blow and the pain in his knuckles doing nothing to satisfy the burning anger inside him. Realizing what he'd done, he stepped back, fists clenched as he fought to rein himself in. "Wilson, gag and blindfold this motherfucker before I kill him."

"You got it, senior chief." Wilson grabbed a wad of gauze

from his pack and shoved it into Al-Nassar's mouth, tying it in place with more gauze.

Al-Nassar began to struggle, trying to pull his head away, blood trickling from his nose and a cut on his cheek.

Zimmerman stood and restrained him none too gently while Wilson tied a tourniquet over the bastard's eyes. "You need to shut the fuck up and leave her alone, asshole. Got that? Yeah, I know you understood me. Went to Oxford, didn't you? Paid the Brits back for your first-class education by trying to blow them up."

Shaking with unspent anger, Javier looked down at Laura again. She probably thought they'd come to rescue her, when the truth was they hadn't even known she was there. If she hadn't shouted out for him, if she hadn't run . . .

Christ!

He didn't want to think about that.

What counted was that she *had* run. She'd found the strength and the guts to break free, to shout out, to let them know she was there.

And now they were taking her home.

CHAPTER 1

February 14, 2013
Manhattan, New York

SANDWICHED BETWEEN THE two deputy U.S. Marshals—
or DUSMs—who'd been assigned to escort her, Laura Nilsson
pushed her way through the throng of reporters gathered outside the federal courthouse in Lower Manhattan, clutching
her gray double-breasted wool coat tightly around her, a chill
inside her that had nothing to do with the icy wind. Reporters
pressed up against the barricades, called out questions, their
mics shoved in her face, cameras clicking around her.

"How will it feel to face Al-Nassar in a court of law?"

"Why did you choose to testify? Are you hoping to encour-
age other victims of sexual violence to speak out?"

"What message do you hope to give the jury today?"

Laura stopped at the top of the stairs, turned to face the
reporters, and willed herself to smile, refusing to let the cameras see inside her.

You can do this.

Pausing to gather her scattered thoughts, she spoke the
words she'd rehearsed. "Thank you all for your support.
Today marks for me the final chapter of an ordeal that began
three and a half years ago. I know that justice will be served
not only on my behalf, but also on behalf of the hundreds of

others around the world who have suffered as a result of Al-Nassar's terrible actions."

Having given them a quote to take back to their editors, she turned to enter the courthouse. But she hadn't taken a single step when another question rang out.

"What is your response to the allegations from Derek Tower of Tower Global Security that negligence on your part led to your abduction and the deaths of your cameraman, your security detail, and the safe house director?"

Her step faltered.

She fought back a rush of rage, turned toward the voice, and met the reporter's gaze, her lips twisting into her best imitation of a smile. "Slow news day?"

The insult made the other reporters snicker.

Laura looked into the cameras once more, fighting to maintain her façade of calm. "The State Department's investigation into my abduction was closed even before I was found alive. It was a random, tragic event perpetrated by a depraved terrorist. No one regrets what happened that day more than I do."

"Not even the families of the men who died trying to protect you?"

She ignored the taunt, turned her back on the crowd, and entered the courthouse, disregarding the shouted questions that chased after her. The trial was closed to cameras and all but a handful of reporters, who'd been selected at random from a pool of news organizations, the solemn quiet inside the lobby a stark contrast to the chaos outside.

But Tower's attack, so unexpected, had Laura's heart thrumming. The bastard didn't know when to quit. He'd been harassing her for weeks, insisting that it was *her* fault she'd been abducted. What did he think he was doing feeding those allegations to a reporter, making them public? Did he really think that dragging her down could somehow make his company look better?

Forget him. It's not important.

She didn't have time to think about that now. Not now. Not today.

A uniformed DUSM motioned her forward. "Put your purse in the plastic bin. Empty your pockets of keys, change, or other metal objects, and pass through the metal detector."

She moved quickly through the security checkpoint, relieved to find Marie Santelle, one of the assistants with the U.S. Attorney's Office, waiting for her. Dressed in a tailored black pantsuit, her dark hair done up in a sleek bun, Marie smiled, took Laura's hand, and gave it a reassuring squeeze. "How are you holding up?"

"I'm fine." What else could she say? That she hadn't slept last night? That her stomach was tied in knots? That she felt terrified?

Today, two years and three days after the SEALs rescued her from a living hell, she would see Al-Nassar again. She would face him in a courtroom, look him in the eyes, and denounce him to the world.

It was the day she'd been waiting for. It was the day she'd been dreading.

It was nearing the end of the second week of his trial, and his face had been all over the news, together with hers. It made no sense to Laura. The crimes he'd committed against her were the least of his offenses, nothing but a footnote in a criminal history that included terrorism and mass murder. And yet the press was obsessed with what he had done to *her*. Reporters had staked her out, called her at work, asked her questions that went beyond the public's right to know, hoping to titillate their audiences with her worst memories, the ordeal she'd been fighting to put behind her fodder for public discussion on every channel, in every newspaper, on talk radio.

Allt kommer att bli bättre med tiden.

Everything will get better with time.

Her grandmother's reassuring words came back to her.

Yes, it would all get better with time. It was already better.

Laura was no longer the terrorized, shattered woman the SEALs had rescued, a woman who barely remembered her own name. A year and a half of living with her mother and grandmother in Stockholm, together with intensive daily therapy, had helped her begin to heal. She might not feel like her old self, but she was slowly defining her *new* self. Or so her therapist had said when she'd burst into tears of frustration one afternoon, angry at herself for still being so pathetically weak, so fearful, so broken.

Her time as a captive made up only eighteen months out of

thirty-two *years* of her life, and yet it seemed to define her. There were still days when the pain inside her was so strong she feared that if she started to cry, she would never be able to stop.

Still, she had so many reasons to be grateful.

She'd regained all the weight she'd lost and was no longer anemic. She was sleeping at night—most of the time. She was back in the States and had a nice loft in lower downtown Denver, or LoDo as locals called it. She had a seat on the I-Team—the award-winning Investigative Team at the *Denver Independent* newspaper. She'd even been on a few dates, though nothing had come of them.

It was a new beginning even if it wasn't the life she'd planned for herself. And yet no matter how good her life was now, she didn't feel whole.

One precious, important piece was still missing.

"Sorry about the mob outside." Marie gave her hand another squeeze, then turned with the two deputies toward the elevators.

The media were the least of Laura's worries today. "They're just doing their job."

She waited in silence with the others for the elevator car to arrive. When the doors closed, Marie spoke again.

"I'm taking you to a private witness room where you'll stay until it's time for you to testify. We'll view the live footage of your abduction first. You're still certain you don't want to see that?"

Laura nodded. "I'm certain."

She didn't want to watch her friends die all over again or hear her own screams. Besides, she didn't need to see it. That moment lived in her nightmares.

"I understand." Marie's brown eyes held no judgment, only sympathy. "When that's done, we'll bring you in."

As Marie went over Laura's testimony, Laura began to feel queasy. By the time they'd reached the private witness room, she felt the first trill of panic.

Marie glanced down at her watch. "Is there anything you need—coffee, water?"

There was just one thing. "Mr. Black has assured me that a certain topic will not be mentioned or discussed in the courtroom."

There was one matter Laura refused to discuss, even in a court of law, a matter she intended to keep secret, private.

"Mr. Black and the team are aware of your concerns, and I want to assure you that every step has been taken to ensure your privacy in that regard. We can't control the defendant, of course. If he chooses to mention it . . ."

Laura nodded, aware of that risk. "Thank you."

Marie took both her hands. "You hang in there. This will be over soon. Thanks in part to you, that bastard is going to spend the rest of his life in prison."

Although the U.S. attorney had an unshakable case against Al-Nassar, Laura had volunteered to testify, certain that confronting Al-Nassar would help her put the past behind her and take the next step in healing. She would see him for what he truly was—a prisoner, a despicable old man, weak and alone. He would no longer loom in her mind as the all-powerful warlord who had controlled her body, her mind, her life. But now that she was here, now that the day had come, she found herself wondering whether she'd made a terrible mistake.

"We'll be right outside the door," one of the deputy U.S. Marshals assured her.

Laura nodded, her mouth suddenly dry.

And then she was alone.

JAVIER CORBRAY SAT in baggage claim at Denver International Airport, his back to the wall, his duffel and guitar case beside him, a cup of coffee from the coffee Automat in his hand. He took a sip, grimaced. ¡Carajo! This shit was worse than the swill they served on submarines. How was that even possible?

He took another swallow, his gaze moving back and forth along the crowded terminal, some part of him on edge. Then again, he was always on edge these days.

It had been five months since he'd decided to let that Pashtun shepherd and his sons live, five months of living with the consequences of that one decision. Warned by the shepherd, the Taliban had ambushed Delta Platoon outside Ghazni with heavy casualties. Javier had taken four rounds. Surgeons had saved his leg, patched up his shoulder, liver, and lung, giving him fourteen units of blood to keep him alive.

Still, he'd gotten off easy. In all, eighteen men had died that day.

Javier had been up and around much faster than they'd expected, pushing himself through the pain of rehab, determined to help his body heal to the best of its ability, regain his strength, and get back with the teams. He'd moved from rehab to PT, passed the post-deployment psych test, and thought he was about to start an active-duty workup. Instead, one of the shrinks had accused him of "playing to the test," whatever the hell that meant, and had benched him.

Post-combat trauma.

It was bureaucratic bullshit. How could he *pass* the test and still get flagged? The screening was useless anyway. They'd borrowed it from a psych test created for the army. But he wasn't some green kid back from his first tour of duty, a young soldier fresh out of boot camp who'd seen his first dead body. Javier had been deploying as a special operator for fourteen years now. He knew the realities of combat, knew his limits, knew what he could handle. He didn't need to talk about his feelings. He sure as hell didn't need some shrink's shoulder to cry on.

Fortunately, Boss had persuaded Naval Special Warfare Command to back Javier, and a compromise had been reached. Javier's medical leave had been extended for another two months, at which time he'd take the psych screening again. If he passed, he passed. He'd move on to an active-duty workup and be back with the teams by summer. If he didn't pass . . .

That won't happen, chacho.

A voice coming from the flat-screen TV overhead caught his ear.

"The trial of accused al Qaeda terrorist Abu Nayef Al-Nassar continued this morning when journalist Laura Nilsson took the stand."

Javier looked up as the broadcast cut away to footage of Laura being waylaid by media outside the federal court building. Flanked by two officers from the U.S. Marshal Service, she made her way up the steps, then turned and smiled.

Javier felt a tug in his chest. He knew testifying wouldn't

be easy for her—sitting in a courtroom with Al-Nassar, reliving the horror he'd put her through—but Javier respected the hell out of her for doing it.

"Today marks for me the final chapter of an ordeal that began three and a half years ago," she said into the microphones. "I know that justice will be served not only on my behalf, but also on behalf of the hundreds of others around the world who have suffered as a result of Al-Nassar's terrible actions."

Gone was the trembling, terrified woman he'd carried on board the Chinook. In her place stood the Laura he'd met in Dubai—confident, polished, beautiful.

Nothing he'd done in his career as a special operator had felt more rewarding than getting her out of that hellhole. Sure, he'd pulled his team out of some pretty tight scrapes, played medic to wounded men, taken out a bad guy or two, earned his share of medals. But the night he'd found her was the only time he'd directly saved the life of an American civilian. The fact that it had been Laura, that she'd been *alive*, had only made it sweeter. He'd gone to bed that night feeling like a hero.

He'd followed the news articles about her as well as he could between back-to-back deployments, and he knew what she'd endured. Repeated rape. Beatings. Daily threats of decapitation. Reading the news stories and watching her interview with Diane Sawyer had made him wish he'd kicked the shit out of Al-Nassar when he'd had the chance, maybe shot the fucker in the balls.

It had also made Javier want to reach out to her, to help her however he could, to let her know that he was there, that he cared. But he'd been downrange in Afghanistan for most of the past two years, and when he'd been home, he'd spent those few precious weeks with his family and his Mamá Andreína, who was ninety-two and had been in and out of the hospital. He hadn't been sure Laura would want to see him or whether she even remembered their time in Dubai City.

Watching her now, he had to give her a world of credit. To go through what she'd gone through and to come out of it in one piece took strength.

"¡Oye, cabrón!" Hey, motherfucker!

Javier turned toward the familiar voice to find Nathaniel

West striding toward him. *"¿Que pasa, cabrón?"* What's up, motherfucker?

The last time he'd seen Nate—whose MSOT, or Marine Special Operations Team, had worked alongside Delta Platoon in Afghanistan—the man had been clinging to life in the burn ward at the Brooke Army Medical Center in San Antonio, the right side of his face and body a mess of second- and third-degree burns from an IED blast. Scars now covered Nate's nose, right cheek, and jaw, disappearing down his neck and beneath his winter coat, but he was alive. More than that, he seemed . . . *happy.*

Javier held out his hand, the lump in his throat making it hard to speak. "Damn, brother, you look good!"

Nate grinned. "It's good to see you, too, man."

They clasped hands—one hand dark, the other scarred—and drew together, slapping each other hard on the back while they embraced.

Nate was the reason Javier had come. Javier had wanted to see for himself that his brother in arms had recovered and was doing as well as his e-mails said he was. He'd gotten married this past summer to some sweet *mami,* but Javier had been downrange and had missed the wedding. He hoped to make up for that now.

They drew apart, both of them grinning, neither able to speak just yet.

Nate broke the silence. "I heard you got hit pretty bad."

"Yeah." There was no denying it. "I pulled through."

Not all of his men had been as lucky.

"Thank God for that." Nate studied him for a moment, a frown on his face, then gave a nod. "How long can you stay?"

Javier had spent three weeks of his two extra months of leave with his family, and had a little over four weeks left. "Trying to get rid of me already?"

Nate laughed, pointed at Javier's guitar case. "If you play that thing, Megan might just throw you out."

"Hey, I've gotten better, man." But Nate's ribbing didn't bother him.

The smile on his buddy's face lifted a weight from Javier's shoulders that he'd carried for three long years. He'd been the first to reach the burning wreck of the transport truck, had pulled Nate out of the wreckage, held his uninjured hand, waiting with him for what seemed an eternity for evac. It had crushed Javier to see him in such agony, his body charred and shaking, his eyes wild with pain and shock.

Nate West had been a natural leader, one hell of a warrior, and a true friend. Now he was Javier's hero.

"Let's load your shit in the truck and get you up to the ranch." Nate reached for Javier's duffel, but something on the television caught his eye.

Javier followed his gaze.

The recycled news footage of Laura again.

"I wish the media would leave her the hell alone," Nate grumbled, slinging the duffel over his shoulder. "She's been through enough."

"You got that right." Javier wanted to say more but couldn't.

No one who wasn't part of that op would ever know that Javier had been the one to find and recover her. OPSEC—operational security—was just a part of his job. He didn't talk about his missions with anyone who hadn't also been a part of them.

"She works at the *Denver Independent* with Megan's sister-in-law, Sophie. We're having a barbecue this weekend to introduce you to some of our friends, and we've invited her. She mostly keeps to herself, but we're hoping she'll show."

Laura Nilsson? At Nate's ranch?

¡Anda pal carajo! Holy shit!

Javier stared after Nate for a moment, then grabbed his guitar and, ignoring the ache in his thigh, followed him out into the chilly morning.

HANDS CLASPED IN her lap to stop them from shaking, Laura did her best to hold herself together. No matter that the queasiness in her stomach had become a sharp ache or that she'd dissolved into tears twice or that she couldn't stop shaking. She'd come here to bear witness to Al-Nassar's crimes against her, to stand up to his cruelty, to make certain that he went to prison for the rest of his life.

She'd made it through two hours of grueling testimony so far, her secret still intact, her composure less so. She'd tried to prepare herself emotionally to see Al-Nassar's face again, to feel his gaze on her, to hear his voice. But what she hadn't prepared for—what she hadn't even *known* to prepare for—was her *body's* response. She could almost feel his hands on her, smell his breath, hear his heavy breathing as he used her, violated her, hurt her. It left her feeling sick.

"When the special operator opened the door to your room and began speaking American English, you did not reveal yourself to him and tell him you were a prisoner. Instead, you remained covered with the burka and kept silent. Why is that?"

Laura had struggled to understand this herself. How could she explain to anyone who hadn't endured captivity what it was like to lose one's identity?

"When I recognized that the language they were speaking was American English, I felt terrified. I didn't know why I was afraid. But I think now that hearing their words made me aware again that I was a captive. It was like waking up to discover that what you thought was only a bad dream was actually real. It took time for me to understand what was happening and find the words to speak out."

"So after months of wanting desperately to escape, you waited till the last possible second to reveal yourself?"

Marie had warned her the defense might take the position that Laura had actually wanted to stay in the compound and had told Laura not to let it rattle her. It was nothing more than a bid to undermine the jury's sympathy for her.

"I didn't *wait*. It just took time for me to comprehend what was happening."

"I see." The defense attorney shrugged. "Is it possible that you delayed revealing yourself for so long because you took your marriage to the defendant seriously and wanted to remain with—what did you call his other wives?—your 'sisters'?"

U.S. Attorney Robert Black stood as if to object, but Laura cut him off.

"No! Absolutely not. I was never that man's *wife*! He kidnapped me, raped me, brutalized me. You want to know why I didn't run straight to the SEALs and beg them to rescue me? I'd been living in terror for so long that I barely knew my own name!"

The courtroom was silent.

Throat tight, tears pricking her eyes, Laura fought to rein in her emotion.

The defense attorney seemed to study her for a moment, what might have been regret in his eyes, then turned to the magistrate. "No further questions, Your Honor."

"You may step down, Ms. Nilsson."

It was over. Finally, it was over.

Thank God!

Laura had just gotten to her feet when Al-Nassar began to shout at her in English.

"I am in chains, but I shall be free in Paradise, while *you* will always live in fear. You will never be safe, nor will anyone you love. I curse you and call upon the Faithful, all who walk the righteous path, to seek to kill you and all—"

The magistrate cut him off. "Counsel, silence your client before I hold him in contempt! Bailiff, remove this man from the courtroom!"

Bailiffs rushed forward, took Al-Nassar, and began to drag him from the room.

But something inside Laura snapped.

She shouted Al-Nassar down, her fury incandescent. "You are evil, nothing but a murderer, an animal who abused me and tried to steal my life! The moment I walk from this room, I'll be free. Before the door to your prison cell has closed behind you, I'll have forgotten your name."

It was only later, after she'd spent ten minutes throwing up in the bathroom, that it struck her.

Al-Nassar had commanded his followers to hunt her down— and kill her.

CHAPTER 2

Cimarron Ranch
In the mountains west of Denver

JAVIER SAT BACK on a plush leather sofa, a glass of single malt in his hand, his gaze fixed on an enormous flat-screen TV where news anchor Gary Chapin cut away to a brunette in a gray trench coat who was giving a live update from New York on Al-Nassar's trial.

"As he was being led out of the courtroom at the conclusion of the day's gripping testimony, Al-Nassar repeated threats he'd made earlier in the day, calling out for 'all who are on the faithful path to seek to kill the infidel Laura Nilsson.'"

¡Puñeta!

Fuck!

"Why the hell does she have to repeat Al-Nassar's threats, make them public?" Javier wanted to punch something. "They've told every jihadist in the world that Laura is a target. Don't they care what happens to her?"

The problem with a free press as far as Javier could see was that some reporters didn't know when to shut the fuck up.

Nate shrugged. "I guess they care more about breaking news."

"It'll be *big* news when some asshole catches up with her and puts a knife in her back." Javier stood and took a few steps, too restless, too damned angry to sit.

Nate pointed toward the television. "Isn't this her old network? Chapin was her anchor, wasn't he?"

"Yeah." Javier glanced up at the middle-aged man on the screen. "He was broadcasting the night of her abduction, covered the whole thing, stayed on the air all night, got all choked up. He won an Emmy, I think. I was impressed then, thought he was all right. Now I want to kick his ass."

"You're really caught up in this." There was a tone in Nate's voice that demanded an explanation.

Javier couldn't tell him the whole truth, so he told him part of it. "She and I met in Dubai City, spent a wild weekend together. That was about two months before she was abducted."

Nate's eyebrows rose, and he grinned. "You . . . and the Baghdad Babe?"

Javier turned on Nate. "Don't call her that. I fucking *hate* that."

"Ooh-kay." There was a note of amusement in Nate's voice. "If I weren't married to the most beautiful woman in the world, I'd be jealous. How did you manage to keep that to yourself?"

"Hey, this brother doesn't kiss and tell, all right?"

"I respect that." Nate grabbed the remote and turned off the television, then stood and walked to the fireplace to toss a few pieces of oak on the blaze. "I think this is about more than Laura Nilsson and the state of the media."

"What do you mean?"

"You've been wound up tight since you got here." Nate poured himself more scotch and sat across from Javier. "Want to talk about it?"

"Ah, hell." Javier sat and took another sip. What was there to talk about? "Not really, man."

Why did everyone from the psych team to his parents to Nate think he needed to talk? Life wasn't an episode of *Dr. Phil.* He didn't want anyone's pity. He didn't need to talk. What he needed was to get strong again and rejoin his team.

Nate tossed back his drink. "I remember when the truck got hit. I'd have burned to death if you hadn't pulled me out of there. Then I was lying there in the sand, wishing I would just die. But you took my hand, and you got me through it. You helped me stay strong. If you need me—"

"I'm *fine*. I got shot a few times, lost a man, watched a helo full of medics crash. It's a hazard of the job. I knew that before I put on the uniform, and so did every man who died that day."

Nate's gaze shifted to the top of the stairs, where his wife had appeared. Javier didn't miss the way his buddy watched Megan as she made her way toward them. With long auburn hair and big green eyes, she *was* pretty, though not in Javier's opinion the most beautiful woman in the world. Then again, all that mattered to him was that she'd brought happiness back into Nate's life, accepting him scars and all. That alone made her one hell of a woman.

"Am I intruding?" Wearing a fluffy white bathrobe over purple silk pajamas, her hair hanging loose, she shuffled across the wood floor and crawled into Nate's lap. "Grandpa Jack is reading Emily a story, but she wants her daddy to tuck her in."

Nate kissed Megan's forehead. "I'll be right up."

Megan looked over at Javier. "Can I get you anything?"

Javier shook his head. "I'm good."

With a smile, she hopped up and disappeared into the kitchen.

"Look at you. You're a family man." Javier grinned. "You've got a wife, a sweet little girl, your old man, the ranch. Things turned out all right for you."

The Cimarron was like nothing Javier had ever seen. Whenever Nate had spoken of "the ranch," Javier had imagined something rustic, like the log house in *Bonanza*. How wrong he'd been! Oh, there were logs, all right, but they were polished and stood like columns, welcoming visitors through a portico that led to a massive three-story house, complete with a library, a home theater, a gym with a sauna, a wine cellar, a five-car heated garage, and enough bedrooms to house Javier's entire family. Outside there were barns where Nate bred prized quarter horses, an indoor riding arena, and bunkhouses for the ranch hands—not to mention mile after mile of open mountain valley and a view of the Rockies that had blown Javier away.

As for Nate's old man . . . Well, he was something else.

Jack West, a decorated veteran and former Army Ranger, had welcomed Javier to the ranch as if he were a long-lost son, crushing him in a bear hug. "Thank you for being there for

Nate. You saved my boy's life, stood by him. As far as I'm concerned, you're family—a son of this house. What's ours is yours."

Strange to think that Nate, the son of a wealthy Colorado rancher, and Javier, a kid from a poor inner-city Puerto Rican family, had become close buddies. But that was what happened when men put on a uniform and served together. Their differences faded in the face of shared duties—and dangers.

"I'm happy for you, man. I really am."

"I'm a lucky man." Nate smiled, not an ounce of self-pity on his scarred face.

It was humbling.

Megan reappeared, a glass of water in her hand. "Days start pretty early around here, so I'm headed to bed. Let us know if you need anything."

Javier gave her a nod. "Will do. Good night."

Nate got to his feet. "Daddy duty calls. I'll be back in a few."

Javier settled back on the sofa, his thoughts turning once again to Laura.

LAURA WRITHED ON the floor in agony, pain wrapping itself around her until she couldn't help but cry out. "Zainab has poisoned me!"

"She is crazy!" Zainab forced her onto her back, her hand pressing against Laura's belly where it hurt the worst. "Be still!"

But she couldn't be still. The pain was unbearable. "I'm going to be sick!"

Zainab motioned to Safiya, who pushed the wooden bowl closer.

Laura pushed herself up with one arm and vomited, her entire abdomen knotted against whatever Zainab had put in her food to kill her.

Why had they done this? Hadn't she made them all promise to shoot her if a time came when they chose at last to kill her? What had she done to anger them, to make them break that promise?

The nausea passed, but another wave of agony had begun.

Moaning, she wiped her mouth on the wet cloth Safiya handed her. She met Safiya's gaze. "Please, sister, help me! I am dying!"

"We are helping you, you stupid woman!" Zainab hissed.

Then Zainab and Safiya stood and left the room, leaving her alone, her pain suddenly gone, her body weak and shaking.

But they had taken something from her. What had they taken? She didn't know, and it terrified her.

Too weak to stand, she screamed after them. "No!"

Laura sat upright, a cry trapped in her throat. In a panic, she glanced around to find that she was home in Denver in her own bedroom, the light she'd left on in the kitchen casting its glow in the hallway outside her door. Shaking, nauseated, and covered in cold sweat, she closed her eyes again, drew deep steadying breaths.

A nightmare. It was only a nightmare.

She glanced at her alarm clock.

Two in the morning.

She'd been asleep for all of an hour.

She ought to have expected this. It had been much harder than she'd imagined to testify, to dredge up old memories and emotions, to see *him* once more. But she'd do it again in a heartbeat just for the chance to confront him.

She wasn't sure what had come over her there at the end, but it had felt . . . good. Rage had surged from her belly, words she'd wanted to shout in his face for years spilling out of her, fury making her feel stronger than she'd felt in a long time.

And seeing shock on Al-Nassar's face . . .

It had felt like a victory.

It *was* a victory. She'd stood up to him, denounced him to the world. The trial was behind her now, her precious secret still intact. Al-Nassar would almost certainly be going to prison for the rest of his life. And she was *free*, the rest of her life ahead of her.

She'd meant what she'd said. She'd flown back to Denver determined to forget Al-Nassar, to reclaim her happiness, to live life to the fullest. Certainly no nightmare, no matter how frightening it might be, would stop her.

And what about Klara? What about Al-Nassar's death threats?

The DUSMs who'd watched over her yesterday had dismissed his threats as mere posturing, the words of a pathetic man who was about to lose everything. They'd urged her not to lose sleep over it, assuring her that the CIA and FBI had everyone believed to be associated with Al-Nassar under surveillance.

Laura wished she could share their apparent confidence.

As for Klara . . .

There was nothing Laura could do but hope and pray.

Knowing she wouldn't be able to fall asleep again soon, she climbed out of bed, slipped into her white chenille bathrobe, and made her way through her three-bedroom loft toward the kitchen, turning on lights as she went, her gaze compulsively drawn to the two dead bolts on the front door.

Locked.

She poured milk into a mug, stirred in a teaspoon of honey—her grandmother's remedy for sleeplessness—and then set the mug in the microwave to heat. While she waited, her gaze came to rest on the postcard. Stuck to her refrigerator with a magnet, it featured colorful photos of the sites that had made Dubai City famous—Sheikh Zayed Road, the Atlantis Hotel, Jumeirah Beach, and, of course, Burj Al Arab.

Javier Corbray.

The nights she'd spent with him in Dubai had left her feeling alive in a way she hadn't felt before—or since. He'd charged to her rescue when a couple of drunk Russian gas moguls had come on to her, and she'd ended up in bed with him. By the end of the weekend, she had known his body intimately—where and how he liked to be touched, what pleased him most—and he'd known hers. But she'd never found out where he lived or what he did for a living. She'd guessed he was military—the man was ripped, more than six feet of lean muscle—but he'd refused to answer.

In his rush to get to the airport that last morning, he'd left the postcard in Laura's hotel room. He'd written a message in Spanish on the back of the postcard, intending to mail it to his Puerto Rican grandmother, who collected postcards from his travels. Laura had tucked it in her handbag, thinking she might use it as an excuse to connect with him again. There it had remained until after her abduction, when the U.S. State

Department had shipped her belongings from Pakistan to her mother. Although her mother had given most of Laura's belongings to charity, she'd kept the postcard, a memento of the daughter she thought she'd lost.

Now it belonged to Laura again—one of the few possessions she owned from the time before her abduction, a reminder of the life that had been hers, of an exciting weekend, of a man she wished she'd gotten to know better.

Did Javier remember her? Did he ever think of her? Never in the past two years had he tried to contact her. Surely he knew she was alive and back in the U.S. Maybe what had happened to her was too much for him. Then again, she hadn't tried to find him either. They'd promised each other no strings, and she had honored that.

She carried her mug of warm milk into her office, sat at her desk, and reached for the phone, dialing the number from memory. As a dual Swedish-U.S. citizen, she had access to help from both the U.S. State Department and the Swedish Ministry for Foreign Affairs, but she'd opted to go through the Swedish government, believing that its more cordial relationship with Islamabad—and its more stringent privacy laws—would serve her better. It was just after eleven in the morning in Stockholm, early enough for her to catch Erik at his desk. Her call was answered on the second ring by a woman whose Swedish carried an unpleasant Skåne accent.

"Foreign Affairs."

"Erik Berg, please."

Her call was put through, Erik's deep voice answering.

Laura set her mug aside, sat up straighter. "Good day, Erik. It is Laura Nilsson. How are you? How are Heidi and the girls?"

Erik loved to talk about his twin daughters, Stella and Anette. He and Heidi had tried for years to have children before turning to in vitro. Now four years old, the girls were his life, and he and Heidi were talking about trying in vitro again or adopting. "We are all doing well. What are you doing calling at this hour? It must be two in the morning."

"I couldn't sleep."

"I understand. We've been following the story. I'm glad testifying is behind you. When is the trial expected to conclude?"

"I was the last witness. They're making closing arguments

today." Then they'd have to wait for the jury's verdict. After that, only the sentencing hearing would remain. "I just wanted to check in. Have you heard anything?"

"It so happens that I have good news. I'd planned to call you later today."

Laura's pulse skipped.

He paused for a moment, as if she needed the added drama. "Pakistani officials have finally admitted they know where Klara is. They say she's with Al-Nassar's wives at his brother's compound outside Islamabad."

Oh, thank God!

Klara was alive! They'd found her!

She fought to control the emotion in her voice. "Wh-what happens now?"

"We're hoping to arrange a welfare check. We've asked to be allowed to send in representatives from the Swedish consulate along with a doctor to check on Klara's well-being, and, if we can manage it, to collect DNA to compare with the sample you left with us. We've only begun negotiating the details, but I hope to have an answer within the next few weeks. I'll forward the communiqués to you in an e-mail."

"Many thanks. I am so happy to hear this." She found herself smiling, tears welling in her eyes.

"You must remember that this doesn't change anything."

Her joy dimmed. "I understand."

"Traditional courts are quite strict about these matters, and you, as an unmarried woman, foreign national, and non-Muslim, are in the weakest possible position. As we told you during the initial briefing, your chances of getting the ruling you want are slim to nonexistent."

Laura heard Erik's words but refused to accept what he was telling her. "I will do whatever it takes. I won't give up. I *can't* give up."

If she did, she would never be whole again. And poor little Klara . . .

"Klara is as much of a victim in this as I am. I will *not* abandon my daughter to be raised in a den of terrorists."

As she finished the conversation and hung up, a voice whispered in her mind.

You already did.

* * *

JAVIER RODE SHOTGUN in Nate's Ford F-150, a load of hay bales in the back, the sun barely up, the temp fifteen below. "Are you sure the cows are going to be awake?"

Cowboy hat on his head, Nate grinned. "These are steers, not cows."

"What's the difference?"

Nate raised an eyebrow. "Seriously, bro? Cows are female. We breed them to grow our herd. Steers are castrated males grown for beef."

"So first you cut off their nuts, and then you fatten them up and eat them." That was a hell of a life. "I shouldn't have asked."

Nate laughed.

"You think there's any real chance Laura Nilsson will come to this barbecue you're having?"

Nate eyed him. "You nervous?"

"Hell, no, I'm not nervous." Okay, so maybe he was.

"It must have been one hell of a weekend if you're anxious to see her all these years later."

It had been.

THE NEWS ABOUT Klara kept Laura awake for the rest of the night. She'd called her mother and grandmother, who'd shared her fragile joy. Now, groggy from lack of sleep, she arrived at the newspaper to find a handful of reporters already waiting for her. Unable to avoid them, she handled it the same way she'd handled it yesterday—ignoring their questions but giving them a quote to take back to their papers and networks.

"I have put this behind me now and am moving on with my life. I thank you all for your concern and ask that you respect my privacy."

She walked inside with deliberate, measured steps, grateful to Gil Cormac, the paper's lone security guard, who held the door open for her. "Thank you, Gil."

"You're welcome. A bunch of vultures is what they are. I don't know why they can't leave you in peace." He looked past her toward the throng, a frown weighing down his round face.

"They're just doing their jobs." If she'd been assigned to cover this story, it would have been *her* job.

She made her way to the elevator and up to the newsroom on the third floor. She'd missed a day and a half of work and wanted to get organized before the I-Team meeting at nine. It was a new day, and she was determined to face it head-on no matter how tired she felt. She'd just go to bed early tonight.

She caught up on e-mail and started in on her messages. There, amid a dozen voice mails, many from reporters hoping to snare an interview with her, was yet another message from Derek Tower.

You're not taking me seriously, Ms. Nilsson. That's a mistake. If you don't contact me, I'm going to find new ways to contact you.

She'd all but forgotten about him and the stunt he'd pulled with the reporter yesterday. He was trying to intimidate her, trying to manipulate her. But she couldn't change the fact that the Pentagon and a host of U.S. contractors had lost confidence in Tower Global Security after her abduction, canceling their contracts and sending the company spiraling into bankruptcy.

Did he truly believe she was to blame for what had happened? Was it possible he knew something she didn't, that he'd seen something in the State Department's report that she'd missed? Had she done something she couldn't remember, something that had put them all at risk?

No! No.

She pushed the twisting thread of doubt aside and willed herself to focus on her work, putting together a list of people she needed to interview to finish her article on the long treatment delays that veterans suffering from PTSD faced at the Denver VA hospital. She couldn't imagine what would have become of her if she'd been forced to wait so long for therapy. Her mental anguish had been every bit as unbearable as physical pain. The thought that men and women who'd served their country were being neglected like this sickened her.

She'd made a point of covering veterans' issues since she'd come back to work. It was a small thing, she knew—little more than a gesture, really—but it was one way to thank the men who'd saved her life.

She didn't know the names of the special operators who'd rescued her or what had become of them since that night. When the choppers had landed at the tactical operations center in Afghanistan, she'd been taken away in a military ambulance, then flown to Germany the next day to be reunited with her mother. She hadn't seen the men again. When she'd asked for their contact information so she could thank them, she'd been told their identities and the mission were classified. Still, there wasn't a day when she didn't find herself thinking about them, especially the tall one.

She hadn't been able to see his face. He'd been wearing a heavy helmet and face camouflage, night vision gear covering his eyes. But he'd saved her life, killing Zainab to protect her and carrying her to freedom. He'd even punched Al-Nassar in the face for harassing her and wrapped a blanket around her shoulders. He'd made her feel safe.

She wasn't a religious person and didn't go to church, but she prayed for him and his men every night, just as she prayed for Klara.

The other I-Team members began drifting in around her. Alex Carmichael, who'd been hired last month to cover cops and courts. Matt Harker, who'd held down the city beat for most of a decade. Sophie Alton-Hunter, who split the environmental beat with Navajo reporter Katherine James, each of them working half time so that they could spend more time at home with their children. Joaquin Ramirez, the photographer whose skill had earned him a Pulitzer.

She was so focused on her work she barely noticed them, their voices and conversation drifting outside the sphere of her concentration. She heard someone cough—and looked up to find them surrounding her desk, Sophie holding a bouquet of pink, yellow, and white roses.

"I was supposed to get here before you did so I could put this on your desk." Sophie set the flowers down. "Welcome back. We're all so glad this is behind you now. We wanted to start today out right for you."

Laura slowly got to her feet, unable to speak, her throat tight. She took the bouquet, inhaled the bright, sweet scent of roses, and then set the vase down on her desk.

"It took a lot of guts to do what you did, Nilsson." Alex

reached out a hand, shook hers. Tall with tousled dark hair and blue eyes, he had a reputation for being relentless when on a story. He'd been arrested five times, shot, and knifed, all in the line of duty. "We're all glad it's behind you now."

Matt, looking as rumpled as ever, pointed to Alex. "What Carmichael said."

Joaquin plucked a pink rose from the bouquet and handed it to her. "You're a hero to a lot of people out there—not just women."

Laura took the flower and looked away, uncomfortable with their praise. "Thank you. I . . . I don't know what to say."

She'd never spoken of her captivity or rescue with anyone on the I-Team. She assumed they'd read the articles. The whole world seemed to know what had happened to her, apart from the most horrific, intimate details—and Klara. Only her doctors, her therapist, her mother and grandmother, the U.S. Attorney's Office, and certain Swedish government officials knew about her daughter. If her coworkers knew, they'd quit thinking of her as a hero.

What kind of woman could trade her helpless two-month-old baby for her freedom?

Sophie beamed. "You don't have to say anything."

"Congratulations, Nilsson."

Heads turned.

Tom Trent, the newspaper's hard-boiled editor in chief, walked up beside them. A few inches over six feet, he was big and beefy and had a temper that intimidated most people, though not Laura. As much of an asshat as he could be, he seemed warm and fuzzy compared to some of the personalities she'd had to contend with in broadcast news.

He met Laura's gaze from beneath a shock of gray curls. "Way to walk tall, Nilsson. But we've got a newspaper to make, and sometime today would be good. Everyone to the conference room."

Laura got to her feet and started down the hallway, notepad and pencil in hand.

Tom held her back. "Not you, Nilsson. Some suits want to speak with you."

And then she saw them. Two men in suits and ties.

FBI.

CHAPTER 3

JAVIER SAT ON the back deck with a bottle of stout, washing down a lunch of Jack West's three-alarm chili with good, cold beer. The mountains rose all around him, stretching their jagged white-capped peaks toward an endless blue sky. Nearby, a herd of elk foraged in the snow, a hawk wheeling overhead.

Everything was so beautiful, so peaceful, so quiet.

He and Nate had spent the day driving hay out to snowbound cattle and seeing to the horses. Despite the near-constant ache in his thigh, it had felt good to get physical. Lifting hay bales and trudging through deep snow had gotten his heart pumping and filled his lungs with fresh mountain air. He'd felt alive again, strong. But the best part about it had been working side by side with Nate.

And still something felt . . . *wrong*.

Javier thrust the feeling aside, refused to let himself go there. If it hadn't been so cold out, he'd have gone back inside to grab his guitar. He'd been playing a lot since getting wounded. Something about it cleared his mind, helped him focus, gave him an outlet for whatever was gnawing at him.

Behind him, the sliding glass door opened and closed, Nate's boots crunching in a foot of new snowfall. He shook off a chair and sat beside Javier.

Javier looked over at him. "Nice view."

"Thanks." Nate grinned from behind his sunglasses, bundled

in a fleece and leather barn jacket, cowboy hat still on his head. "It's home."

Javier could see that. Nate belonged here.

Where do you belong?

Why the hell was he asking himself that question? He already knew where he belonged. He belonged downrange with his men.

He took another swig, savoring the bitterness. "Is the fishing good around here?"

"Yeah. Cutthroat trout. Brook trout. Bass."

"Might have to come back."

Nate leaned his head back and tilted his hat over his eyes, a grin lurking on his face. "Door's always open."

Nate smiled a lot these days. It did Javier good to see him so happy.

Most of the reason for that happiness glanced at them through the sliding glass door, then opened the door a crack, a smile on her pretty face. "I thought I might find the two of you *chilling* somewhere together. Comfortable?"

Nate raised his head, eyeing his wife from beneath the brim of his hat. "Why don't you come on over here, sit on my lap, and warm me up, honey?"

"Thanks, but I think I'll stay inside where it's warmer. Brrr!" Megan pretended to shiver. "Sophie e-mailed to ask whether she and Marc should bring some elk steaks to share tomorrow."

"If they want to do that, it's fine by me, but he's still not touching the grill."

Megan ducked back inside, laughing to herself.

Nate looked over at Javier. "Ever tried elk?"

Javier shook his head.

"My brother-in-law goes elk hunting with a crossbow every fall. It's good eatin'—nice and lean." Nate took a swallow of his beer. "He and McBride brought down a five-hundred-pound cow this year. That's what we call female elk, by the way—cows."

"You're not letting that go, are you?"

"Nope."

But Javier was only half-listening, talk of the barbecue putting his mind back on Laura Nilsson. Would she come?

Would she recognize him? If she did, would she be glad to see him—or would she feel blindsided?

And what will you say to her?

What could he say to the woman who'd been in his thoughts for so long?

He had no idea.

Emily, Megan's five-year-old daughter whom Nate had adopted, stuck her blond head out the door, then disappeared inside, her high little voice drifting back to them. "Grandpa Jack, they're not shoveling. They're just sitting on their asses like you said."

"Hey, old man, quit nagging!" Nate shouted toward the door, a grin on his face.

From inside, Javier could just make out Jack's voice. "Now, Miss Emily, you know there are words that only grown-ups can say, and *ass* is one of them."

Javier chuckled. "Your dad is something else."

"Yeah, he is, and he's teaching Emily to talk like a soldier." Nate took another drink. "Truth is, she's been good for him. He loves that little girl. You should have seen the pride on his face when the adoption was final and her name became Emily West. She and Megan—they've helped fill the emptiness my mother's death left inside him."

Javier could remember the day Nate's mother had died. They'd been in Afghanistan, and Nate had gotten a call from his father. She'd passed suddenly and unexpectedly of an aneurysm. Nate never had a chance to say good-bye.

"You thinking of giving Emily a little brother or sister?"

Nate nodded. "Megan applied to law school. If she gets accepted, we might decide to wait till she graduates. If she doesn't . . . Well, she'll be pretty disappointed. She wants to help young women who get into trouble. She had a rough life and wants to make sure other girls have a better chance."

"That's a worthy goal." Javier knew next to nothing about Megan, but he didn't like the idea that she'd had a hard time of it growing up. Whatever her past was, she certainly seemed to have moved beyond it.

"How about you? You ever going to get married again, raise a few kids?"

Javier glared at Nate. "Are you my mother? She asked me the same thing when I was home."

She wanted him to buy a house somewhere nearby, marry a sweet Puerto Rican wife, and give her more grandkids while she was still alive to enjoy them. But he'd had a wife, and she'd run off with some *cabrón* from Silicon Valley midway through their first married deployment—less than a year after they'd tied the knot. Why would he want to go through that again?

Nate studied him for a moment, then took one last swill. "Well, I guess we'd best get to work if we want to get the patio shoveled in time to get back to the horses."

It *was* a big patio with a built-in gas grill, a fire pit, stone benches, a few outdoor propane heaters, and a couple of picnic tables.

Javier got to his feet, pain shooting through his left thigh. "Tell me again why you have barbecues in the middle of the winter, bro?"

Nate looked at him like he was an idiot. "We like steak."

LAURA MET SOPHIE in the cafeteria for a late lunch, both of them opting for the salad bar over the burgers. They made their way to a table in the back of the nearly empty room, Laura grabbing a bottle of mineral water on the way.

"I can't believe the FBI isn't going to do anything to help you." Sophie stirred sugar into her iced tea.

"That's not exactly what they said." It was close enough from Laura's point of view, but she was a journalist and had to be fair—even if she was furious. "The special agent in charge—Agent Petras—said they had no evidence that Al-Nassar's threats were credible or that I was in any danger. He said they were monitoring the situation and that they would act if they found evidence that a threat existed."

"Having a terrorist leader put a fatwa on your head doesn't count as credible?" Sophie jabbed her fork into her salad. "Good grief! What does?"

What Al-Nassar had done didn't constitute a fatwa, but Laura didn't feel like explaining. Besides, it wasn't *what* the FBI agent had said, but *how* he'd said it.

"Petras was smug, so condescending. He talked down to me as if I were a nuisance, as if I'd cried wolf or something—when he wasn't staring at my boobs."

Sophie rolled her eyes. "Why do men do that? Do they think we don't notice?"

Laura had no idea. "What's so infuriating is that *I* didn't contact the FBI. I wasn't the one who asked them to come."

Sophie frowned. "Who did?"

"The U.S. Marshal Service." Laura wished they hadn't.

Sophie got a knowing look on her face. "I bet that's the problem. There's no love lost between the FBI and the Marshal Service."

Then Sophie told her how her husband, Marc, the SWAT captain, had been deputized by the U.S. Marshal for Colorado a couple years back when Natalie Benoit, a friend and former I-Team member, was in danger from a Mexican drug cartel. She'd just started telling Laura how the cartel had abducted Natalie off a bus, when she caught herself. "Oh, God! Sorry! I'm sure you didn't need to hear that."

"Don't apologize." For a moment, Laura had forgotten about her own situation. "I'm not the only journalist who—"

Her cell phone rang. She glanced down at the display.

Him again.

Something of her feelings must have shown on her face, because when Sophie spoke again, she sounded worried. "Who is it?"

"Derek Tower, the man who owns the company that handled my security detail." Laura told Sophie about him—his phone calls, the accusations he'd fed to the press, his demand that she meet with him. "When I got out of the meeting with the FBI, I had another message from him. That makes three today."

"Have you considered getting a restraining order against him?"

Laura had thought about that. "I'm not sure he's done anything that could be considered threatening. If pestering people with phone calls and e-mails were an actionable offense, you and I and everyone else in the newsroom would be in jail."

"You've got a point there."

For a while they ate in silence.

Sophie set her fork aside. "Can I ask you a personal question?"

"Yes." Laura could always refuse to answer.

"How do you stay so calm? If I were in your shoes, I'd be scared to death."

That wasn't the question Laura had been expecting.

"I *am* scared." She hated to admit that. She was tired of feeling afraid. "I just try not to let it control me. If I did . . ."

If she did, she'd never leave the house.

Sophie took out a pen and wrote a phone number down on a clean napkin. "You and I haven't known each other for a long time, but . . . if you ever need a place to stay, a place where you can feel safe, you're welcome at our house. Marc—Mr. SWAT Captain—wouldn't let anything happen to you. He's armed to the teeth."

"I carry a gun, too." Laura rested a hand on her purse. "I keep it loaded and with me all the time. I even sleep with it under my pillow."

It was a decision she'd made when she'd come back to the States. She would never be defenseless again, nor would she leave the responsibility of protecting herself entirely in someone else's hands. So she'd bought a .22 SIG Mosquito, taken some classes, and then applied for a concealed carry license, which the sheriff had granted.

Sophie reached over and gave her arm a squeeze. "Good. I'm glad. But the invitation is open."

"Thanks."

"You're coming to the party up at the Cimarron tomorrow, right?"

The barbecue at the ranch.

"Oh, well, I . . ." Laura had forgotten completely about it. "I don't know. Parties really aren't my scene. It's been a hard week."

"It's only going to be past and present I-Team members and their families. I know they would all love to meet you."

"It might snow, and I'm not used to driving on mountain roads." She was digging for excuses now, and she knew it.

"You can catch a ride with us." There was a hopeful tone to Sophie's voice, as if it really meant something to her for Laura to come. "The trial will be over. You can get away from the city, see the mountains, meet Marc. It's peaceful up there— no media, no Derek Tower, no one around for miles."

It was on the tip of Laura's tongue to decline, but hadn't she just vowed in front of the whole world to live her life to the fullest? "Okay. I'll come."

"Wonderful!" Sophie's smile broadened. "It will be a celebration."

And despite Sophie's kindness Laura found herself wishing she'd said no.

HE COULD ALMOST smell her fear.

Derek Tower kept to the shadows, watching as Laura Nilsson left the newspaper and crossed the street, hurrying through the parking lot, her head turning from left to right as she kept an eye on her surroundings. Yeah, she was afraid. She'd be stupid not to be after what Al-Nassar had said in court yesterday.

Derek followed her using cars for cover. The little bitch refused even to speak with him, referring his questions to her attorney rather than answering them herself. But he wouldn't let her get away with that, not with three of his men dead and his business in bankruptcy. She owed him.

She held out her keys and clicked the remote, and the hazard lights on her car flashed—revealing to Derek exactly which car was hers.

He moved quickly, silently, opening her passenger-side door and sliding into the passenger seat beside her just as she slipped behind the wheel. "Ms. Nilsson."

She screamed, reached for the door handle, but he had already locked the doors.

He grabbed her coat, forced her to face him. "We need to talk."

She swore in a language he didn't understand, the fear in her eyes flashing into anger. "What the hell are you doing following me?"

"It's just business." He glanced around the parking lot to make sure no one was witnessing this little drama, then turned back to Ms. Nilsson, only to find himself looking down the barrel of a SIG Mosquito.

Damn.

He hadn't been expecting that.

He released her, gave her some room.

She glared at him, her aim rock steady. "Falsely accusing someone of wrongdoing is slander. Following me to my car is harassment and stalking."

"Put the pistol away before you hurt yourself." He reached for it but froze when her finger curled around the trigger.

The woman was serious.

She glared at him, the ferocity on her feminine face pissing him off—and turning him on. "Get the hell out of my car right now, and don't come near me again!"

"I lost three men that day, Ms. Nilsson—three good men, men with families, men who'd been my friends since—"

"Nico, Cody, and Tim were *my* friends, too!"

Cold rage had him leaning closer, the pistol now a mere inch from his throat. "I served with them for a decade in Special Forces. You can't *begin* to understand what that means. Now they're dead, and I want answers."

"Try Ask.com."

"Oh, you're a cold bitch, aren't you?" Beautiful, but cold.

"Or go talk to the State Department. *They* did the investigation. In case you've forgotten, *I* was the target."

"I remember. Except you lived, and everyone *else* died."

Her eyes narrowed. "What are you implying?"

"I've spent the better part of three years trying to piece together how this happened. My sources in Islamabad say that Al-Nassar's men were tipped off by an *American* who said he'd heard from you exactly where you'd be that day."

She glared at him. "That's impossible."

"Is it? How many nights did you hang out with all the other reporters at that ex-pat bar in the hotel? Maybe you got a little tipsy and said more than you should have. Maybe you picked some guy up and let him fuck the intel out of you. Either way, my men paid with their lives. My company probably won't recover from the loss of reputation caused by your disappearance—"

"Loss of reputation? Your *company*?" Her voice quavered. "I spent eighteen months of my life trapped in a living hell!"

"You don't look any worse for wear." He knew what had happened to her, but she had survived, hadn't she? "My men are *dead*. I want answers from you, and I'm going to get them. Now, *put the pistol away*."

She tightened her grip, fear and rage in her eyes. "You're insane! Get out, and stay away from me, or I'll get a restraining order!"

As if that would stop him.

Tired of the bullshit, he grabbed her wrist, angled the barrel away from his body, and wrenched the weapon from her grasp. He held the little pistol for a moment, let her sweat it out. "Nice bit a steel. SIG makes a good pistol, but it won't do you a damned bit of good if you're not willing to fire. Don't draw if you don't plan to kill."

She rubbed her wrist, defiance on her face, only her rapid breathing betraying her fear. "That was assault."

He removed the magazine and racked the slide to expel the round from the chamber, then tossed the firearm in her lap. "You told someone, Laura. Who was it?"

She stared warily at him, still rubbing her wrist. "You really are crazy. I *never* disclosed my travel plans, not even to my own mother. I certainly never talked about them in the bar. As for guys, I wasn't seeing anyone."

Derek was an expert at reading people. It had been part of his training, part of what had kept him alive behind enemy lines for so long. Her shock seemed genuine, nothing on her face to suggest she was lying. Then again, she might not remember.

He deliberately softened the tone of his voice. "I know some of your memories are vague, but you need—"

The shrieking of a car alarm interrupted him.

Her car alarm.

She watched him, a look of dark triumph on her face, the panic button on her keychain gripped in bloodless fingers. "Get out!"

He should have taken the damn keys from her. "You're a journalist, Ms. Nilsson. Don't you care about the truth?"

Out of time, he unlocked the door and opened it. "And, hey, not such a great idea to unlock your car till you're near the door. Those flashing hazard lights give you away, tell an assailant right where you're headed. If I'd been one of Al-Nassar's followers come to kill you, I'd have slit your throat before you even knew I was here."

Ignoring the horror on her face, he climbed out of the car, shut the door behind him, and did his best to disappear.

CHAPTER 4

JAVIER SHOOK ZACH McBride's hand. "It's an honor to meet you. It's not every day a man gets to drink beer with a Medal of Honor recipient."

Javier had read about McBride's heroism and the catastrophic mission that had claimed the lives of McBride's men and had left him gravely wounded. Every SEAL had.

Tall with short, dark hair and a strong handshake, McBride met Javier's gaze through sharp gray eyes. "The honor is mutual. West told me how you were there for him, how you pulled him out of the burning debris, stayed with him."

And Javier knew that McBride and Nate were close. That wasn't a story Nate shared with everyone.

Javier grinned. "He talks too damned much."

McBride chuckled. "How long have you been with the Teams?"

"Fourteen years."

"Going for twenty?"

"That's the plan."

For a while the two of them traded stories—instructors they'd both had in BUD/S, the joys of eating sand with their MREs in Iraq, the scorching heat and freezing cold of Afghanistan. It was always like this when Javier met another SEAL. Each and every one of them was like a brother, the bond between them forged from the unique challenges, risks, and deprivations that came with wearing the Trident.

And for a moment Javier forgot about Laura.

Women's laughter drew McBride's gaze. He gestured with a nod of his head toward a pretty dark-haired woman who was sitting next to Megan, the two of them reading something. "That's my wife, Natalie. She's decided she wants to write fiction—romance novels. I hope that means I get to help with the research."

Two heads came up, and Natalie glared at McBride. "The books are *not* just about sex."

Javier lowered his voice. "I guess you said the wrong thing, man."

The doorbell rang again, and Megan rose to answer it.

Javier's pulse skipped.

You're excited to see her, chacho. *Admit it.*

Sure, he was. Not a day had gone by since Dubai when he hadn't thought of her. Yeah, he was excited to see her again. And more than a little tense.

When Megan returned, it wasn't Laura walking beside her. Instead, Javier was introduced to Julian Darcangelo, a tall son of a gun with a dark ponytail who'd once worked with the FBI but was now head of Denver's vice unit. He'd brought his family—his wife, Tessa, a sweet thing with long, curly blond hair and a mother's soft curves, and a little girl and a baby boy.

The doorbell rang again.

This time it was Reece Sheridan, the state's newly sworn-in lieutenant governor, his wife Kara McMillan, and their three school-aged kids. They were followed not two minutes later by Kat James, a pretty Navajo woman, her husband Gabe Rossiter, and two little ones under the age of two. Then Nate's brother-in-law, Marc Hunter, Denver's SWAT captain, and his wife, Sophie, arrived with their two kids.

Between the adults talking and children running and squealing, it was chaos. It might have bothered some guys, but Javier felt right at home. He came from a big family with two brothers, three sisters, six nephews, and nine nieces, not to mention aunts, uncles, and a few dozen cousins, most of whom had kids. When they got the whole family together—which they did whenever Javier was on leave—the laughter, music, and conversation were loud and lasted late into the night.

He found himself outside on the deck shooting the shit

with Hunter and Rossiter, while everyone got ready for an afternoon of skiing, snowshoeing, and sleigh rides.

Rossiter, who was a climber and former park ranger, was talking about his grand plan for the afternoon. "You can ski some incredible places with a paragliding sail strapped to your back. It's like flying, BASE jumping, and skiing combined."

Ski paragliding wasn't a sport that interested Javier, in part because he couldn't see the point. He shook his head. "I don't know—strapping some kind of 'chute to your back and letting the wind pull you down the mountain? Either ski or jump."

Hunter chuckled, pointing to Rossiter. "You wouldn't believe the sick shit I've seen this guy do. If a sport involves gravity, snow in any form, and a high likelihood of death, he's in."

A flash of short platinum-blond hair—and a body that could kill.

It wasn't Laura Nilsson, but . . .

Javier gave a low whistle.

Hunter and Rossiter looked over their shoulders, then back at Javier.

Hunter shook his head. "Oh, no. No, no. Don't even think about it."

"He's human. He's male. He's going to think about it." Rossiter grinned. "That's Holly Bradshaw. She's one of the paper's entertainment writers. She'll chew you up and spit you out."

That didn't sound so bad.

Hunter looked over at her. "What she needs is to fall for a man who refuses to sleep with her."

Javier was about to say a guy would have to be gay as a daisy to turn down a woman like Holly, when suddenly *she* was there.

His heart skipped again—and gave a thud.

Wearing jeans and a white blouse beneath a blue angora cardigan, Laura shook hands with Nate and McBride, then Natalie, her pale blond hair catching the light, the smile on her face hitting Javier in the gut. She shook Megan's hand, then knelt down to talk to Emily, giving the little girl her full attention.

¡Ea Diablo! She was beautiful!

Hunter and Rossiter saw her, too.

"Oh, hey, she came." Hunter sounded surprised to see her. He lowered his voice. "Sophie said she didn't think Laura was going to make it. Derek Tower—the asshole who owns the security company that was supposed to have kept her safe in Pakistan—accosted her in the parking lot outside the paper last night. He forced his way into her car. She drew on him—a double deuce—but he tore the weapon out of her hands, even left bruises. She filed a report with DPD last night. Uniforms went looking for him but haven't found him."

Javier had heard of Derek Tower, hadn't known what to think of him. Now he hated the bastard. His gaze snapped back to Hunter. "Doesn't she have protection—a bodyguard?"

Hunter shook his head. "Sophie says the FBI doesn't believe she's in any real danger, and she can't afford to pay for protection herself. Sophie wants me to talk to Old Man Irving—Denver's chief of police—and have our local boys fill in."

"Not a bad idea." Javier had never understood how the federal agencies worked. It all seemed like red tape and bullshit to him.

"Let's go say hello." Hunter opened the sliding patio door and walked inside, Rossiter behind him.

Javier followed the two men indoors but hung back, watching while the others introduced themselves.

She probably doesn't even remember you.

"Welcome to the Cimarron. It's a real pleasure to meet you. Make yourself at home." Jack pressed her hand between both of his. "Can I get you something to drink—wine, beer, scotch, soda, some overpriced bubbly water?"

Laura smiled, a genuine bright smile that put dimples in her cheeks. "Overpriced bubbly water would be lovely. Thank you."

Jack turned back to the kitchen.

Hunter stepped forward, held out his hand. "Marc Hunter. I'm Sophie's husband. Sophie has said great things about you."

"Thank you. She's said good things about you, too."

"All true, I'm sure." Hunter grinned.

"I'm Julian Darcangelo. I head up the DPD's vice squad. My wife, Tessa, is a big fan of yours. She's an investigative journalist herself and has written a few books. She used to be on the I-Team before she went freelance. I can't believe she hasn't found some excuse to visit Sophie at the paper so she can meet you."

"Sophie has mentioned her." Laura's eyes narrowed. "You say she's written books? Wait—is her name Tessa *Novak*?"

Darcangelo nodded. "That was her maiden name. She still uses it for journalism."

"I'm a fan of hers. I read the two books she wrote about human sex trafficking. She inspired me to look into the issue in Pakistan and India."

"Hearing that is going to make her day—hell, her entire *year*."

Rossiter pushed his way forward. "Gabe Rossiter. I'm Kat's worse half."

Laura took Rossiter's hand and smiled that beautiful smile of hers. "I've heard about some of your adventures."

"He's the most famous one-legged extreme athlete in the world," Hunter quipped. "Just ask him."

That made her laugh.

Her gaze shifted to Javier. The color drained from her cheeks, and her eyes went wide, her lips parting as she stared up at him. "It's . . . It's *you*!"

LAURA COULD HEAR nothing over the thrum of her own pulse, her gaze fixed on the face of the tall man who stood before her.

Javier Corbray.

Somehow, he was standing right here in this room with her.

"Hello, Laura."

A feeling of light-headedness swamped her, the floor tilting.

Strong hands caught her shoulders, steadied her. "Are you okay? Why don't you sit down for a sec?"

He wrapped a strong arm around her shoulders and led her over to the leather sofa in front of the fireplace, sitting on the coffee table across from her, his gaze fixed on her, his two big hands taking hold of hers.

She found herself staring back at him, this man from her memories—memories from another life. He seemed out of place here, her past now standing right here in her present. A trill of panic shot through her.

She drew her hands away, words spilling out of her. "I didn't think I would ever . . . I never expected . . . I didn't know you'd be here, and . . ."

"Small world, isn't it?" He smiled. "Nate and I are old friends."

It was then she noticed that the room had fallen silent, apart from the chatter of children playing down the hall. She looked up to find everyone watching her. Feeling strangely exposed, she shifted her gaze to the fireplace.

Javier leaned in. "Why don't we find someplace quiet where we can talk?"

A chance to talk with him in private. "Yes."

"Try the library," she heard Nate say.

She got to her feet, following Javier down the hallway and into a spectacular two-story library with its own fireplace. Under normal circumstances the room would have made her smile with delight. Today, it was just a room. She sat in front of the fire in a soft leather wingback chair, her gaze drawn to him. He sat down not in the chair beside her, but across from her, as if to give her room to breathe.

She needed it. For so long he'd been just a memory, a man with whom she'd spent one precious, luxurious, uninhibited weekend. And now he was here.

"Are you okay?" His eyebrows pressed down in a concerned frown. "Can I get you something to drink—that bubbly water Jack promised you?"

"No, I'm fine. I was just . . . surprised." An understatement.

"Sorry to give you a shock. I had no idea there was any connection between you and Nate until he told me you might come to the barbecue."

"Please don't apologize. It's not your fault." She allowed herself to look at him, to really *look* at him. "You haven't changed a bit."

Oh, he was a beautiful man—dark, exotic, sensual. Some men were intelligent. Some were tall. Some were sexy. Some had thick hair or broad shoulders or natural athleticism. Some had lips that made women long to kiss them.

Javier had it all.

His short, dark hair had a bit of curl, his nose straight, his jaw strong. High cheekbones, full lips, and long lashes added a boyish touch to his otherwise masculine face. He was muscular without being bulky, broad shoulders tapering to a narrow waist.

She'd noticed him the moment she'd walked into the restaurant in Dubai. Wearing a dark T-shirt that stretched across the muscles of his chest and shoulders, he'd stood out in a room full of European businessmen in suits and Arabs wearing traditional *kanduras* and *gutras*. When he'd come to her table to rescue her from those drunk Russians, she'd known they would end up in bed. Despite what Derek Tower might think, she didn't make a habit of sleeping with men she met in bars. Javier was the exception, and she hadn't regretted it. He'd been the most giving lover she'd ever had—sensual, focused, attentive to the smallest details.

Something stirred inside her at the memory, something she hadn't felt in a very long time—physical attraction.

And her sense of panic grew.

She'd thought about him for so long, wondered what it would be like to see him again. Now she knew. It was like being slapped in the face with the life she'd lost, with the life that Al-Nassar had stolen from her.

"Neither have you."

She gave a little inadvertent laugh. "We both know that's not true."

"I'm so sorry about what happened. I saw the news broadcast when you were taken. I . . . I've never felt so damn helpless in my entire life."

Laura didn't know what to say. Most people avoided mentioning her abduction and what had followed.

He stood, walked to the fireplace, added wood to the blaze. "I followed your story. What you did took brains and guts. Speaking to them in their own language. Using their culture and beliefs to force them to see you as a human being. Yielding on the outside but fighting to stay strong on the inside."

He spoke the words matter-of-factly, but when he turned back to face her, his gaze was soft with sympathy.

Laura looked away, his praise making her uncomfortable. She didn't deserve it, any of it. "I'm just lucky I was able to speak Arabic and—"

"Luck had nothing to do with it." His tone was adamant, brooking no challenge. "I have a world of respect for you, Laura."

She looked up, willed herself to meet his gaze again. If those words had come from anyone else—her mother, her grandmother, her therapist—she would have dismissed them as nothing more than attempts to distract or console her. But coming from Javier, they seemed to slip inside her.

"I would have gotten in touch with you a long time ago, but I've been out of the country most of the past two years. And when I didn't hear from you, I thought maybe you didn't want contact."

"We said no strings." She changed the subject. She couldn't go there. She just couldn't. "How do you know Nate?"

"He and I served together in Afghanistan."

"So you *are* military." She found herself smiling. "I knew it."

A dark eyebrow arched. "Oh, yeah? What gave it away?"

"You just have that look."

The other brow arched. "What look?"

But there was something important she needed to say. "It's good to see you again, Javier, but you should know that I . . . I'm not the same person I was in Dubai. Too much has happened since then."

She hoped he understood what she was trying to tell him. This wasn't going to be like last time. She wasn't going to rip off her clothes and fall into bed with him. Even if she'd wanted a relationship, a lover, she couldn't have one. She didn't think she was capable of enjoying sex right now. Besides, her body had changed.

If they slept together, he would discover the stretch marks on her belly, and he would know she'd had a baby. She couldn't share that secret with anyone—not yet, not until Klara was safely with her here in the U.S.

"I'm not going to make demands of you. I've got no expectations." His lips curved in a lethal lopsided grin. "But it is good to see you, too, *bella*."

Bella. Beauty.

That was what he'd called her in Dubai.

She looked away. "So . . . what branch of the military were you in?"

"The navy." He seemed to hesitate for a moment. "I'm a SEAL."

"YOU'RE A . . . A SEAL?"

"It's not something I'm supposed to spread around." Javier watched some of the tension leave Laura's body and found himself feeling both pride at her reaction and annoyance at the fact that she seemed more at ease with him as a frogman than as the man who'd made love with her.

"I'm sure you already know this, but a team of SEALs saved my life. I wouldn't be here if it weren't for them." She tucked a strand of hair behind her ear, her motions revealing dark bruises around her wrist where that bastard Tower had grabbed her.

Someone needed to deal with him.

But before Javier could give any thought to that, he found himself in the awkward position of listening as she described her rescue. How she'd woken up to screams. How hearing American accents had made her panic. How the other women had held her back, the one Javier later killed threatening to cut out Laura's tongue if she spoke. How she'd realized with a shock that she was American, too. How the sight of "the tall SEAL" walking toward the helicopter had pushed her into shouting out.

And Javier realized she was talking about *him*.

"I didn't think he'd heard me, and I knew Zainab would kill me, but then he turned. He shouted at me to stop and get down, and I thought he was going to shoot me, but he shot her instead. He killed a woman. He didn't even hesitate. He tore off my burka, and the next thing I knew, he was carrying me onto the helicopter." Laura's hands balled into fists and pressed together tightly in her lap, the only outward sign that talking about this was hard for her. "He punched Al-Nassar in the face when Al-Nassar threatened me again. He was my hero."

How do you like that, Corbray? You're upstaging yourself.

Javier cleared his throat. "I bet he remembers that night, too."

Oh, he did. Yes, he did.

"He and his men were all so kind to me. I never got to thank them."

Javier wanted to forget he'd ever heard of OPSEC and tell Laura that *he* was the tall SEAL, that *he* had carried her out and punched that bastard in the face. He wanted to tell her that no mission had ever meant as much to him as that one, that rescuing her had been the highlight of his career as an operator. God, he wanted to tell her. He knew she wouldn't run to the press or write an article about it, but he'd been ordered not to discuss the mission with anyone who hadn't been a part of it.

He fought to keep his voice and his facial expression neutral, choosing his words carefully. "I was amazed to find out that you were alive—and damned grateful."

Laura's eyes went wide, and she stared at him.

You gave it away, cabrón! She knows. She figured it out.

"You could do it! You could thank them for me, couldn't you?" She looked at him with such hopefulness. "Naval Special Warfare wouldn't give me their names, but they'd pass on a message for you, wouldn't they?"

"Uh . . . You want me to thank them for you?" Okay, this was too fucking surreal. "Yeah. Sure. I can do that."

You bet he could. He had the surviving members of the team on speed dial.

She gave him a relieved smile. "That would mean a lot to me. Thank you."

There was something fragile about her now that hadn't been there in Dubai, a vulnerability that put an ache in his chest. He clamped down on the urge to walk over to her and take her into his arms.

"Hey, no problem."

She looked toward the fire. "I pray for him, for all of them, every night. I'm not religious, but those men are out there somewhere in danger, putting their lives on the line. They risked everything to save me. Who knows? Maybe prayers help."

She had no idea that some of the men she was praying for were already dead or recovering from severe wounds, and he couldn't tell her.

His throat grew tight. "I'm sure they would appreciate that—if they knew."

She looked away again. "I suppose we should get back to the party. Everyone must be wondering what's going on."

"I suppose so." Javier got to his feet. "Hey, you want to grab some dinner, maybe catch a movie? I'm in town for a few weeks."

He knew the moment the words were out that he'd said the wrong thing.

A shadow passed over her face. "I don't know . . ."

"This isn't me trying to trick my way into your bed. Don't insult me, *bella.* I already told you—I've got no expectations."

The wariness on her face eased a little. "Okay. I'd like that."

CHAPTER 5

Laura left the Cimarron right after supper, making her way quickly and quietly to her car while everyone else was sledding down the hill behind the house. She felt bad about not thanking her hosts and saying good-bye, but she just had to get away.

It was harder than she'd thought to be around the children, especially the little ones. Sophie's little girl Addison was about the same age as Klara. Every time Laura had looked at Addie she hadn't been able to help but think about her own daughter, the one she'd never seen except from across a room. Then, when Tessa and Kat had nursed their babies, the sight had made something twist in Laura's stomach, her mind overtaken by a confused memory of swollen, aching breasts, her nipples leaking milk meant for a baby she'd never held, let alone breast-fed.

And then there was Javier.

She'd never thought she'd see him again, and although a part of her had felt true joy at seeing him, he had served only to remind her of how much she had changed. The adventurous, sensual woman who'd enjoyed two days and three nights of crazy, passionate sex with a man she barely knew no longer existed.

Laura spent the rest of the evening swallowing her emotions along with a pint of Godiva white chocolate raspberry ice cream. Then, when it was late enough, she Skyped her mother, who was just getting out of bed in Stockholm. They talked about the trial, Al-Nassar's threats, Derek Tower.

"He says he has sources in Pakistan who told him that an American tipped off the terrorists to my location that day, claiming to have gotten the information from me. Tower thinks I gave away my itinerary. I know that's not true."

"Of course it's not." Her mother let it go.

And then Laura told them about Javier.

"It was *him*, the postcard man? And he's a SEAL? Oh, *älskling*, how wonderful!" Her mother's smile faded. "Weren't you happy to see him?"

Laura tried to explain. "I'm not the person he knew. He looks at me, and he remembers someone else."

"The woman he remembers still exists inside you. You just need to set her free."

Laura wished it were so simple. "He asked me out to dinner."

"I hope you said yes." Laura's grandmother leaned in, her round face appearing in the onscreen image. "You need to get out, to be with other young people."

"I did, but I wish I hadn't. He said he wasn't expecting anything. No sex or—"

"Too bad," her grandmother interjected. "That would be good for you."

"You know I can't sleep with him. If I did, he'd see my stretch marks, and he'd know. I'd have to explain, and then he would think I was the worst—"

"What happened with Klara was *not* your fault." Her mother's voice turned to steel. "Unless he has no heart, he will understand that. *You* are the only one who holds that against you."

"Did you say yes?" Laura's grandmother was not letting it go.

"Yes, Gran."

Her mother and her grandmother shared a smile.

"You are *not* going to back out of it and cancel on him." Her grandmother's blue eyes narrowed, as if she knew that was exactly what Laura had been thinking of doing.

"It is time for you to live again, Laura." Her mother's gaze was gentle, understanding. "This will be a good thing. You'll see."

Laura carried her mother's words to bed with her and through the day on Sunday while she did laundry, cleaned the house, and transcribed interviews for her VA article—a mind-numbingly tedious process she'd never had to deal with as a broadcast journalist.

When her cell phone rang just before noon, she wasn't surprised to find it was Javier. She'd known he would call sooner rather than later.

"You left without saying good-bye." His voice was deep, warm.

"I'm sorry. I just . . . couldn't stay any longer."

There was a long pause.

"I don't want to make you uncomfortable, Laura. If it's too hard for you to be around me—"

"No!" Angry with herself for being so fearful, so timid, so transparent, she spoke more harshly than she'd intended. "No, it's fine. I'd love to go to dinner with you. It's just . . . I haven't been out much since this happened, and I'm not all that comfortable around lots of people."

As true as this was, it was an excuse. Being around him *was* hard for her, but she couldn't bring herself to admit that.

They settled on tomorrow night. Javier would pick her up at her place at seven, and they would go around the corner to the Wynkoop Brewing Company, where she could have her favorite salad and he could sample some of the microbrews for which Denver was famous.

"I'll be with you. It will be okay."

She hoped he was right.

LAURA GOT TO work early the next morning and was grateful to find that she was no longer considered news, the throng of reporters gone, off chasing other stories. She said a quick good morning to Cormack and crossed the lobby to the elevator. She had an interview scheduled first thing with a former soldier named Ted Hollis, who had answered her ad for veterans having trouble with VA claims. He was living with untreated PTSD and claimed he'd been trying to get help from the VA for more than nine months.

"Laura, wait for me!" Sophie caught her at the elevator,

entering just before the doors closed, cup of coffee in hand, handbag over her shoulder, her strawberry-blond hair done up in an artfully messy bun.

The elevator car began to move.

"How was the rest of your weekend?" Sophie asked.

Laura could tell Sophie was trying to decide whether to ask about the barbecue. "I did some work on my VA story, transcribed some interviews I did last week with a couple of former soldiers."

"I'm glad you came to the Cimarron. I hope you had a good time."

"I did. The food was delicious. Thanks for inviting me." There was no way to avoid the topic. "Sorry I left so abruptly. I felt a little . . . overwhelmed."

Sophie gave her a warm smile. "As long as you're okay. I can see how hanging with all of us could be a bit much. We've all known each other for so long. But we were all really happy you were there. I hope you'll join us again."

"I'm glad I finally got to meet everyone."

The elevator came to a halt, and the doors opened.

They stepped out and started down the hallway when Holly hurried up behind them, her heels clicking on the floor.

"Hey, Laura! Hey, Sophie!" She fell in beside them, a colorful Altuzarra sweater and tight black Rag & Bone pants hugging her perfect curves, suede Prada pumps with three-inch heels on her feet. "I can't believe that hunky SEAL is a friend of yours, Laura. If you tell me the two of you have slept together, I'm going to be *so* jealous."

"Holly!" Sophie glared at her.

But that didn't seem to deter Holly one bit. She looked at Laura's face. "Oh, my God! You have!"

Laura had overheard enough conversations between Sophie and Holly in the newsroom to know that Holly had no filter. But how was Laura supposed to respond to that? Fortunately she didn't have to say anything, as Holly went on.

"I've never met a SEAL before. I think it must take so much courage to do what he does. Five months ago he was almost killed, and he still wants to go back."

Laura's step faltered. "Almost killed?"

"He didn't tell you?" Sophie asked.

"No." He hadn't even hinted.

But Holly and Sophie knew all about it. As they made their way toward the I-Team's corner of the newsroom, the two of them told her how Javier and his team had been caught in an ambush, how he'd been shot four times and had barely survived. Now, he was eager to return to active duty.

"I don't even want to go back to places where someone has been rude to me, like restaurants or department stores," Holly was saying. "I can't imagine wanting to return to a place where men were trying to *kill* me."

Neither could Laura. "It takes a special kind of man to do that job."

She set her handbag down on her desk, sat, and booted up her computer.

"So he didn't tell you any of this?" Holly sat on Sophie's desk.

Laura knew what Holly was really asking. She was trying to figure out if Laura and Javier were still connected. "He was concerned about me and didn't talk about himself. But I'll ask him about it tonight. We're having dinner."

Laura spoke the words with an odd sense of satisfaction.

And then it struck her.

You're jealous!

She was.

Javier had told Holly and the others things he hadn't told her.

You didn't give him a chance.

She'd been so busy talking about herself that she hadn't asked him how he'd been these past three and a half years. Clearly, she wasn't the only one who'd suffered.

Holly heaved an exaggerated sigh. "The good men are always taken."

LAURA HAD HEARD stories like Ted Hollis's before, but few had been so graphic—or so wrenching. His job through three tours of duty had included cleaning blood and human tissue from inside vehicles damaged by IEDs so that those vehicles could be repaired and put back into service. The gore he had seen was the stuff of horror films. Midway through his third deployment, he'd had a nervous breakdown and had spent three weeks in a military hospital before being shipped stateside again. Though post-traumatic stress had all but rendered him nonfunctional, he had yet to get treatment and was self-medicating with alcohol.

She'd been speaking with him for almost an hour. His story was one of the most compelling she'd heard so far. She felt sick for him.

"It's the nightmares that bother me most," he said. "They feel so real. When I wake up, I don't even know where I am. But I suppose you know your share about nightmares, don't you, Ms. Nilsson?"

She did, but she wasn't accustomed to discussing such things with strangers. Then again, she was asking Mr. Hollis to bare his wounds for millions of strangers in the form of the newspaper's readership. It seemed only fair to answer.

"Yes, I do."

"I've read the articles about you and watched your interview with Diane Sawyer. I've always wondered what frightened you the most. The daily rapes or the idea of having your head cut off."

Laura's pulse picked up. She reminded herself that she was dealing with someone who needed treatment, someone who was probably trying to empathize with her, one trauma victim to another. "Mr. Hollis—"

"I think maybe being raped every day would be worse than being dead."

That wasn't how it had been for Laura. "I . . . I was more afraid of having my head cut off. I wanted to survive."

"I'm sorry. Was that too personal? Maybe I shouldn't have asked. I guess I wouldn't know. I'm a man. I've never been raped. It must be pretty horrible."

"Mr. Hollis—"

A loud *crack*. A boom like thunder that shook the floor beneath Laura's feet. An orange wall of flame. Shattered glass. Heat.

She was knocked sideways, her head striking the edge of her desk, one word flashing through her mind before she lost consciousness.

Bomb.

* * *

Javier followed Nate through the garage toward the mudroom, his stomach growling. It was just after nine in the morning, and he'd already been up and working for four hours with nothing more than coffee in his gut. "So Wilson starts handing out soccer balls to every kid in the village. One kid drops his ball in the dirt, kicks it, and accidentally hits Wilson square in the nuts. That dawg hit the dirt like he'd been shot."

Nate gave a sympathetic groan. "No good deed goes unpunished."

"Man, I felt for him, but I couldn't quit laughing." Javier took off his gloves, parka, and boots, and made his way toward the scent of eggs and bacon that was wafting toward them from the kitchen.

"Tell me you've got fresh coffee, old man," Nate called to his father.

But Jack wasn't in the kitchen, bacon sizzling forgotten on the stove. They found him in the living room together with Megan, who looked wide-eyed and pale.

"What is it?"

On the television screen was an image of flames and smoke.

Jack glanced over at them, his face grave. "VBIED. It happened just a couple of minutes ago."

Megan turned to her husband. "Someone car-bombed the newspaper."

Laura.

Adrenaline gave Javier a good hard kick, breath rushing from his lungs.

Al-Nassar, you hijo e puta*!*

"Any casualties?" Nate's gaze was fixed on the flames, his jaw tight.

Jack shook his head. "No word yet."

"I've tried Sophie's cell phone and can't reach her." Fresh tears gathered in Megan's eyes. "Marc's on his way there with SWAT, but he hasn't been able to reach her either. Oh, Nate, I'm so afraid for her—and for all of our friends there."

Javier turned back toward the mudroom.

"Where the hell do you think you're going?" Nate called after him.

"I'm going to find Laura."

Nate followed. "How did I know you were going to say that?"

"It's not as bad as it looks. Wounds on the face and head always bleed a lot." Laura dabbed a square of gauze she'd gotten from the cafeteria's first-aid kit to the cut on Holly's temple, her own head throbbing, her stomach in knots, one thought running repeatedly through her mind.

It had happened. It had actually happened.

Someone had tried to kill her *here* in her new hometown.

That had to be it. This couldn't be random. A few days ago, Al-Nassar had called upon his followers to hunt her down and kill her, and today a car bomb had gone off outside her window.

She had already called her mother and her grandmother to let them know that she was safe. Her mother had wanted her to pack her bags and return to Sweden, but Laura couldn't do that. She'd tried to make her mother understand.

"If I let them frighten me away from the life I want, then Al-Nassar wins. I have to show him and his minions that I'm not afraid."

"But you *are* afraid, Laura."

Yes, she was. In fact, she was terrified.

But she wouldn't run.

Holly trembled uncontrollably, tears streaming down her face. "Do you think I'll need stitches . . . or plastic surgery?"

"I don't think so, but I'm not a doctor." Laura's hands were only slightly steadier than Holly's, but it made Laura feel better to help, taking her mind off her own shock and fear. "Just hold it here. There you go. It will stop the bleeding."

Beside them, Sophie spoke with her husband on Laura's cell phone, her own forgotten in her car. "We're in the cafeteria. We had to get out of the smoke. It was rolling in through the broken windows. Laura hit her head and was unconscious for a minute or two, but she seems okay now. We all got cut by flying glass. Apart from that, we're all fine."

Thank God!

If any of Laura's coworkers had been seriously hurt or killed . . .

Already, six people had died because of her. Now her I-Team friends had come into harm's way, too. Sophie, Matt, Alex, Joaquin—they'd all been in the newsroom. If that side of the building had come down, they would have died with her.

The thought left her nauseated, shaky.

Around them, chaos reigned. The high-pitched squeal of the fire alarm. Tom, Alex, and Matt shouting to be heard as they tried to figure out how to get the paper out on time. The murmur of voices as those who hadn't evacuated the building milled about, waiting for the all clear to return to their desks.

It felt surreal, a nightmare.

Sophie lowered the cell phone, her face lined with worry, the bandage on her arm already soaked through with blood. "Are you okay?"

"I'm sorry, Sophie. I'm so sorry."

"It's not your fault." Sophie gave her hand a squeeze, then raised her voice so that everyone could hear her. "Marc said there are undetonated explosives out there. SWAT is coming in to evacuate the building."

"Shit." Tom turned to Matt and Alex. "We need to move fast, get everyone's computers and files moved down here before the cops push us out. If we don't, we're fucked. Alton, Nilsson, want to lend us a hand?"

Sophie shook her head. "Marc said to stay here in the cafeteria, and that's what I'm doing. Didn't you hear me? There are undetonated—"

Ignoring her, Tom turned with Matt and Alex and disappeared out the door—only to reappear a minute or so later, herded by a group of SWAT officers with Marc in the lead, Julian behind him.

Tom was a big man, but Marc was taller. Wearing Kevlar and carrying SWAT gear, he was also more imposing. His gaze rested a moment on Sophie, taking in the cuts on her right arm and cheek, and Laura could tell that more than anything he wanted to go to her. But he had a job to do.

He faced Tom. "You can get the computers as soon as the bomb squad has done its job. Now cooperate, or you're going to put me in the awkward position of arresting my wife's boss."

Done with Tom, Marc turned to the room and raised his voice. "Listen, everyone! There are still undetonated explosives outside. I need you all to leave by the rear exit. Be calm, but be quick. We're evacuating the entire block. Follow the police barricades to safety. No one is allowed to remain inside the building."

While Marc organized the evacuation, Julian walked over to Laura, something in his hand—a Kevlar vest. "Let's get this on you."

Laura's adrenaline spiked. "You think someone's waiting out there for me?"

His expression gave nothing away. "The vest is just a precaution."

She raised her arms and let him draw it on over her head.

"I'm glad to see you're okay." Julian pulled the Velcro straps tight. "I heard you got a bad bump on the head. How are you feeling?"

"I'm fine. Just a headache, maybe a little dizzy."

He frowned, seemed to study her. "We've got a couple of ambulances standing by. I think it's best if we get you, Holly, and Sophie to the hospital, get you cleaned up, make sure you really are okay."

Laura shook her head. She hated hospitals. "I'm fine. I'd rather work to get the paper out. They're going to need all the help they—"

"I wouldn't be doing my job as a law officer and a friend if I let you go back to work without first seeing a doctor. Head injuries can take you by surprise. You can refuse treatment if you want, but at least let a doctor check you out." When she didn't object, he pushed the button on the radio clipped to his Kevlar. "Eight-twenty-five."

A voice crackled back. "Eight-twenty-five, go ahead."

"I need two ambulances at the paper's rear entrance. Someone will need to shift the barricades to let them through." He turned his attention to Holly. He drew her close in a careful hug. "It's going to be okay, honey."

Holly cried harder.

Marc at last came to stand at Sophie's side, his hand resting protectively on the small of her back. "Let's get you out of here. That cut on your arm looks deep."

Julian looked over at Laura. "Can you walk?"

"I walked down here." His hand at her elbow, she headed out of the cafeteria and down the hall, the blaring fire alarm louder in the hallway, the shrill sound making her headache worse.

She stepped out the back door and for one dark second found herself back in Baghdad in the aftermath of a terrorist bombing, the air tinged with the reek of burning fuel, rubber, and wires, men armed with high-powered assault rifles on the rooftop of the building next door, the whir of a helicopter mixing with the wail of sirens.

But this wasn't Baghdad. It was Denver.

How could this have followed her to Denver?

To Laura's left, two ambulances turned down the alley toward them, steel barricades and police cars with flashing lights holding curious onlookers and the media at a distance, officers guiding the other evacuated employees to safety. To her right stood Marc holding Sophie in a protective embrace.

Sophie looked up at him. "Be careful."

He cupped the back of her head with a big, gloved hand and kissed her forehead. "You know I will be. You let them take good care of that arm."

It was an intimate moment, a private moment.

Laura looked away, feeling sick to her stomach to think these good people had been put in harm's way because of her. She looked up at Julian. "Do you have any idea who did this?"

"We will as soon as we can ID the body."

"You mean . . . ?"

Julian nodded his head. "Looks like a suicide bomber."

CHAPTER 6

JAVIER LEANED AGAINST the wall in the emergency room of University Hospital, feeling more restless by the minute. On the television screen, Channel 12 kept going back and forth between the same recycled footage they'd been repeating for the past three hours. The smoking hulk of the car. Firefighters dousing the flames. Police evacuating the area as the bomb squad moved in. An aerial view of the blast site filmed from a news helo. SWAT guys milling around in body armor.

So the FBI hadn't found Al-Nassar's threats against Laura credible.

Idiots.

They were damned lucky the bastard who'd tried to kill her today hadn't known what he was doing. If he had . . .

It had been close, so damned close.

Javier fought the urge to pace, glanced around the waiting area. A thin old man with papery skin and an oxygen tube beneath his nose. A mother and father with a crying baby. A middle-aged woman sitting alone. Two men and a woman who were almost certainly journalists, smartphones out, notepads in hand. They were clearly checking the place out, probably hoping to snag an interview with Laura.

What kind of assholes staked out an ER, for God's sake? And what was taking so long? Maybe Laura was more seriously injured than they'd realized.

Or maybe she doesn't want to see you.

Nate had left with Sophie and Holly almost an hour ago. Both women had been cut by flying glass. Sophie had needed stitches, and Holly had seemed pretty shaken up, her perfect face marred by little nicks. But both of them had wanted to get back to work to help get the paper out on time—a reminder to Javier that courage came in all shapes and sizes.

A woman in blue scrubs walked up to him. "You can see Ms. Nilsson now."

It's about fucking time.

Javier followed the aide through the double doors, aware that the journalists had gotten to their feet the second they'd heard Laura's name and were now watching him. Down a corridor to the right, he saw a cop standing guard outside an exam room.

The aide pointed. "She's in exam room nine."

"Thanks." Javier turned down the corridor, drew his wallet out of his back jeans pocket, and showed his driver's license to the cop, who jotted his name down on a list, then stepped aside.

Javier knocked. "Laura?"

"Come in."

He found her sitting up in the exam bed, talking on her cell phone.

"Thanks for calling. It means a lot to me. Bye." She disconnected the call. "Gary Chapin, my former anchor. He called to check on me."

The left side of her face had a few tiny nicks from flying glass, flecks of blood on her tailored white shirt. A dressing of gauze was taped to the inner elbow of her left arm where they'd hooked her to an IV. Her eyes were swollen, proof she'd been crying.

Seeing her like this—hurt, angry, afraid—made him want to hit someone. How the hell had this been allowed to happen? Al-Nassar, the media, the feds—they'd all played a role in this, through either action or inaction.

But Javier had walked into enough hospital rooms in his life, visited enough wounded men, to know that his anger wouldn't help Laura.

He put a smile on his face. "You're looking good. How you feeling?"

"I just want to get out of here." Her blond brows knitted in irritation. "They say I have a mild concussion. They insisted on doing two MRIs even though I said I was fine. I want to go home, but they're taking their time discharging me."

"They're just trying to take good care of you."

"I suppose so." She looked away, the tension inside her palpable. "I don't like hospitals."

Neither did Javier.

He walked to the bedside. "When I heard the news, I . . . I'm glad you're okay."

"The networks aren't reporting this yet, but it was a suicide bomber."

"Yeah." He'd heard that from Nate, who'd heard it from Marc.

The anger faded from her face, naked fear in its place. "They're going to do it, aren't they? They're going to kill me. I'm going to spend the rest of my life looking over my shoulder, and one day—"

"No, *bella*." Javier took her right hand, gave it a squeeze. He wanted to do more. He wanted to wrap his arms around her and hold her tight, but he wasn't sure she'd feel comfortable being touched like that. "People are going to be asking the feds some tough questions. The FBI is going to have to step up now and do its job. You're a hero to a lot of folks out there. The feds can't let anything happen to you."

"Tell them that. I spoke to them Friday. They blew me off."

Javier hoped whoever she'd spoken to had been handed his ass today. "They won't be able to blow you off now."

"Al-Nassar told me I would live the rest of my life in fear. I told him I would forget him. Now look at me. I'm shaking, terrified. Damn it!" She looked up at him, a kind of desperate fury in her eyes. "I don't want to be afraid anymore. He's stolen *so much* from me. *So* much. I can't give him that satisfaction. I just *can't*."

Javier couldn't begin to understand what she was feeling. He'd never been a prisoner, never been raped. He'd never had control of his body and life ripped away from him. Even when he'd been shot, he'd at least been armed and able to fight back. "You look like you're holding up pretty well to me."

She let out a gust of breath, then shook her head as if he'd just said something ridiculous. "I spent an hour crying on the phone to my mother."

"I'd say you're entitled." If only she could see herself through his eyes.

"She and my grandmother want me to give up my job and move back to Sweden to live a quiet life in some small town up north where everyone knows everyone and there's no place for strangers to hide, but—"

The door opened behind him and two men in suits entered. The first was in his mid-forties, shorter than Javier by a good few inches, his dark hair cut conservatively, his brows dark and bushy, his face round. The man behind him was taller and blander with brown hair and eyes to match, his face expressionless.

It was about time they showed up.

Javier crossed his arms over his chest. "Don't they teach you FBI boys to knock?"

"Ms. Nilsson." The bastard's gaze fixed for a moment on Laura's chest before shifting to his partner. "This is Special Agent Spiteri. We need to ask you a few questions."

Laura's gaze went cold. "Do you find Al-Nassar's threats credible now, Agent Petras?"

"You might believe that you're the center of the terrorists' universe, Ms. Nilsson, but the truth is there are other more tangible threats."

"Whoa, there, buddy." Javier stepped forward. "You're in the emergency room, and regardless of what your priorities are, someone tried to kill Ms. Nilsson today. Show some respect, man."

Petras turned to Javier. "You're Javier Corbray."

It was a trick meant to impress, but Javier knew Petras had simply gotten his name from the cop outside the door.

"I'm an old friend of Laura's."

"You'll need to wait out in the hallway."

Petras could go fuck himself as far as Javier was concerned. He turned to Laura. "Is that what you want, *bella*?"

"No." Laura looked over at Petras. "Javier stays."

Petras glanced from Javier to Laura, cold indifference on his face. He reached into his pocket, drew out a photograph, and handed it to her. "Do you recognize him?"

Laura looked down at the photo, the blood slowly draining from her face. "No. Is he the one who . . . ?"

"The vehicle was registered to him, and he's been reported missing. We're still waiting for DNA confirmation."

She handed the photo back to Petras, then turned her face away.

"You've never seen him before?"

"No. What's his name?"

"Ali Al Zahrani. Eighteen years of age. U.S. citizen born in Denver to Saudi immigrants. College student. His dad is a physician." The agent tucked the photo back inside his pocket.

"So young." The words were a whisper. "Please tell his parents how sorry I am."

Petras acted as if he hadn't heard her, his attitude seriously getting on Javier's nerves. "The FBI is prepared to give you short-term protection while we resolve this case. We don't yet know whether the bomber acted alone or was working with others. It could be that he removed the threat against you the moment he detonated the explosives. Regardless, we're coordinating with the Denver police to have a two-man security detail on duty around the clock."

"What about my car? It's still in the parking lot at the newspaper."

"Give me the make, model, and license plate number, and we'll have a police officer return it to you once it's been cleared."

"Thank you. There's just one thing." Laura's chin went up. "Last week, you ignored my concerns and spent more time looking at my chest than my face. With all *due* respect, I don't trust you enough to put my life in your hands. I want someone else to be put in charge of my security detail."

Javier fought back a grin as Petras's face slowly turned red.

LAURA SAT IN the backseat of Agent Petras's brown Chevy Impala, Javier beside her. She stared out the window, watching the busy streets of Denver pass. The state capitol with its golden dome. The graceful architecture of Civic Center Park. The redbrick walls of Coors Field. The perpetual construction zone around Union Station. It was the same city, and yet it felt different.

"When I got up this morning, this was my new hometown." She'd hoped to make a new start and one day raise her daughter here. "Now it's the city where a teenage boy died trying to kill me."

"You okay?" Javier was sitting so close that she could smell the subtle spice of his aftershave, his voice deep, soothing.

"Sure. It could've been worse, right?" Laura squeezed her hands tightly together in her lap. "Sorry you got dragged into this."

The doctor had insisted that Laura take the next few days off from work and find someone to stay with her for the next twenty-four hours in case her concussion proved to be more serious than they realized. Javier had immediately volunteered. Laura had agreed for purely selfish reasons. She'd feel safer with him nearby.

"Hey, don't apologize." He closed his hands over hers, giving them a reassuring squeeze. "I wouldn't have offered if I didn't really want to be here. Besides, how else am I going to have dinner with you tonight? I just know you'd try to use this whole car bomb thing as an excuse to cancel on me otherwise."

She couldn't help but smile.

They stopped at the Denver Police Station where Nate had left Javier's duffel bag and guitar case, then headed straight for Laura's place, which SWAT and the FBI had already secured. They arrived at The Ironworks, an old redbrick industrial building recently converted to lofts, and parked in the gated underground parking garage, where Laura saw what she hoped would be the last of Petras. She and Javier took the elevator to the third floor to find another FBI agent already waiting outside her door. Laura didn't miss the fleeting look of surprise on Javier's face when he saw the agent was a woman.

"I'm Special Agent Janet Killeen." The agent shook their hands. "I'm taking over your protection detail from Agent

Petras, Ms. Nilsson. I've always admired your courage. I'll do my best to make sure these assholes don't get another crack at you."

Laura immediately liked her.

She was in her early forties, tall and slender with a pretty face, her shoulder-length brown hair sleek and shiny. She wore a brown pantsuit with a crisp white shirt and black pumps, looking more like a real estate agent than a fed. And yet Laura was certain that somewhere beneath her tailored jacket Agent Killeen was strapped.

"SWAT already went through the building and the surrounding streets and alleys to make sure there were no surprises waiting for you. DPD has its two-man detail out front. I'll be out back with another agent, so you'll be covered."

"Thank you, Agent Killeen."

"Call me Janet. Will you be staying here, Mr. Corbray?" She drew a notepad and pen out of her jacket pocket.

Javier nodded. "Yes, ma'am. Like I told your buddy Petras, Laura is a friend."

"Petras is not my buddy." Janet glanced through her notes, her eyebrows going up. "He ran background on you and says you're a Navy SEAL. Are you carrying?"

"I've got a concealed SIG P226 loaded with hollow point and a Walther PPS."

Laura looked Javier up and down, wondering how he managed to hide all of that beneath a gray blazer, black T-shirt, and jeans. She'd had no idea he was armed.

Why hadn't she guessed he was a SEAL? Now that she knew, it seemed obvious, the pieces falling into place. His confidence. The graceful way he moved. His hard, muscular body. His attention to detail, both in and out of bed. His reluctance in Dubai to talk about his job.

"Good to know." Janet looked up from her notepad and smiled. "If we hear weapons fire, we won't shoot the first person we see holding a firearm."

Javier gave a nod. "I'd appreciate that."

Janet took a few minutes to explain the same things that Petras had outlined for them and then went on her way, leaving the two of them alone.

Javier glanced around. "Nice place."

"Thanks." With the original brick walls, polished wood floors, and concrete ceilings with visible ductwork, it had the urban look Laura loved. Big windows let in lots of natural sunlight and gave her a beautiful view of the Rockies to the west. "It's my home, my sanctuary."

Javier walked to the windows and looked out toward the mountains, where a faint pink glow was all that remained of daylight. "I guess you see a lot of sunsets."

"When I'm not working late." Except for midsummer, it was usually dark when she got home.

He glanced around the living room, his gaze fixing on her bookshelves. "Is that your Emmy?"

"Yeah." The golden statuette had an alcove to itself, a reminder of what she'd once accomplished. "It's probably dusty."

He walked over and carefully picked it up. "You got this for that investigative piece about the soldiers who were looting and shaking down Iraqi civilians, right?"

"I'm surprised you remember that."

He set the statuette down. "That was big news to those of us in the military. Some guys were pissed, felt coming down on them was too harsh, but I thought you did a good thing. We can't pretend to be heroes if we're acting like thugs."

It felt strange to be alone with him here in her most personal space. No one had ever been here before. "Want a tour?"

Even as she asked the question, she realized that the adrenaline she'd been running on all day was fast disappearing, leaving her empty, exhausted.

"This is obviously the living room, kitchen, and dining area." She walked through the kitchen toward the hallway.

"Hey, that's my postcard."

She turned to find him standing in front of her refrigerator holding the postcard from Dubai, surprise on his face. "You left it in my room."

"You kept it." His gaze met hers, something in his eyes that made her look away.

She turned and walked down the hallway toward the bedroom area. "This is the guest room where you'll be sleeping. It has its own bathroom. Across the hallway is my office. The master bedroom is at the end of the hallway."

While he glanced around the guest bedroom, postcard still in hand, she walked to the windows and closed the blinds, her head starting to throb again, the day's events weighing down on her, the smiling face of the young suicide bomber stuck in her mind. "I should start dinner."

"You don't need to take care of me, Laura." He set the postcard on the nightstand. "You should rest. Go soak in the tub or lie down for a while. I asked you out, didn't I? Let me take care of dinner."

"SOPHIE AND HOLLY said you'd been wounded, that you're on medical leave."

Javier nodded. "I'll be back on active duty soon."

They'd finished dinner a while ago. Javier had ordered chicken marsala, a dish he knew she loved, from an Italian place down the street, and they now sat on the sofa, a beer in his hand, a glass of white wine in hers. He was trying to keep her mind off what had happened today, though he knew that was probably impossible.

She had changed into faded jeans and a silky blue sweater that hugged her soft curves, the sweater picking up the blue in her eyes. "What happened? Or maybe you don't want to talk about it."

He told her only what he'd told the others. "There's not a lot to say. We were ambushed. They had the high ground, put four rounds in me. I spent a few weeks in a hospital and then a couple of months in physical therapy."

"I'm so sorry." Her eyes were soft with sympathy. "Four bullets? You must have come close to dying."

He shrugged. "It's a hazard of wearing the uniform."

"Have you ever thought of leaving the SEALs?"

"I signed on to do a job that most men can't do. I still want to do that job." The topic was getting close to a raw nerve, so he changed it, returning to an earlier subject. "If you love TV journalism, why did you go to work at a paper?"

"Standing in front of a camera . . . I just feel too exposed. I was looking into that lens, the tally light blinking red to show the camera was live when . . ."

AK fire. Screams. Blood spatter.

Javier had watched that scene explode from the other side of the lens.

She studied her wine. "That probably sounds lame."

"No. It doesn't." It bothered him that she didn't realize how amazing she was just to have survived. "How do you like the newspaper biz?"

"The people are good, but it's . . . It's not the same thing."

They sat together in silence, B. B. King turned down low in the background.

"I kept it in my handbag."

Javier didn't follow. "Kept what in your handbag?"

"The postcard of Dubai City." She took a sip. "You left it in my room. I kept it in my handbag. It was there the day I was abducted."

"Oh."

She avoided his gaze. "It was my memento of you, of that weekend."

Did she understand what she was telling him? Until now, he'd wondered if he'd been the only one who felt that their weekend together had been something different, something special. He'd left Dubai with his head full of her, determined to see her again. Now he knew those three nights and two days had meant something to her, too.

"I'm glad you kept it."

"The State Department sent my handbag and computer back with my suitcase to my mother in Stockholm. My poor mother! She'd just lost a daughter, and then she was faced with dealing with my belongings—my loft in Manhattan, my car, my bank accounts. She sold it all—every bit of it. My furniture, my clothes, the art on my walls. She gave the money to Columbia University in my name."

Javier hadn't known any of this.

"A few weeks after I was rescued, I learned that I had nothing except what had been in the suitcase and my handbag. My mother had kept most of that. She had this postcard hanging on her refrigerator. When I saw it, I remembered that weekend—all of it. I—I took the postcard back."

"It must have been hard to find out everything you'd once owned, everything you'd worked for was gone."

"I was grateful to be free, grateful to be alive. But, yeah, it was hard. It was as if I really *had* died." She took another sip of wine. "Columbia returned most of the money, but I still had to start over."

Maybe it was the beer. Maybe it was the situation. But Javier suddenly couldn't keep his damned mouth shut. "I never forgot you, Laura, not for a day. When they said you'd been executed, I wanted to kill that bastard with my bare hands."

He could count on one hand the times he'd gotten tears in his eyes—and the day they'd announced that Laura had been murdered was one of them.

She met his gaze, eyes filled with regret. "I forgot you. I forgot everything, everyone. I almost forgot myself. Every night during the last prayer I would use the silence to repeat my name in my mind in English and Swedish. I was so sure they would figure it out and that Al-Nassar would follow through on his threat to cut off my head."

"We operators get training on how to survive captivity, but you did it on your own, alone. You won, Laura. You beat him."

"Only because I was rescued." She tilted her head away from him, a sad smile on her face. "Sometimes when I can't sleep, when the nightmares are bad, I close my eyes and pretend that the men from that SEAL team are here in the loft in their gear, armed to the teeth and watching over me, the tall one standing watch over my bed. I know it's silly, but there are nights when it's the only thing that helps me sleep."

Javier felt a hitch in his chest. She'd been comforting herself at night by thinking of him—without knowing she was thinking of him. "That's not silly. You've been through hell, Laura. But tonight I'm here. You'll be safe."

Tonight, she wouldn't need to pretend. Part of that SEAL team would be watching over her for real.

CHAPTER 7

LAURA LEFT JAVIER watching the evening news and went to take a shower, needing to wash the reek of smoke and emergency room off her skin before she tried to sleep. Hot water and facial cleanser stung the nicks on her face, the lump where she'd struck her head tender as she shampooed, her mind dull from exhaustion. Or maybe that was the effects of the concussion. It didn't matter. She didn't want to think anyway.

She didn't want to think about what had almost happened today or the teenager who now lay on a slab in charred pieces or the parents who were grieving the loss of their son. She didn't want to think about her helpless daughter out there somewhere, a prisoner of terrorists. She didn't want to think about what tomorrow would bring. And for a time, Laura let the water pour over her skin, her eyes closed, the heat and the scent of lavender soap soothing her, lulling her into forgetfulness.

She'd just turned off the spray when there came a knock at the bathroom door, startling her, making her pulse spike.

Javier called softly to her. "Laura, the police are here."

"I'll be right out." She dried herself, combed her hair, and dressed, sliding into a pair of gray leggings and a purple oversized sweater, the muffled sound of men's voices drifting from the living room.

There, she found Javier talking with Marc, a man she didn't recognize, and Police Chief Stephen Irving, whom she'd seen on TV but never met before. The four men rose to their feet as she entered.

Marc gave her a nod. "How are you feeling?"

"I'm okay."

Chief Irving, an older man with a bristly white crew cut, held out a beefy hand, regarding her through world-weary blue eyes. "Ms. Nilsson, I'm sorry to meet you under these circumstances. I admire your work."

She took his hand. "Thank you, sir."

"I believe you know Hunter, DPD's SWAT captain." He motioned toward Marc with a nod of his head. "This is Detective Brent Callahan. He left Boston PD behind to head our EOD unit."

Detective Callahan reached out, shook her hand. Tall with dark blond hair, blue eyes, and a deep tan, he looked like a man who spent his life outdoors. "I'm sorry about what happened today. I worked EOD—that's explosive ordnance demolition—for the army in Iraq and Afghanistan. My team and I are heading the investigation on the bombing. I'll do my best to keep you informed and answer your questions."

"I appreciate that." Suddenly remembering her manners, she gestured to the sofa and two leather chairs. "Please, make yourselves comfortable. Would anyone like something to drink?"

They muttered "No thanks" and shook their heads, everyone but Marc taking a seat. He remained standing, arms crossed over his chest.

Laura sat beside Javier, not missing the glance the men exchanged, the room awkwardly silent. "Should I guess why you're here, or would you like to tell me?"

Chief Irving turned to Detective Callahan. "You want to fill Ms. Nilsson in?"

"We found one body in the car—a young male believed to be Ali Al Zahrani, age eighteen. The vehicle destroyed in the explosion was registered to him, and neither his parents nor his friends nor his professors at Metro State College have seen him all day."

The face Laura had tried to forget in the shower came back to her—dark hair, big brown eyes, a wide smile. *So young.*

Callahan went on. "The car had been loaded with metal buckets filled with homemade ANFO, an explosive mixture of ammonium nitrate and fuel oil, in this case diesel. The diesel detonated, but the ammonium nitrate didn't. Whoever mixed the explosive used a grade of fertilizer that comes in large prills, or pellets."

This meant nothing to Laura, but clearly Javier understood.

"The guy was an amateur," he muttered.

Marc spoke, venom in his voice. "It's lucky for all of us the bastard somehow managed to blow up only himself."

And Laura knew he was thinking of Sophie.

Callahan explained. "The larger pellets can't absorb the fuel. When the primer exploded—we believe it was dynamite—the fuel ignited, along with the fumes that had filled the vehicle, causing a gas explosion. If the ammonium nitrate *had* ignited, our bomber would have taken out most of the building."

Laura tried to take this in, the intellectual side of her mind struggling to keep up with the pounding of her heart. "Taken out the building?"

Callahan nodded. "A similar explosive was used in the Oklahoma City bombing."

Oh, God!

Laura felt light-headed, images of the partially collapsed federal building, of the human loss and devastation, coming to her mind. Her head began to throb once more.

Javier's hand closed reassuringly over hers. "You okay? Maybe you should lie down for a minute."

She shook her head. "I'm fine. It's just . . . a horrible thing to imagine."

Chief Irving watched her through sympathetic eyes. "There are some peculiar aspects to this bombing. The coroner did a CT scan of the body and found a twenty-two slug lodged in the alleged bomber's brain. Whoever we pulled out of the wreckage was dead before the explosion. The ME places time of death about two hours prior to the blast—about seven thirty this morning."

"What?" Maybe the concussion was worse than Laura had realized, or maybe all of this was too much. None of it made sense to her.

"I hadn't heard this." Marc frowned. "I'm not an expert, but aren't suicide bombers supposed to kill themselves?"

"Strange, isn't it?" Chief Irving agreed.

Javier shook his head. "Not necessarily. We encountered suicide bombers whose charges were set to detonate both by the bomber and by someone watching nearby. It's insurance in case the bomber gets cold feet, decides that martyrdom is overrated, tries to warn someone. Maybe the kid wanted to back out—and someone wouldn't let him."

Detective Callahan seemed to mull that over. "It's a possibility. Regardless, it proves that at least one other person was involved in this operation."

At least one other person.

"Our other suspect is still out there," Chief Irving said. "He may try to strike at you again, so we've shared all of this with the FBI. Special Agent Killeen is getting hourly updates from my team."

"Right now, we're sifting through all the debris, gathering the bits and pieces of wire and metal so that we can re-create the detonator," Callahan said. "Once we reconstruct it, that will give us a lot of information."

Laura didn't understand. "How can you reconstruct it? Isn't everything melted, incinerated beyond recognition?"

Javier and Callahan shook their heads at the same time.

"An explosion causes an outward burst, a blast wave, which is what produces the damage," Javier explained. "That blast instantly creates a vacuum, which sucks material back in again. Everything you need to know about the bomb is right there."

"All we have to do is pick up the puzzle pieces and put them back together." Callahan drew out a notepad. "I'd also like to create a list of potential accomplices, people with motive who might have been pulling the bomber's strings. Can you think of anyone besides Al-Nassar who might want you dead?"

Laura looked down at her right wrist and the bruises that encircled it. "The only person I've had conflict with lately is Derek Tower. He thinks I'm to blame for my own abduction, the deaths of his men, and his company's demise."

She filled Callahan in on Tower's e-mails and calls, and the confrontation in her car last Friday evening, showing him the bruises on her wrists. "I filed a police report."

Chief Irving glanced over at Callahan. "I'll make sure you get a copy."

Marc took a step toward them, his brows bent in a frown. "Wasn't Tower a Green Beret? He wouldn't make a mistake like that. If he'd wanted to blow up the building, it would be rubble now."

Javier shrugged. "Maybe he got sloppy."

"No." Marc shook his head. "That's beginner stuff."

"Why would Tower start hanging with a teenage terrorist?" Javier asked. "He spent a decade fighting them."

"I want him brought in for questioning regardless," Chief Irving said. "There's still the matter of his accosting Ms. Nilsson in her car. We've been searching for him since Friday night and haven't found him."

Callahan leaned closer to Laura. "I know it can't have been easy for you to hear all of this, but we're doing all we can."

Chief Irving reached out and clasped one of her hands between two of his. "The FBI got caught with its pants down today, but we at DPD will get to the bottom of this and keep you safe, Ms. Nilsson."

And Laura knew both men meant what they said.

The men stood, so Laura got to her feet, too. "Thank you. Marc, thank you for being there for us today."

He gave her a nod. "I was glad to help."

Callahan handed her his card. "We'll be in touch as the investigation progresses."

Laura walked with them to the door, thanked the three of them, and wished them all a good night, asking Marc to tell Sophie hello for her. There was a smile on her face, but behind her breastbone, her heart was still pounding.

Out there somewhere was a man who'd tried to kill her today, someone who wanted to see her dead and had been willing to murder his own accomplice and a building full of innocent people to get to her.

JAVIER WATCHED LAURA struggling to cope, watched her throw her energy into a load of late-night laundry, pretending that she wasn't in pain, that she wasn't afraid. But he knew her head hurt, knew that what she'd learned from the police had shaken her badly. When she poured the third capful of laundry detergent into the machine, he took the plastic bottle from her hands, set it aside, and drew her into his arms.

"Stop, *bella*." He felt her stiffen, then slowly relax, sagging against him. "Where's that prescription the doctor gave you, the one for headaches?"

"I think it's in my handbag."

"You get into your pajamas, and I'll get you water and a pill." He released her, but she didn't budge. "That's an order."

She glared up at him, gave him a mock salute, and walked off to her bedroom, her step seeming to drag under the weight of the news she'd just heard.

He walked out to the living room, found her handbag on a chair, and fished around inside, finding her .22 SIG and a plastic bag holding two prescription pill bottles—one with hydrocodone, the other containing Valium. He carried the bottles to the kitchen counter, took one pill from each, and got her a glass of cold water. He turned to find her standing behind him.

She was wearing a fuzzy blue bathrobe over a nightgown of pale blue silk or satin—hell, he didn't know the difference—her curves delicate beneath the layers of soft fabric. Her hair was almost dry now and hanging in thick, tousled strands. Her feet were bare, her toenails peeking out from beneath the hem of her robe and painted a soft shade of peach. And for a moment all he could do was stare.

She was everything soft and sweet and beautiful in his world, feminine in a way that made his chest ache, his urge to protect her strong.

"I really shouldn't take those." She looked at the pills in his hand. "I need to be alert in case something happens tonight, in case whoever—"

"He won't bother us tonight." Javier handed her the glass of water, turned her other hand over, and dropped the pills into her palm. "Even if he wanted to come after you, he'd need a plan, and he'd need an opportunity. Nothing is going to happen tonight."

She looked at the pills and placed them one at a time on her tongue, washing them down with deep drinks of water. She set the empty glass down on the granite countertop, her fingers finding their way to massage her temple. "This stuff never really works for me anyway."

They settled on the sofa, Laura insisting that she wouldn't sleep, so they might as well watch a movie. She chose *Pride and Prejudice*, and Javier didn't complain, despite the fact that watching guys with goofy-ass hair and prissy clothes walking around speaking in fussy English wasn't exactly his thing. Hell, he'd have spent the night watching *Sesame Street* if it would make her feel better.

He popped the DVD in her player and was about to sit down beside her, when she started to get up again. "Stay put. What do you need?"

"I was going to start a fire. It's chilly."

"I'll do that." He wondered where she stacked her fire-wood, then realized she had one of those natural gas contraptions. "How do you make this thing work?"

"Flick the switch." Her voice, though strained by pain, held a note of amusement.

It was like turning on a light. A fire sprang up between fake logs, putting out a surprising amount of heat. Still, he preferred the kind of fireplace that actually burned wood. What the hell good was this thing if the electricity went out and you actually needed a fire?

He sat beside her, consigned to watching the film. Instead, he found himself watching Laura. Her eyes grew heavy, the lines of pain on her face easing as the medication kicked in, but still she fought to stay awake.

"Come here." He drew her close, resting her head in his lap, his fingers finding their way to stroke the softness of her hair.

In a few minutes, she was sound asleep.

He left her on the sofa, drew down her covers, then went back, lifted her into his arms, and carried her into her bedroom. Her eyes fluttered open for just a moment as he laid her on her bed. He drew her covers up and turned to go.

"Javi?" she said sleepily. "Don't go."

"If that's what you want." Heat pulsed through his body at the idea of being in bed with her, but he ignored it. He pulled off his T-shirt, crawled between the sheets, and stretched out beside her, still wearing his jeans.

"I'm . . . I'm afraid." She turned toward him, snuggled into him.

He knew she was half-asleep and sedated, but he liked that she trusted him. He stroked her hair. "You don't need to explain, *bella*. I am more than happy to be your teddy bear."

JAVIER LAY ON his side, watching Laura sleep, the first weak rays of winter sunshine peeking through the cracks in the blinds. He wished he could say he'd slept well, but he hadn't. Every part of him had been aware throughout the night that she was there. When he had managed to drift off, he'd had the nightmare again—the helo exploding in midair, bits of metal and body parts raining down on him and his element, the stench of charred flesh and burning helo fuel. Only this time, Laura had been on board, and he'd known she was dead. He'd jerked awake, covered in sweat, unable to sleep again.

If he'd been alone, he'd have gotten out his guitar and worked the dream out of his system with music, but he hadn't wanted to risk waking her up. Instead, he'd watched her sleep, grateful she was safe and alive.

She lay curled against him now, her face pressed against his chest, her left leg tucked between his, her hair tangled. She looked serene, untroubled, her sweet face relaxed, her eyelashes dark against the pale skin of her cheeks, her breathing deep and even. Even though she was taller than most women, she felt delicate in his arms, her body soft and slender compared to his, her hands fine-boned, her nails neatly manicured with just a touch of clear polish.

For some time now, a part of him had wondered whether everything that had happened—their weekend in Dubai, her abduction, the false news of her death, his role in rescuing her—had made him see her in some kind of ridiculous, rosy light, exaggerating his feelings for her, leaving him confused. But holding her like this, he knew that nothing he'd felt had been exaggerated.

And what exactly do you feel for her?

Okay, so maybe he *was* confused.

His gaze traveled over the soft curve of her cheek to her jaw and along the silky skin of her neck. He'd once kissed her there, nipped and tasted her there, raising goose bumps on her skin, making her gasp and shiver, the heat inside him like a fever. He'd nibbled his way across her collarbone to the valley between her breasts, then taken her soft pink nipples into his mouth and suckled her, feeling her arch beneath . . .

Blood surged to his groin at the memory, making him hard—not typical morning wood, but a full-blown boner. Pretty certain Laura wouldn't like waking up to find herself being jabbed by his junk, even if it was still encased inside his jeans, he shifted his hips.

Time to think about something else, chacho.

But the moment he moved, Laura stirred, stretched, pressing her belly against his erection. Her eyes opened, her gaze unfocused. She blinked, gave a little gasp, went rigid. Her gaze fixed on his chest, then slid slowly upward until their gazes met.

¡Coño! Damn!

What the hell was he supposed to do now?

Play it cool, man.

"Sleep well, *bella*?"

She nodded, her gaze flicking southward toward his erection, then up to his face again, her cheeks turning pink. "You?"

"Yeah. Like a rock."

Not the best choice of words right now, Corbray.

"I'm glad." Her gaze flicked southward again, and she drew away from him.

"Don't worry about the . . . uh . . . hard-on." He shoved aside the covers, his dick catching awkwardly against the seam in his jeans as he slid out of bed and stood, leaving him a choice between adjusting himself or risking accidental circumcision. "It's just what happens to guys, you know . . . Morning wood."

She sat up, looked straight at his crotch, then looked quickly away again, her face flushed. "You don't have to be embarrassed."

"Oh, I'm not. I just didn't want to you to think . . ."

To think what, pendejo? *That you got hard thinking about having sex with her? Because that's what happened. No, you're not embarrassed. You're guilty!*

She stood, looking hotter than any woman had a right to at

seven in the morning, her hair hanging in tangles, the buttery softness of her robe and nightgown clinging to her curves. "There's a bathroom through there."

"Thanks." He walked in the direction she'd pointed, locking the door behind him.

He lifted the toilet seat, unzipped his fly, and looked down at his dick, which was giving him the one-eyed stare from behind the waistband of his black boxer briefs. Of course, there was *no way* he was going to be able to take a piss with a full-on rocky.

It was time for a shower.

CHAPTER 8

LAURA HEARD JAVIER step into her shower and walked down the hallway toward the kitchen, not sure what to think of what had just happened. She remembered putting her head in his lap, waking up in her bed, asking him to stay. She remembered, too, what his answer had been.

I am more than happy to be your teddy bear.

She'd woken up in his arms. Somehow, she'd curled up against him in her sleep, had known even before she'd opened her eyes that she was with him. It had startled her, but at the same time, she'd felt an unexpected trill of . . . *excitement.*

She found her handbag on the counter, took out her comb, and ran it through her tangles, then walked into the main bathroom, where she kept a spare toothbrush, and brushed her teeth. She found herself smiling at her reflection, amused by Javier's embarrassment over an everyday average morning erection.

Well, maybe not average. From what Laura remembered—and from what she'd felt pressing against her—nothing about Javier was average.

Distracted by her thoughts, she didn't feel it coming. Grief stole up on her quietly, seeping under her skin, sliding over her like a shadow. Her smile faded. She rinsed her mouth, set the toothbrush aside, overwhelmed by a sense of emptiness.

Oh. God.

She missed it. She missed all of it. She missed that entire part of herself—the part that had loved sex, that had reveled in intimacy, that had known how to tease, laugh, and play with a man. Al-Nassar had crushed it, stolen it, beaten it out of her, and she hadn't realized until this moment how much she longed for it, not just the physical pleasure of sex, but the sense of closeness that came from joining with a man, giving her most private self to him, accepting what he gave her.

She inhaled, Javier's scent on her skin, images of that weekend in Dubai sliding through her mind. Endless slow kisses, deep kisses, fierce kisses that stole her breath. Lips, hands, and skin moving over soft skin. The scent and taste of him mingling with her own scent and taste. The hard feel of him moving inside her as he took her against the wall, on the floor, in the sunken tub. The warmth of his muscular body as he lay in her bed, held her, slept beside her.

She squeezed her eyes shut, fought to stop the bittersweet barrage of memories, her life now so empty by comparison. That wasn't how she wanted it to be. She'd never intended to live a sexless, lonely life. Yet she wasn't sure she was capable of enjoying sex right now—with anything other than her vibrator, of course. But seeing Javier again, being close to him, waking up to find his arms around her . . .

No. She couldn't. Especially not with Javier.

The time she'd spent with him in Dubai had been special. If she got into bed with him now, she would tarnish that precious memory for both of them. She didn't want to risk hurting or humiliating him. And then, of course, there were her stretch marks—and the fact that someone out there wanted to kill her.

She closed her eyes, drew a few deep breaths to quash the emotions she was feeling, then turned away from her mirror, walked into the kitchen, and started a pot of coffee. Fairly certain Javier wouldn't care much for the traditional Swedish breakfast of hard-boiled egg, cucumber, and cod roe on *knäckebröd*, she opened her fridge and took out some eggs, then began to search for anything she could use to make omelets.

There wasn't much—green onions, some slightly wilted spinach, mushrooms, a handful of cooked baby potatoes.

She needed to go grocery shopping.

"Don't go to any trouble for my sake."

She gasped and turned to find Javier standing behind her.

His hair was still damp, his jaw smooth and clean shaven. He'd put on a pair of jeans and a dark gray long-sleeved T-shirt that fit over the muscles of his chest like a second skin, its sleeves pushed up his corded forearms to just below his elbows. A heavy watch was bound to his left wrist by a black leather band. He looked masculine—and devastatingly hot.

Laura almost forgot what she'd been about to say. "I . . . I'm just making breakfast. Are omelets okay?"

"As long as there's hot coffee, I'm good." He turned, and she saw the gun holstered on his right side—a cold reminder of her reality.

She ignored it, shut the refrigerator, and retrieved two mugs from the cupboard. "Let me guess—you take your coffee black."

"Only if I have to." He grinned. "Why don't you focus on the omelets, and I'll make you coffee the way we drink it in Puerto Rico? Got milk?"

While he heated milk on the stove, she went to work on the omelets, willing herself to control her thoughts and emotions and focus on this moment instead, the two of them talking about little things. His summers visiting his grandmother and cousins in Humacao. How she'd been born in the U.S. while her father had finished his doctorate at Princeton and therefore had dual citizenship. Why she'd left Sweden when she'd turned eighteen to return to the U.S. Neither of them mentioned yesterday's bombing, her abduction, their time together in Dubai—or the fact that they'd slept side by side last night.

Soon breakfast was ready.

Laura sat and took a sip of her coffee. "Mmm."

"Good?"

"Yes. Mmm. Very good." It was sweet, but not too sweet, the strong coffee aroma rich and satisfying. "Thank you."

"De nada."

Then Laura asked him the question she'd wanted to ask the men who'd rescued her, the question she'd wanted to ask him since she'd found out what he did for a living. What drove some men to put their lives on the line for others, to risk *everything*, when most risked nothing? "Why did you decide to become a SEAL?"

*   *   *

JAVIER TOOK A bite of his omelet, wondering how to answer. There were things about his past few people knew, things he wished he could forget, things he didn't want Laura to know. She was polished, classy, smart. She'd come from a different world. How could she possibly understand?

He told her what he told most people. "I've always been stronger than other guys, faster, had better endurance. After I graduated from high school, I got an associate's degree in sports medicine and landed a job as a certified personal trainer at a gym in L.A. At first, I thought it was the life. My clients were upscale. I was making good money. I had my own apartment, a shiny new Mustang. I always had a date. Life was good."

It was the truth—or part of it.

Laura took another sip of coffee, watching him over the rim of her cup. "I can see you as a personal trainer. Why did you choose to do something different?"

Between bites of his breakfast, Javier told her how he'd slowly come to feel that what he was doing was meaningless. He'd gotten tired of listening to people's bullshit excuses for missing workouts, of bored Hollywood wives trying to get into his pants during sessions their wealthy husbands had paid for, of people saying they wanted to improve their health and change their lives and then giving up without really trying.

"I was twenty-four and going nowhere, doing nothing. I felt restless, like I was wasting my life. I wanted to *do* something, be a part of something that mattered."

Something that would make his parents and *abuela* forget the teenage gangbanger who'd gotten his younger brother killed and see him as a man.

"So you enlisted."

He nodded. "One of the other trainers had a client who'd lost a leg serving with Delta Force in the Battle of Mogadishu in '93. He was in the gym six days a week, working hard, doing his best to stay fit. He never made excuses, never missed a workout, never complained. I was watching him one day when I realized there was a way I could do something meaningful with my physical strength. I talked with a few recruiters, then signed on for the toughest challenge I could find."

She was watching him still, a soft smile on her face. "I think that's noble."

She thinks you're noble, pendejo. *Way to pull the wool over her eyes.*

"Did your family support you?"

Even as a part of him hated himself for hiding the truth from her, another part savored how it felt to sit here talking with her like this, still damp from his shower, Laura still in her nightgown and bathrobe. They'd had a couple of mornings like this in Dubai—except that neither of them had been wearing anything then.

Don't go there, man.

"Once they got over the surprise, yeah, they were okay with it, though my mother and poor *abuelita* were afraid for me. They still are."

"I can't blame them. What you do—it's incredibly dangerous. I've seen a team in action, remember? The men who rescued me almost got shot down."

Ah, hell.

Javier wanted so much to tell her that he'd been on that helo beside her, that he was the one who'd tried to reassure her when the RPG explosions had scared her. He wanted to tell her, but couldn't. "It's a helluva way to make a living, I'll give you that."

"How long have you been a SEAL?"

"Fourteen years. I enlisted in 1998, and earned my Trident in '99 before—"

A knock at the door made Laura jump.

He stood, hating to see fear on her face. "Expecting company?"

They'd buzzed no one in, and neither the DPD nor Agent Killeen had called to say they were coming up.

She shook her head. "No."

"Stay here." Javier walked quickly and silently across the room, positioning himself off to the side of the entrance so he wouldn't be hit if someone fired rounds through the closed door. He drew his SIG. "Who is it?"

"It's Kathleen Parker. I'm Laura's neighbor."

Relief on her face, Laura got to her feet and walked toward the door. "I recognize her voice."

Javier looked out the peephole just to be certain no one was holding a gun to Kathleen's head, then holstered his weapon and opened the door to find a woman—late thirties, maybe five six—standing there in brown yoga pants and a light green fleece jacket, her dark blond hair pulled back in a ponytail. Her gaze shifted nervously from Javier to Laura. "May I come in?"

Laura motioned for her to step inside. "Yes. Of course."

Kathleen eyed Javier's gun. "Are you a police officer?"

Laura opened her mouth as if to answer, but Javier beat her to it. "I'm part of Ms. Nilsson's protection detail."

So this Kathleen is the nosy type.

"Oh." Kathleen turned to face Laura, looking nervous. "First, I just want to say I'm glad you weren't hurt. What happened yesterday was terrible."

She had that part right.

"I appreciate your support. Thank you."

Kathleen's gaze dropped to the floor. "Some of us in the building have been talking. We're concerned that you're endangering all of us by staying here. We think it would be better for everyone if you stayed somewhere else until this was over or maybe even sold your loft and found a more secure place to live."

What the hell?

Javier felt his temper spike, saw the hurt and anger on Laura's face as Kathleen's words struck home.

"You want me to sell my home and move so you can feel safer?"

"That's not what I said." Kathleen shook her head in protest.

Javier crossed his arms over his chest. "Oh, that's exactly what you said."

"Kathleen, I understand it must make you nervous, but everything that can be done to keep me safe—to keep us all safe—is being done. The FBI and—"

"Yesterday, this building was crawling with armed men. SWAT was even here." Kathleen lowered her voice. "My children saw men *with guns*!"

¡Hay que joderse! Holy shit! Good guys with guns?

How could these people be so lacking in courage that the sight of men sent to protect them freaked them out? What a bunch of limp-dick cowards!

Laura's expression had gone sympathetic. "I understand how that might be upsetting, and I'm sorry, but I am not going to be driven out of my home."

But Javier had had enough of Kathleen Parker.

He opened the door. "Visiting hours are over."

Kathleen gaped at him for a moment, seeming to realize that she was being told to leave. She glanced back at Laura, her expression hard. "You're bringing trouble to our doorsteps, and we don't want—"

"Later." Javier shut the door, locked it.

Laura met Javier's gaze, a stunned look on her face. "My neighbors want me to leave, to sell my loft and move out? I can understand why they're anxious, but . . . This is my home."

Javier shook his head in disgust. "It's like my sweet *abuelita* always said—the world is full of assholes."

Of course, a time or two when she'd said that, she'd been talking about him.

LAURA OPENED HER office door, almost shaking from frustration, her head throbbing. She walked into the kitchen, got herself a glass of water, and set it down on the counter, not really thirsty.

Javier stood. "Is everything okay?"

"No." She picked up the glass and drank every drop, then set it down again. "The paper's publisher and board of trustees don't want me to come back to work."

Dark brows bent in a frown. "What?"

She turned, paced the length of the kitchen. "They told me they're afraid for my safety and the safety of the rest of the staff. They want me to take the rest of the week off to recover, but they don't want me back in the office on Monday. They think it would be best for everyone if I worked from home for the time being. They're probably right."

"Sounds to me like they're afraid of being sued."

"They're not brave enough to say that, so they pretend it's all out of concern for me." She pressed her fingers against her throbbing temple. "First my neighbors want me to move out, and now the paper doesn't want me around. I don't want anyone to get hurt because of me, but I can't just run and hide."

She stiffened in surprise to feel Javier's big hands on her shoulders.

He turned her toward him, took her into his arms. "I don't blame you for being angry. But that headache—you need to take it easy. Some time off might not be a bad thing."

She drew back and met his gaze, perilously close to tears, the pounding of her heart a sign that she wasn't far from a full-blown panic attack. "I've fought *so* damned hard to put the past behind me, to start over, to build a new life. No one knows how hard it's been for me to get where I am today. *No one.* And now . . . Now I'm going to lose it all again—my home, my job, maybe even my life."

She fought to calm her breathing, her chest tight, her fear spiraling out of control.

Javier cupped her face, his gaze riveted hard on hers. "No! No, you're not. Your neighbors are cowards, and the newspaper is being run by lawyers. But this won't last forever. When the investigation is over, you'll get your life back."

Conviction was etched into every feature of his face, from the hard line of his jaw to the firm set of his lips to the fierce gleam in his eyes, his certainty giving her something to hold on to, taking the edge off her dread.

From across the room, her cell phone rang, making her jump.

She hurried to the coffee table where she'd left it and got a sinking feeling in her stomach when she saw a restricted number on the screen.

Probably Derek Tower.

She answered but said nothing.

"Ms. Nilsson?" It wasn't Derek.

She let out a relieved breath. "This is she."

"This is Chief Deputy U.S. Marshal Zach McBride, Nate's friend. I met you up at the Cimarron last Saturday."

The Medal of Honor recipient whose wife, Natalie, wanted to write romance novels.

"I remember." She hadn't known he was a chief deputy U.S. Marshal.

He asked how she was doing, passed along Natalie's regards, and then his tone of voice changed. "I'm calling for a few reasons. First, I wanted to let you know that the U.S. Marshal

Service is going to be primary in this case. The Justice Department sees an act of terrorism at a newspaper as falling under our jurisdiction. The FBI and local police will be doing the footwork for a task force that I'll be heading out of our office. We believe we have the best resources to bring this case together."

"Oh. I see." A sense of relief washed through her. The DUSMs who'd protected her before and during the trial had always made her feel safe, whereas the FBI, apart from Agent Killeen, had not. "Thank you. I appreciate everything you're doing to protect me and get to the bottom of this."

"Who is it?" Javier whispered, standing nearby.

"Zach McBride," she mouthed. "U.S. Marshal Service."

Two dark brows rose, and Javier nodded.

Zach went on. "We're going to do everything we can to make sure you're safe from here on out. We're on our way over to talk about protocols and to set up a trap-and-trace on your phone in case Derek Tower contacts you again. Does that work?"

"Yes."

"Tower is officially a person of interest in the bombing, and we've put our Violent Offender and Fugitive Task Force to work tracking him down for questioning. I'm not saying that we think he's behind it, but given his recent actions toward you and his background, I'd like to talk to him."

The idea that Tower might soon be in custody made Laura feel safer. "I haven't heard from him since the night he accosted me in my car."

"I'm not surprised. We'll talk about how we're going to handle any potential contact from him when I get there." Zach paused. "I also wanted to let you know the DNA from the car came back as Ali Al Zahrani."

Laura sank slowly to the couch, the throbbing in her head almost unbearable, the rush of her pulse drowning out whatever Zach was saying, an image of the kid's smiling face burning in her mind. *"Oh, God."*

CHAPTER 9

HEAD STILL THROBBING, Laura sat in the passenger seat of her own car as Javier drove them back up to the Cimarron, the beautiful mountain scenery passing by her window unnoticed. "I want to see his family. I want to tell them in person how sorry I am."

"You'll get that chance, but not today. Today, you need to take care of yourself, take it easy."

Javier was right. They were all right.

When she'd told Zach she wanted to visit Ali Al Zahrani's parents, he'd told her flat out that she needed to wait at least a few days. They were being questioned by the FBI, their house now considered part of a crime scene, their street swarming with media.

"You don't want to walk into that," he'd said.

No, she didn't.

Still, she couldn't quit thinking about them, how they must feel, knowing that the entire nation saw them now as the parents of a terrorist.

"Maybe I can call or send flowers or a card—something to let them know I don't blame them."

Javier glanced over at her. "What if they're proud of him?"

Her gaze shot to his. "I don't believe any mother feels *proud* when her child dies like that. I talked to women in Afghanistan who were devastated with grief over sons who'd chosen so-called martyrdom or who'd died in the fighting. Most were too afraid to let their grief show because the Taliban would beat them."

The kid's parents would now have to live the rest of their lives knowing they raised a son who'd died trying to commit murder. Their child would be reviled across the nation—and so would they. No one would care that they loved their son. They would be isolated in their grief for him. Facebook and Twitter were already teeming with jokes about the suicide bomber who managed to blow up only himself.

Laura couldn't say she understood exactly how they felt, but she *did* know how lonely grief could be. Her heart ached every day for Klara, and yet apart from her mother, her grandmother, and Erik, she could speak of her daughter with no one.

"This is really tearing you up, isn't it?" Javier's big hand closed, warm and reassuring, over hers. "Give it a rest for today, *bella*. You can't do anything now except make this harder on yourself."

Laura drew a deep breath and stared out her window, finally noticing the snowcapped peaks, the stretches of evergreen forest. It *was* beautiful up here, reminding her of the mountains in Sweden where her family had gone skiing every year. Of course, the Rockies were much more rugged, rising to staggering heights, their snowy summits dazzling under the bright Colorado sun.

It had been Javier's idea to get away, to leave her neighbors, the prying media, and all of Denver behind for fresh mountain air. He'd suggested she pack a bag and stay up there with him and the West family for a few days. Laura didn't want to impose on the Wests, but she knew Javier had come here to visit his friends. His decision to help her had taken him away from that. Left with the choice between staying alone at the loft or spending the night up at the Cimarron, she'd chosen the latter, calling Special Agent Killeen, who hadn't yet been relieved of her duties, to let her know about the change in plans. Janet drove ahead of them in her beige Toyota Corolla, another agent following them in a blue Ford Escort.

Laura relaxed into the seat, let her mind go blank, and watched the scenery.

Another ten minutes found them at the ranch's main gate. Recessed from the road, its arch was constructed of heavy logs, a wooden sign that read "Cimarron Ranch" hanging from a crossbeam, the gate itself constructed of steel. It stood open, and there, waiting for them beside a white pickup truck, stood Nate, a cowboy hat on his head.

He grinned, waved them through, then climbed into his truck and followed them, the road dipping downward into a valley.

When the ranch house came into view, Laura was just as amazed as she'd been the first time she'd seen it. "It's so beautiful."

Like a postcard.

Javier grinned. "Home *sweet* home."

Built of rounded river stones and logs, it was as breathtaking as its surroundings, reminding Laura of villas she'd seen in Switzerland and Austria but with some distinct western touches. Its roof was steeply sloped to let snow slide off, smoke curling from one of a half dozen stone chimneys. Rows of wide windows gleamed, reflecting sunlight and blue sky. Beside a row of barns and outbuildings, palomino quarter horses grazed in a large corral, the wind tossing their pale manes and tails.

Javier parked beside Janet's car, handing Laura her car keys. "It's pretty cold. You head on inside. I'll get your bag."

"Thanks." Laura stepped out into a biting wind and hugged her peacoat tightly around her, thin mountain air cutting through the thick wool.

Jack West stood face-to-face with Janet, the two of them locked in some kind of argument. "I know every man, woman, and child on my land, SA Killeen. I don't need you checking IDs or running background on my people. I understand you want to protect Ms. Nilsson. So do I. But I've got twenty men here, every single one of whom knows how to use a firearm. They've all been made aware of the situation. Laura is safe under my roof. I guarantee you that."

Looking uncomfortably cold in a navy-blue pantsuit, Janet held her ground, the other agent standing behind her, his eyes hidden behind Ray-Bans. "I have no intention of running background on every person on your property, Mr. West, but I would like to get an idea of the layout of the ranch and the house in case—"

Jack cut across her. "I'm telling you that's not necessary.

There's nothing you can learn from a map that I can't tell you if it comes down to it. Now, either come inside for a bite to eat, or get the hell off my property."

Janet shook her head, handing Jack her card. "Call sooner rather than too late—and thanks *so much* for your cooperation."

Then she climbed into her car and headed back toward the highway, the other agent following her just as Nate climbed out of his truck.

Nate looked at his father over the top of his sunglasses. "Looks like you sent that pretty FBI agent packing."

"Was she pretty? I didn't notice." Jack walked over to Laura and took her hand between his. "Good to see you again, Laura. I hear your neighbors don't want you bringing trouble to their doorstep. Well, you can feel free to bring it to mine. Anyone who comes looking for trouble here is damned well going to find it."

Laura's throat went tight. "Thank you."

JAVIER PUSHED WITH every bit of remaining strength he had, his muscles maxed, his right pectorals and shoulder screaming, ribs that had recently healed protesting as his body tensed. He ignored the pain, fighting for every inch.

Nate stood over him, spotting. "You got it! You've got it! Come on!"

The bar started to dip on the right, his injured muscles struggling to match the strength on his left side.

"Want an assist?"

"No!" He grunted the word from between gritted teeth, fighting to level the barbell, his right arm shaking.

Slowly, so slowly, the bar leveled, inching upward as he finished his last rep.

Nate took the weight and settled the barbell into place. "Way to tough it out, man. I couldn't manage that on my best day."

Javier sat up, sweat trickling down his temples, his muscles pumped and burning. He grabbed a towel, wiped his face, and stood. Nate might be impressed, but Javier wasn't. He still wasn't benching his max—three-fifteen—and he'd barely made it through this set. Still, he *was* getting stronger.

He rubbed his shoulder, pressed a hand to his aching ribs. "Who are you fooling, West? You're the toughest son of a bitch I know."

Nate hadn't lost only skin in the fire, but muscle and tendons, too. The fact that he was working out every day, lifting weights, working on the ranch was proof that he had a kind of strength few men possessed.

"I sure as hell can't bench two-ninety."

The two of them began to remove weights from the bar.

"How is it being together with Laura again?"

"It's good. It's not like it was before, of course. With all she's been through . . ."

Nate nodded. "A woman who's been hurt like she was hurt needs a lot of time and love to heal. How is she handling the news about the bomber?"

"It's shaken her up pretty badly, but she's hanging in there. She wants to visit his family, express their condolences."

Nate gave a surprised "Huh."

"She's got a big heart. That's what makes her such a great reporter. I just don't want to see her get hurt again because of it. The world is full of people ready to fuck other people over. What if this kid's parents are sorry their son failed?"

"If that's the case, McBride won't let her near them." Nate tightened the clamps on the barbell. "What about you? How are you holding up?"

"I'm going to make damned sure no one gets a second chance at her. They want to hurt her, they have to get through me."

"I respect that, man, but she gets a lot of media attention. If you get too caught up in this, NSW is bound to get wind of it. Think they're going to want you hanging around her, playing bodyguard? If your photo ends up on the nightly news beside hers, you'll find yourself up to your ears in shit."

Nate settled on the bench for his last set, while Javier got into position to spot.

Nate was right, of course. If Javier was connected with Laura, the brass at NSW wouldn't like it. They'd have a lot of questions for him. "What the hell am I supposed to do? I can't turn my back on her and walk away."

There was more to it than that. Being with Laura, watching over her, made Javier feel needed again. It made him feel like he was doing something. It made him feel like a man. But he couldn't explain that to Nate.

"Hell, what would you do if you were in my shoes?"

"Probably the same thing you're doing."

Nate lay back, worked through his set, then sat and reached for his water bottle, drinking in thirsty gulps. Their workout over, he stood, grabbed a spray bottle and cloth, and began to wipe down the equipment. "You've got a lot going on without taking on Laura's problems, too. JG called. He's worried about you."

¡Que mierda! Shit! "Yeah? He's worse than a mother hen."

"You're saying he doesn't have reason to worry, that your refusing therapy is somehow not a problem?"

"I passed the psych screening. Why the hell should I go to therapy?"

Nate set the spray bottle and rag aside. "They say you played to the test."

"What the hell does that even mean?"

"You know what it means. You've been through it before, and you gave them the answers you knew they were looking for rather than telling the truth."

Javier picked up his water and drank, trying not to lose his temper. "I came here to chill and get away from that bullshit."

"And you're welcome for as long as you want to stay, but there's got to be honesty between us. What's going on, Javier?"

When Javier didn't have a ready answer, Nate answered for him.

"I know what happened. I know the whole story. I know about the decision you had to make. I know about the ambush and the medevac helo crash. JG isn't the only one who's called me. Pretty much every surviving member of the squad has either called or e-mailed asking about you."

Javier did *not* want to go there.

"I can't change what happened. I made the call, and I can't do a damned thing about how it turned out. Sitting in some stuffy office crying to some therapist who's never been in combat is not going to change things either." Javier turned to face Nate. "I've been in and out of combat for fourteen years. I know what I can handle, man. I don't need their help. I'm not some fucking pussy."

"Are you saying that JG, Wilson, Ross, Zimmerman—all the guys who *are* getting treatment are pussies?"

"No." *¡Carajo!* That wasn't what he'd meant. "They're good operators, hard chargers, hard-core team guys. They get the job done."

"What's different about you? Why does it make you a pussy if you get help, but not the rest of the team? Oh, I get it. You're the Cobra. You get within striking distance of the enemy, and it's over. But if it all goes sideways and the wrong men die, you don't need help like the rest of us mere mortals."

"Knock it the fuck off, West."

Nate came face-to-face with him. "I know something's not right, and the fact that you won't even talk about it with me scares the hell out of me. A bar fight, Corbray? Yeah, I know about that, too. You're not facing charges only because the man you punched happened to be another operator. He had too much respect for you to turn your ass in."

Okay, this shit needed to end *now*.

"You want to know what's wrong, man? People keep getting in my face, pushing me, acting like I'm going to fall the fuck apart. But I haven't. I won't. They were talking about giving me a *training* job."

"What's wrong with that? Every kid who had the chance to learn from you would be lucky because he'd be learning from the best of the best. What you'd teach them would save lives, ensure the success of their missions."

Nate didn't get it. He just didn't understand.

"Combat is what I do, man. It's what I've done for fourteen years."

"Maybe fourteen years is enough." At the look on Javier's face, Nate let out a frustrated gust of breath. "You know what this is really about? It's about you believing that you have to be perfect just to be as good as everyone else."

Javier let out a laugh. "Is that supposed to make sense?"

Nate jabbed a finger toward Javier's chest. "Somewhere inside, you're still the Puerto Rican gangbanger who's still trying to prove to his parents and himself that he's not the loser they thought he was."

Javier took a step toward Nate. "Watch it, man."

But there was only concern on Nate's face. "Are you going to hit *me* now?"

Javier turned away from him, shocked at the sheer force of the rage surging through him, his heart a jackhammer in his chest, his face burning. He drew a deep breath, willed his fists to unclench. He grabbed his towel and headed for the door. "I think it's time Laura and I headed back to Denver."

"You just got here. You're going to run away rather than talk to me?" There was no condemnation in Nate's voice, just disappointment. "Laura's in the stables with Megan, but give them some time. Megan knows more about what Laura has been through than the rest of us."

Those words and the dark tone of Nate's voice stopped Javier in his tracks. He turned to face his friend, some of his anger bleeding away.

"What are you telling me?"

LAURA PATTED THE mare's velvety muzzle, fighting to hold back her tears. "I just want my life back. Some days I feel like this will never end, like the damage that bastard did will define my life forever."

She was thinking not only of threats against her life, but of Klara, too—the little girl she'd been forced to bring into the world and wanted desperately to protect.

Megan reached out, put a hand on her shoulder. "I want to tell you something."

As they walked to the next stall and the next, Megan told Laura how she'd been only fourteen and in juvenile detention for shoplifting when a group of guards started taking turns raping her. The assaults had happened almost daily and had gone on for weeks, until she'd told a member of the facility's medical staff. But by then she'd been so broken that she'd spent the next decade fighting heroin addiction.

Laura felt sick for her—men brutalizing a child like that. Still, she would never have imagined that the polished young woman who walked beside her had been a victim of something so violent or a heroin addict. "I'm so sorry, Megan."

"I was busted for heroin possession and went to prison, where I found out I was pregnant. They took Emily away from me an hour after she was born. I lost her to Child Protective Services. It took a long time and a lot of hard work to get her back." Megan's voice quavered. "But now I have Emily. I have Nate. I love my life. I'm happier than I ever thought I could be. And one day you'll feel that way, too. They'll catch these bastards, and you'll be able to put all of this behind you."

Megan couldn't know she was treading on Laura's deepest pain—giving birth to a baby in captivity and having it taken from her.

Tears blurred Laura's vision, her throat tight. "Thank you. I hope you're right. The men who hurt you . . . I need to know. Did they pay?"

"Yes. Three are dead. One is serving life in prison, and he won't be raping anyone else. Marc shot him when he tried to kill Sophie, severed his spine."

The same men had tried to kill Sophie?

Why did Laura know nothing about this?

You've never really taken time to get to know your coworkers. That's why.

It was a mistake she intended to remedy—as soon as this nightmare was over.

"I know you must feel alone in this, but you're not." Megan smiled "Jack, Nate, and I want to be here for you. Your I-Team friends are here for you. They really care about you, Laura— Sophie, Kat, Joaquin, Matt, Alex. All of them."

Laura felt touched to the core that Megan had trusted her with all of this. It couldn't have been easy. "Thank you."

They finished their tour of the stables, and then it was time for Megan to meet Emily's bus at the gate.

Laura found her way back inside the house and headed up to her room, unable to take her mind off what Megan had told her, her head aching again, her body chilled from spending so much time in the stables. She was thinking about taking a hot bath when she remembered there was a sauna off the gym. She changed into her robe, grabbed a towel, and headed downstairs. She was passing the library when she heard it.

Guitar music.

She stopped, listened.

It sounded like classical Spanish guitar, the music darkly

passionate with a melancholy feel that put an ache in her chest.
It started slowly, then gathered momentum, notes spilling from
the strings in a rich torrent, braced from beneath by deep,
powerful chords that sounded like a pulse or a heartbeat. She
pushed open the library door a crack—and saw Javier.

He sat on a sofa opposite a lit fireplace. His eyes were
closed, his brow furrowed, his head bowed slightly, guitar in
his arms. The fingers of his left hand moved over the frets,
while those of his right moved over the strings, rich sound
resonating from the polished wood. Then his hands fell still,
and the music stopped.

He was looking at her. "Laura."

Forgetting that she was wearing only her bathrobe, she
walked over to sit on a plush sofa across from him. "I didn't
know you played guitar. Please. Don't stop."

His gaze fixed on hers, he began to play again from the
beginning. Music filled the library's two floors, its emotion
drawing Laura in, holding her. How he could be responsible
for all those notes, all that sound, she didn't know. His eyes
slowly drifted shut as the music began to build, his brow furrowing, the intensity on his handsome face growing as he gave
himself over to his playing.

Laura had seen that naked passion on his face before, only
then he'd been holding her, kissing her, making love to her.
He'd been . . .

No. Don't. Don't do this to yourself.

Despite the music, or perhaps because of it, she couldn't
stop the flow of emotion within her. A lump in her throat, she
found herself unable to take her gaze off him as the music
reached its climax, the power of it sending a shiver up her
spine, stirring something behind her breastbone. As he plucked
the last few notes from the strings, the sound reverberating
through the room, she found herself blinking back tears.

He opened his eyes, his gaze locking with hers.

"That was . . . beautiful." She swallowed hard. "You have
real talent. How long have you been playing?"

The same hands that had once worked magic on her body
plucked idly at the strings, loosing strands of melody. "I started
after graduating from BUD/S. I needed a way to kill time and
clear my mind, something to do during downtime. I took a few

lessons, played when I could, took the guitar with me on deployments when I was able. At one point, Nate threatened to break it over a rock."

Laura couldn't help but smile. "He wouldn't say that if he heard you play now."

Javier's gaze traveled over her, a puzzled expression coming over his face. "You're ready for bed already?"

"I thought I'd go sit in the sauna and warm up."

"Pretty cold out in the stables?"

It was then Laura noticed the shadows in his eyes. "Is something wrong?"

He looked away, strummed the strings. "Nothing's wrong. I just have a lot on my mind. Enjoy the sauna."

The words were out before she realized it. "Why don't you join me?"

CHAPTER 10

JAVIER STRIPPED DOWN to his skin, grabbed a towel from the shelf, and wrapped it around his hips, tucking the loose end in tightly, a sense of heightened excitement humming stupidly through his blood.

This isn't about sex, pendejo. *Think you can handle it?*

By asking him to join her in the sauna, Laura wasn't inviting him to make out. He needed to get that through *both* of his heads before he stepped out of the bathroom and joined her. For her, the sauna was just a social activity. In Dubai, she'd told him how her family—grandparents, parents, uncles, aunts, cousins, and even close friends—often sat together naked in the heat, a way of keeping warm and healthy during the long, dark Swedish winter. Knowing this had helped Javier understand why she'd been so comfortable with nudity, showing not a hint of shame.

She was probably naked now, lying back on the teak benches, utterly and beautifully bare, her hair fanned out around her, her arms stretched languidly over her head. A memory of silky, long legs, full breasts, and sweet curving hips sent a jolt of heat to his groin, threatening to turn his towel into a tent.

You might as well be her brother—or her grandpa.

And then like a nightmare it hit him—an image of his *abuelos* sitting naked in the sauna with the rest of his family, smiling at them all, their faces like wrinkled apples, their bodies . . .

¡Que mierda! Holy fuck!

A shudder ran down his spine.

He took a breath, blew it out, and opened the bathroom door, the heated floor warm against his feet as he crossed the room and stepped into the sauna.

Relief and disappointment hit him when he saw she wasn't naked. She sat in one corner, a fluffy white towel wrapped around her body, concealing her from her breasts to her upper thighs, her legs stretched out on the teak bench, her ankles crossed, her hands lying relaxed in her lap. Her eyes were closed, her hair hanging in a single, pale mass over one creamy shoulder, steam making the ends curl.

He closed the door behind him, the bright scent of warmed wood filling his nostrils. He couldn't help the way his pulse jumped at the sight of her, nor could he fight off a sinking sense of sadness. The Laura he'd imagined lying naked on the bench like some Nordic sex goddess had been the woman he'd met in Dubai. The Laura who sat there now, looking almost fragile by contrast, her back pressed into the corner, was the woman who'd survived eighteen months of brutality.

A woman who's been hurt like she was hurt needs a lot of time and love to heal.

Nate's words came back to him—not just words, Javier reminded himself, but insight based on experience. What Nate had told Javier about Megan had left Javier feeling like an asshole—for blowing up at Nate, for not knowing more about Megan, for getting too caught up in his own shit.

The whole world seemed to be wounded, broken, hurting.

Javier put that out of his mind and sat across from Laura, close enough to see her face clearly in the semidark, but not close enough for contact. He stretched out his legs as she had done, the wood warm and moist against his skin. "This reminds me of summertime in Humacao—hot and humid."

She didn't open her eyes but smiled. "What was the name of that frog you told me about, the one that used to sing you to sleep when you were a little boy?"

She looked completely tranquil, her words spoken in a sleepy voice, but Javier could see the rapid thrumming of her carotid and knew she was anything but relaxed.

"El coquí?" He did his best to whistle its call, so like a bird's.

"Yeah, that one." Her lips curved in a soft smile. *"El coqui."*

Javier couldn't help but grin. "I can't believe you remember that."

She smiled again, a sad smile this time. "I remember everything."

LAURA COULDN'T IMAGINE why she'd asked Javier to join her. She'd been at an emotional edge after talking with Megan, and his guitar playing had touched her, confused her, made her remember things she wished she hadn't. And when she'd seen the sadness in his eyes . . .

Regardless of why she'd done it, he was here now.

She kept her eyes closed, knowing what she'd see if she opened them, knowing that seeing him would bring back bittersweet memories. Just waking up beside him this morning had left her feeling desolate—and they'd both been clothed. It was better not to open her eyes, not to remember, not to see.

Maybe if she pretended to doze . . .

But even with her eyes closed, she could smell him—salt, musk, spice. And then it didn't matter that her eyes were closed. Scents conjured memories, her mind filling with images. Dark eyes gone smoky soft. Full lips wet from kissing her. The beautiful brown skin of his nearly hairless chest. The broad expanse of his shoulders. The planes and ridges of his pecs and abdominal muscles. Big hands that knew how to please. Strong arms that had held her all night long.

Her throat grew tight, an ache filling the dark cavern inside her.

And her eyes opened.

He wasn't watching her. His eyes were closed, his face turned toward the door, his features in profile, a day's worth of stubble dark on his jaw. He wore a towel around his hips, his muscular chest bare, his arms . . .

She sucked in a breath.

Oh, God!

Scars.

Almost without realizing it, she was on her feet. She sat beside him, her gaze fixed on the angry, red lines that carved up the right side of his torso. "Oh, Javi."

His eyes opened, his gaze following hers. "It's all healing really well."

She couldn't imagine what it had looked like before.

He pointed. "I took a round to the liver. It shattered some ribs. I lost a lot of blood. Here's where they got me in the lung. Took one to the shoulder, too—not much more than a graze. And then there was my leg. I came close to losing it."

Laura glanced down, watched as he lifted the edge of the towel, and had to fight to hide her own shock. A deep valley was carved into his upper thigh, dark red scars showing where surgeons had tried to put him together again. It was clear a bullet had ripped through him at an angle, rupturing the muscle and blowing much of it away.

She wasn't a doctor, but she knew he'd come terribly close to dying.

"You must have been in so much pain." She ran her fingertips over the scars on his chest, saw the suture marks, the incision lines still raised and puckered in places. "I'm so sorry."

"Don't be." His voice was soft, deep. "I'm fine now."

At those words, she looked up and found her face inches from his.

From there, it was so easy.

The light brush of lips over warm lips. The slow slide of his fingers into her hair. The hard press of his chest as he sat up straighter, turned her in his arms, and kissed her.

It was a sweet kiss, slow and tender, the heat of it sliding through Laura like honey, warming some empty, dark part of her. Her heart gave a hard kick, a rush of tangled emotions washing through her, filling her chest, making it hard to breathe—elation, nervousness, pleasure, alarm, raw need.

Taken aback by the force of her own reaction, she gave in to the moment, focusing only on him, letting herself feel. The press of lips against lips. The teasing flick of his tongue. The thrumming of her own pulse. Sweat-slick skin against skin. The soft mingling of breath, steam, pheromone.

Ignoring the warning in the back of her mind, she parted her lips, let him inside her mouth, his taste exploding across her tongue, his scent filling her mind. She caught his face between her palms, pressed her lips harder against his, needing more of him, the stubble of his beard rough, his heartbeat thudding against hers.

It seemed a lifetime since she'd been kissed. She'd forgotten what it felt like to be touched like this. She'd forgotten how gentle a strong man could be. She'd forgotten what it was to *want* a man. And it felt to her that she was being kissed for the first time.

But this was no sloppy kiss between teenagers. Laura knew this man, and he knew her. Everything about him was familiar to her, his scent, the feel of his skin, the way he touched her rousing memories.

She slid her hands down his neck to the hard curves of his shoulders, his lips moving to press kisses against the pulse at her throat, his muscles shifting as he slid a hand down her spine, the damp towel falling away from her skin.

Oh, God!

Her stretch marks.

Javier wasn't sure whether he was in heaven or hell.

He'd told Laura he wouldn't make sexual demands of her—and he wouldn't. But being close to her like this, holding her, kissing her, was making it a lot harder for him to keep that promise than he'd imagined. He'd made love to this woman, kissed and tasted every inch of her, been inside her. He couldn't help but want her. He'd just begun to believe this was going somewhere when Laura went stiff in his arms.

"I'm . . . I'm so sorry, Javi. I just . . . I can't." She drew her towel around herself and tucked the end back into place, pulling away from him so fast she almost fell.

He reached out, caught her, his gaze locking with hers.

In her eyes, he saw genuine panic.

¡Puñeta!

"No, *bella*, I'm the one who's sorry." Heart still pounding, he fought to rein in his need for her. "I shouldn't have—"

She held out a hand, pressed a finger to his lips. "Please don't apologize. You didn't do anything. It's just that . . . It's . . . hard to explain."

"You don't owe me any explanations."

But she seemed to think she did.

She sat down by his feet, one arm across her breasts as if to make certain her towel stayed in place. "I . . . I'm just not ready for this. I'm not sure I ever will be."

Did she think he was upset with her?

"Hey, it's okay. You hear me? It's okay."

Any rage he felt was set aside for Al-Nassar and his thugs. Seeing her like this—unable to enjoy being touched, trembling out of fear when she should be trembling for a much different reason—made him wonder how easy it would be to break into the supermax facility and kill Al-Nassar. The prison was located here in Colorado outside Florence. And certainly Al-Nassar deserved it. The *hijo e la gran puta* had stolen something precious from her.

He willed himself to lock that anger down, to listen to what she was saying.

"You were the last man I was with before . . ."

God, he wasn't sure he could handle hearing details of what had been done to her.

If she can live through it, you can listen to it, cabrón.

But she didn't go there.

"When you left that morning, a part of me wished we'd exchanged numbers or e-mail addresses. I thought I'd use the postcard as an excuse to track you down. I thought I'd have time to . . ." She squeezed her eyes shut, turned her face away from him.

He'd felt the same way. He'd thought there'd be time, too.

But then she'd been gone.

"Dubai was special to me, Javi. You're special to me." She opened her eyes. "Being close to you like this after all these years . . . The way you make me feel . . . I want to get closer to you, and that scares me."

So he hadn't been misreading her signals when he'd thought she was enjoying kissing him. That was good to know. "Hey, you're safe with me. I would never push you to do anything you didn't want to do."

"I know." Her expression grew troubled, her hands moving to shield her lower belly. "But it won't work. I'm . . . I'm different now."

When she'd first told him she was different, he'd taken her to mean that she had changed emotionally. But something in the way she'd just said it, the way her hands seemed to shelter her pelvis, made him wonder whether she'd suffered physical wounds—some kind of mutilation or internal damage that made sex impossible or painful. He knew that some of the tribes in the area where she'd been held practiced genital mutilation on girls, a brutal way of ensuring chastity. And he'd heard of more than one woman maimed by rape, their insides battered to the point where sex was agony and motherhood impossible.

Could something like that have happened to Laura?

¡Carajo!

The thought made his skin shrink, something twisting in his gut.

Forget breaking into prison. Maybe he could ambush the prison transport and kill Al-Nassar before he reached Florence.

Laura went on. "As much as I wish we could go back to how things were in Dubai, I just can't. You'd only end up getting hurt. I couldn't bear it if I did something to destroy our memories or our friendship."

He dropped his feet to the floor and moved to sit beside her, taking her hand in his, caressing her fingers. "That is *not* going to happen. Do you hear me, *bella*? No matter what he did to you, no matter how you've changed, nothing—and I mean *nada*—can change the way I feel about you."

And how do you feel about her?

He wasn't sure. He only knew he couldn't leave her alone with this.

"Thank you." She gave him a wobbly smile, squeezed his hand. "I should go."

And in a heartbeat she was gone, leaving Javier alone in the heat.

LAURA LAY IN the dark, her tears spent, an ache in her chest. She'd pleaded a headache and had gone to bed early, certain that Nate and his family would enjoy some time alone with Javier. Besides, she needed to think, to make sense of what had happened in the sauna, of what she had *allowed* to happen.

She ran her finger over her lips, conjured up the memory of Javier's taste, his scent, the sweet heat of his tongue teasing hers. Her pulse spiked, warmth sliding through her. But the rush of pleasure was short-lived, only to be followed by an overwhelming sense of emptiness.

She'd always been afraid that having sexual contact with a man would make her think of Al-Nassar and leave her feeling revulsion. She'd avoided men for that reason alone. But that hadn't happened today. She hadn't thought of that bastard once while Javier had been kissing her. Maybe the fact that she and Javier had been lovers before her abduction somehow made a difference. Or maybe Javier was such a fantastic kisser that it was impossible to think of anything else once his mouth touched hers.

Kissing him had felt like coming home, everything about it precious, familiar—his scent, his taste, his ability to make her lips burn. Yes, she had enjoyed it. She'd enjoyed it so much she'd forgotten about everything else, an almost desperate need overtaking her. Not lust. It had been far more than lust. A need to touch and be touched. A need for intimacy. A need to reclaim her sexuality, to put bad memories to rest, to feel like a woman again.

She'd sat through dinner watching Megan and Nate, catching their glances. The love in Nate's eyes as he looked at his wife. Megan's absolute devotion to her husband. Their shared love for little Emily, the daughter Megan had lost and reclaimed, the child Nate had adopted, not caring how she'd come into this world. And some part of Laura had dared to hope that she could have the same thing—her daughter, a man who would love Klara no matter who her biological father was, a family.

But Megan deserved her happiness. She'd fought like hell for Emily. She hadn't turned her back and walked away from her.

Nothing—and I mean nada—*can change the way I feel about you.*

Javier believed that, but if he knew . . .

God, how she wished she could go to him right now. She'd walk to his room, take off her nightgown, and show him the faint silver lines on her belly. She could tell him how she'd turned her back and left her two-month-old baby girl in the hands of terrorists to flee with the SEALs.

He would stare at her, a horrified look on his face, and he'd ask questions.

Yes, of course, she'd known the baby girl was hers. How

could she not? What woman could carry a baby for nine months and not realize she was pregnant? Or give birth on a dirty floor and not understand that she'd just had a baby? She would have to be crazy, wouldn't she?

Wouldn't she?

Laura rolled onto her side, a bitter torrent of regret surging through her, followed by an overwhelming sense of loathing for the weak, broken woman she'd been. If only she'd taken time to think before she'd run. If only she'd grabbed Klara from Safiya's arms. If only she'd told the SEALs.

If only . . .

Whatever mistreatment Klara suffered, she suffered because of Laura.

Oh, Klara, I'm so sorry! I am so sorry!

Laura's cell phone rang, startling her, making her gasp.

She sat and reached for it. "This is Laura."

"Hi, Laura."

Her heart gave a thud.

Derek Tower.

"What—"

"Here's what's going to happen. Tomorrow, you're going to find out that the U.S. Marshal Service has taken me off its list of fugitives and issued an apology. You'll read in the paper how I offered to consult with federal authorities on the car bombing in an effort to help them find whoever it is who wants to kill you, and you'll issue a statement thanking me for my help." He paused for a moment. "Okay, maybe not that last bit, but the rest of it *will* happen. Then you and I are going to meet face-to-face and have a nice, long conversation about the good old days in Pakistan."

Her temper kicked in. "So you're psychic now as well as psycho?"

"You disappoint me, Ms. Nilsson. I had you figured for a smart chick, but maybe what they say about blondes is true. Or maybe it's that bump you took on the head. Do you really believe I'm mixed up with terrorists and trying to kill you?"

If he'd wanted to kill her, he could have done it that night in her car. Then again, he'd gone away angry that night.

"Are you?"

"I want the truth about why my men are dead. Since you're the key to my getting that info, terminating you wouldn't make much sense, would it?"

Laura started to answer, only to realize Tower had already ended the call.

CHAPTER 11

THEY STAYED UP at the Cimarron for the rest of the week. Surrounded by the stillness of the mountains and the hospitality of the West family, Laura felt herself begin to relax. She slept away hours of each day, likely a result of the concussion, spending the rest of her time getting to know her hosts, savoring Jack's amazing home-cooked meals, and enjoying the fresh mountain air.

While Javier helped Nate tend the ranch's horses and its herd of Angus, Laura spent time with Megan and Emily. She found herself fascinated by Emily's sunny smile, her quick mind, and her imagination, whether Emily was trying to braid her hair, drawing pictures with crayons at the kitchen table, or showing Laura how to feed treats to her favorite horse, a big palomino gelding named Buckwheat. Watching Megan and Emily together put an ache in Laura's chest, the love between mother and child sharpening her regret—and her determination.

That was how it would be for her and Klara one day.

Laura and Megan had lots of time to talk. Laura found that despite the dramatic differences in their upbringings, she felt a deep connection to Megan, the violence they'd survived marking them as women in such a way that their differences didn't matter. How strange that something horrible could lay a foundation for friendship.

Time seemed to stand still up at the Cimarron. After reporting Derek Tower's call to Zach, she'd turned off her cell phone and wasn't even checking messages. Apart from checking in with her mother via e-mail a couple of times, she ignored the Internet, too. She didn't want to know what was going on in the world. Monday would come soon enough and with it a return to so many things she didn't want to think about. Besides, there were too many fun distractions here.

On Wednesday, they went on a sleigh ride, Laura and Javier sitting in the back under a warm wool blanket while Nate held the reins, Megan and Emily beside him.

On Thursday, she went cross-country skiing for the first time in years, sticking to easy terrain both because she was out of practice and because she didn't want to fall and bump her head again. On Friday, she went out with Nate and Javier to see the north herd, watching while the men spread hay for the hungry animals.

When they got back to the house, Jack told them the news: Al-Nassar had been found guilty by the jury on all charges against him, with a sentencing hearing set for the middle of March—a month from now. Jack made a big chocolate cake to celebrate the news, even putting candles on the top for Laura to blow out. Turning the verdict into a party wasn't something that would have occurred to Laura, and it felt special to share that precious, hard-fought triumph with them.

The only downside of being at the ranch was spending so little time alone with Javier. The kiss they'd shared in the sauna had reignited something inside Laura, a raw current seeming to arc between them with every touch, every glance, every word they shared. All Javier had to do to make her heart beat faster was smile. She felt like a schoolgirl in the throes of her first crush—except that there was nothing childlike about her feelings for him and nowhere for her feelings to go. And yet, apart from the times when he was out on the land with Nate, he was never far away. He sat beside her at meals, put his arm around her shoulder when they watched DVDs in the evening, walked her to her room and kissed her on the cheek every night when she went to bed.

Their last afternoon at the ranch was spent grilling on the porch, the day unusually warm, the sky bright and blue. They'd just finished eating when Emily got down from her booster seat, took her grandpa Jack's hand, and disappeared into the house, a secret smile on her cute little face. When they returned, they were each carrying a big gift-wrapped box topped with a bright red bow. Emily brought hers to Laura, while Jack handed his to Javier.

"What is this?" Laura asked Emily, who popped a finger in her mouth and smiled, looking over at her grandfather.

"Open it and find out," Jack offered.

Laura tore through the wrapping paper and ripped open her box to find a white cowboy hat. She laughed, lifted it carefully from the box, and realized it was the real thing. "Will you show me how to wear it, Emily?"

Emily nodded, stood on the picnic bench beside Laura, and helped Laura settle it on her head. "Now you're a cowgirl like me."

Laura hugged Emily, the little girl precious in her arms. "Thank you, sweetie."

"Now we're talking." Javier's was black. He took it out and settled it on his head, pulling it low over his eyes. "How do I look, *bella*?"

He looked incredibly, unbelievably . . . *hot*.

Laura met his gaze, saw the warmth and humor in his brown eyes, and found herself struggling to form a coherent sentence. "He . . . um . . . looks very handsome, don't you think, Emily?"

Emily looked over at Javier and gave a shy smile.

Javier grinned. "Maybe the ranching life is for me— getting up early to feed the cows, fixing fences, eating steak."

"Steers, bro. Those were steers."

Laura laughed along with the others.

"I bet some of your best rodeo stars are Puerto Rican. Am I right?" Javier adjusted the hat on his head. "We *Boricuas*— we are everywhere, man."

"That's the Javier I know." Nate rolled his eyes, shook his head.

"We wanted you to know you're always welcome here, come rain or shine, tarnation or hellfire," Jack said. "You're both a part of this place, and it's a part of you."

Laura smiled. "Thank you, Jack. Thanks to all of you."

* * *

"I saw you playing with that little girl," Javier said as they drove toward the highway, his gaze warm. "You're going to make a wonderful mother some day."

He had no idea how deeply his words cut her.

They arrived back in Denver Sunday evening to find that Tower had told Laura the truth, the backlog of e-mails and news articles like an onslaught after five days of quiet. Laura read through them one by one, determined not to lose the sense of peace she'd gained from her time at the ranch, but it wasn't easy. The media were making Tower out to be the selfless hero who was helping to keep Laura safe despite her suspicions toward him. He was no longer a suspect in the bombing, and the Washington office of the U.S. Marshal Service had, indeed, apologized in what must have felt like a smack in the face to Zach and the Colorado office.

Laura called her attorney and left a message asking her to begin the process of getting a restraining order against Tower. He might not be behind the bombing, but that didn't mean she had to put up with him.

"Don't let him get to you, *bella*," Javier said when he kissed her good night, leaving her to sleep alone while he took the guest room.

Monday morning found Laura sitting at her desk, joining the morning I-Team meeting via Skype, while Javier took a shower. As much as she had enjoyed her time up at the Cimarron, it felt good to be getting back to work again, even if that meant enduring the image of Tom Trent's scowling face on her monitor.

"You're late, Harker. What's on your plate?" he asked Matt.

Matt's voice came from somewhere nearby. "The city is moving to condemn a stroke palace on Colfax—a place called Candy's Emporium."

"A stroke palace?" Kat asked. "What's that?"

Laura had no idea what that meant either.

"Uh, yeah . . ." Matt stammered.

"Candy's is basically a cross between a porn arcade and a strip club." That was Alex. "Men go there to jack off."

Stroke palace?

Ew.

"Apparently, customers get a helping hand at Candy's. Police have been trying to shut it down for years but have never been able to prove what was happening there, so the city decided to take a different approach and went after the building's owners for violating fire codes. I'm guessing about fifteen inches."

"Can we get photos?" That was Syd, the managing editor.

"Done." Joaquin said. "I went by there yesterday. That place is pretty seedy."

"See if you can get interviews with some of the working girls," Tom said. "Find out what impact this has on them."

"I'll be happy to take that on if you don't have time, Harker," Alex offered.

Laura rolled her eyes.

"Carmichael, since you seem to have energy and spare time, you're next." Tom's gaze shifted to his left. "You've got follow-up stories about the bombing and the Al-Nassar verdict."

"The feds aren't sharing anything new at this point. I can see what the talking heads at the alphabet soup agencies have to say, write an update, but I'm pretty sure it's going to be the same as Friday."

Judging from his expression, Tom didn't like this. "I want the bombing on the front page every day until it's resolved. Some asshole tried to take out one of my reporters and damned near killed the entire I-Team staff. What about an interview with the kid's parents?"

"I've called four times. I'll try again." Alex sounded irritated.

Then Tom looked directly at Laura. "Are you privy to any info the feds haven't felt like sharing with the public?"

Laura stiffened. "No. I haven't spoken with anyone from the FBI or the Marshal Service since last week."

Surely Tom realized she couldn't share information from an active investigation just because she worked for the paper.

His gaze shifted back to Alex. "Get me something—an interview with a source close to the investigation, the kid's parents, witnesses. I want at least ten inches on this, enough for a decent headline."

"Whatever you say." Alex was definitely irritated. "There was a gang-related killing in the state pen overnight. The suspected head of one of the Mexican nationalist gangs was found dead in his cell this morning with his throat slit. Word is that the head of the white supremacist group green-lighted the murder from his cell in D-seg. I'd like to report this— maybe ten inches—and use it as a springboard for a bigger piece about gangs in Colorado prisons."

While Tom and Alex discussed possible angles for Alex's proposed story, Laura looked over her notes, knowing it was almost her turn in the hot seat. She heard footsteps and looked up to see Javier. Her breath caught, her mind going blank. He stood in her office doorway wearing nothing but a towel. In the sauna, seeing him dressed like this had been one thing. But seeing him standing in her office, daylight highlighting his muscles, making his dark skin gleam . . .

"Can I use your washer?" he asked quietly.

She nodded, unable to keep from raking him with her gaze.

"Nilsson, you there?" Tom looked into the computer screen.

"Yes." Laura glanced down at her notes. "I need to finish my interview with Ted Hollis, the man I was speaking with when the bomb went off. I've got two more soldiers I'd like to interview after that. I'm slated to talk to the local coordinator for the VA's PTSD program tomorrow. I'd like to talk to the regional VA director, as well, but he keeps shunting me over to the PR flack. I hope to have a story by Friday."

Laura glanced back over her shoulder, but Javier was gone.

McBRIDE SHOWED UP with Callahan at fifteen hundred hours to brief Laura on the investigation. Javier could tell the man was pissed. So was he.

"I've never known the Marshal Service to back down like

this. Tower must have powerful friends in Washington. He also has an alibi. A friend of his claims he was in D.C. at the time the bomb went off. I'm sure it's false, but I can't prove that. He came in voluntarily and answered our questions, even offered to help, which makes him look good. Officially, he's no longer a person of interest in this case, but unofficially . . ."

Laura nodded. "I understand."

Javier stood to her right, the tension inside him making it impossible for him to sit. "What about all the phone calls, the way he followed her to her car? What about the bruises he left on her wrists?"

McBride didn't seem to take Javier's frustration personally. "The district attorney has declined to prosecute the case. He bought into Tower's claim that Tower would never have touched Laura if she hadn't held a gun on him. He says one incident of following Laura to her car doesn't constitute stalking. But if Tower continues to call you or comes near you again, Laura, we'll arrest the son of a bitch and charge him with violating the restraining order. He won't be able to squirm out of that."

The order, signed by a judge on his lunch hour, thanks to Laura's very determined attorney, sat on Laura's coffee table beside half-empty coffee cups.

Tower was making the most of his fifteen minutes of fame to repeat his lies about her being to blame in some way for her own abduction and the deaths of his men, and this time some of the papers had taken the bait, dredging up old news stories, reexamining the State Department's report. The bastard was a master schemer, and he'd taken advantage of the bombing to manipulate the media.

But Javier was willing to bet Laura knew more about the media than Tower did—and she had her own contacts. She'd already been interviewed by her editor for a piece in tomorrow's paper, and she'd left a message for her former anchor, who'd been more than happy to give her a segment on Thursday's prime-time broadcast.

Laura reached out, touched McBride's hand. "Thanks. This isn't your fault."

McBride turned to Detective Callahan. "I believe you wanted to update Laura on your investigation."

Detective Callahan nodded, dark circles beneath his blue

eyes proof he'd been putting in long hours. "We've collected debris from the bomb site and from the body and have been able to piece together the explosive device."

"Have you learned anything definite so far?" Laura asked.

Callahan nodded. "We know that the bomber used dynamite stolen from a construction site in Adams County to use as a primer. The dynamite was detonated by cell phone. A call was made to a cell phone connected to an SCR switch."

When it was clear that this meant nothing to Laura, Javier knelt down beside the coffee table, took her reporter's notepad and pen, and began to sketch. "A call to the cell phone sends current through the phone. The current passes through a nine-volt battery that is wired into a blasting cap. The blasting cap is what sets off the dynamite, which in turn ignites the ANFO. We saw shit like this all the time in Iraq and Afghanistan."

She studied the drawing. "Can you trace either cell phone?"

Callahan shook his head. "The one used to make the detonator was a burner bought solely for this purpose. It received only one call—and that call came from a burner phone, too."

She looked disappointed. "I guess there's not much to go on."

Callahan's brows bent in a frown. "Not true. We've got serial numbers and may be able to locate the store where the phones were purchased. Same with some of the detonator's components. That might give us an idea where this person lives—in Colorado, out of state, Front Range, Western Slope. We might also luck out and get some footage from security cameras. Obviously, this won't yield results overnight, but we *will* find him."

"In the meantime," said McBride, "we know for certain another person or persons was involved. We know that the materials they used are consistent with the materials used by AQ, the Taliban, and other terrorist groups to build and detonate IEDs. And we know that Ali Al Zahrani wasn't the shot-caller here. Whoever detonated the explosives probably never intended for Al Zahrani to set off the bomb himself. He probably used Al Zahrani to help mix the ANFO and get the car into position, and then killed him to eliminate witnesses or prevent him from backing out and warning someone."

"That poor kid!" Laura closed her eyes, then looked up at

them. "He was murdered. Someone pumped him full of hatred, brainwashed him into doing their dirty work—and then shot him in the head. What if he had second thoughts? Maybe he remembered at the last moment that killing was wrong. Maybe he realized he wanted to live and—"

"Hey, don't do this to yourself." Javier rested his hand on her shoulder. "We don't know what happened for sure."

"But we are going to find out." McBride pressed a finger to his earpiece, then glanced toward the door. "This is going to be fun. Excuse me."

He walked out the door, closing it behind him. A few seconds passed before Javier heard the sound of arguing.

"This is still a multi-agency operation. I don't see why I can't remain a part of Ms. Nilsson's protection detail." That was Agent Killeen.

McBride's voice was so deep he could barely make out what McBride was saying. "The marshals are handling that aspect of the operation. The FBI—"

"With all due respect, sir, I don't give a rat's ass where the brass have drawn the lines. I promised to keep her safe, and I want to fulfill that promise."

"You kept that promise, and now you've been relieved."

"Damn it, sir, I don't *want* to be relieved! I fought hard to become a part of her protection detail, and now—"

"You're letting your emotions get the better of you, Agent Killeen."

Javier knew Laura liked Agent Killeen, trusted her. He knew the moment he looked at Laura's face what she was going to do. He followed her as she got to her feet, walked to the door, and opened it.

"I know it's probably unusual, but can't I request that Agent Killeen remain part of my detail?"

McBride seemed to consider Laura's words—not altogether cheerfully. "I could deputize you, bring you into the Marshal Service temporarily. It won't make you popular with your colleagues."

From the look on Agent Killeen's face, the idea didn't appeal much to her either.

And Javier wondered how the government functioned at

all when the federal law enforcement agencies spent so much time caught up in dick fights.

Agent Killeen's chin went up. "Yes. Deputize me."

"All right." Zach drew out his cell phone, a frown set on his face. "I'm going to catch hell for this."

Laura smiled. "Thanks, Zach. I really appreciate it."

They walked back inside, McBride shutting and locking the door behind them.

Laura offered Agent Killeen a glass of water, then settled back in her chair. "There's something else I wanted to ask you."

Javier knew where this was going.

McBride clearly didn't. "Go ahead."

"When can I visit Ali Al Zahrani's parents?"

McBRIDE ARRANGED FOR Laura to visit the kid's family Wednesday night. That gave the security detail two and a half days to plan. They didn't know it yet, but Javier was determined to be a part of that effort. Not that he didn't trust the Marshal Service. He did, especially with McBride in the lead. But none of them cared about Laura the way he did. Javier was willing to lose everything for her—including his life.

JAVIER FINISHED HIS call with McBride, then walked back to the guest room to fold his newly washed and dried clothes, listening to Laura as she interviewed a disabled Marine in her office. From what Javier had been able to piece together, the veteran, a woman who'd served two tours in Iraq, had lost both legs and been badly burned when a suicide bomber had blown up a car at a checkpoint near the Green Zone.

It was a helluva thing to live through.

"What did they say when you told them you were having thoughts of suicide?" Laura asked, periodically injecting "I see," or "How upsetting," or "Mmm-hmm," as she listened to the woman's answer.

It was interesting to hear her work after watching so many of her broadcasts. She was cool and collected on the air, but in person she was warm, sympathetic, always letting the person she was interviewing know that what they told her mattered to her. Even when the interview was what Javier might consider hostile, like her interview with the VA flack this morning, she was warm and caring—at least until she had them by the jugular.

"I know it's difficult to talk about this, but it would really help my readers understand the issue better if you could describe for me what you're experiencing—the nightmares, the flashbacks, the anger you feel."

Nightmares.

Flashbacks.

Anger.

The words hit Javier, sent ripples through him.

Knock it off, cabrón.

He did *not* have PTSD. A few post-combat nightmares, a bar fight, and a handful of strange adrenaline surges did not constitute PTSD. If he was on edge all the time, it was only because everyone kept hassling him, as if they expected him to fall the fuck apart. But he was stronger than that. If they would back the hell off and let him get on with an active-duty workup, he'd be fine.

"You jumped out of bed? You mean without your prosthetics? Oh, I'm so sorry. I can only imagine how frightening that was."

¡Sí, claro!

After what she'd been through, Laura knew damned good and well how bad it could get. Javier knew she'd had another nightmare last night. He'd heard her in the kitchen mixing that milk-and-honey brew of her grandmother's. He'd almost gone to her, offered to sleep with her again. But after what had happened in the sauna, he'd thought the better of it. She'd been coping without him all of this time. It was better not to fan the flames.

That was probably another reason he was on edge. His mind knew he and Laura were not going to enjoy a repeat of their weekend in Dubai, but his body wasn't getting the message. He'd tried to blame it on the fact that he hadn't gotten laid since before his most recent deployment—four months in Afghanistan followed by five months that included a stay in ICU, rehab, and medical leave. He might even have believed that excuse if it hadn't been for the inconvenient fact that the only woman he wanted was Laura.

But no way in hell did he want to see that same panicked look in her eyes that he'd seen after he'd kissed her in the sauna. He'd be damned before he'd upset her like that again or make her regret spending time with him.

He focused on folding his clothes and squaring his gear away. He'd finished and was in the kitchen making a sandwich as an afternoon snack when she emerged from her office. She walked past him to the fridge, opened the door, and bent down, reaching for something in the back, the sweet curves of her ass outlined in butter-soft denim. He managed to lift his gaze just as she turned to face him, her long-sleeved pink V-neck doing nothing to hide the fact that she wasn't wearing a bra.

He willed himself to quit gawking.

Mind over balls, bro.

"That sounded like a tough interview."

"I feel so bad for her. She's grappling with uncontrolled neuropathy and PTSD at the same time, and no one seems to be helping her."

He put the lid back on the mayo. "You are. You're helping her."

"I just hope the article lights a fire under someone's butt at the VA." Laura walked to the fridge, took out a container of yogurt, and grabbed a spoon out of the silverware drawer. "You must be bored out of your mind. It can't be fun to be stuck inside with me here all day long."

He grinned, shook his head. "Bored? No way."

There was still doubt in her eyes.

He carried his plate and a glass of water to the table. "You think life as an operator is all combat and thrashin' through jungles and shit?"

She sat across from him and popped a spoonful of yogurt in her mouth, her lips curving in a sweet smile. "You mean it's not?"

"A lot of it is training—predeployment workups. Uphill runs in full combat gear. Jumps, jumps, and more jumps. Night surf landings. That's all good." He took a bite of his sandwich, chewed. "But between that and actual combat ops, there's a lot of waiting. We jock up, then get told the op is off.

We jock up again. They call it off again. In the meantime, we hang around the TOC with no running water, sweating or freezing our balls off in our BDUs, living off MREs, checking our gear—and staring at each other's ugly faces."

She smiled again, pointed her spoon toward him, a hint of playfulness in her eyes that made his blood heat. "And you *love* every moment of it."

Okay, so she had him there. It wasn't always comfortable, but he loved hanging with Team guys, waiting for the next tasking, letting the adrenaline build.

"Here, I've got a real bed, a bathroom with a door that closes, great food, and a hundred channels on the TV. But you know the best thing, *bella*?"

She took another bite of yogurt, shook her head.

He met her gaze straight on, let his lips curve in a slow grin. "The scenery here is *so* much better."

Her pupils dilated—and damned if she didn't blush.

CHAPTER 12

JAVIER SAT IN the passenger seat, keeping an eye out for trouble while Laura drove, his SIG Sauer P226 in a shoulder holster hidden beneath his jacket, the Walther in an ankle holster. There was only one reason why he'd gone along with this.

It was important to Laura.

He glanced over at her, could see she was afraid despite her attempts to hide it. She wasn't wearing any makeup, her skin almost translucent, her face pale. "I respect what you're trying to do, but I wish you'd let McBride arrange a meeting with them at a neutral site."

Laura kept her eyes on the road. "I'm tired of sitting around and waiting. Besides, the marshal office is hardly neutral. These people have lost their son. They've been raked over the coals by the FBI and the media. Every corner of their lives has been probed. The last thing they need is to be dragged from their home again."

"You have such a soft heart, but your compassion might be wasted on these people." Javier knew only too well how an act of compassion could blow up in a person's face. He'd spared that shepherd's life and those of his sons, and eighteen men had died as a result. "They raised a son who tried to *kill* you."

The FBI had found exactly what Javier had expected they'd find. The kid's laptop had a secret user identity filled with extremist rants about the U.S., downloaded videos of Osama

bin Laden and other terrorist leaders, and photographs of terrorist bombing sites. His browser history showed that he'd
made frequent visits over the past two months to Internet sites
that gave instructions on how to mix ANFO, build detonators,
and buy supplies. The fact that the attempt on Laura's life had
followed so closely after Al-Nassar's call for her death made
it an open-and-shut case as far as Javier could see. But who
had put the kid up to this?

That was the critical missing piece of intel.

"Zach told me the parents aren't religious extremists. He
says the FBI believes they had nothing to do with their son's
actions. I can't imagine how hard this has been for them—
loving their son, discovering what he'd done, learning that
he'd been murdered. Besides, no one knows we're here except
Janet and the deputy marshals working my detail."

"And his family—they know you're coming." Javier was
willing to bet they hadn't kept that fact secret. The Baghdad
Babe visiting their home? Their relatives in Riyadh probably
knew by now.

Ahead of them, Agent Killeen turned right, making her
way through a middle-class neighborhood in Aurora. An
unmarked car with two deputy U.S. Marshals followed closely
behind them, another deputy marshal already at the house.

Laura steered her car around the corner, and Javier watched
her expression grow more determined as her headlights spilled
over the media vans and reporters that filled the street before
them. But the media's attention was focused on a small brick
ranch-style home, where an older man was making his way up
the front steps. They didn't notice Laura drive by, take a right at
the alley, and drive up behind the house. Nor did they see
Killeen block the far end of the alley with her car, while the
two deputy marshals who followed them blocked the other end,
effectively sealing the alley from media encroachment.

A deputy marshal stepped out of the backyard through a
wooden gate, waiting for Laura, who parked the car and slipped
the keys into her handbag. She was dressed entirely in black, a
black blazer over black pants and a black shirt, a black scarf
tucked into her neckline.

She drew a deep breath, exhaled. "I can't believe I'm doing
this."

Javier thought she was talking about her visit with Al Zahrani's parents. He was about to remind her that she could still change her mind when she took the scarf from around her neck and began to draw it over her beautiful hair.

"I swore after I was rescued that I'd never wear cover again."

Something clenched in Javier's stomach. He'd ripped that burka off her two years ago. He knew what this must bring back for her, and he didn't want to see her put herself through this. He reached out, stopped her. "Coming to pay your respects is enough. You don't need to go that far, *bella*."

She looked over at him. "Their son is dead. I'm coming into their home. I'm not so weak that I can't respect their culture."

She drew the scarf into place and secured it beneath her chin, veiling both her hair and the last of her emotions, her face expressionless.

They stepped out of the car and followed the deputy marshal through the gate and up a back walk to the rear door, light spilling from the windows. Javier instinctively scanned their surroundings for any hint of danger, possible exits, cover. From overhead came the thrum of a police helo McBride had requisitioned to monitor the neighborhood.

Javier glanced up at it, its lights illuminating the entire block.

Pain in his chest and his leg made him want to puke, his body shaking from shock and blood loss. He reached out, took Krasinski's hand, squeezed. "Hear that? Medevac is almost here, buddy. We're going to be pumped full of morphine, and flirting with nurses, before you know it."

"Y-eah?" Krasinski sounded far away.

"Stay with me, Crazy K. Come on, man. Not long now."

A helo appeared to the south. He blinked cold sweat out of his eyes and watched it approach, the thrum of its rotors growing louder. "Just a few minutes, bro."

"Cobra, I . . ."

"Yeah?"

Krasinski started to say something, the word disappearing in a groan and a rattling exhale.

Christ, no!

Javier tried to shout, but couldn't. He squeezed Krasinski's hand. "Krasinski? Hey, K, come on, man."

The helo was looking for a place to land. What was taking them so fucking long? If they didn't put down fast, more men were to die.

The helo exploded in a ball of flame, shrapnel hitting the ground all around them.

A hand touched Javier's shoulder.

He gasped, found himself looking into Laura's worried eyes. "Are you okay?"

Javier nodded, the tang of blood and reek of smoke still in his nostrils, his heart thudding. "Yeah. Of course."

She watched him for a moment, then turned and headed up the sidewalk.

What the hell had just happened? One minute he'd been here. The next . . .

Lock that shit down, cabrón*!*

He wouldn't be any good to Laura if he didn't.

He sucked air into his lungs and followed her, beating back his memories and the sense of dread that came with them, forcing them out of his mind, the helo's rotors beating in his memory like the thrum of a pulse.

The back door of the house opened, and a tall, beefy man with short gray hair and a neatly trimmed gray mustache stepped outside. He wasn't wearing the white robes and red-checked headscarf Javier was used to seeing on Saudi men but was dressed in a dark gray sports jacket, a white shirt, and black trousers. Heavy bags hung beneath his red-rimmed eyes, weariness lining his face.

Laura looked up at him and spoke in Arabic.

He answered, reached for Laura's hand, and switched to English, speaking with only a faint Arabic accent. "Come in! Come in! Welcome to our home."

So this was the kid's father, Yusif Al Zahrani.

Naturalized citizen. Works as a cardiologist. Pays his taxes. Votes. No arrests.

Laura followed Al Zahrani indoors, Javier close behind her.

Apart from the somber mood, what Javier found inside was not what he'd expected. Men sat on chairs and couches in the living room, wearing sports jackets or nice sweaters, some with trimmed beards, others clean-shaven. Women bustled in the kitchen, some wearing scarves over their hair, some not, one clad in a black abaya, her face exposed. He'd been inside a lot of homes in Afghanistan and Iraq, but he'd never seen men and women mingle casually like this.

The dining room table was covered with serving dishes heaped with food—pastries, dates, cheeses, breads, salads, sliced pineapple, grapes, olives, desserts, rice, meats, and a big pot of what looked like lamb stew. The spicy aromas of the different dishes mingled with the exotic scent of incense.

All conversation stopped.

Javier was still on edge from his little flashback, or whatever the hell that had been, and his instincts kicked in hard, his gaze taking in the entire room at once, watching for sudden or suspicious movement as the women turned to face Laura, the men rising to their feet. Still speaking Arabic, Laura was introduced to them one at a time. Some shook her hand, gave her polite nods, the men as well as the women—but not all of them.

An older man with a trimmed beard refused. He spoke to Laura in Arabic, his tone of voice gruff. Javier moved closer to Laura, uneasy about the way the man was looking at her, his eyes cold, rage on his face.

Laura replied, her voice soft.

Javier was about to ask who the man was and what the hell he'd said to her when a door opened, and a woman appeared in the hallway. She wore a long tunic of embroidered gray silk with matching silk pants, an ivory scarf draped loosely over her long, dark hair. Her eyes were red from crying, the grief on her face unmistakable. Behind her, women stood in the doorway of what appeared to be a bedroom, peering out at Laura.

Karima Al Zahrani, the boy's mother.

Naturalized citizen. Teaches Arabic at CU-Denver. Votes. No arrests.

The house fell silent.

The woman reached for Laura with both hands.

Laura went to her, again speaking in Arabic.

The woman replied, took Laura's hands in hers, bent down, and kissed them.

LAURA WASN'T HUNGRY, but she made herself eat the food she'd been offered, washing down Medjoul dates and bread with sips of strong coffee while her hosts and their other guests spoke about young Ali, the boy they'd all lost. Zach had been right about them. They weren't extremists. They weren't even strict.

Many were U.S. citizens, had teaching jobs with the university, and maintained very progressive attitudes. Most of the women didn't cover, and few of the men had beards. Rather than being separated, men and women mingled freely. They reminded Laura of some of the families she'd met on her one and only trip to Saudi Arabia, families that adhered to the strict laws and traditions of their country while in public but lived a very different life behind closed doors. At the same time, they embodied everything she loved about Middle Eastern culture—warmth, generosity, hospitality.

"We are most anxious to get his body back for burial," said Hussein Al Zahrani, the boy's paternal uncle, who ran a halal grocery store on East Colfax. More conservative than the others, he had declined to shake her hand and was furious that his nephew's remains hadn't yet been returned. "When will his body be released to us?"

Laura wished she had an answer for them. It was Islamic tradition to bury the dead before sunset on the day they died. "I'm sorry. I wish I knew, but I don't."

"Come." Karima, Ali's mother, rose to her feet.

Laura walked beside her down the hall and into Ali's bedroom, Yusif, the boy's father, and Javier following behind them. Laura wasn't sure why they were bringing her here. Maybe it was their way of sharing their love for Ali, of trying to show her that there was more to their son than the act of violence that had led to his death and would now come to define his life.

It was clear that federal investigators had combed through the room inch by inch, searching every nook and cranny. There was no computer at the desk, no cell phone plugged into the charger. The shelves had been stripped of books. A small black metal filing cabinet stood open, its drawers empty. The closet door was open, too, a young man's clothes—jeans, hoodies, T-shirts—pushed to the side, their pockets turned out, board games lying in a haphazard pile on the closet floor.

And then Laura began to notice the details. Little League trophies on the shelf. A ball and glove in the corner, a bat propped up beside them. A framed high school diploma. A plaque for making the honor roll all four quarters of his senior year. A poster of a young Marilyn Monroe on one wall. One of the Avengers on another.

How had he gone from all-American boy to suicide bomber?

Laura ran her fingers over the Little League trophies, over the frame of the diploma, mementos of a young boy's achievements, now reminders of a wasted life.

Karima's quiet weeping came from behind, interrupting Laura's thoughts.

Laura turned to see Karima sitting on the edge of the bed, her hands pressed over her face. Laura sat beside her and wrapped an arm around her shoulders, speaking in English now. "I'm so sorry."

"He was a good boy, a good boy. I loved him so much. My son." Karima sobbed out the words. "There was no hate inside him. He was born here. He was a citizen. He loved America."

Karima's grief cut through Laura, touched close to her own deepest grief. And yet Laura couldn't imagine what Karima was feeling. Karima had raised her son, watched him grow from the day he was born. Laura had never even held Klara.

She pushed her own sadness aside. This wasn't about her.

Then Yusif spoke, chin quivering. "Ali wanted to join the army, but I didn't want him to go. He is our only son. Our only child. I didn't want to lose him. He accepted our decision. He stayed and went to college. And now he's dead."

Karima looked up at Laura through tear-filled eyes. "He would never have tried to hurt you. When you were taken, when we saw on the news that you'd been killed, my boy cried. He was only fourteen then. He was angry at the men who'd hurt you. He told me that no true Muslim would harm a woman like that. He felt no respect for Al-Nassar. I cannot believe that he did what they say he did. I cannot believe it."

Yusif wiped tears from his face with a big hand. "He was never in trouble. He worked hard at school and at his job. Every afternoon after classes he went to work at my brother's grocery, stocking shelves, cleaning. He never complained, even when he worked late. How could such a fate have befallen him?"

Laura swallowed hard, tears sliding down her cheeks, her heart feeling as if it might burst. She looked from Karima to Yusif to Javier, who stood in one corner, arms crossed over his chest, a grave expression on his face. "I . . . I don't know. But I'll do my best to find out."

CHAPTER 13

"I DON'T UNDERSTAND it. How could the kid cry when he heard I'd been killed and then a few years later try to kill me himself? How could he be on the dean's list in December and a terrorist by February? It doesn't make sense."

"When does terrorism ever make sense?" Javier watched Laura battle with her emotions while she attempted to make coffee, her mind distracted, her movements wooden. Truth be told, he felt more than a little shaken up, too.

First, whatever had happened when he'd seen that helo, and then . . .

He'd been to more funerals than he cared to count, lost men who were like brothers to him, and yet something about today had hit him hard. The kid had died for nothing, the life he'd been given wasted, his parents' lives destroyed by his actions.

Now Javier understood why this had been so important to Laura. Somehow she'd realized how terrible his parents must feel about what their son had tried to do. She'd let them see that she held no grudge against them or their religion or culture, bringing them a sense of redemption. She'd enabled them to grieve without guilt.

"You did a good thing tonight. You were right. It *was* important."

"I didn't do anything. Their son is gone. They'll never see him again, hug him again, hear his voice again. It's not even their fault." She pushed the brew button on her coffeemaker and turned to face him, fingers pressed to one temple. "They have to live with what he did and what was done to him, but they didn't teach him to hate."

"What about the kid's uncle? I didn't like the way he looked at you. What did he say to you? He seemed so angry."

"He was upset because Ali's body hadn't yet been returned. He—"

It was then Javier noticed her mistake. He pointed, but it was too late.

"You forgot . . ."

The coffeepot.

Coffee hissed as it poured straight onto the burner, steaming liquid spilling onto the granite countertop and the floor.

"Helvete!" Laura seemed to freeze for a moment before flying in all directions at once, unplugging the machine and grabbing an entire roll of paper towels.

Javier rounded the counter, picked up the glass coffeepot, and slid it into place on the burner, where it could catch the rest of the coffee.

Laura stared at the mess on the counter and the floor, then dropped to her knees and began to wipe it up. "God, what's wrong with me?"

He knelt down in front of her, caught her wrists. "You're upset. Why don't you go sit by the fire for a minute while I clean this up?"

Her gaze slid to his, her eyes filled with despair that had nothing to do with spilled coffee. "It's my mess. I made it. I should clean it up."

"I came here to help you, *bella*. Now let me help. That's an order."

She stood and backtracked out of the kitchen, careful not to step in the puddle.

Javier made quick work of it, then washed his hands and started heating milk. If he was going to make the coffee, he'd make it the *Boricua* way.

He carried the steaming mugs to the living room, where he found Laura curled up on the sofa and clutching a small pillow to her chest. He set her mug down on the coffee table and sat near her feet.

"Thank you." She sat up, picked up the mug, and sipped, closing her eyes and making an "mmm" noise that sent Javier's thoughts running in the wrong direction.

Get your mind out of your pants, Corbray.

When she opened her eyes again, her gaze was fixed on the fire. "They have to find him. They have to find the person behind this. Not just to keep me safe, but for Karima and Yusif's sake—and Ali's."

"They will." And when they *did* get him, Javier hoped it was with a high-caliber weapon. "Tearing yourself apart over this isn't going to help anyone."

He got to his feet, moved to stand behind her. "Lean back."

She looked over her shoulder at him but did as he asked.

"You've got a headache again, don't you?" He moved the silk of her hair aside, baring the graceful length of her neck. He couldn't touch her in a sexual way, but that didn't mean he couldn't touch her.

"What are you—the Headache Whisperer?"

"Just relax."

Laura closed her eyes as Javier began to knead the muscles of her shoulders. "Mmm. Don't tell me this is something they teach you in BUD/S."

"Nah." He chuckled, the sound deep and warm. "It's something I learned as a personal trainer. Your upper trapezius and scalene muscles are tight. It makes your headache worse."

She sank into his touch as he searched out knots and sore spots she didn't know she had, his fingers working their way along her nape, raising tingles on her skin. And the pain inside her skull began to lessen.

She decided to ask him. "What happened in the backyard tonight?"

His fingers stilled for a moment. "What do you mean?"

"I heard you gasp like you'd been hurt, and when I turned to look, you were staring up at that helicopter as if it were about to crash or something." She'd never seen fear on his face before.

No, not just fear. Terror.

His fingers began to move again. "The sound of it . . . For a second, it reminded me of the day I was wounded."

A flashback?

She turned her head to look back at him. "You told me you'd been ambushed. Did they attack by helicopter?"

"No." He withdrew his hands.

"I'm sorry. I don't mean to pry. If it's too hard for you to talk about—"

"It's not a problem." He rounded the sofa and sat in a chair across from her, elbows resting on his knees, his hands folded together. "We ran across a shepherd and his sons on our way to infiltrate a village outside Ghazni. I had to decide whether to let them live or to kill them to prevent them from warning anyone. We gave them food, water, a little medical help. We tried to show them we weren't the enemy. They promised not to give us away. I let them live. They warned the Taliban anyway. Taliban fighters ambushed us. We called for exfil. The medevac helo sent to retrieve the wounded was hit by an RPG and blew up before it could land."

"Oh, God." Laura stood and took a few steps toward the fire, the memory of the narrow escape from Al-Nassar's compound coming back to her. She turned to Javier and asked the question, pretty sure she knew the answer. "What happened to the medics?"

A muscle clenched in his jaw. "Everyone on board was killed."

"That's terrible." She found it appalling that anyone would attack medical personnel.

Then the truth of what Javier must be dealing with dawned on her. A decision he'd made had resulted in an ambush that had ended in the deaths of some of his men—and the crew of the medevac chopper, too. Did he blame himself?

"It wasn't your fault—those men's deaths, the medevac chopper."

"I know that. I don't sit around lamenting my choice." His denial came too quickly, and Laura wasn't sure she believed him.

She sank into a chair, an image of his scars in her mind. "All of you who were wounded—you had to wait for another chopper, didn't you?"

He gave a single wooden nod. "Not everyone made it."

"I'm so sorry." Her words seemed empty, inadequate. "It

must have been horrible to lie there in so much pain and to watch those men get shot out of the sky, knowing it meant some of you would probably die, too."

He stood, walked over to the window. "We all knew the risks when we signed on, even the medics. Besides, it's over."

She rose, followed him, slid her arms around him, rested her cheek against his back, his body tense, rigid. "It's not over, not if it still affects you like it did today. Are you getting therapy?"

"I passed the post-combat psych screening. I don't need therapy." He drew her hands away and stepped out of her embrace. "I'm not some weakling who can't get his shit together."

"I saw a therapist every day for almost a year, and I still can't say I'm over what happened to me. Am I a weakling?"

"You're a civilian."

"Oh. Thanks for clarifying."

He turned, faced her. "You were abducted, held prisoner for a year and a half, beaten, raped. You weren't trained to endure that. Getting shot, killing, watching other men die— that's part of my job description. It's the downside of what I do for a living."

"So that was just another bad day at the office?"

He shook his head, muttered something in Spanish, his eyes gone cold. "Just drop it, okay? What happened today wasn't a big deal. I just . . . got confused."

But it hadn't been confusion Laura had seen on his face.

"You're entitled to be human."

Without another word, he turned and walked down the hallway toward the guest room. She sipped her coffee and paced the length of the room, debating whether to go after him, to apologize. She'd pushed him, striking some kind of nerve.

But then she heard the sound of guitar music, first just tuning chords, then music so melancholy it made her heart ache.

So this was how he dealt with it—what had happened, his emotions.

And she knew he wanted to be alone.

THEY HAD A late supper of carryout Thai delivered by the U.S. Marshal Service, neither of them bringing up what had happened earlier. Javier seemed distant, closed off, and Laura knew he was still angry. They watched the news together. Then, pleading a headache, she went to bed and lay awake in the dark, the events of the day running through her mind.

Her interview this morning with the VA flack. Karima and Yusif's tears. Javier's reaction to the helicopter and his anger with her.

I'm not some weakling who can't get his shit together.

Oh, Javi!

She hadn't realized she'd fallen asleep until the nightmare woke her. Shaking and drenched in cold sweat, she crawled out of bed, slipped into her robe, and walked to the kitchen for a glass of warm milk, only to find Javier still awake, the television on, the volume down low.

He took one look at her face, turned off the TV, and stood. "Bad dream?"

She nodded, the sound of her own screams still echoing in her mind.

He left her then, walked back to the guest room without so much as saying good night, the distance between them leaving an ache behind Laura's breastbone.

But by the time she put her empty mug in the sink, he was back, wearing only his jeans, gun in one hand. "Come."

She met his gaze and felt a rush of relief to see warmth in his eyes again.

They walked to her bedroom together. Laura crawled into bed, making room for Javier, who shucked his jeans on her floor before stretching out beside her.

Strong arms closed around her, drawing her close. "I'm sorry, *bella*. I shouldn't have gotten angry with you."

"It was my fault. I pushed you. I'm sorry."

He kissed her hair. "Sleep."

She curled up against his bare chest and within minutes fell fast asleep.

JAVIER WOKE WITH a start the next morning, the whir of helo rotors and reek of burning oil and smoke fading as he came fully awake. Laura lay beside him, still sound asleep, her hair spilling over both of them, her sweet scent surrounding him. He brushed a strand from her cheek, his gaze traveling over her sweet face with its dark lashes and high cheekbones, the satiny curve of her bare shoulder, the soft curves of her breasts, their tips like little pebbles beneath the silky cloth.

Every instinct in him wanted to kiss her awake and pick up where they'd left off in the sauna. But he couldn't go there.

Instead, he slid out of the bed, drew the covers up to her chin, and left her to sleep. He took a leak, brushed his teeth, and put on his workout clothes and a jacket. He left Laura a quick note to tell her where he was going, checked in with her security detail, then slipped out of the loft, her key in his pocket. With a quick search on his smartphone, he headed up 20th Avenue toward City of Cuernavaca Park and the South Platte River Trail. And then he ran.

He barely noticed the half-frozen river, the early morning cyclists who sped by him, or the sun, which hovered above the eastern horizon, spilling its rays over the drowsy city. He ignored the pain in his thigh, the ache in his ribs, his mind focused on respiration, the beating of his heart, the rhythm of his feet on the concrete.

What do you want to do with them, senior chief? If we let them live, they might warn someone and bring the whole op down around our ears.

No, he wouldn't go there.

He ran faster, pushed himself harder.

There are more than a hundred fighters up there, senior chief. Somehow they knew we were coming. We need to start our exfil now!

His lungs burned. The muscles in his thigh screamed in protest. He ignored the pain, drove himself harder.

Hear that? Medevac is almost here, buddy. We're going to be pumped full of morphine and flirting with nurses before you know it.

And still Javier ran.

LAURA HAD JUST finished with the I-Team meeting when Janet arrived. One of the advantages to working from home was that she could take a break whenever she wanted. She made Janet a cup of coffee, then sat across from her in the living room and told her what she needed her to do—and why.

"I know it's a lot to ask of you, but I have to do all I can. It makes even less sense today than it did yesterday."

Janet met Laura's gaze. "I don't know what you think you're going to discover that FBI investigators won't."

"I'm a trained investigator, and a good one. Maybe I won't find anything. But maybe I will."

"You give me your word you won't leak the contents of the file in a news story or reveal where you got the documents?"

"I promise—and I've never broken a promise to a source."

Janet drew a deep breath, clearly considering it. "All right. I can probably get the file to you by this afternoon before we head to the television station. I'm trusting you with my career."

Laura felt a rush of relief. "Thank you. I won't let you down."

"I know you won't. I know where you live." Janet smiled, then looked toward the door. "Corbray is on his way up. I didn't know they made men like him. He is . . ."

Janet didn't finish the sentence, so Laura finished it for her. "He is strong, thoughtful—and incredibly hot."

Janet smiled. "Yes. That's the word I was looking for. Hot."

Didn't Laura know it?

Sleeping beside Javier again had left her painfully aware of her own sexual attraction to him, filling her head with fantasies that were going to make it very hard to get any work done today.

"Where did you two meet?" Janet asked.

"In a restaurant in Dubai. He saw a couple of Russian guys bothering me and—"

A key slipped into the lock and Javier entered.

His face was wet with sweat, his expression guarded. He gave them both a nod, his gaze lingering for a moment on Laura before he disappeared down the hallway, probably to take a shower.

Janet stood, her gaze following him. "We've got a security briefing in about an hour to prepare for your trip to the news studio tonight. I'll see you then."

JAVIER SAT IN the backseat of a bulletproof Chevy Tahoe beside Laura, who pored over her notes in preparation for her interview, pencil and highlighter in hand. She wore a sweater and jeans, Kevlar beneath her coat. Her face was still free of makeup, a makeup bag the size of a tool chest and a sleek little blue dress in the cargo space behind them. She'd styled her hair the way she'd always done before her abduction—loose and long with lush waves that were drawn away from her face and pinned back with a barrette. One way or another, he was going to find a way to get his fingers into that hair when they got home from this little adventure.

He leaned closer to her and spoke quietly, catching the soft, sweet scent of her skin. "After this is over, you're going to spend tomorrow and the weekend resting. That's what you're supposed to be doing, remember?"

"You can't give me orders. I may look like one of your men with this on," she said, glancing up at him and tapping the Kevlar with her knuckles, a slight smile playing on her lips, "but I'm not."

He leaned closer still and nuzzled her hair, lowering his voice to a near whisper. "Oh, believe me, *bella*, there's no way I could mistake you for one of my men, not even in pitch dark."

She canted her head, looking up at him from beneath her lashes. "Don't distract me. I'm going on live TV for the first time since . . . I need to be prepared."

He could tell she was genuinely nervous about this interview—and he knew why. Still, he was doing his best to keep the mood light, hoping to take the edge off her stress. "Were you this grumpy when you reported from Baghdad?"

"Oh, much worse."

Javier chuckled, turning his gaze back to the street. Ahead of them, an unmarked vehicle carrying two DUSMs turned the corner, another vehicle following behind them, its headlights illuminating the backseat. The Marshal Service had jocked up for a fight. It was the first time since the car bombing that the killer stood a chance of knowing *exactly* where Laura was going. The idiots at Channel 12 had been plugging the interview all day, clearly trying to drive up ratings, but also giving the killer exactly what he needed—an opportunity to strike and time to plan.

Tonight, Laura Nilsson joins Gary Chapin for an exclusive interview about her new life and the recent car bombing that could have killed her.

There was a chance that someone stupid enough to fuck up would be stupid enough to think that Laura had flown to D.C. to do the interview in person, but there was also a chance the bastard had been watching the Channel 12 studio all day, waiting.

Javier wasn't officially part of Laura's security detail. He didn't get to wear a lip mic and earpiece to keep up with the action, and they hadn't armed him. But he'd come ready to play rough. He wore his SIG in a shoulder harness beneath his jacket, five spare fifteen-round magazines loaded and ready, the Walther in an ankle holster.

He rubbed his thigh, the muscle still aching from his run. He must have gone six miles before he'd found himself kneeling on the riverbank, breathing hard, his mind filled with images he couldn't escape, echoes he couldn't silence—the rattle of AK fire, the cries of wounded men, the blazing orange of the exploding helo.

They had died—Krasinski, Johnson, Grimshaw, the men in the helo—because of a decision he'd made.

He hadn't been able to outrun his memories, but kneeling there on the riverbank, he'd locked them down once more, shutting them in a part of himself he vowed not to open. He couldn't change the past, and Laura needed him in the present.

"We're almost there." Agent Killeen looked back at Laura, who slipped her notes, pen, and highlighter inside her handbag. "You head straight inside as we discussed. Don't stop to talk in the doorway. One of us will bring your belongings shortly. There's already a team at the studio. They've been checking IDs, making sure the parking lot is secured. They'll man the doors while you're there. We'll have a team out here watching the vehicles and the building perimeter. I'll accompany you inside the building and onto the news set. Corbray, I understand you plan to remain close to Ms. Nilsson, also."

"Yes, ma'am."

He sure as hell did.

DEREK TURNED INTO the parking garage north of the Channel 12 studio, pushed a button for his ticket, then drove slowly up to the top level.

Tipped off by the station's constant ads about the interview, he'd spent yesterday doing recon around the building and knew that the uppermost level offered an unobstructed view of the station's rear entrance—perfect for getting within striking distance and squeezing off a couple of fatal shots from a high-powered rifle.

He pulled into a parking space, angling his rearview mirror to give himself a view of the entry ramp, his loaded AR-15 beneath his parka on the passenger seat beside him, an HK Mark 23 in his hip holster.

Now there was nothing to do but wait.

CHAPTER 14

BELLY FULL OF butterflies, Laura hurried from the vehicle through the station's rear entrance, Javier on her right, Agent Killeen on her left, and found herself in a long, brightly lit and crowded hallway, where two deputy marshals motioned her forward, their gazes focused on the entryway behind her.

A man with thick brown hair, a boyish face, and wire-rimmed glasses stepped into her path and shook her hand. "Welcome to Channel Twelve, Ms. Nilsson. I'm Jim Temple, the station manager. We're so happy to have you here with us. This is John Martin, our news director."

John Martin looked like every news director Laura had ever met—thin, lines on his face from stress, graying hair. But whereas most news directors were perpetually irritable, he seemed almost giddy. "It's great to meet you. Having you here on the last day of February sweeps—it means so much to us. I think it's going to do great things for our ratings. Viewers can't get enough of you or your amazing story."

"Thanks for having me." Laura wasn't shocked to hear him talk about her appearance in terms of blatant self-interest.

That was TV news. Ratings were everything. If the station performed well in the sweeps, they'd be able to demand more money from their advertisers. A good February meant a great start to the year and job security for everyone.

But apparently Javier *was* shocked. He muttered something

in angry Spanish, one of his hands coming to rest protectively against her lower back.

"I'm Special Agent Janet Killeen." Janet, apparently having forgotten she was temporarily a deputy U.S. Marshal, shook hands with Temple and Martin. "I'll be accompanying Ms. Nilsson throughout the building to ensure her safety while she's here at the station. This is Javier Corbray. He's—"

"I'm Ms. Nilsson's bodyguard." Javier held out his hand.

Laura had to fight back a laugh. She could tell from the expressions on Temple's and Martin's faces that Javier was all but crushing their fingers as they shook his hand.

Sometimes men could be so predictable.

A young woman with dark curly hair stepped up to them, clipboard in hand. "It's an honor to meet you, Ms. Nilsson, Agent Killeen, Mr. Corbray. I'm Tania Clarke, the senior producer. I'll show you to your dressing room, Ms. Nilsson."

Laura quickly found herself alone staring at her reflection in the lighted mirror. The last time she'd sat in a makeup chair, she'd been about to tape her interview with Diane Sawyer. She'd been nervous then, too, knowing what Diane was going to ask her, well aware that she'd be sharing deeply personal pain with the entire world. But somehow this felt worse, her pulse rapid, her palms damp, her mouth dry.

She hadn't done *live* TV since the day she was abducted.

She met her own gaze. "You can do this."

She was *not* going to let fear get the better of her. Derek Tower had repeatedly assaulted her reputation in public. It was her turn to speak out—and to show him exactly what she could do given a camera and a microphone.

She reached for her makeup kit, which Janet had brought in for her, and began what had once been her daily routine, taking care to cover the healing nicks on her cheek. She'd always done her own face and hair, in part because she'd spent so much time reporting from abroad where no makeup artists were available, and in part because she preferred a more natural look. As she worked, she went through the interview in her mind again, the act of concentrating on her answers helping her to control her fears.

Gary had e-mailed her a list of questions earlier in the day.

It wasn't something a journalist would normally do. Telling the subject of an interview ahead of time what you planned to ask gave him or her time to prepare, to create canned answers, eliminating the element of surprise and all possibility of controversy, which was so vital to live television news. But this wasn't an ordinary interview.

This was one friend doing a favor for another.

Not that Gary's agreeing to give her an interview was a selfless act. His career, like that of any other news anchor, depended on ratings. He wouldn't have agreed to have her on the program if he hadn't believed it would give him a boost.

Chaos reigned in the hallway beyond the dressing room as Laura finished putting on her makeup. How familiar the environment felt—and how foreign.

The door opened and Tania appeared. "There's the water you asked for. We go live in ten minutes."

"Thank you."

Laura took a deep drink, then finished her makeup. She studied the results in the mirror, a familiar face from long ago staring back at her, the pearls on her earlobes understated, her blue dress with its princess neckline sexy, but not too revealing. She wanted viewers' attention on what she was saying, after all, not on her boobs.

The butterfly sensation in her belly grew more intense. She drew ten deep, calming breaths, then stood.

She was ready.

She found Tania waiting for her out in the hallway, Javier and Janet standing beside the door.

"This way." Tania led her toward the news set. "You'll be on for ten minutes with one commercial break. Gary will introduce you, bring our viewers up to date, and then head into the questions. Will you need help with your earpiece or mic?"

"No." Laura hadn't been out of the game for that long. "I can handle it."

They entered the studio, which was dark apart from one set—the main news set. It featured a desk with the newspaper's logo and a backdrop of Denver's nighttime skyline. A dark-haired woman named Diane introduced herself as the floor director and then left Laura to get settled, while Tania disappeared into the booth.

Laura quickly clipped the mic to her dress and put in her earpiece, hiding the wire beneath her hair and letting it trail down her back. She nodded in the direction of the booth—bright lights made it impossible to see far beyond the edge of the set—then spoke, enunciating clearly so they could set sound levels. "This is Laura Nilsson. I'm here for my interview with Gary Chapin."

"That's great," a man's voice said in her ear.

Laura glanced over at Javier one last time and saw encouragement in his eyes. He and Janet stood just out of range of the cameras. Beyond them, off the edge of the set, she could just make out the station's management—Temple, Martin, and others in suits watching her as if she were a celebrity interview. Maybe she was.

She willed herself to smile, her heartbeat racing as she faced the camera. It stared at her, lens dark, the teleprompter screen blank, the tally light off.

Gary's voice came on in her ear as he closed one segment and the station cut to a commercial break.

"Two minutes," Diane said.

Laura's heart was beating so hard now that she could hear it over the chatter in her earpiece, a rapid thrum.

Slow breaths. Slow breaths.

She would *not* panic on live television. She would hold herself together and show Derek Tower and that son of a bitch Al-Nassar that they could not control her, could not frighten her.

The director's voice sounded in Laura's earpiece, counting down the last few seconds. The tally light blinked red. Diane's hand dropped beneath the camera.

And they were live.

JAVIER FELT HIS chest constrict as Laura spoke easily with her former anchor, who introduced her and welcomed her back to the news program. He knew she'd been nervous about this, but she was handling it like a pro, her smile warm, her eyes bright, her voice clear and strong.

From the moment she'd stepped out of the dressing room, Javier hadn't been able to take his gaze off her. Her blue dress hugged her sweet curves, its color bringing out her eyes, its neckline giving him a hint of what was hidden beneath. Her long, slender legs were sheathed in sheer panty hose, her feet in dressy heels. She looked sophisticated, polished, good enough to eat.

It was interesting to see how it was all done. Laura sat alone, looking at the camera, but what viewers saw on the television screens at home was a split-screen image with Gary Chapin, who was in Washington, D.C., on the left and Laura on the right, the two seeming to make eye contact when they weren't even in the same state.

"Laura, your abduction happened in the middle of a live broadcast, terrifying the millions of viewers who witnessed it. Let's go back to that moment. What we are about to see is quite disturbing, so viewer discretion is advised."

What the hell?

The side-by-side image of Laura and Chapin was replaced by footage Javier remembered only too well, Laura's face in a small frame at the top right of the screen where viewers could see her reaction.

"In the past five years," said the Laura from the video footage, "Sabira Mukhari's organization had documented more than seventy-five hundred cases of women being burned in 'stove accidents' within a two-hundred-mile radius around Islamabad and—"

A nearby door burst open, the room exploding with AK fire.

Rat-at-at-at-at-at!

Laura screamed, dropped to the floor.

Men's shouts in English and Arabic.

"Cover her! Cover her!"

A man in a black T-shirt threw himself over Laura, M16 rifle fire answering the AKs—only to stop short as her security detail was slaughtered.

Rat-at-at-at-at-at!

A man cried out, groaned, blood spraying across the camera lens.

Women's screams came from the background, gunshots drowning out Laura's shouts for the women to flee.

Two men in olive-green jackets with scarves around their

heads blocked the camera's view. They lifted Laura off the floor, dragged her toward the door.

She kicked, fought, screamed, her desperate cries sending chills down Javier's spine. "No! No!"

¡Puñeta! Son of a bitch!

This wasn't supposed to be part of the broadcast. Javier had seen the questions, had heard Laura talk through them with Chapin on the phone. He had agreed that he wouldn't ask her about her abduction or the shit she'd survived in Afghanistan.

Chapin had ambushed her.

The heartless son of a whore.

Javier's gaze shifted to the real, live Laura. She was pale, her pupils dilated, her face frozen into an expressionless mask. One of her hands rested lightly on the desk, but from where he was standing, he could see that the other was clenched tight in her lap.

Chapin's image returned to the screen. "This is the first time you've seen that footage, isn't it?"

Somehow she managed to answer. "Yes."

"Can you tell us what was running through your mind three and a half years ago when that door burst open and your attackers opened fire?"

"I was just trying to comprehend what was happening. It was over so quickly."

Beside Javier, Martin whispered. "Oh, this is great stuff. Great stuff."

It took every bit of willpower Javier possessed not to turn and slam his fist into Martin's face. He didn't give a damn about Chapin's ratings, the station's ratings, or the sweeps. If Laura gave him any sign she wanted to leave, he would take her by the hand, and they would go, live broadcast be damned.

"When they dragged you from the room, you must have been terrified." The false sympathy in Chapin's voice sickened Javier.

If the bastard truly cared about her, he wouldn't be putting her through this.

"Of course."

"What did you think they would do to you?"

Laura's voice held no emotion when she answered. "I

assumed I would be killed or held hostage for ransom, as other journalists had been."

"But that's not what happened, is it?"

"No."

No way was he going to make Laura repeat details of her ordeal on live TV.

"Can you tell our viewers what *did* happen?"

¡Hijo e la gran puta!

Laura's voice was calm, steady. "As your viewers already know, I was held captive for eighteen months, beaten, sexually assaulted, and threatened almost daily with beheading. I was eventually rescued by a team of Navy SEALs."

Chapin seemed to wait, hoping she'd say more. When she didn't, he looked gravely at the camera. "Beaten. Raped daily. Threatened with beheading. It's been a long, hard healing process for you, I'm sure."

The man warped Laura's words. She'd said she was threatened with beheading daily, but he'd said she was raped daily. Obviously, he was trying to titillate his viewers.

¡Que clase e cabrón! What a bastard!

Laura's chin went up, a glint of anger in her eyes. "I put that behind me when I testified at Al-Nassar's trial. I have a wonderful life now."

When she said nothing more, Chapin went on. "We've all just seen that horrifying footage of your abduction. As incredible as it may seem, Derek Tower, CEO of Tower Global Security, says he believes *you* may be to blame for what we just witnessed. More on this when we return."

The moment the broadcast cut away to a commercial, Javier headed straight for Laura, ignoring Martin's attempts to block him.

"You can't go on set!"

"Try to stop me." Javier strode over to Laura, who was staring down at the desk, her hand still clenched in a fist. He took it, held it, found it cold. "You okay, *bella*?"

She looked up at him, anguish and fury in her eyes. "He promised he wouldn't do this. He promised. He didn't even mention the car bomb. This first part was supposed to be about Al-Nassar's trial and the car bomb."

"You don't have to put up with this. Just say the word, and we're out of here."

She shook her head. "If I leave now, I'll burn a bridge with the network, and I'll lose credibility with—"

"Twenty seconds!" a dark-haired woman called to them.

Javier squeezed Laura's hand. "All right. You're doing great. Just finish it."

He stepped off set again as the camera once again went live.

It was almost over.

"One last question before we go: Is it possible that one of Tower's men made a fatal mistake that day?"

Laura heard the one-minute warning in her earpiece.

She focused on her answer, careful not to rush her words. "I refuse even to speculate. These men were my friends. We'd traveled the world together for more than two years, and they lost their lives trying to save mine. Did security measures fail that day? Yes, but not because any of us were negligent. To paraphrase the State Department report, we were in the wrong neighborhood at the wrong time."

"The wrong neighborhood at the wrong time. A dark day." Gary paused for effect. "Thanks for joining us this evening, Laura. It's great to have you back. It's been a long time."

"Thank you, Gary. It's good to be back in the studio." Laura gave the camera her warmest smile, held it.

The tally light went dark.

She shot to her feet, yanked out the earpiece, ripped off the microphone, letting both fall on the desk, her heart still pounding, her stomach in knots.

"Great show!" Martin walked over to her, his face split by a wide grin. "That was fantastic. I can't wait to see the numbers. I bet they're through the roof."

Everyone was smiling, laughing, talking.

But not Laura. She felt sick. Enraged. Hurt.

She tried not to take her anger at Gary out on them. This wasn't their fault. She shook hands, people seeming to crowd in on her, names and faces blurring together—Martin, Temple, Diane, Tania. "Thank you. Thanks, everyone."

Then Javier was there beside her. He leaned in and spoke for her ears only, his presence giving her something to hold on to. "Do you want to change first, or do you just want to get the hell out of here?"

She was too upset to think, let alone make a decision, her hand reaching for his. "I . . . I don't know."

"Let's go."

People moved aside for him, seeming to want to get out of his path as Javier led her back to the dressing room, where Janet was waiting for them.

"We're going to grab her things and go," he said to Janet, who passed the message on to the deputy U.S. Marshals in the hallway beyond.

Laura entered the dressing room and walked over to her clothes, which hung on a hook beside the empty garment bag. "That jerk! He said he wouldn't show the footage, that he wouldn't ask for details about my captivity."

She hoped no one was listening outside the door, because she couldn't keep her voice from shaking, repressed anger and adrenaline surging through her.

"I used to like the guy. He used to be my favorite news dude. Now I want to bust his nuts." Javier pointed to the vials and tubes of makeup sitting next to her makeup kit on the dressing table. "Are these yours?"

She nodded, wadding her jeans and shoving them into the garment bag. "He's never forgiven me for giving that interview to Diane Sawyer. He wanted to be the first one to interview me after I returned to the U.S., but I went with Diane because she agreed to respect my boundaries. He wouldn't."

"Yeah? Well, he's a grade-A piece of shit if you ask me." Javier opened her makeup kit, held it edge to edge with the dressing table, and swept everything—every vial, brush, tube, and bottle—into the kit with his forearm.

Laura gaped at him. "That stuff is worth hundreds of dollars."

He shrugged, then shut the kit. "That's how SEALs pack makeup."

The absurdity of his words made her smile.

Only Javier could do that—make her smile when she felt this shaken.

She grabbed the rest of her clothes, shoved them into the garment bag, and zipped the bag shut. She turned to find Javier holding her Kevlar vest. He'd just finished helping her fasten it in place when Janet appeared at the dressing room door.

"There's a lot of media out there. Ready to go?"

"Just about." Javier grabbed Laura's coat and held it for her. She slid her arms into the sleeves, then turned to face him. Their gazes met, locked.

"Thanks for being here, Javi."

He ran a finger down her cheek. "You bet."

With Janet in front of her and Javier behind her, Laura walked out of the dressing room, down the hallway, and out the back door into the cold night, the two DUSMs who'd watched over the station's rear entrance following them.

The night exploded with flashes and the *click-click-click* of cameras.

"Did you know Gary Chapin was going to play the footage from your abduction?"

"Do you plan to sue Derek Tower for slander?"

"Look this way, Laura! Just one shot!"

Thankfully, the engine of the SUV was already running, its back door open for her, a DUSM sitting in the driver's seat.

Half blinded by the light, Laura caught the heel of one shoe in a crack in the asphalt and stumbled—just as a distant *crack* rang out, something whooshing above her head, striking the wall beside her, a spray of what felt like pebbles hitting her face. She didn't even have time to react before she found herself on the ground, breath knocked from her lungs, Javier on top of her, firearm in his hand.

"Sniper!" he shouted in a deep voice she'd never heard before. "Nine o'clock!"

Gunfire. Screams. Running feet.

It was happening again.

CHAPTER 15

¡PUÑETA! FUCK!

On a single inhale, Javier weighed his options. He had no infrared drone overhead to give him the big picture, no radio contact with the DUSMs, and no damned assault rifle. There were ten feet between Laura and the station's rear entrance and a couple of lateral feet between her and the SUV's open door. But judging from the hole that first shot had left in the building's concrete wall, these were armor-piercing rounds. Bulletproofing was *not* going to stop them from penetrating the vehicle—which meant they couldn't take shelter inside it—and lying here on the ground and trying to use it for cover was a fucking bad idea.

They had to move *now*.

But moving was risky, too. If this sniper had any training, he'd be watching, waiting for Laura to pop into his sights again in her attempt to flee.

"Stay low!" Javier caught her hard around the waist and dragged her up with him, lunging for the studio's back door, Agent Killeen behind them.

"Get back!" he shouted to the station's staff, who stood just inside the door staring in horrified surprise. "Get back, goddamn it!"

Two more shots, and Killeen went down with a cry.

Javier didn't stop. He couldn't.

Laura would be dead if he did.

The best thing he could do for Killeen and the others was to get Laura out of the line of fire. As long as she was in the shooter's sights, he would keep firing, putting every DUSM, reporter, and bystander out here at risk.

Javier threw himself and Laura through the open doorway, the two of them landing on their hands and knees just as the shooter opened up on the entrance.

More screams.

Javier jumped up, dragged Laura to her feet again, and hurried her down the hallway. "Everyone get out of the hallway and away from the door! Those rounds can penetrate concrete. Go! *Move!*"

He didn't stop moving until they reached the dressing room. Both hands gripping her coat, he pressed her up against the wall. "Are you hurt, *bella*? Talk to me."

She looked at him with dazed blue eyes, blood running down her temple, her entire body shaking. "I-I'm fine."

Shit.

"Like hell you are."

She was in psychological shock—acute stress reaction.

He quickly removed her coat, checked her for other injuries, and found abrasions on her palms and right knee from hitting the asphalt so hard.

God*damn*, that had been close! If she hadn't stumbled . . .

His stomach lurched at the very thought.

She reached up, pressed her hand to her bleeding temple, and looked down at the blood on her fingers, as if she couldn't understand what had happened, the expression on her face reminding him of the expression she'd worn in the helo after he'd carried her out of Al-Nassar's compound. Slowly, she sank to a sitting position on the floor.

He draped her coat over her to keep her warm and pulled out his cell. "McBride, it's Corbray. Yes, she's safe but in shock with contusions on her right temple, her hands, and one knee. She'll need an ambulance. We're inside the building. Killeen is down. I think the shots came from the top of a parking garage to the north of our position. He's probably using a flash suppressor."

Through the walls of the station Javier could hear the wail of sirens, but it sounded as if the shooting had stopped. Oh, how he wished he were out there, rifle in hand. He would run that fucker down and catch him trying to make his getaway.

But Javier couldn't leave Laura.

"We'll stay put. Roger that." He hung up and slipped the phone into his pocket, then walked to a nearby sink, grabbed a paper towel, and wet it. "One of the deputies is taking care of Killeen. Ambulances are on their way."

Laura was silent, her gaze focused on nothing as he knelt beside her.

He pressed the wet paper towel to her temple, gently wiping away the blood, something in his chest constricting when the light pressure made her flinch. "Sorry. I don't want to hurt you. I just want to get a look."

Her temple had a few deep abrasions, and it looked as if some debris had embedded itself in her skin, probably from ricocheting bits of concrete. Once it was cleaned out, it would heal fine. She was lucky it hadn't struck her eyes.

"Look at me, *bella*. Talk to me."

She met his gaze, her eyes still unfocused, pupils dilated, body trembling, her arms wrapped protectively around her middle. But she said nothing.

And Javier understood.

She'd been forced to watch the footage of her abduction and had then stepped out the door into a hail of gunfire. Together, it was just too much.

He pressed his forehead to hers and looked straight into her eyes. "Laura, do you hear me? You're safe. You're here with me, and you're safe."

A voice came from the dressing room doorway. "Is there anything we can do to help?"

Javier looked up—and found himself staring into a camera lens.

"Turn that fucking thing off!" He reached out, put his palm over the lens, got to his feet, and slowly pushed the cameraman out the door. "You got any shame, man? She's one of yours. If she were lying there bleeding to death, would you film that, too? Yeah, you probably would. Ratings, right?"

Martin spluttered, glaring at him. "Do you know how expensive that piece of equipment is? You can't—"

"The hell I can't." Javier stepped back, slammed the dressing room door in the cameraman's face, and locked it. He sat beside Laura and drew her trembling body into his arms. "It's going to be all right."

IT WAS THE reassuring sound of Javier's voice that reached her.

"Javi?"

"I'm right here, *bella*. You're safe now. I'm not going to let anyone hurt you."

Head throbbing, Laura realized she was in the station's dressing room. She'd done the broadcast. Gary had played the footage of her abduction. And . . .

Oh, God! Someone had tried to shoot her!

"Wh-what . . . Who . . . ?" Her heart pounded as if she'd been running, her stomach churning, her body shaking uncontrollably.

He looked into her eyes. "You don't need to worry about that. McBride, the cops—they've got this locked down. It's over. You're safe."

It was then she remembered, her heart giving a hard knock, the breath leaving her lungs in a rush. "Janet. Agent Killeen! She was shot!"

It was happening again. People were dying because of her.

"The ambulance is almost here. There are marshals with her now. She's not alone, *bella*. Just take deep breaths."

Laura closed her eyes, tried to do as he said, but the sound of gunshots and screams echoed in her mind, memories of another time, another place.

Cries. AK fire. So much death.

Cover her! Cover her!

No. No. No!

She clung to Javier, the strength of his embrace and the reassuring tone of his voice holding her together, horror from the past threatening to drag her under. She lost any sense of time, aware only of Javier and the thrum of her own pulse.

A knock.

"Paramedics!"

"They're here, *bella*." Javier pulled away from her, reached over, unlocked the door. "They've come to help."

Two men in paramedic uniforms entered, both carrying red medical kits.

"She's got some abrasions, and I think she's in shock—acute stress reaction," Javier said.

The paramedics knelt down beside her. "You've had a rough night, but we're going to check you over and take good care of you, Ms. Nilsson."

One of them clipped something to the end of her finger and wrapped a blood pressure cuff around her left arm, puffing it up until it was tight.

But Laura wasn't the one who needed help. She tried to draw away. "Go to Janet—Agent Killeen. She's been shot."

Javier took her right hand and leaned in close where she could see him. "There's already a team with her, Laura. These men are here to help *you*."

They were here to help her? There was nothing wrong with her.

"I-I'm fine."

None of them seemed to agree with her.

"Those contusions aren't serious, but she's definitely shocky. Pulse is ninety-eight. BP is seventy-five over forty."

"We'll get some fluids in her, give her some IV Ativan and some oxygen, and get her under transport."

It took a moment for their words to hit her, but when they did, she shook her head.

"No. I'm not going to the hospital."

"You're in shock, *bella*. You need—"

"No! Take me home. I just want to go home."

IT WAS ALMOST midnight by the time they reached The Ironworks and parked in the secured underground garage. Zach opened Laura's door, Javier meeting her at the rear of the vehicle. Marc and Julian pulled into a visitor's space near Laura's car, which sat looking abandoned and forlorn, not having been driven in almost a week. Two other unmarked vehicles, each carrying two deputy marshals, slowly circled the garage, while the security detail that had her building under surveillance kept watch on the street.

She ought to feel safe, but she didn't. Maybe it was recounting the details of what had happened for Alex for his news story. Or maybe it was just stress or exhaustion. Regardless, she couldn't shake the sense of dread that had crept over her. She felt hunted, the world closing in around her.

They walked to the elevator, Laura sandwiched between the men, their footfalls sharp against the concrete floor, the echo eerie. She pushed the elevator call button, and they waited.

Ding.

Laura gasped, jumped.

It was just the elevator car arriving.

Javier slipped an arm around her waist.

She let herself lean into him, needing him, needing his strength, his confidence. How could anyone live with this kind of violence as part of his job? She glanced up at the men around her, each of them willing to risk his life for hers, each of them ready and able to kill, each of them . . . so much taller than she was.

She let out a laugh, surprising herself as much as anyone else.

"What's funny?" Javier asked.

"I don't think I've ever been the shortest person in the room before."

The men didn't say a word, but Laura saw grins on their faces.

The elevator door opened, and they stepped out, crossing the small hallway to her door. Laura fished in her handbag and drew out her keys.

Zach held out his hand. "Hunter, you and I will clear the place. You two stay here with Laura."

Laura gave him the keys and waited, Javier and Julian beside her. She heard the click of the dead bolt and looked up to see Kathleen Parker and her husband peering out of their front door.

"Yes, I'm still alive. I know you don't want me here, but this is my home."

The door shut hard, the bolt turning with a quiet *click*.

"What the hell was that about?" Julian asked.

Laura was about to explain, but Javier beat her to it. "The day after the car bomb, Ms. Nosy Yoga Pants there came over to tell Laura that she and her hubby and some other folks in the building would sleep better at night if Laura sold her flat and moved somewhere else."

"I guess I can understand why they're nervous, but seriously?" Julian rested a hand on Laura's shoulder. "Sorry you had to put up with that, Laura."

Zach returned. "The place is clear."

Laura walked inside—and stepped on something. She looked down to find a large manila envelope with her name on it lying on the floor. Pretty sure she knew what it was, she bent over and snatched it up, tucking it beneath her arm.

But Javier had seen. "What was that?"

"Oh, just some files I requested." She hoped he would assume she was talking about her job. "You all feel free to make yourselves comfortable. Grab whatever you want from the kitchen. I'm going to take a shower and call my mother."

She walked into her bedroom, closing the door behind her. She set her purse aside and looked down at the envelope. There on the front, Agent Killeen had printed her name with black marker.

Poor Janet!

Laura sat on the edge of her bed, ran her fingers over the letters, and found herself blinking back tears. Janet had fought to stay on Laura's protection detail and had ended up taking a bullet for it. Was she out of surgery yet? How badly had she been hurt?

What if Javier had been shot, too? What if he'd been killed?

Laura couldn't stand to think about it, the very idea making her stomach knot.

And suddenly she felt weary to the bone.

She was tired of being afraid, tired of seeing good people get hurt and killed, tired of feeling like every day was an uphill battle. Life had been challenging enough just trying to put body and soul back together, hold down a job, and find Klara.

But now . . .

What had happened today had reopened something dark inside her, punctured a deep hole in her sense of self, and exposed the brokenness that was still inside her. For a time, she'd been shut down. She hadn't been able to think clearly.

Had she made any true progress? How could she still be a prisoner of this terror?

Allt kommer att bli bättre med tiden.

Everything will get better with time.

Would it?

Laura got to her feet, tucked the thick envelope into one of her drawers, then walked toward the bathroom.

JAVIER HEARD THE water go on in the shower and nodded to the others.

McBride spoke first. "Our guys found Derek Tower with a bullet in his chest on the top level of the parking garage. He was armed—an HK Mark 23 and a tricked-out AR-15 that was loaded with five-five-six green tip."

Armor-penetrating rounds.

"Is he dead?"

McBride shook his head. "He's in surgery at University Hospital. No word on his condition, but it doesn't look good."

A cold sense of loathing settled in Javier's chest. "So Tower is our man after all."

"What's the first rule of assassination?"

"Kill the assassin." Javier didn't like the way this was coming together. "Maybe Tower was the shooter and someone showed up to take care of him, or Tower came to take out the shooter and it went sideways big-time."

"How would a former Green Beret get mixed up with terrorists?" Hunter asked.

McBride shrugged. "Regardless of how it went down, there has to be at least one more person involved, someone bad enough to get the better of Tower."

"If Tower isn't our shot-caller, he must know who is." Darcangelo ran a hand over the day's worth of stubble on his jaw. "I just hope he survives."

"How about Agent Killeen?" Javier knew Laura would ask.

"She made it through surgery. They had to transfuse her, but she made it. The round shattered her hip, broke her pelvis, and severed her sciatic nerve. They had to replace the joint. They're not sure how much nerve function she'll regain."

"Jesus!" Javier hated to think of the long road that lay

ahead of her. If Tower was behind this . . . "It'd be best not to tell Laura yet. She really likes Killeen. She's going to take it hard, and I don't think she can handle anything else tonight."

"Obviously, it was a mistake for us to let Laura do the interview at the studio," McBride said. "We asked the station not to announce it, but they couldn't resist. That gave our shooter a couple of days to plan. He got the studio's address, was probably watching when she arrived, using the hour she was inside to get into position."

That made sense to Javier. "Whoever he was, he had good night optics, and he knew how to shoot. If Laura hadn't tripped . . ."

He let it go, unable to say it, the very thought making his heart trip.

"So the shooter sucks with ANFO, but he's got some solid sniping skills." Darcangelo seemed to consider this apparent contradiction.

"Not just solid, buddy. Rock fucking solid." Hunter looked over at McBride. "I stood where he stood when he took those shots and scoped them myself. It was a good three hundred yards, but he hit everything he wanted to hit—except for Laura. He wasn't just firing random shots, at least not until the end. He fired at her, missed. Then he took out the SUV's engine and its tires, immobilizing the vehicle, clearly hoping she'd take cover inside."

And then he'd have had her.

McBride pointed to Hunter. "He's not just making shit up, Corbray. Hunter here served as an army sniper. Earned himself some medals, too. For a while he held the record both for confirmed kills and long-distance marksmanship."

"So the guy we're looking for can shoot, but somehow missed Explosives 101. That's strange." Then it dawned on Javier. "Do we know for certain that the shooter is the guy behind the car bomb?"

McBride shook his head. "We can't be sure these two attempts on her life were made by the same person. We have no idea how many suspects might be involved or whether they're part of a cell. We have no clue how Tower is connected to this or why he was shot. All we have are more pieces to the puzzle, and that puzzle keeps getting bigger. We're pulling surveillance video on the parking garage. Hopefully it will give us some answers."

"DPD is canvasing for witnesses," Hunter said. "This happened in the middle of downtown Denver. Someone must have seen something."

Javier hoped so. "The pieces need to start coming together—and fast. It was close today, man, too close."

"Hell, yeah, it was," Darcangelo said. "We got ahold of the news footage, then slowed it down. That round missed her head by no more than an inch."

Javier's stomach seemed to hit the floor.

McBride met his gaze. "You saved her life. You realized what was happening before anyone else. She'd have been dead the moment she regained her footing if you hadn't been there."

Somehow that didn't make Javier feel better. "So what's the plan?"

"We work the case," McBride said. "We pull surveillance video, question Tower if and when he wakes up, and strengthen security around this building. Until we know for certain Tower is our shooter, we cover all adjacent rooftops and keep this place under tight surveillance. Laura can't set a foot outside her own door. They took a shot at her today because they knew exactly where she was going to be and when. But they haven't tried to hit her here, which tells me they've scoped it out and decided it's too risky."

Javier would see to it that the risk level got even higher.

"Any chance it would be safer for her in Sweden?" Darcangelo asked. "She's got family there, right?"

"She'd have to give up the life she's built for herself, and she doesn't want to do that." Javier couldn't blame her. She'd already lost more than most people could comprehend. "Besides, what's to stop these guys from boarding a plane and taking a little trip to Stockholm? You think they can provide security in Sweden that we can't?"

"Good point." McBride glanced at his watch. "We need to get some sleep."

They stood.

"Just a warning," Hunter said, pointing to Javier. "You made prime time."

"That's what I hear." Javier already knew.

Nate had called an hour ago to tell Javier that his face was all over the television. Thanks to Channel 12, where he'd made the mistake of introducing himself, all of the stations had reported his name, broadcasting it to the world together with live-action footage and still shots of him throwing Laura to the ground, covering her body with his, and getting her out of the line of fire.

"You're in it now, bro," Nate had said. "All the same, I'm glad you were there. You were the first one to react. You saved her life."

Javier hoped the brass at NSW felt the same way.

Yeah, right. You'll be lucky if they don't hand you your ass.

"Thanks for what you did today, Corbray." McBride shook Javier's hand. "Nate said you were the best, and now I see why. I'm glad we've got you on our side. If you ever leave the Teams and need a job, you know where to find me."

CHAPTER 16

LAURA SAT ON the edge of her bathtub hugging her bathrobe around herself, fighting hard to hold herself together. "Was anyone else hurt . . . or killed?"

Javier knelt on the floor in front of her with a first-aid kit, dabbing antibiotic ointment on her skinned knee, his hands in white sterile gloves. "A reporter got creased by a ricochet, but he's going to be fine. McBride says he's already home."

"So many people might have been killed. *You* might have been killed. Oh, God, Javi, if you'd been shot—" The thought stopped her breath cold.

"I wasn't." He looked up at her, his brown eyes warm. "Let's stick with the positive, okay?"

"Okay." She would try.

He studied the scratches and bruises on her knee. "I think you need to ice this. I didn't mean for you to get scraped up."

"Next time you shove me out of the path of a bullet, be gentle, okay?" She gave him a smile, fighting the urge to reach out and touch him. "You saved my life."

"Walking in those damned shoes saved your life."

"I've never been graceful in heels."

"Thank God for that."

From somewhere out in her bedroom, her cell phone rang.

"Who is calling this late? Did you talk to your folks?"

"Yes." Her mother and grandmother had been asleep, so they'd gotten the news from her. They'd been very upset, of course, and had asked her again to come back to Sweden. "It's probably Gary calling to apologize—or make excuses for himself. I should have known he wouldn't keep his promise. I've seen him do that before. I just didn't think he'd do it to me."

"That bastard is lucky he was in D.C. and not in the station tonight." Javier peeled the tabs off an oversized adhesive bandage and stuck it carefully over the wound. "He and I would have had a serious confrontation."

Somehow Laura doubted the confrontation would have been verbal. It touched her that Javier cared that much about her. He cared so much that he'd put his life on the line for her today. But she didn't want that.

If anything happened to him . . .

She said the words she'd been meaning to say since they got home, words she'd thought about in the shower. "It's probably best for you to go back to the ranch tomorrow. You came here to visit Nate and so far—"

"Whoa! What did you just say?" Javier's gaze shot to hers. He sat back on his heels, his dark brows bent in a frown. "You want me to *leave*?"

She nodded, struggling to keep her tears at bay. "I-I don't want you to get hurt, Javi. I couldn't live with myself if you were hurt or killed."

"Looks like we've got a problem." He reached out, ran a gloved thumb down her cheek. "I couldn't live with myself if you were hurt or killed when I was here and had the power to do something about it. I've seen that footage of your abduction at least a dozen times. Every time, I wished I'd been there to stop them. When I heard you'd been killed . . . *Shit*." He shook his head. "Nah, I'm not leaving you, Laura. I *can't*."

She closed her eyes, turned her face away, the guilt she felt for putting him in danger at odds with an overwhelming sense of relief to know he was staying.

He pulled off his gloves, twined his fingers with hers. "Hey, is my sweet *bella* worried about a big, bad operator?"

She nodded. "You're not bulletproof, you know. I feel so selfish keeping you here. This is *not* why you came to Colorado."

"I think maybe it is, even if I didn't realize it. I . . . care about you."

Something in the way he said it made her look at him, the concern in his eyes putting an ache in her chest. That ache grew sharper when she realized that she and Javier might have had a real chance if things had gone differently after Dubai.

He took her hand, turned it over, ran his finger over the deep scratches on her palm. "I wish you'd gone to the hospital. I've had training as a medic, but the doctors and nurses would have done a better job of this."

"I hate hospitals." They were desolate, lonely places. "Besides, there's nothing wrong with me. I'm not really hurt. I'm not sick. I'm just . . . *pathetic*."

She'd heard gunshots, and she'd fallen apart.

Javier came eye to eye with her. "Don't say that about yourself. You've already lived through more shit than most people face in a lifetime, and you've overcome it. You're one of the strongest women I know."

She shook her head, tears finally spilling down her cheeks. "No. No, I'm not. I'm not nearly as strong as you think."

As tonight had proven, she hadn't overcome anything. She'd merely gathered the shards of herself together, plastered a façade over the ruins, and pretended to the world that she was whole again. Beneath the surface, she was shattered. Her weakness had cost a helpless little child her freedom.

Javier needed to know the truth. If he was going to be risking his life for her, he needed to know the truth.

Her pulse began to race at the thought of what she was about to do. She'd worked hard to keep this secret, but she wouldn't keep it from Javier any longer.

She drew her hand away from him and stood. Trembling, she opened her bathrobe and exposed her naked body to his gaze—stretch marks and all.

JAVIER WAS HIT by two things at once—the sight of Laura's beautiful body and the distress and fear on her pretty face. One sent a jolt of heat to his groin. The other set off alarm bells in his brain. The result was a short in his wiring.

"Uh . . ." he said.

He couldn't keep his gaze from raking over her, taking in the sight of her full breasts with their light pink tips, the satiny curves of her hips, the soft golden curls between her thighs. The sight of her awakened memories of touching her, tasting her, losing himself inside her. He remembered her scent, the silky texture of her skin, the little mole on her right breast.

But she wasn't trying to seduce him. Something was wrong.

He looked up to see tears streaming down her cheeks. "Why are you doing this?"

She took his hand, pressed it against her lower belly, drawing his gaze.

There on her skin he saw faint silver lines.

Not scars.

Stretch marks.

It took Javier a good long moment to understand, but when he did, it hit him like a body blow. His heart gave a hard knock, pain knotting his gut, one emotion colliding with the next—astonishment, rage, sadness. "Oh, God, Laura. No."

Laura had been pregnant. She'd had a baby.

Al-Nassar's baby.

Jesus!

A thousand questions chased through Javier's mind, but now wasn't the time. Laura was shaking uncontrollably, her arms now crossed over her breasts, her face turned away from him. He got to his feet, pulled her robe around her trembling body, and tied it in place, then drew her into his arms.

She stiffened as if she didn't want to be touched. "I-I'm cold."

He stepped back, his mind and emotions still reeling. "Want to sit by the fire? I can make some tea."

"Okay." She followed him out to the living room and sat on the sofa, her gaze far away, her eyes haunted.

He turned on the fire, grabbed a throw from her sofa, and wrapped it around her, then went to the kitchen, his gaze never wandering far from her while he heated water and steeped tea bags. She'd been in shock earlier, and she'd refused treatment. What she needed was rest, not more emotional turmoil. Why she'd chosen tonight to tell him about this he couldn't say, but he wasn't sure it was best for her.

God, Laura!

She'd had a baby in captivity.

The force of it hit him again.

When she'd been rescued, there'd been a few articles in the tabloids and some online chatter asking why she hadn't gotten pregnant during the eighteen months she'd been Al-Nassar's prisoner. The idea hadn't even occurred to Javier, maybe because he knew from their time together in Dubai that she was using some kind of long-term contraceptive—or maybe because the possibility was too terrible for him to imagine.

She'd suffered enough, damn it. But to get pregnant by that bastard?

He carried two mugs into the living room and set his down on the coffee table, placing hers in her hands. "It's hot."

She sipped, the tea seeming to bring her back to the moment. "Thanks."

He sat down beside her, deliberately giving her space, doing his best to lock down his own emotions. "You should just take it easy, *bella*. We can talk in the morning."

But she didn't seem to want to wait. "That's why I stopped you in the sauna, you know. If you'd seen me naked, if we'd had sex, you would have seen my stretch marks, and you would've known."

"I wouldn't have rejected you, if that's what you're thinking." In fact, Javier doubted he would have noticed anything. Yeah, he'd been trained to be good with details, but once his dick started working, his brain generally shifted to standby. Still, this was an interesting revelation, one he tucked in the back of his mind.

But she wasn't listening to him. Her eyes drifted shut, regret sharp on her face. "I . . . I didn't know. Most women know. Most women see the signs."

"You didn't know you were pregnant?"

"I'm sure that seems strange to you, but I didn't have periods when I was on Depo-Provera, so . . ." She opened her eyes and stared into the fire. "The shots last for four months, and it's supposed to take a while for your body to go back to normal."

Javier did the math and realized it couldn't have taken too long for Laura to become fertile again. She'd spent half of her captivity pregnant.

If only they'd known she was still alive . . .

¡Carajo! Fuck!

"He was always so rough with me, even when I didn't fight him. He didn't want to have sex with me. He just wanted to hurt me. I was a symbol of something he hated, and he wanted me to suffer. Every time he . . ." She paused as if searching for the words. "It's like he was stabbing me again and again and again."

Javier tasted bile in the back of his throat, his stomach revolting at the horrific images her words brought to mind, hatred like venom in his veins. He swallowed, fought back his rage. "I'm so sorry."

You're sorry, bro? What the fuck good is that?

"After a while, some part of me tried to forget my physical body. I just . . . moved out, blocked it out."

Javier could understand that.

"I never thought about getting pregnant. There was so much else to worry about—getting enough to eat, beatings, rape, being killed. Every day they told me they were going to execute me soon. Every day I woke up thinking I was going to die. I . . . I made them promise to shoot me instead of cutting off my head."

Javier could only imagine what it was like to live each day in that kind of terror, unable to fight back, depending only on your wits to survive. He knew men who'd lived through it as prisoners of war. None of them had come back without emotional scars.

"I . . . I thought it was poison."

He didn't follow. "Poison?"

"The pain." Laura opened her eyes, her hands pressing protectively against her lower belly as they had that night in the sauna. "I thought Zainab had poisoned me."

It took Javier a second to understand what she was talking about, the knot in his gut tightening when it hit him.

"I . . . I didn't know I was having a baby. I didn't know what was wrong with me. If I had known what was happening . . . How could I not have known?" She looked up him through tear-filled eyes, as if she expected an answer, her expression of despair slowly turning to self-loathing. "I should have known."

"After what you'd been through? Your mind was doing all it could to protect you, to keep you alive. You can't blame yourself, *bella*."

Laura didn't seem to hear him. "It was terrible. The pain

was tearing me apart. I was sure I was dying. I begged Zainab to help me. I asked her why she had poisoned me. She called me stupid."

Javier didn't know much about women having babies beyond what he'd heard his mother and sisters say. The thought of Laura going through that much pain without medical attention or so much as a loving hand to hold was horrible enough, but to know that she'd been so brutalized that she'd had no idea what was happening to her . . .

He wanted to hold her. He wanted to comfort her. He wanted somehow to take all of this away from her. But he couldn't. Nothing could.

NAUSEATED, LAURA COULDN'T bring herself to look at Javier's face, fighting to put her worst nightmare into words. "I felt like my insides were being torn apart . . . like everything inside of me was being ripped out. And then . . . I heard a cry. I lifted my head, saw Safiya holding something in a blanket. The blanket moved. Until that moment, I'd had no idea I was having a baby. It almost didn't seem real."

She could still remember her confusion, her shock, the rush of adrenaline that had jolted her to a momentary awareness.

Javier's warm fingers stroked hers. "You can finish telling me about this tomorrow after you've had some sleep. You've been through—"

But Laura needed to get it out. "They took her from me. I tried to get up and follow, but there was so much blood. I . . . I fainted."

Laura told Javier how she'd almost bled to death, how she'd lain there on that bloodstained blanket for days, desperately thirsty and barely able to hold her head up, how she'd asked about the baby, only to be ignored.

"My breasts swelled and ached and started to leak milk." The discomfort had been almost unbearable. "When I asked to see the baby, to nurse it, they told me I was crazy, but I could hear it crying. Then they said my baby had been stillborn. After a while, I began to wonder whether I had just imagined it all. My doctor says it was traumatic amnesia. When I was strong enough to walk, I tried to get close to her, tried to see her, but they wouldn't let me, saying she was Safiya's child and that I was unfit to be a mother."

"How do you know it was a girl?"

"Angeza told me. She was the only one of Al-Nassar's wives who was ever kind to me. She was Afghan. Her father had given her to Al-Nassar to settle a debt when she was only fourteen. I think she hated the others as much as I did. She said Al-Nassar had named the baby Yasmina. I call her Klara."

"What happened to the baby, Laura? What happened to Klara?"

Laura shook her head, her pulse ratcheting. She stood, crossed the room, and gazed unseeing through the window onto the rooftops of a sleeping city. Why had she started this? Why had she told him? *"Oh, God."*

Javier came up behind her and rested his hands gently on her shoulders. "It's okay, *bella*. I'm right here."

But it wasn't okay.

It wouldn't be okay until Klara was free and safe.

And once Javier knew the truth . . .

"About two months after the birth, the SEALs rescued me. I heard them speaking American English, and something in me woke up, some part of me that remembered who I was and why I was there. I wanted to survive, to escape. I didn't mean to forget her."

Oh, Jesus!

"Your baby was left behind."

Laura whirled about to face him, knowing what he must think of her. How could she explain it? There was no explanation, no excuse. "I didn't think . . . I didn't remember . . . Something inside me just *snapped*. I had to get away. I didn't mean to leave her there. I didn't mean to leave her. I didn't even remember she was mine."

"How soon before you remembered?"

She looked away. "The doctor at the hospital in Germany did an exam. Afterward, he told me that it looked like I'd recently given birth. And then it all crashed in on me—all the memories. But it was too late. It was too late."

She looked up, expecting to see disgust or anger on Javier's face.

Instead, he drew her close, held her tight, whispered to her in Spanish, words she didn't understand, his voice not angry but soothing.

She resisted. She didn't deserve this. "What kind of mother leaves her baby with terrorists? What kind of mother does something like that?"

Javier drew back and caught her face between his palms, forcing her to meet his gaze, his expression fierce. "Don't you dare blame yourself. You'd been brutalized, violated, terrorized. You had a baby alone and almost died. They never even let you hold her. Then some men with guns drop from the sky and offer you a way to survive and come home. How could you expect yourself to remember she was your baby in the middle of that chaos?"

Laura heard his words, saw beyond the intensity on his face to the sympathy in his eyes, but some part of her couldn't accept the absolution he offered. "She was my baby, and I left her behind."

"It's *not* your fault, Laura. You didn't leave her. She was taken from you."

"You . . . really believe that?"

"Yeah, I do."

"You forgive me?"

"There's nothing to forgive."

Tears Laura had held back for what seemed an eternity poured from her, grief and regret as sharp as pain cutting through her. Strong arms lifted her up, carried her to her bed, held her together until pain gave way to numbness and numbness to exhaustion—and sleep.

UNABLE TO SLEEP, Javier lay in the darkness, feeling gutted, torn between his need to do all he could to help and comfort Laura and a bitter rage that simmered in his chest. Memories of the night they'd raided Al-Nassar's compound moved through his mind frame by frame. Al-Nassar lying almost naked in the dirt. Women huddling together with their children, some holding babies. Laura looking fragile and pale in the helo.

Now he knew why she'd seemed so weak. She'd been only

about eight weeks away from having had a baby and hemorrhaging.

What he wouldn't give to go back in time and have the
presence of mind to ask her if anyone else was being held captive. He'd take Laura's baby and get them both safely on that
Hercules. But that was just a fantasy. He'd barely had time to
rescue Laura as it was. Had he delayed any longer, the combatants who had fired those RPGs would probably have hit them
and brought them down. But what kept him awake was wondering what had happened *after* they'd left.

Where was Laura's baby now?

JAVIER JOLTED AWAKE to the sound of his cell phone ring-
ing. He opened his eyes to find Laura snuggled up against him
and still asleep, clearly exhausted. He reached for his phone,
saw that it wasn't yet oh-dawn-hundred. He hadn't even had
three hours of sleep. Then he saw the number.

Shit.

He'd known this was coming.

He muted the phone, slipped from the bed, and walked out
into the hallway, shutting the bedroom door behind him.
"Hey, Boss."

"Want to tell me why I saw you on prime-time news last
night playing bodyguard for Laura Nilsson?" Lt. O'Connell
sounded pissed. "Word is all over base—hell, it's all over
town. I just got a call from the commander, who was out for
his four A.M. run and wants an explanation."

How in the hell was Javier going to explain this?

He decided to keep it simple. "Laura and I are old friends.
I was in Denver to hang with Nate West, and when that car
bomb went off, I just had to help her. I was there when the
shooter opened fire and was able to save her life."

"Let me get this straight. You violated OPSEC by frater-
nizing with a civilian you rescued while part of a classified
mission, then you made matters worse by exposing yourself
in the media when you decided to moonlight as her bodyguard. They're going to drag you in—"

"No, sir, I didn't."

"You didn't what?"

"I didn't violate OPSEC. I knew Ms. Nilsson long before that rescue mission. To this day, she has no idea that I'm the one who pulled her out of there."

"You expect me to believe you haven't told her?"

Six years on the Teams together, and O'Connell had the nerve to talk to him like this? "Have I ever lied to you, man? Have I *ever* lied to you?"

Not that Javier hadn't wanted to tell Laura. Last night, he'd had to bite his tongue to keep from telling her that he'd been there, that'd he'd carried her out, that he'd seen how terrified and confused she was. But he'd upheld OPSEC and kept his mouth shut, even when he'd known that telling her would have helped her forgive herself.

"So you're friends with the Baghdad Babe."

"*Don't* call her that, man. I fucking *hate* that. I really do."

"More than friends, maybe. That's the kind of thing a guy might tell his buddies, especially given how famous she was."

"Some guys, maybe, but not me."

"Did West know?"

Everyone knew that Javier and Nate were best buds. "Not till this week, sir."

"Now I understand why you were gunning so hard for Al-Nassar."

"That mission went off without a hitch." No one could say that Javier's feelings for Laura had compromised that op in any way.

"Did you know she was alive?"

"If I'd even *suspected* she was alive, I'd have raised hell to get her out of there long before that mission."

"How did you get mixed up in her shit? You're supposed to be recuperating, preparing yourself for a return to active duty, not starring in the latest episode of *Celebrity Bodyguard*."

"Is there a reg somewhere that says I can't help a close friend when she's in trouble? I'm staying with her because she needs me right now. She's terrified, man. I don't know about you, but I didn't pull her out of that compound just to let these assholes kill her on *our* soil."

"Ms. Nilsson has the Marshal Service and the FBI to protect her. It's their mission. Your mission is to recover and rejoin your platoon."

"True. But who saved her life last night? I did."

Boss drew a deep breath. "Okay. I'll call the commander back, explain it to him like you explained it to me. But I can tell you right now, he's not going to like it. I just hope he doesn't revoke your leave and haul your ass back here for a disciplinary hearing. You've been a huge pain in the ass lately, you know that?"

That sounded more like the O'Connell Javier knew.

"Thanks, Boss. Sorry he woke you up and chewed your ass."

"You'd better be. And, Cobra—good work. The guys are proud. They're kind of attached to Ms. Nilsson themselves."

The call ended.

Javier turned to find Laura standing behind him.

"You're in trouble for helping me, aren't you?" She watched him through worried eyes still swollen from crying, her hair in long tangles, her feet bare.

How much had she heard? Not much. If she'd overheard him talking about rescuing her from Al-Nassar, she'd be staring at him wide-eyed and full of questions.

"Naval Special Warfare just doesn't like its operators on prime-time news."

"Oh, God. I'm so sorry. I didn't even think about that."

He drew her into his arms, held her close, caressed her hair. "Don't apologize, *bella*. That wasn't your fault."

"Is everything going to be okay?"

"Yeah, it's going to be fine." He didn't want her worrying about this. "The sun's not even up. Let's get some sleep."

CHAPTER 17

LAURA AWOKE, SAW bright daylight through her blinds. Beside her, the bed was empty, the sound of running water telling her Javier was in the shower. She stretched, yawned, body and mind strangely lethargic. It wasn't until she saw the abrasions on her palms that she remembered.

She sat bolt upright, her pulse tripping.

Someone had tried to shoot her yesterday. Someone had tried to kill her, wounding Janet in the process. Javier had saved her life and . . .

Laura had told him about Klara.

Oh, God.

He hadn't reacted the way she'd thought he would. Like her mother and grandmother, he'd refused to blame her, offering her comfort and understanding she didn't deserve.

You forgive me?

There's nothing to forgive.

She remembered how caring he'd been, holding her while she cried her eyes out, carrying her to her bed, staying with her through the night. Some of her lethargy lifted.

She got out of bed, grabbed her bathrobe, and walked out to the kitchen to make coffee. She'd just gotten off the phone with University Hospital when Javier stepped out of the bedroom wearing only jeans, his short hair wet.

He poured himself a cup of coffee. "Was that the hospital?"

She set down her smartphone. "Janet has been upgraded from critical to fair."

"I'm glad to hear that." He leaned against the counter, his gaze meeting hers, his brown eyes warm. "How are *you*?"

"I'm fine. I'm okay, I guess. I don't know."

In truth, she felt awkward, exposed, nervous. Javier had seen a part of her no other man had seen. It was one thing to be sexual with a man. It was another to break into pieces in front of him. But Javier had seen the shattered core that she'd kept hidden, and he had accepted her, comforted her. He'd even seemed to understand.

Still, she couldn't help but wonder. Did he feel some kind of obligation toward her because of Dubai? "You don't have to stay, Javi. I don't want you to waste—"

"Shh." He pressed his fingers against her lips. "I'm right where I want to be, *bella*. Why don't you take a hot shower while I make us some breakfast?"

A HALF HOUR later, Laura sat down to a cup of hot coffee and a plate loaded down with a breakfast burrito and freshly sliced cantaloupe. "This smells delicious. Thanks."

They spoke of inconsequential things while they ate— their favorite things to eat for breakfast, how well they'd slept, the weather.

It was Laura who finally brought it up. "I'm sorry I fell apart like that."

"Give yourself a break. You've been through hell. There aren't many people who could even imagine what it was like." He reached across the table and took one of her hands in his. "It can't be easy keeping Klara secret. I feel honored that you trusted me. No one else here knows, do they? Not even your friends."

She shook her head. "I feel so *ashamed*. What I did—"

"You survived against all odds. There is no shame in that."

She looked up at him. "I thought you would think less of me."

"You thought I'd leave. That's why you told me, isn't it? Somehow you truly think you did something unforgivable."

He narrowed his eyes. "Sorry, *bella*, but you can't shake me off that easily. But I have to ask . . . Where is Klara now?"

Laura found herself telling him about her long battle to find her daughter and bring her home. How she'd decided to work through the Swedish foreign ministry rather than the U.S. State Department to better protect her privacy. How they'd found Klara living with Al-Nassar's younger brother. How they hoped to arrange a welfare check with Klara soon. How everything was stacked against her when it came to custody.

"Even if they're able to get DNA and the DNA proves she's my child, the fact that I'm a non-Muslim, a woman, and a foreigner means that the courts will likely rule against me. But I'm not giving up. Klara is a victim, too. She was abducted straight from my body, and I won't feel whole again until she's safely home."

Javier laced his fingers through hers. "You'll get her home."

Laura nodded, fighting back her doubts, refusing to acknowledge any other possible outcome, regret swamping her once more. "If only I'd told the men who rescued me that she was there . . . If only I'd remembered . . ."

"I can't stand to see you blame yourself. I know what war is like. Even if you'd remembered she was yours, even if you'd told the squad leader, there's no guarantee they could have made it out with her alive. You did all you could."

She looked up from their twined fingers. "Have you ever left a man behind?"

Javier opened his mouth as if to speak, but nothing came out. He didn't need to say a word. The answer was plain to see on his face.

STILL REELING FROM all that Laura had told him, Javier spent the afternoon in his own special hell, wanting desperately to tell her that he'd been the man who'd rescued her. If she could only see that night from his point of view, she'd quit blaming herself. But if he told her, he'd violate OPSEC and turn himself into a liar.

He was in enough hot water already.

Then the paper called, Laura's editor insisting she drop

everything to do an interview. The asshole didn't seem to give a damn about what Laura had been through, as far as Javier could tell. He just wanted the paper to have the most complete coverage, given that Laura worked there.

By the time McBride called to say one of his teams had seen a man with a spotting scope on the roof of the building across the street, Javier was restless, pissed off, spoiling for a fight. Thinking the worst, he left Laura, who was still on the phone, with Deputy U.S. Marshal Mike Childers, who had taken Killeen's place, and met McBride, only to find the spotting scope was actually a telephoto lens and the sniper was a shooter of a different kind.

He fought to keep his trap shut while McBride cuffed and Mirandized the bastard. McBride's team had apprehended the guy in the act of trying to take photos of Laura through her living room and bedroom windows. Now he lay on his fat belly on the black rubber roofing, arms behind his back.

"You have the right to remain silent. Anything you say can and will be used against you in a court of law. You have a right—"

"You can't arrest me! I'm a photojournalist! I—"

"A photojournalist? You're nothing but paparazzi. What kind of whiskey tango fuck-ass editor wants to publish the shit you call photos? You were spying on her, man. You're no better than a peeping Tom."

McBride shot Javier a warning glance and went on. "You have a right to an attorney. If you cannot afford an attorney, one will be appointed for you. Do you understand your rights as I have explained them to you?"

"You're gonna make headlines, buddy." The man twisted his head around and glared at McBride. "Arresting a reporter for trying to report the news—you'll be lucky if they don't sue your ass! Ever hear of the First Amendment?"

Javier bent down, looked the *cabrón* in the eyes. "Remember that part about staying silent? You should try that shit out, dawg."

McBride stepped back, making room for a cop who began to pat the photographer down. "The First Amendment doesn't give you the right to trespass on private property, and trying to photograph someone inside the privacy of their home sure as hell isn't journalism."

The cop pulled something out of the photographer's vest. "A lock-picking kit? Is that how you got up here? That's a felony."

"I keep that in case I get locked out of my car."

"Yeah, right." Javier wanted to kick the man's ass. "Tell that to the jury."

McBride turned his back on the photographer and walked a short distance away, motioning for Javier to follow. He stopped, turning to face Javier. "You need to chill. I don't blame you for being angry, but I can't let you harass people in my custody no matter how badly they deserve to have their asses kicked."

"Got it. Sorry, man."

McBride lowered his voice. "How is she?"

"She's coping."

It bothered Javier that none of Laura's friends knew the full weight she was carrying on her shoulders. How lonely these past two years must have been for her, keeping her heartbreak and worry for her little girl to herself, living with a sense of guilt and shame that should never have been hers to carry.

"Does she know about Tower yet?"

Javier shook his head. "I've kept the TV off, and she's been staying away from her laptop except to connect with her mom through Skype. She hasn't read the papers either because I recycled them."

"Good call. How much does she know about Killeen?"

"She's called the hospital twice to get an update on Killeen's condition, but they won't release any details. The last we heard, doctors had upgraded Killeen to fair. That seemed to ease her mind."

McBride squinted against the bright sunlight, his gaze fixed on the city beyond. "Killeen was good at her job. I hate to think her career might be over."

Javier knew from experience the regret McBride was feeling. Killeen had been wounded on McBride's watch, and he would carry that with him. "She knew the risks, and she asked to be assigned here."

"Yeah." McBride didn't sound convinced.

Neither was Javier.

Javier had spoken those words more times than he could count—for wounded men, maimed men, dead men. He'd said the same thing about himself.

Just words.

"West tells me you might be facing a disciplinary hearing for getting yourself involved in Laura's situation."

"West has a big damned mouth."

McBride grinned. "I just wanted to let you know that I'd be happy to speak on your behalf if it comes to it. I still have a few connections inside NSW."

For a moment, Javier didn't know what to say. "Thanks, man. I appreciate it."

"You let me know."

"Will do."

Nearby, two uniforms escorted the photographer across the roof toward the exit, one of them carrying the bastard's hardware.

"I swear if you break my camera, I'll sue for every dime you got!" The photographer was still shouting by the time they all reached the street seven stories below, his threats now laced with profanity. "I'll have your fucking badge!"

As they walked past, Javier couldn't stop himself. "Moth-erfucker."

LAURA HAD JUST hung up from talking with Alex at the paper when her cell phone rang again. Thinking it was Alex calling to clarify something, she answered without checking the display. "Hey."

"Hello, Laura. Am I catching you at a bad time?"

"Gary." He was the last person on earth she wanted to talk to.

"You've been ignoring my calls."

"You ignored your promise."

"I was just doing my job. You'd have done the same thing."

"I'm sorry you think so."

"Hey, you came to me, remember?" His voice was soothing, as if he were speaking to an upset child. "You asked for help in countering Tower's allegations, and I did my best to provide that. By showing that footage, I generated sympathy for you. Yes, it helped boost our ratings, but all that means is that more households got *your* message. What's wrong with that?"

He'd never understood the human element of journalism.

"You forced me to watch that footage on *live* television."

"Well, it paid off for you. The poll on our website shows that ninety-six percent of our viewers believe Tower is simply trying to save face with his accusations against you—not that I suppose any of this means much to him now. Do you think he was behind it all, some kind of vendetta? He must be involved somehow."

"What are you talking about?"

"You haven't heard?"

"Heard what? And this is all off the record, by the way. No interview."

"Tower was found shot in the parking garage where the sniper hid."

Laura got to her feet. "Tower was *shot*?"

"Your handlers really are sheltering you, aren't they? Yes, he was shot. He's on life support in ICU. They're not sure he's going to make it."

Derek Tower. Shot. On life support in intensive care.

Laura was so stunned that it took a moment for Gary's insult to sink in. Her face flushed, cheeks burning with anger. "Is there anything else?"

Her *handlers*?

"Mostly, I wanted to say I'm sorry the interview put you in danger. If I'd had any idea what was going to happen, I would've insisted we send a crew to your place rather than having you go to the studio. I care about you, kid."

Yeah? Well, I think you're a jackass.

"Thanks, Gary. I need to go." Not bothering to wait for his good-bye, she ended the call and sat on the edge of her bed.

Why hadn't anyone told her about Tower?

As soon as she asked the question, she knew the answer. They'd been trying to protect her, trying to prevent her from becoming emotionally overwhelmed. How weak she must seem to them, how helpless, how fragile.

She'd thought she had her life together again, but the past two weeks had proved her wrong. She needed to be stronger, to quit waiting for Al-Nassar's goons to attack her or kill her. She needed to fight back somehow.

How would she have handled this four years ago?

She would have investigated the bombing and the shooting, doing her best to uncover the perpetrators and expose their motive.

Her thoughts turned to what Gary had told her. It couldn't be a coincidence that Tower had been shot at the parking garage. Was he working with Al-Nassar's men? If he was, why would they shoot him? Maybe he'd gone there to tidy up loose ends by killing the shooter and had been shot himself. Or maybe he *was* the shooter and he'd been the loose end. But why would Tower want to kill her?

I want the truth about why my men are dead. Since you're the key to my getting that info, terminating you wouldn't make much sense, would it?

None of this made sense.

There was only one place she knew to start looking for answers.

She walked to her chest of drawers and took out the thick manila envelope Janet had left for her.

JAVIER FOUND LAURA in her office reading something, a look of intense concentration on her face, her hair twisted into a knot at her nape, a purple highlighter in her hand. Documents were spread across her desk.

"Working on your VA article?"

She didn't look up, her gaze fixed on the page in her hand, her blond brows bent in a frown of concentration. She answered almost absentmindedly, still focused on whatever she was reading. "Something happened two months ago. He must have met someone new or fallen in with the wrong crowd."

"Who?"

She didn't say. "Or maybe I don't have all the files."

He walked over to her and reached for a stack of documents. They were intel communiqués of some kind, memos about Ali Al Zahrani. On the back, each was stamped "Classified" in bright, bloody red. "Where did you get these?"

Laura's head snapped up, her gaze colliding with his, an unmistakable look of guilt on her face. "Uh . . ."

Busted.

"Did McBride leak these to you?"

She took the pages from Javier's hand. "I can't reveal my source."

He saw the envelope on her desk, recognized it—and it clicked. "Agent Killeen. She gave them to you. They were in that envelope that you found on the floor when we got back home last night."

Laura glared at him. "You can't breathe a word to anyone, especially not Zach."

Javier was an expert at keeping secrets, but he wasn't used to keeping them from his team, and for the moment, McBride and the others were his team. "What are you hoping to do with all of this?"

She sat down, began to arrange the piles. "I just want to understand. I need to know how a good kid like Ali could wake up one morning and decide to be a terrorist. What could make him suddenly turn his back on his family, his community, his life?"

"Maybe it wasn't as sudden as it seems." In Javier's experience, the seeds of terrorism were planted early in a kid's life.

"His browser history was full of searches about video games and topless Hollywood stars, and then two months ago, he created a new subdirectory on his computer and started searching for information on jihad and how to mix ANFO."

"The kid moved from boobs to bombs fast."

"Too fast." Laura tucked the papers back inside the envelope and turned to her computer. She opened her browser, typed in a URL. "My gut tells me something must have happened to send him over that edge, and I need to know what it was. I want to create a list of the stories I was working on a couple of months ago. Maybe I wrote something that offended or provoked him."

Javier sensed the tension in her. He could feel how hard she was fighting to be tough, to hold herself together. He bent down, looked at her computer screen, and saw that she was on the *Denver Independent* website. "You're making this way too personal. "

"His mother said he cried when he thought I'd been killed. So why would he try to kill me himself three years later?"

"Who knows?" Javier sat on the edge of her desk, caught her hands, and held them, turning her to face him. "Are you sure this is a good idea, *bella*? You've been through a lot and—"

"I have to *do* something." She glared at him, but behind the anger in her eyes he saw desperation. "I can't just sit here, hidden away, waiting for Al-Nassar's goons to get it right next time and kill me. If I could just understand *why* Ali did this . . ."

"Would it fix anything? Would it?"

Her gaze dropped to the floor, worry on her pretty face. "I . . . I don't know. I hate unanswered questions, and I think his parents deserve an answer. Don't you?"

Sure, he did. "When it comes to shit like this—kids getting radicalized, wanting to kill and die—there are no easy answers."

Her chin went up, that defiant look coming over her face. "I'm going to do my best to figure it out."

"What do you think McBride will have to say about you digging through classified, leaked documents and working your own angle on his case?"

"Who's going to tell him?"

Javier opened his mouth to speak but said nothing.

Her lips curved in a deliberately sweet smile. "That's what I thought."

She has you figured out, hermano.

She clicked Print. "I also need to find out how Derek Tower is tied to this."

"You heard about that."

She took a few sheets of paper from her printer tray. "Gary told me. I called the hospital. Tower is still in ICU in critical condition."

Chapin again.

How Javier hated that *pendejo*. "What Gary doesn't know is that Tower was armed with an assault rifle loaded with armor-piercing rounds. We've got no clue what he was doing there or how he's mixed up in this, but if he's not the sniper, it's a good bet he knows who is."

"I hope he makes it." She stood, the defiance she'd worn on her face moments ago crumpling. "I need this to be over. I need it to end."

He drew her into his arms, kissed her hair, savored the feel of her, her fear and vulnerability rousing a fierce protective instinct inside him. "What you said earlier about waiting for Al-Nassar's goons to get it right and kill you? That won't happen. I won't let it happen."

"I don't know what I did to deserve you, Javi. You've missed out on time with Nate and put yourself in danger for my sake, and now you might be facing a disciplinary hearing. You're sacrificing so much—*too* much."

How could she think that she didn't deserve him? If anything, it was the other way around. "Let me worry about that, okay?"

She looked up at him. "I feel bad saying this, but I'm so glad you're here. I don't know what I would have done without you."

Then she stood on her tiptoes—and kissed him.

A jagged bolt of heat shot through him, stirring up the hunger he'd spent the past week trying so hard to suppress. He'd told himself he wouldn't let this happen again, his pulse like thunder as she brushed his lips with hers, teased their outline with her tongue.

If only he didn't want her so damned bad . . .

And she seemed to want him, too.

CHAPTER 18

LAURA HAD MEANT to kiss Javier's cheek, a quick kiss to thank him for all he'd done, to show him she cared. Instead, her lips found his, the fleeting contact sending a warm shimmer through her, stealing her breath, making her worries vanish. She heard Javier's quick intake of breath, felt his body tense as she kissed him again.

He began to kiss her back, submissively at first, letting her take the lead, ceding control to her. But Laura knew from experience that Javier was not a submissive man. He'd been the only man she'd ever had sex with whose drive matched hers, the only man she'd known who was strong and skilled enough to top her and bring out *her* submissive side. Clearly, he was holding back, trying to respect the boundaries she'd set, doing his best to make sure she felt safe. Except that she didn't want to feel safe.

She wanted to feel alive again, exhilarated, vibrant.

She drew his head down, brushed her lips across his, whispered, "*Kiss me.*"

With a groan, he began to kiss her back, slow and deep, one big hand sliding inch by inch up her spine, the other splayed across her lower back, drawing her closer, his body so hard against hers, strong and male.

Laura's blood seemed to ignite, a bolt of heat piercing her belly, raw need for him making her pulse skip, delight surging inside her like a sunrise, driving away the darkness.

He drew back, looked down at her through warm eyes. "Do you feel that—the way your touch makes me shake? God, *bella*."

His mouth claimed hers again, this kiss as fierce as the first had been gentle, his hand fisting in her hair, his heart thudding hard against hers.

Laura felt her knees go weak.

With slow, drunken steps, Javier backed her up against the wall, his lips and tongue relentless, his fingers working her hair from its twist, his erection hard against her hip. The feel of his arousal and the hard press of the wall behind her elicited delicious memories of the afternoon in Dubai when he'd picked her up, wrapped her legs around his waist, and fucked her up against the wall.

The memory and the man and the moment came together, naked desire flooding Laura's veins like a drug. She arched into him, her fingers caressing the shifting muscles of his back, the stubbled line of his jaw, the steel of his shoulders.

He lowered his lips to her throat, possessing the sensitive skin beneath her ear, caressing, nibbling, teasing. A hand closed over her breast, the delicious shock of it making her jerk and gasp. His thumb flicked her hardened nipple through the cloth of her shirt, unleashing a flood of liquid heat between her thighs. "Were your stretch marks the only thing holding you back from letting me touch you like this?"

His breath was hot against her throat, his voice strained.

"Yes. No!" She looked into Javier's eyes, her pulse still racing, his words resurrecting old fears. She wasn't sure how she would react if they actually tried to have sex. "What if I'm not ready for this?"

His lips, wet from kissing, curved in a smile. "I guess we'll have to take it slow."

He'd just lowered his mouth to hers again when his cell phone rang. He squeezed his eyes shut and drew reluctantly away from her, seeming to recognize the ring tone. "I'm so sorry, *bella*. I have to take this."

Disappointment almost made her moan. "NSW again?"

He nodded, reached into his jeans pocket. "My platoon commander."

* * *

JAVIER HAD JUST gotten off the phone from having his ass chewed by the platoon commander, who'd let him off with a warning, when his folks called to find out why they'd seen him on the news and how he was connected to Laura. That call had been interrupted by one from McBride, who said he was on his way over to update Laura on the investigation and to ask her to view the surveillance video from the parking garage.

So much for picking up where he and Laura had left off.

"You think she's up for it?" McBride asked.

Javier looked over to where Laura stood, frozen in the act of making a salad as she listened to Javier. "Yeah, I think she is."

Fifteen minutes later, McBride sat in Laura's living room, a cup of freshly brewed coffee in hand. "The photographer bonded out."

So the *hijoeputa* was back on the street.

"If he shows up here again, I'll—"

McBride's gaze narrowed. "If he shows up here again, you'll call the cops."

"That's what I was going to say."

"Right."

Laura poured herself a cup of coffee and sat beside Javier, her hand sliding easily into his, her fingers cold. He'd known she was nervous, but he hadn't realized how nervous. He got up, turned on the fire, and sat down beside her again.

"First, this isn't for the paper," McBride said. "Agreed?"

Laura nodded.

"Tower wasn't our shooter." McBride held up a clear plastic bag with spent shell casings. "We recovered these at the site. Whoever tried to kill you, Laura, was firing 7.62 NATO AP rounds, not five-five-six."

Laura looked puzzled. "I'm sorry. I don't know what that means."

"Tower was carrying an AR-15 armed with five-five-six green tip, a specific armor-piercing round. The shooter's weapon used a different caliber."

"I understand."

McBride held up a DVD. "We'd hoped the surveillance

video from the parking garage would give us all the answers we want, but so far we just have more questions. Laura, if you don't mind, I'd like you to watch this."

"Of course." Laura took the disk and popped it in the player, then turned on the television and handed the remote to McBride. When she sat down beside Javier again, her fingers were even colder.

McBride leaned closer to Laura. "I know this won't be easy for you to see, but I'm hoping you'll recognize something about the shooter—the way he walks, how he's dressed, or something he does. Even the smallest detail might help us identify him."

Javier had to hand it to McBride. He was doing his best not only to catch a killer, but also to keep from traumatizing Laura further. Then again, Nate wouldn't have considered McBride a friend if McBride had been an asshole.

"I'll do my best," Laura answered.

McBride pushed Play, and a greenish image flickered to life, showing the entrance of the parking garage with a time stamp of sixteen hundred hours—a good two hours before Laura had arrived at the television station.

"What you're seeing was taken from hours of footage we spliced together from several different cameras at the garage. In a moment you'll see Tower drive up. Here he comes."

Tower appeared at the wheel of a metallic bronze BMW X3, rolled down his window, and took a ticket, disappearing as he headed into the garage. The footage cut to the top floor of the garage, where he emerged moments later, parking directly across from the position Javier thought the shooter must have taken.

McBride pointed at the television. "He drives straight to the upper floor of the parking garage. He doesn't get out. He doesn't do anything but sit there."

"So the bastard must have known what was about to go down."

"It seems so."

The footage cut back to the entrance of the parking garage, the time index in the corner showing that about forty minutes had gone by.

"Here's our shooter," McBride said.

Javier felt Laura tense as a blue Honda Civic pulled up, a man with a white glowing ball for a head at the wheel.

She frowned. "He's hiding his face using infrared LEDs."

"How did you know about that?" Javier was fairly certain this wasn't common knowledge.

"Oh, please." She gave him a look. "Investigative reporter?"

McBride paused the playback. "Does anything about him look familiar to you?"

Laura studied the image, leaning toward the TV. "No."

"We ran plates on the car, but it was reported stolen from in front of a private home Thursday afternoon. There are no city surveillance cameras in that neighborhood, so we're hoping to find witnesses." McBride pushed Play again. "Watch where the shooter goes. He stops on the fourth floor—one floor down from Tower."

Javier watched as the shooter parked facing south. He climbed out of his G-ride, range finder in hand, and began to scope his shot.

McBride paused once more. "Does anything seem familiar to you?"

Laura watched intently, then shook her head. "No. I'm sorry."

"Here's where it gets interesting." McBride pushed Play again. "If this gets too difficult for you, let me know, okay, Laura?"

McBride fast-forwarded through an hour's worth of footage, the image getting darker as the sun set. When it slowed again, there was a split-screen image, one side showing Tower, the other showing the shooter.

Tower stepped out of his Beemer, looked around, then walked to the southern side of the garage and looked in the direction of the television station, the AR-15 in hand. He glanced at his watch, then looked down at the television station again through his night scope. Meanwhile, one floor down, the shooter got into position with an M110 sniper rifle equipped with a bipod—and a suppressor. He flipped out the bipod, rested the weapon on the concrete ledge, and began adjusting his sights.

It sickened Javier to think the shooter was about to focus on Laura.

Minutes ticked by, both men in position, Tower periodically checking his watch.

"Here's where the shooting began," McBride said.

A knot of dread in her stomach, Laura watched as the shooter, with his eerie ball of light for a head, held absolutely still—and pulled the trigger. That was the shot that had nearly killed her and sent concrete fragments spraying into her face. It was quickly followed by four more.

On the other side of the screen, Tower turned and ran for the stairs, while the shooter kept firing, the jerk of the rifle the only sign that he'd pulled the trigger. One of those bullets had hit Janet, Laura realized, dread turning to nausea.

Abruptly, the shooter stood and began to pack his gear. He froze and glanced toward the stairwell.

"He's made Tower. He can see him there." Javier pointed to a section of the stairway that was exposed. "See?"

The split-screen image became one as Tower reached the fourth floor, his weapon raised. But the shooter was ready for him, squeezing off two shots just as Tower fired. Tower fell back, arched and writhed on the concrete, then went still, a pool of blood spreading around him, while the shooter got quickly into his car and drove away, leaving Tower for dead.

"Stop, please!" Laura had seen enough, the sight of Tower's suffering and the memories it roused too much. "I can't."

Zach stopped the DVD and retrieved it from Laura's machine. "I'm sorry, Laura. I was hoping that you might recognize something about him."

Laura wished she had, but without so much as a glimpse of his face, the man who'd tried to kill her was nothing more than a ghostly headless body.

Javier sat in silence for a moment, seeming lost in thought. "So we know Tower knew what was going to happen, and we know he wasn't the shooter."

Zach took a gulp of his coffee. "Like I said, the footage raised more questions than it answered."

"Was he there to take the shooter out and clean up loose ends?"

"If he was, why did he do such a bad job of it?"

While the two men discussed the footage, Laura found herself reliving her last conversation with Tower.

I want the truth about why my men are dead. Since you're the key to my getting that info, terminating you wouldn't make much sense, would it?

Laura spoke, interrupting Javier and Zach. "What if he was trying to stop the shooter? What if he was trying to protect me?"

Zach seemed to consider this. "I suppose anything is possible, but the best way to protect you would've been for him to share what he knew with law enforcement. He's in extremely critical condition. Apparently the wound and blood loss were so severe that he was thrown into something called adult respiratory distress syndrome and is close to pulmonary failure. But we've got him under guard. If he survives, we may get some answers. If not, we'll have to find those answers ourselves."

For a time there was silence, each of them lost in thought, the puzzle pieces shifting in Laura's mind without coming together. Most of the time, the details of an investigation fascinated her. This time, she just felt overwhelmed.

Javier broke the silence. "Whoever the shooter is, he moves like a man with military training."

"Interesting you should say that. I got the same impression. So did Hunter." Zach held up the plastic bag with the spent casings once more. "Whoever our terrorist is, the rounds he used all had U.S. military headstamps."

"Headstamps?" Laura had never heard the term before.

Zach pointed to the flat bottom of one of the casings. "Those are the markings pressed into the bottom of a casing showing when and where it was manufactured."

Javier shrugged. "That doesn't tell us a damned thing. He could've bought the ammo anywhere—online, at a gun show, on the black market. He could have stolen it. Someone could have bought or stolen it for him. But why would a skilled sniper or hired gun leave his shell casings behind? That's just sloppy."

"The casings were clear of prints, so perhaps he didn't think they mattered. Or maybe the firefight with Tower made him rush. Like I said, lots of questions, not a lot of answers." Zach pulled out a notepad and glanced through it. "As for the bombing investigation, the FBI has confirmed that all of the bomb components were purchased in the Denver metro area, so our guess is we're talking someone local, perhaps Al Zahrani."

Laura had a hard time believing it could be Ali, but she didn't say that. She knew Zach and all the members of the task force had been working tirelessly to solve this case. "Thank you, Zach. I appreciate everything you've done."

Zach stood, concern in his gray eyes. "I can't imagine how hard this has been for you, Laura, but we are doing our best to catch the guys responsible for this and put them behind bars. We're all working through the weekend, and we won't stop until you're safe again."

Javier held out his hand, and the two men shook. "Thanks."

"Thank you. Call if anything comes up."

Laura watched as Javier locked the door behind Zach, then stood and, without saying a word, walked into his embrace.

JAVIER HELPED LAURA finish making supper, keeping the conversation light. She was quiet, almost withdrawn, understandably upset by what she had seen. But she didn't want to be alone. She came easily into his arms when he reached for her, holding his hand while they ate, as if his touch alone made her feel safer.

The surveillance footage had upset him, too. But he wasn't afraid—he was pissed off. Whoever that son of a bitch was, Javier wanted him dead. If he was the one to put a bullet through the bastard's skull, so much the better.

After supper, they did the dishes, then stretched out together on the sofa to watch another episode from season one of *Downton Abbey*, one of Laura's favorite shows. He stroked Laura's hair, her head pillowed on his chest, the fingers of his other hand twined with hers. Being close to her like this was the most natural thing in the world, and yet it wasn't easy. The silky feel of her hair, the scent of her skin, the soft press of her body against his, triggered memories of this afternoon's kiss, made him burn for her.

What a strange kind of intimacy they shared. It was like nothing he'd had with a woman before. They were closer than they'd been in Dubai, and yet they hadn't done more than hold each other at night and kiss a couple of times. Granted, that last kiss had blown his mind, but the longing for more was there.

Oh, hell, yes, it was.

She'd taken a big step today, but he didn't want to push things and make her uncomfortable. Of course, she had nothing to worry about. Javier had been a special operator for most of his adult life. He'd gone long stretches without a woman, making do with the occasional combat jack to take the edge off. He could handle this.

It was enough to hold her, to sleep with her at night, to know that some part of her wanted him. Why else would she have kissed him?

"Yo, Bates, man, you'd better watch your six!" Javier shouted at the TV, surprising himself as much as Laura. "Thomas and O'Brien are going to bury your ass if you don't. O'Brien, man, she's one nasty, conniving bitch."

His outburst made Laura laugh. "You're getting into this, aren't you?"

"Hey, don't tell West. He would never let me live it down."

She smiled up at him. "I bet Nate watches it, too. I know Megan does."

That was a revelation.

Laura listened to Javier's heart beat beneath her ear, her fingers stroking his forearm. They hadn't talked about the kiss that had been interrupted. It was as if it hadn't happened. But it had.

She could still feel the heat of it, her lips tingling, her blood warm, her body in a state of heightened awareness. She was mindful of every breath he took, his scent seeming to surround her, the feel of his hard body beside hers so arousing that she could hardly concentrate on the show.

Her thoughts drifted from one sexual scenario to the other, each more titillating than the last. She could take off his shirt, kiss her way down his body, and go down on him. Or lead him by the hand to her bedroom and make love with him. Or ride him like she'd done in Dubai, feeling him thrust into her from below.

All it would take was another kiss, a few words, a touch. *Javi, I changed my mind. I want to be with you.*

Or maybe something sexier.

You kept your promise, Javi, but now I really need you to break it.

No, that was stupid, not sexy.

I trust you, Javi. I want you. Make love to me.

Too corny.

But no matter how many times she imagined it, she couldn't bring herself to act, anxiety like heavy chains, holding her back, leaving her torn between what she desperately wanted and what she desperately feared.

Still, she couldn't let herself remain stuck in this rut. Soon, Javier would be leaving. If she didn't at least try to explore the desire she felt for him, she would regret it for the rest of her life.

THEY LAY TOGETHER on Laura's bed in the dark, her head resting on Javier's bare chest, her fingers tracing his scars, the outline of his muscles, the veins in his arms. He held her close, caressing her bare skin with his fingertips.

"Is it hard for you to be close to me like this without having sex?" she asked.

"Yeah."

"It's hard for me, too. I want *so* desperately to reclaim that part of my life, to put all the bad memories to rest, to feel like a sexual being again, like a woman and not a victim, but I don't know how."

"Maybe we should do something about that."

CHAPTER 19

THEY SLEPT IN the next day, taking turns in the shower, then making breakfast together. While Javier changed to go for his morning run, Laura carried a cup of coffee into her office and began putting together a list of questions to ask Ali's parents, uncle, and friends.

Had there been any new friends or new influences in Ali's life in the past few months? Had he attended any meetings or events where he might have been radicalized? Had he traveled, spent time away from home? Was there any sign that his views had changed? Had he seemed upset or afraid or depressed?

"You working today? It's Saturday."

Laura looked up to see Javier wearing a dark blue fleece jacket and a pair of black running pants. "Zach and the task force are working through the weekend. Why shouldn't I? Besides, I can't really work on this during the week because I'm too busy with stories for the paper."

Javier didn't look convinced. "Childers is sitting in the living room, reading the paper and drinking coffee. I'm headed out. I've got a few things to do after my run, so I'll be gone for at least a couple of hours. Can I pick up anything for you?"

Oh, how she wished she could go with him! It was bright and sunny outside, the crystalline air giving her a perfect view of the Rockies. But she was stuck indoors, and she'd been stuck indoors for what seemed forever.

"How about an order of fresh air and sunshine with spring-time on the side?"

"I'll see what I can do." Javier bent down, kissed her soft and slow on the mouth, then turned and disappeared down the hallway.

Laura found herself pressing her fingers against her lips where they still tingled, her gaze fixed on the doorway where he'd just stood, the words he'd spoken as they'd fallen asleep coming back to her.

Maybe we should do something about that.

It seemed to her that their relationship was on the brink of turning a sexual corner. She didn't know whether she should feel excited—or terrified.

She sipped her coffee and willed herself to focus on writing up her list of questions. When she had her list ready, she called Ali's parents.

They were surprised to hear from her, but gracious, asking about her safety in the wake of the shooting. Still, they were reluctant to speak with her, having been cautioned by their attorneys not to talk to reporters.

"I'm not calling you for an interview. I'm just trying to piece this together, to make sense of what happened. I want to understand why Ali did what he did, and I want to do my part to find the person who killed him. I won't be writing an article about it."

After twenty minutes it was clear to her that they didn't have any information that could be helpful to her—no recollection of new friends or influences in Ali's life, no knowledge of any meetings or activities where he might have been radicalized, no notion of what might have set him off.

"Ali was a good boy." In tears, Karima spoke the words with a mother's undying love. "He got up early every morning and went to school. When he was done with class, he rode his bike to his uncle's store, where he worked hard every weekday from three in the afternoon until the store closed. He worked weekends, too. He worked at the store every day but Friday."

Friday was reserved for prayer, Laura knew.

"His uncle, my husband's brother, was helping him earn money to save for tuition. After work, he came home, ate a late dinner, and studied. He had no time for meetings or making trouble. He would not hurt a fly."

"Thank you, Karima. Once again, I'm so sorry for your loss."

Shaken by the depth of Karima's grief and her unwavering faith in her son, Laura took a minute to compose herself, then went to the kitchen for a fresh cup of coffee. She talked with Childers, then excused herself, steeling herself for a conversation with Ali's uncle. She wished she could interview him in person. She'd be able to get so much more from his answers if only she could see his face, his body language, his eyes.

She sat at her desk, dialed the number, and he answered. "Mr. Al Zahrani, it's Laura Nilsson. I'd like to—"

"I am not talking with reporters! I am sorry for your troubles, but please—"

Laura switched to Arabic, speaking quickly. "I am calling on my own behalf, not as a reporter. Please, if I might, I would like to ask a few questions. I am trying to understand what has happened."

"Why do you need to ask questions, too? The FBI—they came in, tore my store apart, took my computer, asked me questions. The reporters who stand out in the street scaring away my customers try to ask me questions. What do you want with me?"

Laura reminded herself that the man was grieving, just like his brother and sister-in-law. "I want to find the person who killed your nephew. That same person is trying to kill me. Please, if I could just have ten minutes of your time."

"You are not writing an article?"

"Nothing you say to me will be part of a newspaper article—not one word."

Taking his silence as consent, Laura asked him her questions one at a time. "Have any new employees come to work for you in the past three months?"

"No. Everyone who works for me has been with me for years."

"What were his hours?"

"He worked three to nine after school every day but Friday and on the weekends during the daytime. I told the FBI this already."

"Did anyone—new friends or someone from his college—

come to visit Ali at the store and spend time talking with him privately?"

"He worked hard the entire time he was here. No, he had no visitors."

"Did he ever leave in the middle of a shift for any reason?"

"Leave the store? No! I already told you. He worked very hard. He was my right hand. My nephew was hoping to take over the store when I got too old. Now there is no one."

"Did he ever ask you about jihad or seem interested in extreme—"

"You are wasting my time. As I told the FBI, my nephew would have nothing to do with such things. I have customers waiting."

With that, he hung up, leaving Laura with no more information than she'd had before.

JAVIER CUT HIS run short and got busy on his cell phone launching Operation Laura. McBride, Nate, Megan, and Sophie constituted Javier's intelligence collection, but he had no on-call support assets, no tactical operations center. He was going in alone.

It was a high-risk op with significant potential for failure. He couldn't mitigate the risk factors by running scenarios, training, or bringing in a combat support package. He would have to improvise.

To complicate the situation further, this operation would be carried out on what most men found to be treacherous and unfamiliar terrain—a woman's heart. A wounded heart at that. Once he stepped off, anything could happen.

Unfortunately, the one who was most likely to get hurt should the whole thing go sideways was the woman he was hoping to help. Still, he had to try.

He knew his dick wasn't a magic wand, and he realized there was a selfish element to this—if it went the way he hoped it would. But he and Laura had a connection. He knew she felt it every bit as much as he did.

What was it Nate had said?

A woman who's been hurt like she was hurt needs a lot of time and love to heal.

Javier would be leaving in nine days, so there wasn't much time. But no man on earth cared about her the way he did. He wanted to give her this chance.

If he opened the door, would she trust him enough to walk through it?

JAVIER GOT BACK to the flat, relieved Childers, and went looking for Laura. He found her still in her office, documents from the leaked FBI file spread out on her desk, a troubled look on her face. "How's it going?"

"It's not." She tossed down the document she'd been reading and motioned to the hundreds of pages before her. "I talked to Ali's parents and his uncle. I even called two of his instructors. They still insist he's innocent. They can't think of anyone he might have met or anything that might have happened to radicalize him. When I listen to them, he sounds like a great kid. Then I look at the file the FBI compiled on his online activity . . . I went to some of the websites. It's terrible—films of people being killed, murdered children, decapitated bodies."

Javier knew what those sites carried, hate and violence turned into a kind of pornography. "I wish you hadn't. You didn't need to see that."

She rubbed her temple, the telltale sign she had a headache. "What makes a kid turn away from studying accounting to launch a career as a terrorist?"

"If I had the answer to that, I'd have the corner office at the Pentagon. Why don't you take a break and let the FBI and the Marshal Service do their jobs?"

"We *know* at least one other person has to be involved. That person must be to blame for—"

"Or maybe Ali himself is to blame." He walked over to her and began to massage her shoulders. "This isn't good for you. You need to let this go, at least for a while. Your muscles are tight again."

She tilted her head to the side, her eyes drifting shut as he gently kneaded her upper trapezius muscles with his fingertips. "Mmm."

He saw his first chance to improvise. "You know what you

need? A massage. It would help you relax, loosen up your muscles, ease that headache."

She smiled. "That sounds perfect, but somehow I don't think Zach will let me visit a massage therapist."

"A massage therapist? Hey, I am perfectly capable of giving a good massage. It was part of the curriculum for my degree—anatomy, therapeutic modalities, and shit."

Of course, that had been a lifetime ago.

She opened her eyes. "Are you sure that's a good idea? I don't want to make things harder for you."

"Put yourself in my hands, *bella*. You won't regret it."

And Operation Laura was off the ground.

LAURA LAY FACEDOWN on a blanket on her living room floor in front of the fireplace, naked apart from the sheet she'd pulled up to her hips. The blinds had been drawn to give the room a dark, cozy feel. A mix from Javier's iPod played quietly in the background—soft Spanish classical guitar music. It was almost like being in a spa, except that she'd never felt this combination of anxiety and anticipation at a spa.

She felt strangely self-conscious. Before her abduction, she'd never been body shy, never felt the need to cover herself. Now it was her natural instinct to shield her naked body, to protect the part of her that was most vulnerable.

But this was Javier. They'd been lovers, and she knew she had nothing to fear from him. Despite her anxiety, she longed to feel his hands on her again, her pulse picking up at the very idea.

It's just a massage.

Yes, it was. But it had been a long time since Laura had wanted a man to touch her, even in a nonsexual way. And if this massage turned erotic?

Some part of her hoped it wouldn't—and prayed it would.

Javier knelt beside her wearing only his running pants, a bottle of sweet almond oil he'd bought in his hands. He opened it and poured some into his cupped palm, the soft scent filling her head. "I'm going to start with your back and shoulders. Let me know if the pressure is too much for you."

The idea that she was about to get a massage from an elite military operator made her smile. She wanted to make some joke about him giving massages to his fellow SEALs. Then big, warm hands settled in the middle of her back, sliding slowly upward, unleashing delicious sensations. And her thoughts unraveled on a slow sigh.

With deep, slow strokes, he moved his hands up to her shoulders, then down to her lower back, which was surprisingly sore. He zeroed in on the place where it hurt and pressed against it with his thumbs in deep, firm circles. "You're really tight here. It comes from sitting at that damned desk all the time. How is this pressure?"

She wanted to speak out in defense of her desk, but she could barely answer his question. "Good."

His hands were magic. That was the only explanation. As they worked over her back, they found sore spots she didn't know she had—the base of her spine, between her shoulder blades, an area on her right shoulder where she'd hit the ground the night of the shooting—then teased those sore spots away with gentle pressure.

She began to drift, anxiety and anticipation slipping away, yielding to a feeling of drowsy bliss, her sense of place and time fading, her mind aware only of Javier's soothing touch.

He massaged her arms to her fingertips, earning a whimper when his fingers found the knotted muscles in her forearms—the result of typing all the time. He moved on to her legs, rucking up the sheet to expose her upper thighs, then massaging her ankles and feet with his thumbs. And she was in paradise.

JAVIER BENT DOWN, kissed Laura's temple. "Time to turn over, *bella*."

He watched as she turned onto her back, his gaze taking in the sight of her—her long, silky hair, her creamy smooth skin, the fullness of her breasts, the sweet spot where her narrow waist met the curves of her hips. He'd known that touching her like this would turn him on, but what he hadn't expected was the rush of tenderness.

She settled onto her back, her white-blond hair fanned out around her head, her eyes closed. The sheet had slipped off, but she didn't seem to care, whatever shyness she'd felt before having melted away.

He lifted her head into his hands, smoothed silken strands of hair away from her face, and began to explore the muscles of her neck with his fingertips. "Just let the full weight of your head rest in my hands."

She did as he asked, making a little "mmm" sound as he began to work her tight upper trap muscles with his fingers. "You're so good at this."

"Thanks."

He turned her head slightly to one side and then the other, stretching muscles that had knotted up under stress, his gaze falling on her throat. Something twisted in his gut to think that Al-Nassar had threatened daily to decapitate her. His fingers caressed that sensitive skin, and he found himself wanting to feel her pulse against his lips.

He'd done this to help her feel comfortable with being touched, to prove to her that her body was a safe place to be. But while she grew steadily more relaxed, he became more aware of the suffering she'd endured, the true horror of it becoming visceral for him in a way it hadn't been before. It was bad enough to read about it in the paper or hear her speak about it, but to see proof of it . . .

He'd seen her stretch marks last night. What he hadn't seen were the other marks her ordeal had left on her body—faint lines on her back that could only have come from being beaten repeatedly with a strap of some kind.

He knew he couldn't take away the pain she'd suffered or erase the memories she carried. They would be with her for the rest of her life, just like his memories of Krasinski's death and the medevac crash would always be with him. Still, he'd found himself trying to soothe away those scars, to wipe away her suffering.

Then he'd remembered a story Mamá Andreína had told him of old Taino healers, men and women who had the ability to heal others by taking the pain and suffering of the sick into their own bodies and overcoming it. Well, Javier was no healer. He killed for a living. But in a way, that was what he'd been trying to do, even if he hadn't realized it until now.

Maybe that explained why his chest had gone tight. Or

maybe seeing the cruelty of what Al-Nassar had done to her written on her skin was more than he'd been prepared to take on. Or maybe . . .

He was in love with her.

¡Anda pal carajo! Holy shit!

The realization hit him with the force of a fist, unleashing a rush of adrenaline. Even as he tried to deny it, he realized it was true.

He was in love with her.

His hands froze for a moment, the realization transforming the act of touching her into something . . . sacred. It seemed amazing to him that she should trust him, that he should be here with her now, her precious body in his care. Pulse pounding in his veins, he found his rhythm again, moving slowly over her skin, careful to avoid her breasts, uncertain how she'd feel about being touched so intimately.

By the time he finished, she was sound asleep, her face relaxed, her lips slightly parted, her breathing deep and even. He drew up the sheet and draped the throw from the sofa over her to keep her warm. Then, with nothing else he'd rather do, he stretched out beside her and watched her sleep.

CHAPTER 20

LAURA WOKE TO find Javier looking down at her, a soft smile on his face, his head propped up on his elbow. She smiled. "Javi."

"Hey." He brushed a strand of hair off her cheek. "How do you feel?"

"Wonderful." She stretched, her body feeling warm, languid, relaxed.

It was then she remembered she was naked. She took hold of the sheet and discovered he'd drawn a blanket over her, too. It was so like him to do something thoughtful like that. "How long have I been asleep?"

"A little over an hour."

Clutching the sheet to her breasts, she sat up, alarmed to think she'd lost track of time. She glanced at the clock and saw that it was just after three in the afternoon. How could the day have gotten away from her like that?

"Hey, it's Saturday. You're going to spend the rest of the day chilling, *me entendiste*?" He brushed a knuckle over her cheek. "No more work. No more worry."

If any other man had said that, Laura probably would have found it patronizing. But there was something about Javier—his absolute confidence, his ability to understand her needs, his genuine concern for her. He wasn't trying to control her. He truly cared.

The man had shielded her from bullets with his own body, after all.

"So we're just going to spend the whole weekend being together?"

"Sounds good to me." He grinned, got to his feet, her gaze drawn to his broad shoulders, his bare back, the shifting muscles of his incredible butt as he walked into the kitchen. He returned with a glass filled with cold filtered water from her refrigerator dispenser. "Massage can release toxins into your bloodstream. You need to stay well hydrated."

"Thanks." Laura took the glass and drank, only to realize she was intensely thirsty. She drank the entire glass and was about to stand up to get more when she remembered she was naked apart from the sheet. She hesitated, sure he would refill her glass if she asked. And in that moment, she made a choice.

Javier had seen every inch of her body—more than once. There was no reason to hide herself from him.

Heart pounding, she let go of the sheet, stood, and walked naked to the kitchen. She felt the heat of Javier's gaze on her skin as he followed her. She refilled her glass, drank, then turned to face him, some part of her wishing he would just reach out and touch her.

He didn't. "Uh . . . You asked for air and fresh sunshine . . . I, uh . . . managed to get some for you. You might want to . . . put something on."

She watched the direction of his gaze—decidedly south of her chin—and couldn't help but smile. She'd forgotten the thrill, the sense of power, that came with knowing she could arouse a man. "Air and fresh sunshine?"

Ten minutes later, Laura stood with him in the elevator, dressed for the outdoors in jeans, a T-shirt, and a thick hoodie.

"Where are we going?" She watched as he used a special key to bypass the controls and take them to the roof. "Does Zach know about this?"

Javier raised a dark eyebrow. "Would I do anything to put you in danger?"

"No." Yet she knew that, beneath his fleece jacket, he was armed.

He leaned against the wall of the elevator car and crossed

his arms over his chest. "If it makes you feel better, I already cleared it with McBride."

"I trust you, but thanks." It touched her that he had taken time from his day to plan this for her.

The elevator opened onto a landing that led to a flight of stairs ending at a heavy steel door. Using another key, Javier unlocked the door—and they were outside.

A cool breeze caught her hair, sunshine warm on her face as she glanced around at her strange surroundings. Laura had never been on the roof of the building. It spread out around her the length of a city block, air-conditioning units and ventilation ducts jutting out of a surface that resembled pitch.

"Here you go, *bella*—fresh air and sunshine."

She took a few steps, tilted her face toward the sun, filled her lungs. It felt good to be outside, to see the sky, to hear the thrumming of the city around her. She glanced over at Javier, who stood nearby watching her, his gaze warm. "Thank you."

He took her hand, kissed it, slid his fingers between hers. *"De nada."*

THEY WALKED SLOW laps around the roof, Javier savoring the feel of Laura's hand in his as Laura talked about her memories of growing up in Sweden. She didn't seem to notice the DUSM teams in place on the nearby rooftops. Then again, they were trying to be inconspicuous.

"Every summer, we spent five weeks in our summerhouse on Sandhamn, a little island in the Stockholm archipelago. The house is just off the beach, so I spent a lot of time playing near the water. My grandmother and I would go into the forest to pick berries, which she would make into jam or serve fresh for dessert. Some nights there would be bonfires on the beach. My grandmother would sneak out a bottle of akvavit and get tipsy. I think my mother had to carry me inside more than once after I'd fallen asleep beside her."

Javier could imagine that—little white-blond Laura curled up like a kitten at her mother's feet. "Your grandmother drank akvavit?"

Laura smiled and nodded. "She still does."

"You don't mention your father much."

"He died when I was six. A traffic accident. My mother never remarried."

Way to go, chacho.

"I'm sorry."

She shrugged it off. "It was many years ago. Enough about me. Tell me more about your summers in Humacao."

"You picked berries with your grandmother. My grand-mother had a big vegetable garden. She put us all to work in it. Whenever I complained that I didn't want to pull weeds or dig, she would tell me I didn't have to help with the entire garden, just the parts I hoped to see on my dinner plate."

Laura laughed, the sound sweet to Javier's ears. "She sounds very clever, your Mamá Andreína."

"She is. Most of the time we just ran wild with our cousins—playing baseball, lying down in the grass to watch the clouds, listening to drums play bomba. I think those sum-mers saved me—that and joining the Teams."

"What do you mean?"

Javier had never shared this story with anyone but Nate. But Laura had his heart, so there was no point in keeping anything else from her.

"In high school, I got mixed up with a bad crowd—one of the local Bronx gangs. My little brother Yadiel—he thought I was the shit, man. He followed me around like a puppy. One night, I got into it with a rival gang, started shooting off at the mouth. It got ugly—fists, knives. Then when we were walk-ing home, a car drove by, and I heard a gunshot. They were firing at me but hit Yadiel."

Javier could still remember the shocked look on his broth-er's face, the helplessness and terror he'd felt as his brother's blood spread in a pool of crimson on the sidewalk. "I tried to help him, tried to stop the bleeding, but . . . He was dead before the ambulance arrived. He hung around with me because he thought I was cool, but it got him killed. He was fourteen."

Laura looked up at him. "Oh, Javi!"

He avoided eye contact, gazing out over the rooftops of LoDo. "I'll never forget the sound of my mother's scream when she heard he was dead. My father yelled at me, told me it had been my job to keep him safe, that Yadiel had only gotten killed because he'd been hanging with me. I was sent off to Humacao the next day, spent the rest of that year living with Mamá Andreína. She put me back in line, put me to work. She told me I needed to become the hero Yadiel believed I was."

Laura's voice was quiet, sympathetic. "That's a lot of pressure to put on a troubled teenager's shoulders."

"Sometimes it's the weight of responsibility that makes a person stronger. I left the gang, graduated, went to college, became a trainer."

"That's the real reason you became a SEAL, isn't it?"

"I suppose it is. I've carried a photo of Yadiel with me on every mission."

She gave his hand a squeeze. "Your grandmother must be very proud of the man you've become."

"Yeah. She keeps a candle lit for me, prays novenas to Santa Clara for me whenever I'm deployed."

"And your parents? What happened wasn't really your fault. The blame lies with the person who pulled the trigger. They must know that."

"They've forgiven me." But Javier would never be able to make up for his brother's death in their eyes.

For a time they walked in silence, the sun now low on the horizon, spilling golden rays over the mountains, making all the colors richer—the pale blond of her hair, the rosy flush of her cheeks, even the ice blue of her eyes. They went to stand on the western side of the roof, Laura in front of Javier, his arm around her waist, the street below them busy with people headed out on the town.

Javier glanced at his watch. "Time to get inside, *bella*."

Tonight, he had special plans.

LAURA STARTED THE fire again. "I want to take a shower before I start supper. Think you can wait, or are you starving?"

"Don't worry about me. Take your time." His gaze narrowed. "And, hey, put on something really pretty afterward."

"Something pretty?"

"Yeah. Just put on . . . you know . . . an evening gown or something formal—whatever you would wear to a fancy restaurant."

"Are we going out on a *date*?"

His lips curved in a slow smile, making her pulse skip. "Go take your shower."

Okay, so he was keeping secrets.

Laura showered and shaved her legs, a sense of anticipation humming through her as she tried to guess what Javier was up to. She dried her hair, put on eye shadow and mascara, then walked naked to her closet, wondering what to wear. If only she knew *why* she was dressing up . . .

She looked through her small collection of cocktail and evening gowns. Before her abduction, she'd had dozens. Now, she had only a few, each one seeming less appealing than the last. The dark blue beaded velvet dress she'd bought for the symphony was too much. The black lace dress might work, but it was short—great for happy hour and parties, but maybe not a formal restaurant. Her yellow silk sheath dress was meant for summer. That left only the floor-length gown she'd bought for the foreign ministry dinner in Stockholm.

She searched the back of her dress rack and found it still in the garment bag. She unzipped the bag and removed the dress from its hanger, her gaze taking in the richness of the cloth—black silk that was adorned with gold beading. She'd fallen in love with it the moment she'd seen it, but she'd never worn it. When she'd put it on the night of the dinner—her first public event since her rescue—she'd felt uncomfortable with the plunging neckline and the male interest it would bring. But now . . .

It had been a long time since she'd *wanted* to attract a man's attention.

She walked to her chest of drawers and searched for a bra that could handle the neckline, then found the matching panties. The beading made the dress heavy, and getting into it was a bit of work, involving a hidden back zipper, lots of shimmying, and little beads that caught in her hair. But when she was done, the results were worth it.

She looked into the mirror and found herself smiling at her reflection, a feeling of giddiness running through her as she imagined Javier's reaction. The gown fit her perfectly, enhancing her curves, the gold beading glinting as she moved.

She touched up her makeup, added a deep red lip stain,

dabbed scent behind her ears and between her breasts—and then she was ready. Or she *hoped* she was ready.

She stood at her bedroom door, one hand on the doorknob, her heart beating fast. She knew she was safe with Javier. Why did she suddenly feel afraid?

Her mother's words came back to her.

It is time for you to live again, Laura.

Wasn't that what she'd vowed to do in that courtroom?

Subduing her fear, she turned the knob, opened the door, and walked toward the living room, her feet stopping when she saw. "Oh, Javi!"

He stood near the table wearing a charcoal-gray three-piece suit over a white shirt, the colors of the fabric bringing out his coal-black hair and brown eyes. His face was clean shaven, his hands in his pants pockets, a black tie hanging untied from his neck. She'd never seen him in a suit before, the sight of him taking her breath away.

His gaze met hers, then dropped, gliding slowly down her body and up again, his brow furrowing, the breath leaving his lungs in a slow exhale. "You look . . . *beautiful.*"

She felt heat rush into her cheeks. "Thank you."

It was only then she noticed the rest of it—the scent of something delicious, the candles, Latin music playing softly in the background, champagne chilling on the counter, the bouquet of red roses on the table, which had been set for two.

She stared, amazed. "What . . . ?"

How had he managed all of this by himself today?

He walked slowly toward her, took her hand in his, and held it to his lips, his gaze locking with hers. "Last night, you told me you wanted to reclaim your life, to feel like a woman again, but you didn't know how to make that happen. I thought maybe if I paved the way, it might be easier for you to take the next steps. But there's no pressure. If we just enjoy a nice dinner together dressed in these very fine threads, that's great. This is your night, *bella.* Whatever happens—it's up to you."

JAVIER SAW TEARS well up in Laura's eyes, watched her blink them back, an expression of surprise and anxiety giving way to a wobbly smile.

"I . . . I don't know what to say. Thank you." She reached up with one hand, caught a curl at his temple, and teased it with her fingers. "You look so handsome. I've never seen you in a suit."

"There's a reason for that. I don't own one. This belongs to McBride." He'd dropped it off, together with the wine, when Laura was in the shower.

"It fits like it was made for you." She fussed with the shoulder seams, ran her palms down the vest, caught the loose ends of the tie. "Going for the casual look?"

"Yeah. Nah. I . . . I have no clue how to tie it." He'd tried looking up directions on the Internet, but he'd run out of time.

"I'd tie it for you, but I don't know how to do it either."

"To hell with it." He drew the tie off and tossed it onto the sofa. "Hungry?"

She smiled. "Starving!"

He drew out a chair for her, his gaze drawn to the gentle curve of her shoulder as she sat, the subtle musk of her perfume filling his nostrils.

He bent down and pressed a kiss to the side of her throat. "You smell incredible."

Watch it, pendejo.

It was important that he let Laura set the pace, and that meant keeping his hands and his mouth off her until she asked him to touch her—not an easy job when she smelled this sweet, her creamy skin gleaming like satin, the swells of her breasts . . .

Oh, no, he was *not* going to spend the evening staring at them.

"I'll get our food." He walked into the kitchen, grabbed a hot pad, and took the serving dishes out of the oven where they'd been warming. "I hope you like it. I slaved in the kitchen all day."

He set the two dishes down on the table, tossing the hot pad onto the counter, his gaze fixed on her face. With Megan's help, he'd found a restaurant that served a meal that almost matched the last dinner they'd shared in Dubai—roast duck breast, wild rice with mushrooms, asparagus.

Laura's eyes went wide. "Where did you get all of this?"

"That's classified. Champagne?"

"I would love some."

"This is . . ." He lifted the bottle out of the ice bucket, glanced at the label, and realized he couldn't read a thing. ". . . French."

He wished he knew something about wine, about cuisine, about the classy side of life, but his expertise was limited to firearms, explosives, covert ops.

She smiled up at him, a glint of humor in her eyes. "Perfect."

He poured them each a glass, then sat across the table from her, the surge of emotion he felt when he looked into her eyes making it hard for him to speak. "To everything you want in life."

She raised her glass and clinked it against his, a telltale sheen in her eyes.

With a Spanish guitar mix playing in the background, they started on their supper, the conversation awkward at first. Laura complimented the food, the wine, the music. And for a few minutes Javier was afraid he'd gone overboard and had only managed to leave her feeling overwhelmed.

Then she reached across the table and took his hand. "This is the sweetest thing anyone has ever done for me. Thank you."

He wanted to tell her he loved her but couldn't. He didn't want to add to her confusion or put her on the spot tonight. She had enough to work through without dealing with his emotions. So he kept his words simple. He kept them true.

"I would do anything for you, *bella*."

CHAPTER 21

FEELING WARM AND tipsy, Laura rested her head against Javier's chest, her arms around his neck as they danced barefoot in slow circles. He sang along to the music in soft Spanish, one big hand at her waist, his other arm holding her close. He filled her senses, his body hard and strong against hers, his voice smooth and beautiful, his masculine scent as heady as the champagne.

Some part of her had melted hours ago under the force of this subtle but sensual seduction, her desire for him undeniable. Never had any man made her feel so cared for, so special. And still she hesitated, not wanting to start something she wouldn't be able to finish. He'd said that whatever happened was up to her, but how would he feel if she got into bed with him only to shut down?

Don't think about that. Just enjoy the moment.

She closed off her mind, determined to feel her way through this night, to let her heart and body guide her. She breathed him in, let her mind drift, savoring the experience of being in his arms, his heartbeat steady against her cheek, his embrace a refuge from the tumult of her life. Somehow her lips found their way to his Adam's apple, his singing ending on a quick exhale as she kissed him there. That kiss led to another and another, her lips tracing a path up the side of his throat to the sensitive skin beneath his ear, his pulse quickening against her mouth.

But giving herself a taste of him only made her hungry for more. She turned his face toward her, drew his head down, and kissed him.

He gave a soft moan, his lips responding to hers, matching every nip, every caress, every flick of the tongue without taking control of the kiss from her, his restraint both arousing and sweet. She yielded, arching against him, parting her lips for him, welcoming the heat of his tongue. He slid a hand into her hair to cradle the back of her head as he angled his mouth over hers, taking the kiss deeper.

Lost in the moment, she slipped her hands inside his jacket, sliding her palms over the rough fabric of his vest to feel the hard muscle beneath. She had never touched Al-Nassar, never put her hands on him, the act of caressing Javier resurrecting only good memories. One by one she undid the buttons, sliding off his vest and his jacket with it, the white cloth of his shirt a stark contrast to his dark hair and brown skin.

"I want to undress you," she whispered against his mouth. "I haven't touched a man since . . . *since you*."

"Come." He took her hand and led her to her bedroom.

Her heart gave a nervous skip as she turned on her bedside lamp, being in the bedroom more intimidating than the living room. And for a moment she stood with her back to him, trepidation snaking its way up from her belly. She did *not* want to hurt him, didn't want to disappoint him.

His hands came to rest on her shoulders, his mouth brushing butterfly kisses against the side of her neck, the sensation making her shiver. She dimmed the light and turned to face him.

He ran a thumb down her cheek, emotion burning in his eyes. "Do whatever you want with me."

Under the heat of his gaze, she began to unbutton his shirt, the cloth giving off a pleasing starchy smell that mingled enticingly with the scent of his skin—salt and fresh linen. She pushed the shirt over his shoulders and down his arms, letting it fall to the floor, leaving his chest bare.

She stepped back, let her gaze feast on the sight of him, heat flaring to life in her belly. The play of light on his satiny brown skin. The twin bulges of his biceps. The sculpted curves of his shoulders. The slant of his collarbones. The smooth planes of his pecs. The red lines of his scars. The flat brown disks of his nipples. The deep groove that bisected his abdomen. The firm ridges of his six-pack. The angles of his obliques as they sloped toward his groin.

God, he was beautiful.

She reached out with both hands, letting them follow the same path her gaze had taken, indulging in the male feel of him, warm, smooth skin stretched over hard muscle. She heard his quick intake of breath as she ran her thumbs over his nipples, felt his abdomen tense as she grazed it with her fingertips, watched his hands slowly clench as she stroked the length of his obliques.

But she wasn't finished.

She grasped the waistband of his trousers with trembling hands, struggling with the hidden button. His hands closed over hers and dealt with the button, leaving the zipper to her. She unzipped him, then pushed his trousers away from his narrow hips and down his thighs. He kicked the trousers aside, standing before her wearing nothing but black boxer briefs, the hard ridge of his erection outlined in sharp detail.

The breath left her lungs.

The closest she'd come to sex since her rescue was fantasizing about this body, about Javier, and now here he was, standing before her, ready to do whatever pleased her.

But what was that? She wasn't sure.

If this had been that weekend in Dubai, he would have already picked her up and laid her down on the bed or pinned her against a wall, his sexual assertiveness like nothing she'd experienced before. But this time he was waiting for her.

Don't think. Just feel.

Ignoring her fears, she turned her back to him and drew her hair aside. "Unzip me?"

She felt Javier tug at the zipper, felt her gown fall open in the back. He lifted the gown over her head, let it fall to the floor, a finger tracing down her spine, making her gasp and shiver. Wearing only her bra and panties, she turned in his arms, his gaze sliding over her like a caress, the heat that emanated from his body warming her.

She thought he was about to kiss her again. Instead, he slowly sank to his knees, grasped her waist, and pressed his lips to her belly.

Her stretch marks. He was kissing her stretch marks.

Tears stung her eyes, her throat tight, the sweetness of his gesture as overwhelming as it was unexpected, his complete acceptance of her body and what she'd been through feeling like redemption.

JAVIER WANTED TO take it all away—the pain she'd suffered, the violence, the fear. But he couldn't. Instead, he kissed the part of her that had been hurt.

He'd always been closer to the Puerto Rican side of the family than the Cherokee side, but his father had taught him when he was still a boy that men should always show respect for women because women carried inside them the place where life began. Laura had been violated, this sacred part of her abused and exploited, the baby she'd been forced to bring into this world stolen from her.

If only he could give back what had been taken and heal that pain . . .

Her fingers curled in his hair as he pressed his lips against the faint silver lines on her skin again and again, her breath catching on a little sob.

But he hadn't meant to make her cry.

He slid his way up her body, wiped the tears from her cheeks with his thumbs, and kissed her slow and hard and deep. She wrapped her arms around his neck, kissed him as if her life depended on it. And he remembered.

She had asked to touch *him*.

He stretched out lengthwise on the bed, watching as she crawled onto the bed beside him. She was like a vision from a sailor's wet dream, her breasts swelling over the cups of her bra, the dark lace making her skin seem impossibly pale. He ached to touch her, to kiss her, but she hadn't asked him to do either—yet.

He'd rather eat his own balls than ruin this for her.

She knelt beside him and slid her hand slowly over his chest, a look of sensual tension on her face, her hair spilling over one shoulder. "You are so beautiful."

He was already so turned on that he had no idea how he was going to get through the night without humiliating himself, and her touch only made it harder, need for her drumming in his chest like a heartbeat. Unable to stop himself, he reached out and caught the weight of her hair in one hand. "I'm glad you like what you see."

But *she* was the beautiful one.

Holding her hair aside, he watched as she bent over him and began to scatter kisses across his chest, her lips scorching a trail on his skin, the sight every bit as arousing as the sensation. Her hot tongue flicked one of his nipples and then the other, making his breath catch, the lace of her bra abrading his skin where she brushed against him. And the ache in his groin grew sharp.

Staying passive like this was new for him—and it wasn't easy. Whether it was the old *Boricua* machismo or the drive that had pushed him up to the top of the enlisted ranks, it was in his nature to take control, to lead. Instinct told him to get her out of her bra and panties, draw her beneath him, and taste every inch of her until she forgot to be afraid. But he willed himself to remain still, yielding control to her. And yet as difficult as it was to surrender, there was something erotic about it, too.

Frustratingly, aggravatingly, maddeningly erotic.

¡Puñeta!

Did she have any idea what she was doing to him?

She nipped the ridge of one of his obliques, making him jerk, her lashes fluttering as she looked up at him, her mouth curving in a teasing smile.

So she *did* know—and it was clear she was aroused, too, her pupils dilated, her breathing fast, her nipples puckered beneath black lace.

Somehow that made it harder to endure, her kisses more sensual now, her warm tongue sliding over his skin, her teeth nipping him as she kissed her way with unbearable slowness across his belly. He'd been hot for her before she'd kissed him, days and nights of holding her and sleeping beside her fueling his desire. Now his skin was so sensitive that the slightest brush of her fingers made his muscles jerk, his cock straining against his boxer briefs and hard enough to split wood.

She traced the line of body hair that ran southward from

his navel, her fingertips teasing the skin at the edge of his boxer briefs. Slowly she drew them down, his cock springing free. "I want to taste you."

Did she expect him to object?

"Are you sure, *bella*?" He smoothed her hair back from her face, her lips wet and swollen from kissing him.

"Yeah." She smiled, a sweet, sexy smile that made his heart skip.

She took him in hand and began to stroke him slowly from root to tip, a look of curious fascination on her face as if he were terrain she was exploring again after a long absence. Her motions were cautious at first, almost awkward. He would have reached down to guide her, but giving a hand job must have been a lot like riding a bike, because she got the hang of it quickly.

Hell, yeah, she did.

Javier found himself holding his breath, his hips rising to meet her strokes as she built up a rhythm, his body already perilously close to orgasm. Then she bent down and took him into the heat of her mouth, and he knew he was in trouble.

¡Diache! Hell!

It felt so damned good, her tongue swirling around the aching head of his cock, her mouth and fist moving in tandem up and down the shaft. He caught her hair with his fists, held it back to give himself a view—and instantly regretted it, the sight of her devouring him bringing him to the brink. He fought to relax, to keep his hips from bucking against her, to enjoy the feel of it for as long as he could—or at least long enough not to embarrass himself.

You're a SEAL, damn it, not a minuteman.

"You are *so* good," he managed to say. "If you don't stop now . . ."

Those were the last coherent words out of his mouth, his eyes drifting shut, his breathing ragged as she brought him to the brink, then finished him with her fist, pleasure scorching through him as he came, leaving him out of breath.

He felt the bed shift and opened his eyes to see Laura reaching for a tissue. She wiped off her hand, dropped the tissue in the trash, then reached for another. He took it from her, cleaned himself off, then drew her into his arms.

"If tonight was supposed to be about you, why am I the one who just came?"

LAURA NESTLED AGAINST Javier's chest, wanting him to understand but not sure she could explain. "If you think I didn't enjoy that, you're wrong. I haven't been able to *give* anything to a man since we were together. It was all just . . . taken."

Taken, stolen, beaten from her.

But tonight she'd been able to bring pleasure to a man she cared deeply about while staying in control. It had been intensely erotic to see his muscular body straining against her touch, to watch him come apart when he'd climaxed, his muscles tensing, his body arching off the bed, his eyes squeezed shut.

"Watching you, seeing the effect I had on you—I loved it."

It had been more than a little arousing. The aching wetness between her thighs was proof of that. She hadn't felt this sexually alive since . . .

Of course, it had been much easier to focus on him than to have his attention—and his hands—on her. This way, she hadn't had to worry that she might freak out and make him feel rejected.

She could see on Javier's face that he didn't understand, but that was probably because she hadn't explained it very well.

He stroked her hair. "What would you say if I told you I wanted to do to you what you just did to me?"

She felt a clench deep in her belly, her pulse spiking partly out of fear and partly out of raw sexual need. It had been so long since she'd viewed her body as a source of pleasure rather than a weapon to be used against her. "I . . . I don't know."

"Would you let me try?"

Her pulse raced faster. "I don't want to hurt your feelings or—"

He propped himself up on his elbow. "I would never do anything you didn't want me to do, but it would help me if you told me what you're afraid of."

"I'm afraid of hurting your feelings, of damaging our friendship."

"And I told you that is never going to happen."

She might as well come out with it. "There are . . . some things you should know. You don't have to worry about getting me pregnant because I had my tubes tied. I had never planned on having children anyway, and after what happened . . ."

He could understand that.

"Also, I don't know how I would feel about you being on top of me or inside me and . . . and no anal play."

"I thought we agreed in Dubai that neither of us was into that last one." Understanding dawned on his face. "Aw, God, Laura, *no*. I'm so sorry."

She blinked back tears, willing herself to look straight into his eyes. "My body was a battleground for so long, and I . . . I don't know how to let you get closer."

He sat up and ran his knuckles over her cheek. "I can think of a thousand ways to make love to you, *bella*, a thousand ways to satisfy you. Forget about everything but us. Just let me touch you. Tell me what feels good."

His words sent a tremor through her, hope warring with despair inside her.

He teased her lips with his, traced their outline with his tongue, nipped them with his teeth, tiny bites that brought only pleasure. And her lips began to burn. Then he claimed her mouth with a slow, deep kiss that she knew would drive darker thoughts from her mind—if she let it.

Don't think. Feel.

She leaned into him, her lips parting for him, her tongue accepting his, the warmth of his body and his strength seeming to surround her. By the time he broke the kiss, they were both breathless, Laura's heart pounding so hard she was certain he could feel it against his chest.

"Laura, mi amor." One of his hands slid into her hair, tilting her head back to expose her throat, his lips pressing kisses against her cheeks, his tongue teasing the whorl of her ear, his teeth nipping the tender skin just above her pulse.

Shivers danced across Laura's skin, her breath coming in sighs.

"I want to see you. I want to feel you. Can I take this off?" One hand tugged on her bra strap.

"Yes."

He sought for the clasp, unhooked it, then tossed her bra aside, leaning back to look at her. His brown eyes went black as he stared at her breasts, her nipples drawing tighter under the heat of his perusal. "So beautiful. I want to touch and taste you the way you touched and tasted me."

She nodded.

Don't think. Feel.

He cupped and lifted her breasts, his thumbs making slow circles over her areolas, the sensation sweet, shards of heat splintering through her, the ache between her thighs growing stronger. "Do you like that?"

"Oh, yes!"

He teased her nipples with the pads of his thumbs, caressed them with his palms, pinched and rolled them with his fingertips. Then with a moan, he arched her back, bent down, and began to suckle her, the wonderful sensation making Laura gasp.

She heard herself exhale in a long, trembling sigh, feeling the heat of his mouth and the friction of his tongue all the way to her womb. She grasped his shoulders and held on, every tug of his lips heightening her need for him, until her hips began to shift impatiently beneath her, the ache inside her begging to be answered.

Javier withdrew his mouth, making her moan in frustration. He turned her, brought her hips square with the edge of the bed, then knelt between her thighs. "Now I can reach all of you."

"Yes, Javi, please!"

He leaned in, cupping one breast with his hand, holding it for his mouth, his tongue flicking lightly over the aching, puckered bud while the other hand slid slowly, agonizingly down her side, over the curve of her hip, along the outside of her thigh and up the inside again, his fingers teasing and tickling her skin. "Is it okay if I touch you—"

Before he could finish asking the question, her hips answered for her, moving against his hand.

He grinned, his finger seeking and finding her clitoris. "I

don't get why women are afraid of how they look here. You are so damned hot, Laura, and so wet. I can't wait to get my mouth on you."

Her heart gave a hard knock.

He began to stroke her, teasingly at first, his mouth finding her nipples and suckling her again, the two sensations together almost more than she could handle, the ache inside her making it impossible to hold still. Her hands moved restlessly over his shoulders, her anticipation building.

When his mouth left her breasts it was almost a relief because she knew where he was headed. But he wasn't in a hurry to get there. He trailed kisses over her rib cage and down to her belly, flicking her overly sensitive skin with his tongue, making her body jerk just as she'd done to him earlier.

Without breaking the rhythm he'd built with his hand, he ducked one shoulder down and then the other, catching her thighs, nudging them farther apart. "Mmm . . . Beautiful."

But rather than putting his mouth on her, he began to kiss and nibble her inner thighs, the exquisite sensation raising bumps on her skin, making her shiver.

She sank backward onto the bed and lifted her feet onto his shoulders, all hesitation fading in the face of his sensual onslaught.

"Oh, yeah, *bella*, open for me." He parted her labia, lowered his mouth to her, and tasted her with a single long lick.

She gasped, her back arching, her fingers curling in his hair.

He licked her again and got the same response, his groan proof that he was enjoying the sight and taste of her. He flicked her clit with his tongue, drew it into his mouth, and sucked, tugging on her with his lips.

Laura had forgotten what it felt like to have a man's mouth on her, had forgotten the staggering pleasure of it. She buried her fingers in his hair, let her knees fall open to give him more room, and was rewarded with a deep groan, the low sound sending vibrations through her swollen flesh.

She was trembling now, her breath coming in pants and gasps, his mouth working magic. Some part of her had longed for this, longed to give herself to him, to be strung out on him, to reel out of control at his touch. Oh, God, it was sweet!

But that delicious ache inside her—it wouldn't go away. She felt a throbbing emptiness, her body yearning to be filled, needing to be filled.

She panted out the words. *"Inside me."*

With a moan, he slipped a finger and then two inside her, stretching her, filling her with slick, deep strokes, driving her toward the edge.

And then she was flying, orgasm shimmering through her in blazing, golden waves, the bliss of it tearing a cry from her throat as she was lifted skyward, then left to float breathless and weightless among the clouds.

After a time—she couldn't say how long—Javier drew her into a sitting position, scooped her into his arms, and lowered her to her pillow, stretching out beside her. His gaze was warm, his lips wet, his skin drenched in her scent.

"A thousand ways?" Tremors of pleasure still shivered through her.

He smiled, ran a finger over her lower lip. "That was just one."

CHAPTER 22

JAVIER DIPPED THE strawberry first into melted chocolate, then into brown sugar, and then into the dish of sour cream. He held the strawberry to Laura's lips, watched her take it with her tongue.

Her eyes drifted shut as she chewed. "Mmm."

She sat beside him wearing her bathrobe over hot-pink panties and a white cotton tank top that left little to his imagination, her hair still wet from their shower.

He leaned in and licked a spot of chocolate off her lower lip. "That good, huh?"

She opened her eyes, smiled. "Your turn."

She selected a fat, red strawberry for him, dipped it in the three small dishes, then held it to his lips.

His gaze fixed on hers, he took her offering and chewed, the sweet-tart-chocolate taste combination surprising him as it exploded across his tongue. "Mmm. Amazing."

She'd been right when she'd said it was a culinary orgasm.

They'd already polished off their eggs Benedict—which, Javier had discovered, was just a name for poached eggs served on an English muffin with Canadian bacon and some kind of lemony sauce—and were finishing their mimosas and the strawberries he'd grabbed on the way back from his run. He hadn't had many breakfasts as nice as this, and he knew he would never forget it, not only because of the food and the company, but also because it had followed one of the most incredible nights of his life.

He would remember every moment of last night until the day he died. Last night, he had watched Laura come back to life in his arms. She had trusted him, and together they'd found a way to break through her fear. No, they hadn't had conventional sex—no tab A in slot B—and yet it had been one of the most sensual nights of his life. If he'd doubted that he was in love with her, those doubts had been blown to bits.

Wouldn't the guys get a kick out of this if they knew? The Cobra was hopelessly, helplessly in love—and happy about it.

You are in deep shit, chacho.

As for Laura, she'd slept through the night without a single nightmare—which was more than he could say for himself—and seemed more like her old self than she had since he'd arrived in Denver, more playful, more lighthearted, a smile on her beautiful face more often than not. Just seeing her happier made him happy.

They'd already made love once this morning, making creative use of touch and tongues and tile walls—not to mention Laura's pulsing showerhead.

"That's two," he'd whispered when she'd sunk against him in a boneless, postorgasmic stupor.

There was nothing like sex to wake up a man—or a woman—in the morning. And, despite his nightmare, this was the most relaxed he'd felt in months.

He reached for another strawberry, dipped it, and held it out for her. "Where'd you learn this? Is this the way your grandma serves strawberries, because, man, if it is, I got to figure out how you stay so skinny."

She raised a hand to her mouth, fighting not to laugh while she chewed. "I learned this from my college roommate. She learned it from some other woman and used it to try to seduce some guy she was seeing."

"She went to all this trouble for that? All she had to do was tell the man he'd be getting puss—" The annoyed look on her face cut his words short. "Uh . . . I mean . . . did it work?"

The corners of Laura's eyes crinkled, and she burst into laughter. "Just so you know, the p-word doesn't offend me provided you use it for the correct body part and not to insult people. And, honestly, Javi, I think all women understand that about men. In this case, she was looking for more than sex."

"Oh." Okay, that made sense. "She was?"

Laura dipped a strawberry for him and held it. "I think Kim wanted to do the traditional thing—marriage, kids, the dog."

"You got something against dogs?" He took the fruit from her and was again blown away by the taste.

"I've always been focused on my career."

And Javier's mood dropped a notch.

They fed each other the rest of the strawberries, the conversation drifting while Javier tried to sort through his feelings. Yeah, the nightmare had sucked. It had been the same nightmare he'd been having off and on for the past three months. He'd been lying wounded in the dirt, holding Krasinski's hand, trying to keep him conscious, only to discover as the medevac helo went up in a fireball that it was Yadiel bleeding out beside him. But Javier didn't think the nightmare was to blame for how he felt right now.

Then it hit him.

When they'd met in Dubai, Laura had been clear that she didn't plan on getting married and having kids. He'd felt the same way. They'd both agreed—no strings.

But now Javier found himself wanting strings.

How was Laura going to feel about that?

She looked into the small dipping dishes. "I wish we had more strawberries. We've got leftover chocolate."

Javier set his thoughts aside and smiled. "I know just what to do with that."

Oh, yeah. She was going to like number three.

LAURA LEANED BACK against Javier's chest in a tub of hot water, feeling languid and sleepy, little tremors of pleasure still shivering through her, her body replete, the chocolate that hadn't been licked off her skin now washed away. "I hope you're enjoying this as much as I am."

He kissed her hair, one arm encircling her just above her breasts, his fingers caressing her shoulder. "You know I am."

"How did I get so lucky?" She trailed her fingertips over his forearm.

"Hmm?" he asked.

"One night in Dubai, a man steps in to save me from two drunk Russians, and the next thing I know, I'm in bed with him."

"Nah, not in bed."

He was right. The first time *hadn't* been in bed.

"The next thing I know, he's shagging me against the wall."

"It's a miracle we weren't arrested."

True. But that wasn't the point.

"Now, more than three years later, that same man steps back into my life and changes *everything*. I never thought I could have this again. I thought . . . I thought this part of me was dead. Thank you, Javi."

He kissed her hair again. "Hey, all I did was open the door."

"Oh, you did more than that."

By some miracle, Laura felt almost whole.

He nuzzled her ear. "Well, I am pretty good in the sack— or so you've said."

She smiled. "You're very humble about it, too."

Javier wasn't just the most creative lover she'd ever had or the most confident, but he was also the most thoughtful. She'd seen that side of him in Dubai, but she'd come to appreciate it even more last night, perhaps because that was what she needed most this time. He'd been patient with her, getting her consent each time, making certain that she felt comfortable—and then driving her wild.

It amazed her to think that he was still holding back. If she'd just met him, she would have no idea how forceful he could be, how physical sex could be with him. As much as she treasured the gentleness he'd shown her, some part of her was beginning to long for the thrill of his more aggressive side— and the feel of him inside her.

She hadn't found a way to tell him yet, still afraid that she would freak out the moment she felt him thrust into her. But the ache was there.

She wanted him—all of him.

But there was still time for that. In Dubai, they'd had only three nights and two days, and that had been magical. They still had more than a week to be together, and . . .

Her pulse spiked.

More than a week.

That was no time at all.

In the blink of an eye, this would be over. He would go back to the dangerous job that had almost cost him his life, and she would stay here in isolation, waiting for the cops to catch this killer, working at the paper, fighting to get Klara back. And God only knew whether they'd see each other again.

No, she couldn't let that happen this time.

She decided to come right out and ask. "Can we stay in touch this time?"

"Are you asking for my phone number?"

"E-mail, phone number, address—and your grandmother's, too."

"You want to call my *abuelita*?"

"If anything were to happen to you, I would want to know."

"Well, it's kind of sudden. You're talking about taking our relationship to a whole new level." He kissed her cheek, his voice going soft. "You got it, *bella*."

By Sunday evening they'd made it to number seven. Laura knew it was humanly impossible to reach a thousand in the time they had, but that didn't mean they couldn't try.

Javier had made love to her with his mouth, his fingers, her massaging showerhead. He'd even made them both come by rubbing her clitoris with the hard length of his erect cock. They'd tasted each other on the bed, in the shower, on the table, on the floor, and still Javier kept coming up with ideas that were new to her.

Ice cubes. Side-lying sixty-nine. A dab of minty mouthwash on his tongue.

She was just finishing the supper dishes and thinking about the start of the workweek when she heard a buzzing sound. She turned to find him standing there, one dark eyebrow arched, her blue jelly vibrator buzzing and rotating at high speed in his hand. Heat flooded her face. "Oh, my God! Where—"

"You left one of the bathroom drawers open."

Helvete! Damn!

She reached for it.

He angled his upper body away from her and held it out of her reach. "Hold on. I've got a right to check out my competition. Are you blushing? You are."

She pressed her palms to her cheeks. "I don't blush."

He leaned in, still holding the vibrator out of reach. "The hell you don't. Look—your cheeks are all pink."

She lunged and tried again to grab it from him, torn between amusement and irritation. "Give that to me!"

"You want it, *bella*?" He grinned, took a step back. "You're going to have to let me use it on you."

She gaped at him, heat suffusing her face—and other parts of her body. "Fine. On one condition."

"Sure." He grinned, so sure of himself, so smug. "What's that?"

"I get to use it on you, too." The look of shock on his face made her laugh. "What's the matter? Is the big, bad special operator afraid of a little sex toy?"

His eyes narrowed. "You got a deal."

She hadn't expected that.

Next time he was here, she would hide the damned thing.

He grinned again. "You didn't think I'd call your bluff, did you? Now get on into the bedroom—and get naked."

She walked to her bedroom, anticipation beginning to build despite her embarrassment, Javier one step behind her. She'd never imagined doing something like this, but then Javier had always managed to surprise her. She undressed, dropping her clothes on the floor. "Not sure why I bothered to put clothes on at all today."

"You complaining?"

"Absolutely not." She looked over her shoulder at him, then crawled onto the bed, teasing him with a view of her from behind. "Maybe I should just stay naked."

"I like that idea." He nodded, his gaze fixed right where she knew it would be.

She sat facing him and reached for the vibrator. "I'll show you how to use it."

"No, I got this." Javier turned both switches on, activating both the vibration and the rotating steel balls. He ran a finger down the translucent blue shaft. "The dick part with the rotating balls goes inside you, while the part that looks like a bunny with long ears vibrates against your clit."

Okay, so he had figured it out.

"Don't look surprised. I know how to operate some very tricky weapons systems. I can even fly a helo if I have to. This"—he held it up—"is easy."

Laura lay back on her pillows, expecting him to put the vibrator to work between her legs, but he didn't. Instead, he brought it up to her neck, running the little buzzing rabbit ears along the tender skin there. It certainly wasn't what she was used to doing with it, but it felt good. She turned her head to give him better access, the delicate sensation raising bumps on her skin.

He traced a line down her neck, across her clavicle, and down to her breastbone, amused curiosity mingling with desire on his face. He was having fun with this.

Laura felt her nipples tighten and wondered what the vibrations would feel like there. She didn't have to wait long to find out. He made circles around one breast and then the other, tickling the sensitive undersides before touching it to her aching nipples.

She gasped, her eyes drifting shut as frissons of arousal skittered through her. The jelly texture tugged at her skin more than his tongue did, the heightened friction and the vibrations creating an intense new sensation. She felt herself grow wet, sexual need flaring to life inside her.

But he was just getting started.

He bent down and began to use the vibrator in tandem with his tongue, suckling her nipples, then rubbing the vibrating shaft over the wetness he'd left behind.

Laura arched her back and reached her arms above her head to give him unimpeded access to her breasts, the vibrations seeming to settle deep in her belly. He switched from one breast to the other until she thought she might go out of her mind. By the time he finally nudged her thighs apart, she was on the brink.

He touched the shaft of the vibrator to her clit.

"Oh!" Her hips jerked, the sensation almost too much.

He eased off, stroked her lightly, the vibrations like a thousand flicks of a feather, his lips scattering kisses across her sensitive inner thighs. "Like this?"

"Yes." She was certain nothing could possibly feel better.

He proved her wrong, penetrating her with his fingers, taking her with slick thrusts, heightening her pleasure even further.

She cried out, dug her nails into the comforter, fought to hang on.

"Mmm." He kissed her inner thigh again. "You are *so* wet."

Oh, how she wanted him inside her!

Not the vibrator—Javier.

But some part of her held back. "Please, Javi. *Now.*"

He chuckled, withdrew his fingers, nudged the vibrator inside her inch by slow, unbearable inch—and turned it on high.

JAVIER WATCHED, SO turned on by Laura's erotic responses that he thought his balls might burst. He slid the shaft in to the hilt, felt the friction of her inner muscles, then slowly withdrew it, those same muscles gripping it tight. He thrust it inside her again, imagining that the vibrator was his cock as he slowly built a rhythm, his gaze fixed on the most private part of her body as he gave her what she craved.

God, how he wished *he* were inside her now. He was a hell of a lot harder than this made-in-China plastic dick—that much was a fact. But he wouldn't push her.

It was enough to know that he was pleasing her. And he *was* pleasing her. She was lost now, her legs wide apart, her eyes squeezed shut, an expression of sensual abandon on her face.

But he wasn't done—not by a long shot.

On the next thrust, he slid the toy into its intended position, the little bunny ears resting on either side of her swollen clit. Her hips jerked off the bed, a stream of breathy "ohgods" spilling from her lips, her hands clenched into fists.

Oh, yeah, his balls were going to blow.

She was slippery wet now, the musky scent of her arousal driving him loco. He needed another taste. He lowered his head and began to flick the tip of her clit with his tongue, keeping up the in-and-out rhythm of the shaft.

She was close to orgasm now, all whimpers and moans, her head tossing from side to side, her muscles drawing tighter around the vibrator. Then her breath caught, bliss on her sweet face as she came, her inner muscles clenching so hard around the vibrator's shaft that it jerked in his hand.

¡Coño! Hell!

Lucky damned toy.

He kept up the rhythm until her climax had passed, then turned the gadget off and set it aside, teasing her with light strokes of his tongue, savoring the moment, giving her time to recover. "That was eight."

Eyes closed, she lay still, lost in the aftermath of what had clearly been an intense orgasm. Slowly she stirred to life. Her eyes opened, and she smiled at him, speaking in a soft, sexy voice. "Your turn."

"I'm not sure how you think this is going to work. This is a toy for *las chicas*. It looks like a dick, for God's sake."

But he'd been raised to keep his word. He duly shucked his clothes, then climbed onto the bed, ready for the silliest sexual experience of his life.

She picked up the vibrator, its jelly shaft still slick with her juices and drenched with her scent. "Lie on your back."

"*¡Oye!*" He did as she asked, his cock standing at attention, clearly eager for whatever she had in mind.

Rather than teasing him as he'd done to her, she went straight for the sweet spot, rubbing the wet shaft against the sensitive underside of his erection.

Javier gasped, his hips jerking reflexively at the strange and intense feeling.

She smiled and continued to caress him root to tip, letting the rotating steel balls rub against the ultrasensitive underside of the head.

It was unlike anything Javier had felt before, enough to keep him hard and make him horny as hell, but probably not enough to get him off. Still, she didn't relent, running the buzzing toy up and down his cock. Then she wrapped both hands around his cock and the vibrator, holding them together, shaft to shaft, using pressure to enhance the sensation. And in the blink of an eye, Javier was on the edge.

Still naked, she bent over him and began to circle her tongue around the engorged head of his cock, still holding the vibrator and his erection tightly together.

"*Jesus.*" Javier thought he would go out of his mind, one

sensation spilling into the next, making him jerk and buck, until climax hit him, pleasure making him groan, hot semen blasting onto his belly.

It was a while before he could speak again.

Laura sat beside him running her fingertips over his chest, a smile on her face. "A toy for *las chicas*?"

It was a little after midnight when Laura's cell phone rang. She'd just fallen asleep but the sound brought her immediately awake. She recognized the ring.

It was Erik.

She hurried into the living room, hoping not to wake Javier. "This is Laura."

"They've agreed to a welfare check," Erik said. "I thought you wouldn't mind me waking you up to tell you good news."

Laura was so stunned she had to sit. "That's wonderful!"

She felt a hand on her shoulder and looked up at Javier, smiling, only to realize he couldn't understand a word she was saying because she was speaking Swedish.

"A consular official and the embassy doctor will visit the family tomorrow to examine Klara, bring her up to date on her vaccinations and address any health problems she may have. They also hope to collect a DNA sample from her—and to take photographs."

Photographs?

"Would . . . Would I be able to see the photos?"

Erik chuckled. "My dear, that's the reason we're taking them."

"Thank you!" Laura hadn't even dared to hope for this.

"You should know that Safiya claims to be Yasmina's— that is to say Klara's—biological mother. She says your baby was stillborn and was taken from you to be buried. Al-Nassar's younger brother, who is now Safiya's guardian, backs up her story, though we know he was nowhere near the compound when Klara was born."

Erik was still talking—something about DNA being essential for her case—but Laura barely heard him, his words drowned out by the thrumming of her pulse.

Was it possible Safiya was telling the truth? Could Laura still be so confused about what happened that night that she didn't realize her baby had died? Could the baby she'd been forced to bring into the world lie buried in the dirt in Afghanistan?

No. *No!*

"Safiya is lying. Klara is *my* child. She was born alive. I saw the blanket moving in Safiya's arms. I heard her cry."

It was that tiny cry that had cut through Laura's shock and trauma and had made her realize, at least for a moment, what had just happened.

"That's why we want DNA. We want to be able to prove in court that she's your biological daughter. The Pakistani representative who met with the family said she did not resemble Safiya at all, but had lighter hair than Safiya's other children and blue eyes. But that alone won't be proof."

Lighter hair. Blue eyes.

It was the first description Laura had gotten of her daughter.

Somehow, those few words made Klara more real to her, heightening her anxiety, sharpening her regret.

I am so sorry, Klara!

Laura's stomach knotted. She looked up to find Javier watching her, a worried frown on his face. "I know you'll do your best. Please give the consular officials and doctor in Pakistan my thanks."

"I will." Erik paused. "We're doing all we can, Laura. I wish I could tell you that we'll get her back, but I cannot make that promise."

"We will get her back. We must."

Laura refused to consider any other possibility.

CHAPTER 23

LAURA WAS QUIET and subdued at breakfast, and Javier knew she was worried about her daughter. He couldn't blame her. She'd shared her news with him—some of it good, some of it bad—and he'd realized that the chances of her getting her little girl back through official channels were next to none.

"Why don't you bring in the U.S. State Department?" he'd asked as they'd gone back to bed. "They've got a lot more international muscle."

"They've got more enemies, too. Besides, if I do that, it won't be long before someone in the media picks it up, and the coverage will make it harder to free her. She'll be a prized pawn. It's better to keep it quiet, work behind the scenes. Also, I'm not ready for the whole world to know what I did."

He'd taken her hand. "Laura, you didn't *do* anything."

"Exactly," she'd said, turning out the lights.

If he hadn't just sworn to the commander that he'd kept OPSEC intact, he might have told her right then how he, as the man in command of the squad who'd rescued her, saw what had happened that night. Instead, he'd kept his mouth shut.

When she went into her office for the Monday morning I-Team meeting, he went for his morning run, leaving her with Childers again. Outside, the wind was biting cold, snow in the forecast. He ran hard, his leg giving him less grief. On the way back, he stopped at a grocery store to grab some food and other supplies.

He was standing in the vegetable aisle when he got the feeling he was being watched. He glanced to his left and saw a white guy—brown hair, brown eyes, close to six feet, maybe two-fifteen—staring straight at him. The man looked quickly away, smiling, one hand in his pocket.

Was he carrying?

Javier couldn't be sure. He walked down a few random aisles just to make sure he was truly being followed. The man stuck with him.

What the hell?

He carried his basket to the express checkout lane and picked up a tabloid, pretending to give a shit about celebrity baby bumps. He glanced over the top of the magazine to find the *hijo e puta* standing in the next lane, still watching him. There was something off about him, something odd. Javier set the magazine back, drew out his wallet and his cell, and sent McBride a quick text.

Being followed. @ Grocery on 20th & Chestnut.

He had no idea what this guy wanted or whether he was connected in any way to the attacks on Laura. But he was taking no chances.

He got an immediate reply.

Walk S. on Chestnut to 19th. Turn left. Units en route.

Wanting the bastard to believe that Javier wasn't on to him, he made conversation with the cashier, a friendly woman with sandy brown hair and brown eyes. He paid, picked up his bags, and headed out the door, using the mountains in the west to orient himself. He turned left, heading south. He didn't have to look behind him to know the guy had followed.

What the hell did the bastard want with Javier?

Spare change? A date?

Sorry, cabrón. *Can't help you either way.*

Javier reached 19th Street and turned left, no sign of the cops. They'd be running silent, of course, maybe even riding in unmarked cars. He slowed his pace a little, wanting to give the cops more time, his senses trained on the man walking behind him. The man began to laugh.

And Javier had had enough.

He turned—and found himself staring at the working end of what looked like a toy replica of an M1911, its tip fluorescent orange to distinguish it from the real thing. "What the—"

A smile on his face, the man fired.

BAM! BAM!

Javier felt searing pain as a very real round creased his rib cage. "What the fuck?"

The weapon was real.

He dropped to the concrete and rolled, drawing his concealed SIG. "Drop it!"

The man laughed, smiling as he aimed at Javier again.

Javier took him out with a double tap—two rounds, center mass.

He stared at Javier, fear in his eyes, a look of shock on his face, then fell to the ground. Javier didn't have to check his pulse to know he was dead.

Then Javier heard the sound of running feet as the cavalry arrived at last. He tucked the SIG back into its holster and stood, sliding a hand beneath his jacket and pressing it against the pain in his left side. His hand came away bloody.

¡Puñeta!

Four cops approached, weapons drawn.

"On your knees! Hands above your head!" one of them shouted.

And Javier realized they were talking to him. He'd been in this situation—walking up on a shoot-out, unable to tell who were the good guys and who were the bad guys. It was better to comply and explain later than get shot again.

He had just dropped to his knees when an unmarked vehicle tore around the corner and drew to a stop at the curb.

Darcangelo stepped out, called off the officers. "What the hell happened?"

Javier stood. "No clue. This *cabrón* was following me. I heard him laughing and turned to find him pointing that piece at me. The tip is orange. I thought it was a toy, but the bullets were real enough."

Darcangelo pulled Javier's jacket open. "You've been shot."

"He fired two rounds before I dropped him. One caught me. It's just a graze. I'll take care of it at Laura's place."

Darcangelo shook his head. "I hate to say it, but you're not going anywhere. I need a statement from you, and I'm going to have to confiscate your firearm. In the meantime, you might as well humor me and let the Band-Aid boys check you out."

An SUV turned the corner behind them, tires squealing, and stopped beside Darcangelo's car. Hunter stepped out of the vehicle. "You okay, Corbray?"

Javier nodded.

Hunter looked over at Darcangelo. "How'd you get here so fast?"

"I was setting up that solicitation sting down on Colfax when the call came in. What took you so long? Getting your nails buffed?"

"Hey, fuck you. It's my day off."

"Your day off? What is that shit? Why don't you see what you can do to keep Corbray out of the limelight while we clean this mess up? Any minute now the media are going to show up and start taking photos of him again."

¡Puñeta!

What a clusterfuck!

The commander was going to love this.

LAURA MADE COFFEE for Deputy U.S. Marshal Childers, then retreated to her office, turning to her job to keep her mind off Klara. But that was impossible.

Safiya was lying, doing all she could to keep Klara, and there was little Laura could do about it. Once Erik had exhausted diplomatic options, she would have only the courts to turn to. And the courts would rule against her.

Despair welled up inside her, Erik's words running through her mind. If it hadn't been for Javier, she wasn't sure how she'd have gotten any sleep last night. He'd held her, assured her everything would be all right. His confidence had seemed to lift some of the burden—and some of the worry—off her shoulders.

Determined to have a productive day, she slogged through transcribing her most recent interviews. She had worked only four full days over the past two weeks, the newspaper seeming distant, part of another life. If she didn't produce something soon, Tom would lose patience with her, though his temper didn't bother her the way it bothered other people.

Done with that, she began to run through her notes on the VA story, only to find that she still couldn't concentrate. Her gaze fell on Ali Al Zahrani's FBI file. She set her VA notes aside, reached for the file, and looked through the list of articles she'd written over the past few months to see whether any of them might have provoked Ali. But none of them had touched on any topic remotely related to the Middle East or terrorism. There were, however, a lot of articles *about* her both in the *Denver Independent* and in other papers as the media focused on Al-Nassar's upcoming trial.

Could that be it? Could that coverage have persuaded him somehow to think of her as an enemy, a threat that needed to be eradicated? Could there be some connection between Al-Nassar and Ali or his family of which the FBI wasn't aware?

If Laura had read this report without having met Ali's family and without having spent so much time in the Middle East, she might have bought that story without a second thought. Page after page painted a damning picture—a young man who'd gone from model teenager to terrorist in a matter of months, turning his back on society to carry out one fatal act of violence. But nothing in the report explained how Ali might have become radicalized or who might have influenced him. Could he have spent his afternoons radicalizing himself in his own bedroom?   •

Laura's reporter instincts, instincts she'd learned to trust, told her that something was off here.

His afternoons.

Her heart gave a hard kick.

She grabbed her notes from her interview with Ali's uncle together with a fistful of pages from Ali's browser history and began to compare.

According to FBI's interview notes and her own, Ali went from class to his uncle's grocery store, where he worked every afternoon until the store closed. He got out of class at roughly two in the afternoon and then reported to work by three, usually getting home at about nine thirty at night. And yet all of the suspect Internet searches he'd made using his desktop computer and home IP address—*every single one of them*—had taken place between one and four in the afternoon.

That made no sense.

Laura double- and triple-checked the documents, page by page, and confirmed it. The condemning Internet searches had all been made from Ali's home during the hours he was supposed to have been at school or working at his uncle's grocery store.

That could only mean one of two things. Either his uncle was lying about Ali's whereabouts in the afternoon—or someone else had been using Ali's computer.

Had FBI investigators noticed this?

Surely, they had. Then again . . .

Just to be cautious, she read through the browser history for a fourth time, noticing things she hadn't before. His afternoon searches were strictly related to bomb making and terrorism. There wasn't a single search for naked women, no clicks on news articles, no visits to chat rooms, no detours to iTunes. Also, he'd never done any Internet searches about her. In fact, there was nothing in his browsing history that involved her at all, not even articles about Al-Nassar's trial. To make matters stranger, he'd visited some of the sites—many of them, in fact—for only a matter of minutes before clicking on the next link and the next.

"Ms. Nilsson?"

Laura gasped, startled. She looked up to see Childers standing in her office doorway, smartphone in hand.

"Sorry to startle you, but I just got word that Mr. Corbray has been shot."

It was late afternoon by the time Javier was discharged from the hospital and free to head back to Laura's place. He'd been questioned first by Darcangelo and then by two homicide detectives while waiting for the doctor to appear and stitch the graze. He'd been about to stitch the damned thing himself when the doctor had finally walked in and gotten the job done, leaving nine stitches in all.

Now, all he wanted to do was get back to Laura.

She'd put his phone number to use and called him the moment she'd heard he'd been shot, panic in her voice. He'd reassured her he was fine, but he knew she wouldn't believe that until she saw him.

He walked with Hunter, Darcangelo, and two officers to the hospital's parking garage. The two men had offered to accompany him back to Laura's flat even though it wasn't really their job.

"Why don't you ride with that loser?" Darcangelo pointed to Hunter with a jerk of his head. "He's got tinted windows that might give you more privacy if we run into media on the way."

Hunter grinned. "He's just jealous."

Javier recognized close male friendship when he saw it. He climbed into Hunter's SUV and put on his seat belt. "How long you and Darcangelo been married?"

Hunter grinned. "We met about six years ago. I'd broken out of prison, and Darcangelo was the one who found me."

"Prison?" Javier listened while Hunter told him how he'd been convicted of a murder he didn't commit. He'd broken out of prison to save Megan and Emily, and Darcangelo had put the pieces together, first bringing him in and then helping him prove his innocence.

"If it had been anyone else, I'd probably still be in the joint—or dead."

Javier understood that bond. That was what he had with Nate. Except that he'd been awfully hard on Nate when he'd been up at the Cimarron, keeping him at a distance, keeping things from him.

Maybe you should set that right, cabrón.

Maybe he should.

LAURA WAS ABOUT to go out of her mind by the time Javier finally got home. She met him at the door, took in the sight of him. He smiled when he saw her, but she could tell he was troubled. Was he in pain? "Thank God you're okay!"

She wanted to wrap her arms around him but stopped herself. He was carrying two grocery bags, and she wasn't sure where he'd been hit. She didn't want to hurt him.

He set the bags down and drew her into his arms. "I told you not to worry, *bella*."

She hadn't been able to help it. She'd felt nauseated since she'd gotten the news, afraid in her heart that Javier had become a target because of her. His photo had run in the papers and been on all the news broadcasts, after all. Maybe the same people who wanted to get rid of her had now decided to go after him, too.

"Where were you wounded?"

Javier stepped back and slid out of his jacket to reveal a bloodstained T-shirt, the left side torn a few inches above his waist. He lifted the shirt and pressed his hand against a dressing that was held in place by medical tape. "Nine stitches. No big deal."

"No big deal?" Fear for him flashed into anger. "You could have been killed!"

Childers stepped forward. "Glad to see you're in one piece."

"Thanks, man." Javier shook Childers's hand. "Sorry to keep you so late."

"No problem. It was good to see you again, Ms. Nilsson." Childers gave Marc and Julian a nod and left.

It was then Laura remembered her manners. "I'm so sorry. Please make yourselves at home. Can I take your coats, get you something to drink?"

Marc and Julian shook their heads.

"Don't worry about us," Marc said. "We'll be heading out in a minute."

She looked at the three men. "So will one of you please fill me in? The TV news isn't saying much. A shooting in LoDo. One man dead. Another wounded."

Javier slipped out of his coat and sat on the sofa, drawing Laura with him, Marc and Julian sitting across from them. She listened as Javier told her what had happened, feeling sick to think that he would be dead right now if the man who'd fired at him had simply been a better shot.

"He was laughing?" Chills shivered down her spine

Javier nodded. "It was the damnedest thing I've ever seen. He had this look on his face like he was having fun. And when I shot him, he looked . . . surprised."

"Was he psychotic?"

"We hope to have some answers soon." Julian got to his feet. "Old Man Irving sent homicide to execute a search warrant at his residence this evening. In the meantime, the firearm he used has been sent to the lab."

Marc stood. "It looked to me like someone had painted the tip to make the weapon look like a toy. It could be the shooter *wanted* to fool you, Corbray. That way he'd get off the first shot."

"If his aim had been better, it would have worked." Javier touched a hand against his wounded side.

"How did they know where to find you?" Laura didn't understand that part. The grocery store wasn't usually part of Javier's routine.

"My guess is he knew I went for a run every morning and planned to catch me on my way back. When I took a detour to the store, he followed me."

"That's as good an explanation as any." Julian stood. "We'll let you know what the search warrant turns up."

Then Marc and Julian left, leaving Laura and Javier alone.

Laura checked to make sure the door was locked and turned to find Javier standing behind her. "The media are going to pick this up. My paper will pick it up first. Someone on the news crew will remember your name, and they'll connect you to me. Then the national papers will grab it and the TV news stations. I'm so sorry."

He nodded, a muscle clenching in his jaw. "It's not your fault."

"Your commander can't penalize you for defending yourself, can he?"

"Probably not."

"You'd be dead if you hadn't fired back."

But Javier's thoughts seemed to be elsewhere.

He reached for her. "I killed a man today, *bella*. I've killed men in combat, but this was different. I had no choice. I know that. He tried to kill me. But why?"

"I'm so sorry." She sank into his embrace and held him as tightly as he held her, one thought running through her mind, the same thought that had haunted her all afternoon.

She'd almost lost him. She'd almost lost Javier.

That simple realization had cut through her, opened her

eyes to the truth. Despite all that had happened to her, despite the terrible situation with Klara, she had something precious in her life now, something beautiful, something she could not bear to lose.

And that was Javier.

She loved him.

He drew back, a hand against his injured side. "You think you can help me find a way to take a shower without getting this wet?"

She smiled up at him. "I bet I can think of a thousand ways."

It was only later, when she and Javier lay in bed together on the brink of sleep, that Laura remembered what she'd discovered about Ali.

She would call Zach tomorrow.

CHAPTER 24

LAURA RAN NAKED into her office and booted up her computer, then rushed back to her bedroom and grabbed something out of her closet. It turned out not to be the blue dress she'd aimed for but a blue blouse. *"Helvete!"*

Javier stood in the hallway naked, apart from the dressing on his side, glancing down at the watch in his hand. "You're not going to make it. It's zero-nine-hundred and thirty seconds."

She slipped into the blouse, buttoning it as she ran back toward her office, still totally bare from the waist down.

"Is this your new professional look, because, I gotta say, *bella*, I like it."

Torn between laughter and irritation, she glared at him as she passed. "This is your fault, Javier Corbray."

"My fault? Hey, you started it." He followed her. "Don't get me wrong. I'm happy to be your morning lollipop, but I need to eat, too."

Her simple good-morning blow job had turned into a round of crazed sixty-nine that had sent pillows flying—and was about to make her late for work. Oh, but it had been worth it. Her body was still purring.

She sat at her desk and clicked on Skype, doing her best to work the tangles out of her hair, the clock on her computer telling her that she was now a full minute late for the I-Team meeting. She grabbed her notepad and was about to log on when she realized Javier had followed her into her office. "Go, or my editor is going to see you naked!"

Chuckling, he disappeared out the door.

A click and a few rings later, she found herself staring at Tom's face.

"Nice of you to join us, Nilsson."

"Sorry I'm late." She felt the urge to laugh, knowing that to him she looked normal—a bit less polished than usual, but normal—when she was only half-dressed.

"Hey, Laura!" That was Sophie.

Tom went on. "Harker, can you indulge Nilsson's tardiness by repeating yourself?"

"I've got an e-mail trail of two city council members who appear to have been taking kickbacks from a labor union. I'm guessing twenty inches with head shots."

"Alton?" Tom's gaze shifted.

"Windsor became the tenth Colorado town to ban fracking. I'd like to pull something together on the lawsuits challenging the bans and include the latest EPA studies on air and water pollution at fracking sites. Joaquin got some great shots of the rigs out along the Poudre River. I'd need probably fifteen to twenty inches."

Tom looked into the camera. "How about you, Nilsson? Make any progress on that VA story?"

"I have an interview scheduled for later today with the regional VA director, and then I'll be ready to pull it together." Laura had never quite gotten the hang of thinking in column inches. She did a bit of mental math. "It will be a good twenty inches."

"What about photos?" That was Syd.

Joaquin answered. "I've got shots of most of the soldiers she's interviewed as well as the PTSD coordinator."

"Carmichael—your turn. What's the latest on the bombing investigation and last Thursday's shooting?"

"That depends." The camera moved until Laura found herself looking at Alex, who had a black eye and lacerations on his cheek. "Any word from the DPD as to whether yesterday's shooting of your SEAL friend is related to the attacks on you?"

He already knew.

"No."

Alex looked directly into the lens. "Are you sure about that?"

"Of course, I'm sure."

"I'd really hate it if some other paper scooped us on any of these stories because you held out on your own coworkers."

Laura's face flamed. "If I knew something and sharing it wouldn't place my life or his in danger, I would tell you. In this case, I haven't heard anything. The shooter might have been just a random psycho."

She understood now why Alex got punched in the face so often.

Alex looked up at Tom. "Javier Corbray, the SEAL who's shacking up at Laura's, was shot yesterday in broad daylight on Nineteenth Street between Chestnut and Wewatta. Minor wound. Corbray fired back and killed his assailant with two slugs to the chest. DPD is being very close-lipped about it. Also, my sources with the FBI says they're getting close to making an arrest in the bombing."

"What?" Laura hadn't heard that. "Who told you that?"

But Alex ignored her. "I'm looking at six inches on both pieces."

Laura was glad when the meeting was over. She walked to her bedroom to finish dressing, then found Javier sitting in his running pants on the sofa staring out the window at the mountains, his cell phone on the coffee table across from him.

She sat beside him. "Did your commander call?"

He shook his head, one hand coming to rest on her thigh. "I called him. I decided it was better he hear it from me than the newspapers."

That made sense.

"What did he say?"

"He wants me to fly back to Coronado this afternoon."

Laura felt the color drain from her face. She stood, turned her back to him, walked to the kitchen. "So . . . you're leaving."

"Laura, I—"

"It's probably for the best. Since you got here, you've been filmed and photographed, had your name in the paper. You've been shot at—twice. You were almost killed yesterday." She averted her gaze, not wanting him to see how upset she was. She'd never cared for women who used their emotions to blackmail. Javier needed to do what was right for him without pressure from her. "You came to Colorado to recover, not to get sucked into my mess."

"I did not get *sucked* into anything." He walked over to her and took her hands. "I made a choice, *bella*, and that choice was to stand by you. I'm not leaving now."

She stared at him. "But your commander—"

"He didn't give me an order. It was more like a strong suggestion."

"A suggestion?" Laura shook her head. "I don't want you putting your career on the line for me. You've already done so much for—"

He pressed his fingers to her lips. "I've made up my mind. I'm staying here with you until my leave is up."

Laura sank into his open arms and held on tight, hoping with all of her heart he wouldn't have a reason to regret his decision.

JAVIER LOOKED OUT over the rooftops of Denver, trying not to feel anything as he spoke. "We came across a shepherd and his two sons on our way in. You know the choice—kill them or let them live and risk them giving us away. I did what I felt was right. We gave them chocolate and water, even fixed blisters on one boy's foot. The moment we left, they must have hightailed it to the village. We were ambushed by Taliban fighters. Eighteen men died."

"You can't blame yourself." Nate stood beside him in his fleece barn jacket, cowboy hat pulled low to keep the wind from catching it. "I'd have done the same thing. Most of us would."

Nate had called shortly after Javier and Laura had finished breakfast to say he'd heard about the shooting and was on his way over. The two of them had retreated to the rooftop so as not to distract Laura, who was still on the clock.

"That's what I tell myself." He'd been telling himself that for more than five months. "My squad agreed with my decision. No one wanted to put a bullet through those kids, man.

The boys couldn't have been much older than nine or ten. But then I see that helo flying in, getting blown to bits along with medics inside . . . They died trying to save our lives."

He could still hear the rotors, feel the blast wave, smell the burning fuel oil.

"I tried to help Krasinski hold on, but . . . I took another round, lost consciousness, woke up in a hospital. In my dreams, Crazy K is lying beside me, bleeding out in the dirt."

"Just like your brother."

Javier nodded, his throat tight. "Krasinski trusted me. He was a tough kid, a hard charger. He gave it a hundred and ten percent. He was a warrior. I guess he reminded me of Yadiel—that enthusiasm, that deep loyalty, you know?"

"Yeah, I know."

Javier drew a deep breath, then turned to look at his best friend. "You were right. I've been acting like an ass. I'm sorry, man."

"You got no reason to apologize. You've always been there for me. I just wanted you to trust me enough to let me be there for you. I know it's not easy for you to admit that you need anything from anyone. Thanks for opening up, for letting me in."

And Javier finally understood.

He'd tried to be the one that everyone could count on, the one who didn't need help. He'd felt that's what he'd had to do to be strong. But this kind of brotherhood—it was a two-way street. It had been arrogant of him to try to help Nate when he refused to let Nate help him.

"Thanks, man."

"You going to see a therapist when you get back?"

That was a completely different question. "I don't know. The nightmares have always stopped eventually. If they don't . . ."

If they didn't, he might talk to someone then.

The conversation drifted. Nate shared his news. Megan had gotten into law school and would be starting at the University of Colorado School of Law in August. Jack was getting ready to head out for a forty-fifth reunion with his platoon of Army Rangers. Emily had lost her first tooth.

Then Javier told Nate about the commander's phone call and his refusal to return to Coronado until his leave was up.

"He asked me if I was trying to make a name for myself as

an individual by hanging with a celebrity. After fourteen years of service, a Silver Star, two Purple Hearts, and a half dozen other medals, I didn't feel I deserved that kind of bullshit." A handful of SEALs had risen to individual prominence in recent years, giving the Pentagon a headache when it came to national security, but Javier had never sought to cash in on his Trident. "I got pissed, told him I wasn't doing this so someone could buy the book rights. I love her, Nate."

Nate grinned. "Tell me something I don't know. How does she feel?"

Javier wasn't entirely sure. He knew she trusted him more than any other man. He knew she cared about him, felt sexual desire for him. She wanted to stay in touch after he left. For now, that was enough.

"She cares about me. She was really shaken up yesterday."

"I don't blame her."

Javier's cell rang. He fished it out of his pocket. "It's McBride."

"On my way over," McBride said. "A couple of these puzzle pieces just came together."

LAURA DIALED TED Hollis's number to complete the interview that had been cut short by the car bomb and was relieved when he answered on the second ring. "Hi, Mr. Hollis. This is Laura Nilsson from the *Denver Independent*."

"Hello, Laura. It's good to hear your voice."

"It's been a while since we last spoke. I'm sorry our interview was interrupted. I meant to get back to you sooner, but things have been busy."

He laughed. "You couldn't help that."

"How are you doing these days?"

"Oh, I'm hanging in there. I'm still having nightmares. I tried to quit drinking myself to sleep, but that just meant I didn't sleep."

"I'm so sorry to hear that. I called to see if you had anything else you wanted to add to your interview."

"Oh, well, I can't remember what we talked about. How are you? You've had a lot happen in your life since we spoke. The bomb. Some guy trying to shoot you. That must be very

scary. I watch the news at night. I saw your interview and saw
how afraid you were when they showed you that footage. I
never did like Gary Chapin."

"I'm doing fine. The U.S. Marshals are keeping me safe."

"That's good. I'm glad to hear it."

Javier appeared beside her.

"McBride is here," he whispered.

She said a quick farewell to Mr. Hollis, thanking him for
his willingness to share his story with her readers, then ended
the call. "Did they say why he's come?"

He shook his head. "He's waiting for you."

She was glad he was here, regardless of the reason. She
needed to speak with him about Ali. She got up from her desk
and walked with Javier down the hallway. "Alex said this
morning in the I-Team meeting that the FBI was close to making an arrest in the bombing case. Maybe that's what they've
come to tell us."

She found Zach sitting in her living room.

He stood when she entered. "Sorry to interrupt your work,
Laura, but I've got some news for both of you."

She sat, her hand instinctively finding its way into Javier's,
his warm fingers closing reassuringly around hers. "Go ahead."

"First, I wanted you to know that Derek Tower might pull
through after all. He's been upgraded to critical but stable. He
hasn't fully regained consciousness, and he's not yet breathing
on his own. Hopefully, we'll be able to question him soon."

That was good news.

"How's Janet?" Laura hadn't had time to call and check on
her this morning.

"She may be looking at another surgery, but she's recovering." Zach took a photo out of a file folder and slid it across
the coffee table toward Laura. "We've identified the man Corbray shot yesterday. Do you recognize him at all?"

Javier leaned in. "That's him, all right."

Laura looked at the image, feeling revulsion to think that
this was the man who had tried to kill Javier. She looked at
the man's lifeless face and vacant eyes. He had lost most of
his hair, his face fleshy, his mouth gaping open. "No, I don't.
Should I?"

"He was Sean Michael Edwards, age forty-one," Zach said.

Sean Michael Edwards.

The name sounded vaguely familiar, but she couldn't say why.

Zach went on. "DPD sent a team to do a search of his residence last night. They completed that search this morning, and what they found will interest both of you. In addition to an arsenal of *toy* firearms, we found an AR-15, an M110 sniper rifle, and two double-deuce pistols. We also found a wall covered with photos of you, Laura."

"What?" Laura's stomach sank.

Javier gave her fingers a squeeze. "So he's not just some random nut job. He's a part of this somehow?"

"We can't be sure of anything yet, but it certainly seems that he had an obsession with you. He had photos dating back three years. They'd been cut from newspapers and magazines and stuck on a bulletin board until they overlapped—dozens of them. Also, the rifle in the surveillance footage from the parking garage was an M110. It's hard to imagine this could all be a coincidence."

"Why would he go after Javier?"

"We can only speculate," Zach said. "Given that Corbray was featured alongside you in news coverage of the sniper attack, perhaps he felt that getting Corbray out of the way might make it easier for him to get to you. We're sending the weapons in to ballistics for testing and should have an answer by tomorrow."

"Wait a sec." Javier looked confused. "Are you saying *this guy* is our sniper? I just can't believe that he could miss Laura's head by less than an inch from more than two hundred yards and then almost miss me when he was standing just fifteen feet away."

Zach shook his head. "There's more. We did an extensive background check on him. He served two deployments as an RTO—a radio telephone operator—with the army infantry in Iraq. His first was in 2007, while you were there, Laura. He suffered a traumatic brain injury near the end of his second deployment and was given a medical discharge. What we found more interesting was the fact that he was disciplined for his involvement in a protection racket. It seems that he and a few of his fellow soldiers were shaking down residents in a neighborhood in Baghdad. You broke that story, Laura."

Sean Michael Edwards.

Laura's heart gave a hard knock. *"Oh, my God."*

She tried to remember the details of the investigation. It had been so long ago. Four soldiers had run a shakedown racket against residents of one Baghdad neighborhood, promising protection in exchange for money and other favors—cigarettes, liquor, sex. She'd been tipped off by a woman, a pediatrician, who lived in that neighborhood and had filmed the soldiers looting with her phone. They'd been disciplined—each of them sentenced to fines and a reduction in rank.

She glanced down at the photo again, his face that of a stranger. "His name sounded familiar, but I didn't make the connection. I don't recognize him at all."

Javier looked down at the photo again. "A lot of us felt those guys got off easy. They should have gone to prison."

Zach looked from Laura to Javier. "Clearly, this connection constitutes a motive for murder. We took the liberty of looking up the other soldiers who were a part of that scheme. One—Theodore Kimball—was reported MIA and declared dead not long after Laura's investigation. The other two—Paul Mortimer and Tyler Robb—are in Miami and Detroit. We looked into them, but neither of them has been to Colorado, so it looks like Edwards was carrying this grudge on his own."

Javier pointed to Edwards again. "So this guy is one of the soldiers Laura busted with that investigation, and he wanted revenge. I get that. But what I don't get is where Derek Tower fits in—or how the guy I shot could be connected to Ali Al Zahrani."

And then Laura felt pieces fall into place, insight riding on a surge of adrenaline. "He isn't. I think Ali Al Zahrani was framed."

The two men stared at her.

Javier spoke first. "I know you care about what happened to this kid, but you've got to have strong evidence to say something like that."

Zach's eyes narrowed. "I've got a feeling you've been investigating this on your own. Maybe you should start talking."

CHAPTER 25

JAVIER WAITED WITH McBride for Laura to explain. When in the hell had she reached this conclusion? She hadn't said a word about it to him.

She sat up straighter and looked from him to McBride. "You should know that I won't divulge my sources, so don't even ask."

McBride's gaze grew hard. "I could subpoena that information under federal law, and the state's journalism shield law wouldn't protect you. You'd be forced by the court to divulge your sources or face prison time."

She nodded. "It wouldn't do you any good. I'd choose prison."

The two of them sat in silence, their gazes locked, and Javier knew they both meant what they'd said, the tension between them seeming to fill the room.

It was McBride who blinked. "I don't want to go that route. Just be sure you don't impede our investigation or give the wrong information to the wrong person. Then I might not have a choice."

"I understand." She excused herself and went to get her notebook from her office, then sat beside Javier again and glanced through what she'd written. "I reviewed all the available documents on Ali Al Zahrani, and I discovered that he could not have made those incriminating Internet searches."

"Why do you say that?" McBride asked. "They were on

his computer. They all originated at his IP address. No other prints were found on his keyboard or his computer."

"I'm aware of all of that. Just hear me out." Laura began to explain. "Ali worked at his uncle's halal grocery store after class every weekday afternoon except Fridays and all day on the weekends. His uncle says he was very dedicated and never missed a day. He also said Ali didn't leave during his shifts. The Internet searches began abruptly two months ago. They all originated from his home IP address, but here's the problem. They all occurred during hours when he was known to be at work—never on Fridays when the store is closed and never on weekends when his parents were home."

That *was* strange.

"Are you sure?" There was a note of doubt in McBride's voice.

"I went through the documents four times, checked each and every search. But there's more." She looked at her notes. "The terrorism-related searches were all saved in a browser under a different user identity on his computer. Investigators probably think that serves to incriminate him because it looks like he was trying to hide his activity from his parents. But what if someone was trying to hide those searches from *him*?"

"You got any proof of that?" McBride asked.

"No," she admitted. "But stay with me for a minute, okay?"

"I'm listening."

As Laura went on, Javier felt himself growing more impressed with her intel abilities. None of the evidence she presented was the obvious sort that would have jumped out at investigators. It required some thought. Like the fact that the kid's browser had recorded searches pertaining only to explosives, jihad, and terrorism—no T&A, no music, no sports, nothing about Laura or Al-Nassar. And the fact that Ali had visited some of the sites for only a handful of seconds—just long enough for the page to load—before he'd apparently moved on.

"I read fast," Laura said, "but even I can't absorb the content of a web page in a single glance."

McBride was still playing devil's advocate, but it was clear to Javier that he saw where she was going with this. "Maybe he was downloading the pages to a flash drive that we haven't found. Or maybe he was printing them. There could easily be a logical explanation."

"If you find one, let me know." Laura looked down at her notes again. "As I see it, there are two possibilities. Either his uncle is lying and Ali wasn't at the store when he was supposed to be, or someone else was using his computer during hours when no one in the family was home, creating an Internet history to make him seem guilty."

"You're forgetting that the explosives were found in his car, along with his body," McBride added.

"True." She frowned and seemed to mull this over. "What if that setup was just another part of the plot to leave the blame at Ali's feet? Investigators found no trace of explosives at the Al Zahrani home. If he'd actually built the bomb, wouldn't they have found *something*? And don't forget that he'd been dead for hours before the explosion. Someone might have set him up to look guilty and then murdered him to put both him and his car at the center of the crime. What better way to hide a motive than to make it look like the explosion was the result of Al-Nassar's call to kill me?"

The hair stood up on Javier's neck, his instincts telling him she was right. "What you're saying is that the kid might not have had anything to do with this."

Laura nodded. "When I realized that he couldn't have been responsible for those Internet searches, I began to wonder. Now that we have Edwards here, I'm almost certain."

"I don't often find myself in the position of defending the FBI," McBride said, "but don't you think they've checked into some of this?"

"I have no idea." Laura shrugged. "Why would they? A VBIED goes off outside the newspaper near my window a short time after Al-Nassar called on his followers to kill me. A young Muslim man is found in the car, making the blast look like a suicide bombing. The suspect's computer reveals a browsing history of do-it-yourself bomb and terrorism sites. In other words, investigators found *exactly* what they expected to find. Why dig any further?"

McBride seemed to consider this.

Laura went on. "They have a dead body, a car packed with explosives, and these Internet searches. But they don't know where the ANFO was mixed. They can't find any ties between Ali and any known terrorist elements. They can't explain why he was shot before the bomb went off or find the man who killed him and detonated the explosives. They're ignoring the missing and contradictory evidence because the rest of it fits together so nicely."

Javier's gaze dropped from Laura to the photo of the man he'd killed yesterday, Laura's theory opening up all kinds of new possibilities. "Maybe this has nothing to do with Al-Nassar at all."

For a moment, there was silence.

McBride chuckled. "I can't wait to see Agent Petras's face when I go over this with him. I can't stand that son of a bitch."

Neither could Javier. "That makes two of us, bro."

"So you'll take this to the task force?" Laura asked.

"You've painted a compelling picture. I'm impressed. Yesterday's shooting adds weight to your theory. You bet I'm taking it to the task force."

"Do you think they'll listen?"

McBride grinned. "I'm the chief deputy U.S. Marshal for the Colorado territory. They have no choice *but* to listen."

THE MEETING WITH Zach had left Laura on edge. It wasn't just the revelation that a man she'd exposed five years ago had tried to kill Javier and might have been behind the plot to kill her, too. It was also the investigation of Ali Al Zahrani. Her mind kept drifting back to the boy—and the horrible thought that he might have been murdered just to serve as a kind of decoy.

She did her best to focus on her work, answering a few e-mails from Tom and Syd and reviewing her questions for her interview with the regional VA director. The interview itself turned out to be as unrevealing as it was brief. She'd just hung up the phone when Javier came up behind her, his big hands resting on her shoulders.

"How did it go?"

"Short and uninformative." Laura swiveled her chair and stood, sliding into his embrace. "He basically read me a press release over the phone and then declined to say anything else. I might as well have interviewed a rock."

"I've got some news that will cheer you up." He smiled down at her. "You've got company."

She found Sophie, Matt, Alex, Kat, Joaquin, Holly, and Megan whispering together in the living room, carryout Thai food spread out in containers across her coffee table.

"Surprise!" Sophie gave Laura a bright smile. "We brought lunch for you both."

Laura felt a swell of happiness to see them, even Alex.

Javier leaned down and spoke for Laura's ears alone. "You have a good time with your friends. Mind if I borrow your computer to catch up on e-mail?"

"Feel free. The browser should be open."

He thanked Sophie and the others for the food, then disappeared down the hallway. Laura soon found herself enjoying panang curry with chicken, spring rolls, and rice—and catching up with her coworkers about events at the paper.

Repairs had been completed so that no one could tell there'd ever been a car bomb. The cafeteria's new healthier lunch menu had everyone in an uproar—everyone except Holly, who said she no longer had to feel jealous of what the others were eating. Matt and Tom had gotten into a blowout in the newsroom over a headline. Alex had been roughed up by a few members of a prison gang who were living on the outside and hadn't appreciated his questions. Kat and Gabe would be leaving for two weeks on the Navajo reservation to help with the *kinaalda*, or coming-of-age ceremony, of one of Kat's nieces. Joaquin had put together a photo spread of some of the working girls from Candy's, but the publisher and Tom were fighting over whether the package could run, given what the women did for a living.

"It's bullshit, man." Joaquin was clearly furious. "Since when is our job only to pass on G-rated news?"

This led to a long discussion about editorial autonomy.

Then Megan announced that she'd been accepted into law school.

Laura felt a rush of joy for her. "Oh, that's wonderful! When do classes start?"

"They start in August, but I've got a reading list that I'm going to work through this spring and summer."

Megan talked a bit about her plans after graduating, how she planned to open a resource center that provided guidance and support to women who were being released on parole in hopes that fewer of them would wind up behind bars again.

Laura was struck by Megan's courage, her moral fiber. "What a beautiful way to turn your own suffering into something positive."

"How are you doing, Laura?" Sophie asked. "We all know what happened to Javier yesterday. I'm so glad he wasn't seriously hurt."

"Sorry to interrupt." Alex stood. "Where's your bathroom?"

"Down the hall and on your left." Laura returned to Sophie's question. "I'm fine, I guess. I was pretty shaken up when I heard. I'm just glad Javier was able to defend himself. If he hadn't been armed . . ."

She didn't want to think about that.

"Do they have any idea why this guy tried to shoot him?" Matt asked. "It must be related to the attacks on you, right?"

And Laura remembered that her friends were reporters.

She answered carefully. "We assume so, but we don't know anything for sure."

Holly leaned forward, looking gorgeous in a blue and white Prada print suit. "So have you and your sexy SEAL *reconnected*?"

"Holly!" Sophie rolled her eyes.

Kat looked up from her lunch. "That's your business, Laura, not ours. Please don't feel you need to answer."

Then Laura heard Javier's voice.

"Hey, get the hell out of here. Are you wearing a wire, man?"

She set her plate on the coffee table and hurried down the hallway to find Javier standing face-to-face with Alex in the doorway to her office, his fists clenched.

"What's going on?"

"I was sitting at your computer, and he walks in, starts asking questions about the shooting, pretending to give a shit. I look up to find him looking over my shoulder at the files on your desk, and I start asking myself whether he's just talking to me because he's your friend or whether he's trying to grab a quote."

Laura took one look at Alex, and she knew that was exactly what he'd been doing. She touched a hand to Javier's arm. "Javier can't give interviews. You know that. Give me the recorder. Give it to me!"

Javier moved closer, crowding Alex. "You'd better do what the lady asks."

Alex drew a digital recorder out of his pocket and handed it over. "This is bullshit, Laura. I'm just doing my job."

It was one thing to wear a digital recorder in an interview. It was another to wear it into someone's home when no interview was taking place in hopes of stealing a quote or two in the guise of casual conversation.

She scrolled back, deleted the file, then handed it back to him. "I thought you were a friend coming into my home, Alex, not a journalist working a story. I guess I was wrong. You need to leave. Now."

Alex walked off, muttering profanity.

Laura turned to find the others standing down at the end of the hallway, watching, looks of astonishment on their faces.

"I guess it's time for us to go," Alex said.

Sophie glared at him, crossed her arms over her chest. "No, just you."

Joaquin glared at him. "What the hell were you thinking, man?"

And Laura felt a rush of relief to know that the rest of her friends from the paper hadn't been a part of Alex's scheme.

JAVIER AND LAURA had a quiet dinner, did the dishes together, then settled on the couch, Laura's head resting on Javier's lap.

"I'm sorry Alex was such a jerk today. In the I-Team meeting this morning he implied that I was keeping information from him—which I suppose I am. I didn't think he'd join us for lunch only as a pretext to snoop in my office or to try to steal a quote from you. That's low."

Javier stroked her hair, the feel of it like silk, being close to her making it impossible for him to feel angry. "The stupid *cabrón* is lucky I didn't give him another black eye to match the one he already has."

"Can you imagine what might have happened if you hadn't

been in my office? He would have been free to look around and read everything. He might have found the FBI file. What would I tell Zach then?"

"Why aren't you like that? I always say that I can't stand the media. You're part of the media, but you're not like him or that *pendejo* Gary Chapin."

"Gary and to some degree Alex live to break a story. It's not the content of the story that matters to them. It's the thrill of being first, of winning that race to make news. For me, journalism is about people. It's about the human element."

"I guess that's what sets you apart, why you're so good at what you do."

"When I was a new reporter straight out of college, I was sent with a cameraman to a house where a father had just run over and killed his own eighteen-month-old daughter. He'd been pulling out of the driveway on his way to work and didn't know that she'd gotten outside. She died before they reached the hospital. My job was to stake out the house and try to get an interview with him or the child's mother.

"When I got there, the place was already surrounded by reporters and photographers. They stood in the driveway, on the sidewalk in front of the house, and spilled into the street. After a few hours, the parents returned from the hospital to find that they couldn't even get into their own driveway. They ended up having to park down the street and walk through a media gauntlet to their own front door.

"The mother was so grief-stricken she could barely walk. And the reporters—they didn't seem to care. They kept shouting questions. 'When did you realize you'd run over your daughter?' 'Where were you in the house when you heard that your husband had run over your daughter?' 'Did your little girl scream or cry out?' 'Was she alive when you discovered her under your vehicle?'

"I was so sick to my stomach, so disgusted, that I didn't ask a single question. I got back to the station with nothing. I almost got fired that day, but I didn't care. I made up my mind that night never to accept an assignment that I felt compromised my integrity."

He ran his knuckles over her cheek, wondering what he'd

done to deserve this time with her. "I've never known anyone like you, *bella.*"

His cell phone buzzed.

"Hey, McBride, what's up?"

"Tower has regained consciousness. You said you wanted to be there when we questioned him. I can have Childers there in ten to watch over Laura if you want to come along."

"I'll be ready."

LIGHT, PAIN, AND noise seemed to crash in on Derek all at once—a steady beep, a mechanical sound like breathing, and voices.

A sea of women's faces. Were they nurses?

"Is your pain under control?"

"This IV has started to infiltrate. We're going to insert a new one in your other arm, okay? You'll feel a little prick."

"If you don't stop thrashing, we're going to have to sedate you!"

He was in the hospital, but he had no idea why. He couldn't speak, could barely open his eyes. He drifted in and out, lost somewhere between oblivion and a world of clashing sounds and bright, blazing lights.

And then there were other voices, men's voices.

"I'm Chief Deputy U.S. Marshal Zach MacBride, and I need to ask you a few questions about the shooting that put you in this bed. Can you understand me?"

So Derek had been shot. That explained a few things. It must have been bad for him to be in this kind of shape.

He nodded.

"Can you write your name for us?"

He felt a pencil in his hand. He spelled it out—*D-E-R-E-K.*

He opened his eyes, men's faces swimming in and out of focus. He thought he recognized them, but he couldn't remember.

"Can you remember who shot you?"

So he had been shot. Yes, he'd been shot. They'd just told him that.

What was the last thing he remembered before this place?

He'd been waiting. Yes, he'd been waiting in his car. He'd been waiting for someone . . . He'd waited for a long time. He'd had to get there early because he'd wanted to be in position in case anyone showed up.

"Mr. Tower, can you remember who shot you? It's very important that you try."

Images slid through his mind. A parking garage. The sky. A building down below. The weapon in his hand.

"Why were you at the parking garage, Mr. Tower?"

A parking garage. Yes, he'd been at a parking garage. He'd been waiting.

"He's completely out of it. We're not going to get a damned thing from him."

"We've got to try. In a few minutes, they're going to send us away. Try to remember, Tower. Remember who shot you, and spell his name."

Spell his name?

D-E-R-E-K.

"Hey, Tower." This one sounded angry. "Who tried to kill Laura Nilsson?"

Laura Nilsson.

He felt a spark of adrenaline, his eyes coming open.

The little bitch had refused to meet with him. He'd needed to speak with her about her abduction, to find out whom she'd had contact with in the weeks prior. But she'd gotten a restraining order. She'd thought he was trying to kill her, but it wasn't him. He needed her. He needed her alive, and so he'd gone to the parking garage.

One second it seemed to make sense, and the next . . .

A man with short, dark hair and angry brown eyes was leaning over him, his hand giving Derek's an impatient squeeze. "Who tried to kill Laura Nilsson? Spell his name. That same person shot you, man."

But Derek didn't know the shooter's name. He couldn't even remember his face. So he spelled the first thing that came into his mind.

F-U-C-K Y-O-U.

CHAPTER 26

LAURA KNEW THINGS hadn't gone well with Derek the moment she saw Javier's face. "He wouldn't tell you anything."

Javier shook his head. "Either he's still too out of it, or he doesn't want to cooperate. He managed to write his own name twice and then spelled *fuck you*."

The little bubble of hope that Laura had carried inside her since Zach's call popped. She wanted so much for this to be over. By answering their questions, Tower could have made that happen. "Maybe he'll be more alert tomorrow."

"Yeah. Maybe." Javier tossed his jacket onto the chair and drew her into his arms. "Come here. I think it's bedtime."

She glanced at the clock and saw it was nine. "It's too early for me to go to sleep."

He lowered his voice. "Oh, *bella*, who said anything about sleep? Now, where did we leave off?"

All it took was one look from him, and her blood began to heat. "I think we were at twelve."

"That's right. A dirty dozen. Now for lucky thirteen." He grinned, planted a kiss on her mouth. "Follow me."

Soon the two of them were sharing a tub filled with steaming hot water. He reached for her shaving gel and her razor.

Her pulse spiked. "What do you think you're doing with those?"

"Just watch." He filled his palm with lather, then rose to his knees and began to shave himself, slowly and carefully removing the hair around the base of his penis and on his testicles, leaving himself smooth.

Laura watched, both fascinated and more than a little aroused. She'd never watched this process before, never had a lover who'd gone all the way with manscaping, never watched a man handle himself so casually. And it turned her on.

He rinsed the foamy gel away to reveal his half-hard cock. She never would have asked him or any other man to do this, but now that he had, she kind of liked it. Somehow it made him seem . . . bigger. The skin of his pubic area and testicles was darker than the rest of his body, the sight of his bare package deeply erotic.

He tossed the razor cartridge and put on a new one. "Now I'm going to take care of you."

"Me?" Her belly clenched.

He had her stand with first one leg raised on the side of the tub and then the other, his shaving her becoming an act of foreplay. The stroke of the razor over sensitive skin. The pressure of his fingers as he held her skin taut. Hot water as he rinsed her again and again. And what he was saying to her . . .

"I want to taste you so bad. I want to bury my tongue inside you."

She barely had the patience to wait for him to finish, but standing as she was, her balance precarious, his hands between her thighs with a razor, his face so close she felt the heat of his breath on her inner thighs, all she could do was hold on.

When he'd rinsed her one last time, he scooped her into his arms, his mouth coming down on hers as he carried her to her bed in long, fast strides. He tossed her onto the mattress, grabbed her ankles, and dragged her toward him until her hips cleared the edge of the bed, forcing her legs apart. And then his mouth was on her.

"Oh, yes!"

This was the Javier she remembered.

She dug her fingers into his hair, so aroused by these exquisite new sensations that she found herself already hovering on the edge. Bare like this, every inch of her vulva was available for him to lick and nip and taste. He drew her glossy pink labia into the scorching heat of his mouth, tugged and sucked on her aching clit, teased her entrance with the tip of his tongue until she thought she would come apart. And then she shattered, orgasm singing through her, leaving her breathless and trembling.

She felt the mattress shift as Javier stretched out beside her. She opened her eyes, smiled at him, then rolled onto him and slid down his body and off the bed, coming to rest on her knees on the floor. "I want to make you feel good—just as good as you made me feel."

He sat up, his erect cock bobbing as he shifted, his gaze locked with hers. He reached out, traced a finger down her cheek. "Oh, I know you will."

Without breaking eye contact, she licked him a few times, base to swollen tip, and heard his breath leave him in a slow exhale. Certain his newly shaved skin would be just as sensitive as hers, she lowered her mouth to the root of his cock, kissing and licking him there. He stiffened, his body jerking when her tongue slid over the bare skin of his testicles, his reaction encouraging her. She took them into her mouth one at a time, teasing their underside with her tongue, feeling them draw tight.

Javier's breath caught, his fingers sliding into her hair.

She sat up taller and went to work on him with her tongue, circling the engorged head, flicking its satiny tip, her fingers encircling him, stroking him lazily. But he was just as impatient as she had been. She followed his cues, sliding her mouth and hand as one up and down the length of him, moving faster, increasing the pressure, and bringing him to a quick finish in her hand, his hips jerking off the bed as he came.

He fell back onto his pillow, his chest heaving, his fingers still tangled in her hair. And there he lay, spent.

Laura wiped off her hand, then handed him the box of tissues, gratified to see that she'd managed to exhaust him the way he so often exhausted her. There was nothing quite like a sex coma. She was about to lie down beside him when her cell phone rang.

Erik.

The home visit.

She ran to the living room where she'd left her phone,

answering on the fourth ring, questions darting through her mind. Had they been able to get Klara's DNA? Had Klara seemed healthy and well fed? Had they been able to vaccinate her?

"This is Laura."

"Hi, Laura. Yesterday was the day of the scheduled home visit."

"How was it? What happened?"

"A consular official and one of our doctors went with two Pakistani officials to the home." Erik paused. "And they were gone. They had disappeared—the whole extended family. The house was empty."

"What?" Laura's heart began to pound, her pulse beating against her eardrums.

"I'm sorry, Laura, but they have vanished. Their neighbors say they haven't seen them for a few days, and no one knows where they've gone. They must have left immediately after our last contact."

"Can't the police find them and detain them? They can't just vanish."

"You know what it's like there. It took us more than two years to find them when they were in Islamabad. If they've fled to the countryside or crossed into Afghanistan, we might not be able to locate them again."

"No." Laura shook her head, panic making her nauseated. "No, that can't be. I can't lose her, Erik. I can't lose her."

"I'm very sorry, Laura. I know how much this meant to you. You must be devastated. But she is missing, and we don't have any idea where they took her."

This couldn't be happening. It could *not* be happening.

Laura fought to hold herself together. "I understand. Thank you for all you've done."

"We will start searching at once, of course. We have already filed a complaint with the Pakistani government and are demanding action."

"Thank you."

"I told you at the beginning this would be a very hard fight. It seems it will continue to be a fight for some time to come. Good night, Laura."

Laura disconnected the call and slid slowly to the floor.

* * *

WEARING A PAIR of flannel pajama bottoms, Javier stood in the bedroom door watching. He hadn't understood a word Laura had said, but he knew the call hadn't brought good news. He went to her where she sat huddled naked on the floor, took a throw off the couch, and wrapped it around her bare shoulders, reaching over to turn on the fireplace so she wouldn't get cold.

She looked up at him, tears welling in her eyes, the panic on her face echoing the expression she'd had the night he'd rescued her. "They took my little girl. They disappeared. No one knows where they went or where she is."

¡Puñeta! Fuck! Son of a bitch!

The news hit Javier with the force of a bullet. He wanted to hit something, wanted to rip Al-Nassar's balls off, wanted to kill. What kind of stupid, dick-faced, baby-raping, jihadist piece of shit would kidnap an innocent newborn and do everything possible to keep her from her mother?

Heart thrumming, he drew a couple of deep breaths, fighting to get his shit under control so he could be there for Laura. He drew her onto the couch beside him and held her. "I'm so sorry, *bella.*"

"They have to find her. If they don't . . ." She squeezed her eyes shut and pulled away from him. "This is my fault. If I had been stronger . . . If I'd believed what I knew in my heart, that Klara was mine . . . If I'd taken her from Safiya when I'd run or told the SEALs about her . . . But I didn't. She's two years old, and she's lived every one of those days as a captive."

"Laura, you *can't* blame yourself for this."

But she wasn't listening.

She stood and took a step toward the fire. "If they don't find her and bring her back, she might never learn to read. She might spend years of her life hungry. She could get polio or tetanus. I've seen little girls married off to men in their thirties and forties when they were only nine years old. *Oh, God!*"

Javier had spent enough time in Pakistan and Afghanistan to know that Laura's fears for her child were real. Disease and hunger were a part of life for too many people there. Little girls faced the added burden of child marriage, too many of them forced to have children with men they didn't love when they themselves were still children. The thought of Laura's child enduring any of this made him sick.

But he couldn't let Laura take the blame for this on her shoulders.

He rose, caught her face between his palms, and forced her to meet his gaze, knowing she was on the brink of true panic. "Listen to me. This is *not* your fault."

"I left her, Javier. I turned my back on her, and I left her— my own baby!"

"They took her from you the moment she was born. You never got to hold her. They did their best to brainwash you into believing she wasn't yours. You didn't even remember you'd had a baby until later. They're to blame for this, not you."

She shook her head. "You're just saying that to make me feel better."

He switched tactics. "Okay, fine. It's your fault—all of it. Why don't you explain to me what you should've done better?"

She gaped at him for a moment, and then her face crumbled. "I should have realized I was having a baby. I shouldn't have let them take her from me."

"I'm betting that having a baby hurts a helluva lot, but if you'd have been stronger, maybe you could have fought the two of them off between contractions or some shit, right? Or if you weren't able to do that, you could have at least dug deep, toughed out the hemorrhaging, and gone after her."

Laura glared at him. "When you say it like that—"

"Hey, I'm just speaking the truth here. So tell me, what else should you have done? Out with it. I want to hear."

She turned her gaze away from him. "I should have taken Klara when I ran. If I had just pulled her from Safiya's arms—"

"You think that crazy bitch who tried to stab you might have noticed a move like that? Do you think Al-Nassar's other wives might have noticed? You said they were holding you back, that they left bruises on your arms trying to control you. Could be they'd have slit your throat right there or slipped that knife between your ribs. Could be they'd have fought you and torn that little baby girl to pieces."

She glared at him. "At the very least, I could have told the tall SEAL, the one who carried me onto the chopper, that I had a baby. I could have remembered her and asked for his help. The women were so afraid of the operators that they'd have done whatever he said."

Javier nodded. "Well, there is that. Why didn't you tell him?"

"Because . . ." Her gaze dropped to the floor. "Because I didn't remember. I . . . I just knew I had to go with them if I wanted to live."

"You barely remembered your own name." He didn't see why she couldn't understand. "How could you have remembered a baby you'd never held, a baby they wouldn't let you believe was yours? Maybe it's easier for you to blame yourself than to admit how badly they'd brutalized you and how helpless you truly were."

Her gaze snapped back to his. "How can you say that?"

Javier saw the despair and self-loathing in her eyes—and he made a decision. "Because I was there, Laura. I saw what happened. I was in command of the squad that hit Al-Nassar's compound. I'm the one who carried you out of there."

Her face went pale, her eyes wide as she gaped at him. *"You?"*

"I just violated my orders by telling you this, so don't repeat it, understand? That mission is still classified."

"You were the tall SEAL?"

"Yeah." Now at least he wouldn't have to compete with himself.

She shook her head. "That couldn't have been you. I watched him. I listened to him. I would have recognized your voice."

"That *was* me, Laura. I was there. You shouted out, 'I'm an American, too.' Ross warned me one of the women was running up behind me. I turned, told you to get down, but you were already on your knees. I saw the other one running toward you, saw the knife in her hand, and I killed her. Then I ripped that burka off you and saw your face. I couldn't believe it was you." Javier's throat went tight, a surge of emotion taking him. He tucked a strand of white-blond hair behind her ear. "You were *alive*."

She sank to the couch, her gaze locked with his. "That was really you?"

"Yeah." Some part of him had wanted to tell her that for a

very long time. He sat beside her. "When I learned a SEAL team was being tasked with taking down Al-Nassar, I did everything I could to get our guns into that fight. I wanted to be the one to catch the *pendejo* who'd killed you. Our mission was to bring him back alive if we could, and I was hoping that motherfucker would do something, anything, that would justify my putting a bullet through his skull."

Javier stopped himself, pretty sure she didn't need to hear any of that. "I'm telling you this, because I saw how it was. I know what happened that night. It's clear as crystal in my mind. Do you want to know what I saw?"

She didn't answer, still watching him through wide eyes.

"I saw a woman run from people who had tried their best to break her. I saw the bruises. I saw how weak she was—pale, thin, terrified. She mustered all the courage she had and did what few hostages dare to do. She ran."

She seemed to consider this, her gaze dropping to the floor again. But there was grief on her face now, not self-loathing, not blame. "I didn't mean to leave her. I didn't mean to forget her."

"I know you didn't." He took her hand, stroked her knuckles with his thumb. "I've thought about this a lot since you told me about Klara. Here's what I think would have happened if you *had* remembered. I'd have grabbed a few men and gone after Klara, and those combatants with their RPGs would have blown us to bits. They barely missed as it was. Another minute or two and they'd have had us."

He caught her chin and lifted her gaze to his. "Do you hear what I'm telling you, *bella*? There wasn't time for me to go after Klara. We barely got out of there alive."

She looked into his eyes, and he could almost feel the struggle going on inside her. "I feel like I remember that night so well. It was as if the world became color again instead of just black and white, and yet, when I hear you talk, I realize I'm only remembering small pieces of it."

"Then listen to me, *bella*. See yourself through my eyes."

"Why didn't you tell me it was you? Why didn't you visit me at the hospital?"

"I couldn't. Operational security. I spent two days after the mission being debriefed and getting the materials we confiscated into the right hands. Besides, I wasn't sure you'd recognize me. I didn't want to make things harder for you."

Her lips curved in a sad smile, and she gave a little laugh. "What?"

"Thanks for saving my life—and for punching Al-Nassar in the face. That's one of the nicest things anyone has ever done for me."

"I wish I'd killed him." It was the truth.

"I wish I'd known it was you."

"You were never supposed to find out."

"I won't tell anyone. No one at NSW will know."

"No worries. I trust you." Javier didn't say it because he knew it would upset Laura, but NSW *would* find out. He would tell them himself. Not right away, of course, or they'd drag his ass back to Coronado. Unless they asked him point-blank, he'd wait till he was back in California. He respected his uniform too much to mislead or lie to his superiors. It was a matter of honor.

Do you hear that, cabrón? *It's the sound of your career circling the drain.*

Maybe so. But he didn't regret what he'd just done. Laura had suffered enough. He couldn't let her waste years of her life blaming herself.

Laura smiled, laughed, ran her fingertips along his jaw.

He caught her hand and kissed it. "What?"

She looked into his eyes, still smiling. "I was just thinking how lucky I am. The man I've held in my heart as my hero for the past two years, the man I've prayed for every night—he turned out to be the man I love."

Javier thought his heart would punch a hole in his chest. Had she just said what he thought she'd said?

¡Ea Diablo!

Sweet adrenaline sang through him, took the breath from his lungs as he looked at her tearstained face, the love he felt for her shining back at him in her perfect eyes.

He did the only thing he could.

He kissed her.

CHAPTER 27

LAURA DRANK JAVIER in, the warmth of his lips dispelling the tangle of grief and rage inside her, sexual need so recently satisfied flaring to life again.

She loved him. God, she loved him.

She'd told him, and she'd seen love on his face.

Javier. Her hero.

He'd come into her life, turning her world upside down in a single weekend, showing her a kind of passion she'd found with no other man. But it had been more than a physical connection even then. She'd never felt that close to another soul. He'd reached a place inside her no other man had touched.

Why hadn't she recognized it for the miracle it was in Dubai?

How arrogant she'd been, so sure of herself, so certain she knew the path her life would take. She'd thought she had all the time in the world. She'd been wrong. She'd come close to losing everything—the past, the future, her identity.

But that didn't matter any longer because she was alive and free. Because of him, she was alive and free. And they were together again.

She let her lips go pliant, wanting him to take control, wanting to feel the raw side of him, the side of him ruled by instincts. She didn't need to be afraid—not any longer. She knew this man, knew where he could take her if they both let go.

He slanted his mouth over hers, his tongue teasing hers, his fingers in her hair. But still he held back.

How could she let him know she was ready for more?

Without breaking the kiss, she let the throw fall from her shoulders and straddled his thighs, her hands grasping the waistband of his pajama bottoms and giving them a rough yank.

He took his lips from hers, a questioning look in his eyes as he reached down to shuck the pajama bottoms, kicking them off his feet.

And then they were both naked.

Laura raked her nails down his chest, scraping gently. "I don't want to be afraid anymore. I don't want to hide from this. I want this to be what it should be."

He traced a finger down the valley between her breasts. "There is no 'should,' *bella*. There are no expectations or rules for us to follow. All that matters is what we feel, what we want—your desire and mine."

She felt a hitch in her chest, that precious flame of love she felt for him growing brighter. "What I want is you—all of you."

His eyes went dark, a muscle clenching in his cheek.

And she knew he understood.

Still looking into his eyes, she leaned forward and brushed his lips with hers, traced their outline with her tongue, needing him, wanting him. He accommodated her kiss with his own gentle response, but that wasn't what she wanted. She kissed him harder, brushing her nipples against his chest, grinding herself against his erection. His response rose to match hers, but it wasn't enough. Frustrated, she dug her nails into his shoulder and gave him a little shake, biting gently down on his lower lip, trying to provoke him. His body tensed, all that muscle going taut.

And she felt his restraint break.

In a heartbeat, he took control from her, claiming her mouth in a fierce kiss, his tongue dominating hers, strong arms crushing her against him.

Oh, God, yes!

She let herself go, desires she'd thought she'd never feel again exploding to life inside her. She dug her nails deeper into his skin, challenging him with her own response, resisting him, forcing him to use his strength, the masculine power of his body delighting some hidden part of her until she had no choice but to yield.

JAVIER GAVE IN to the animal in his chest, his need for Laura driving every other thought from his mind. She was back. His Laura, his sweet *bella*, was back.

He wanted to taste nothing unless it was the sweetness of her mouth, the musk of her arousal, the salt of her tears, wanted to touch nothing unless it was the silk of her hair, her soft curves, wanted to breathe nothing unless it had come from her lungs.

Her nails dug into his skin, ten precious points of pain, her body trembling and pliant in his arms, her vulva slick and hot against his cock. And he knew neither of them wanted to wait. They'd already waited so long.

He caught her weight with his arms and stood, her legs locking around his waist, putting pressure on his stitches. But he didn't care. His first thought was to take her on the floor in front of the fire. But Al-Nassar had raped her on the floor. He didn't want to dredge up those memories.

Not the floor.

His mouth still on hers, he crossed the room to the dining room table. But the vase of roses he'd given her sat at its center.

Not the table.

He carried her toward the bedroom, but the bedroom was too damned far away, her tongue clashing with his, the little motions she was making with her hips driving him crazy. He turned and pressed her back into the wall, shifting his hips so that the head of his cock nudged against her entrance.

Wanting to be certain, he dragged his mouth from hers, somehow managing to speak. "Is this what you want, *bella*?"

"*Yes!*"

And with a single slow thrust he was home.

She gasped, her eyes drifting shut on a moan. She was so wet, her body taking all of him and gripping him tight. He tested her response with a few deep, slow thrusts, saw only pleasure on her face, her inner muscles tightening around him.

And then his body took over, his hips thrusting hard and fast, the sheer bliss of it blowing his mind. His mouth sought and claimed hers again, catching her little moans and sighs, her arms wrapped tight around his neck, her thighs clamped like a vise around his waist.

He had imagined this moment a thousand times, but he hadn't envisioned it like this. He'd imagined tender kisses and caresses, taking her with gentleness and finesse, not fucking her up against a wall. But then sex with Laura had never been what he'd imagined it would be, the chemistry between them volatile.

He'd hoped that coming earlier would have taken the edge off, made it easier for him to last, but he was dick-deep in paradise, his male anatomy threatening to betray him. He was already on the edge, his balls drawing tight against his body, the shimmering tension in his groin growing brighter with each thrust. He fought to relax his ass muscles, shifting his stance and his hold on her hips so that every thrust made the root of his cock graze her swollen clit.

Her head fell to the side, her lips parted, her breath coming in pants as he kept up the rhythm. He lowered his mouth to her throat, biting and nipping the sensitive skin above her pulse, the mingled scents of his sweat and her arousal filling his head.

She gasped, her body going tense, her inner muscles drawing tighter around him, and he knew she was moments away from orgasm. He tried to hold on, thrusting harder, faster, willing to go to the edge for her, his sweet Laura, his *bella preciosa*.

She came with a cry, ecstasy on her beautiful face, her inner muscles clenching hard around him. And he surrendered, climax overtaking him in a liquid rush, carrying him over the edge and into heaven.

LAURA AND JAVIER held fast to each other, their bodies slick with sweat, as he carried her to the bed. Javier got his guitar and, still naked, played for her, singing romantic love songs to her in Spanish, his voice deep and smooth. Then, contented and replete, they kissed each other to sleep.

* * *

Laura jerked awake.

Just a nightmare.

It was the same nightmare she always had. Only this time it had been different. She hadn't been alone. Javier had been there. When Zainab had tried to take Klara from her, he'd shot her. But when Laura had reached for her newborn baby, the blanket had been empty.

She glanced down at Javier and watched as he stirred, reaching for her in his sleep, his dark lashes resting against his cheeks. He was such a beautiful man, such an incredibly brave man, the most courageous man she knew.

It still hadn't sunk in. Javier was the nameless, faceless warrior she'd always thought of as the tall SEAL, the man who had saved her life. She looked back and tried to see beyond the night vision optics, the weapons, and the face camo to recognize the man she knew, but couldn't, her memories colored by confusion, terror, adrenaline. He'd seemed larger than life that night, invincible, he and his men the only force in this world capable of bringing her tormenters down.

She thought through what he'd told her about that night, his perception so different from her own. She'd blamed herself for so long for the fact that Klara was still in the hands of terrorists that she didn't know any other way of thinking. But listening to him run through the different scenarios of what might have happened—Zainab stabbing her the moment she tried to take Klara . . . the women fighting her for the baby, hurting or maybe even killing her little girl . . . the RPGs blowing the chopper to bits—she'd realized he was seeing things more clearly than she had.

And a dark weight she'd carried for so long seemed to lessen.

She glanced at her clock and saw that it was just after five in the morning. Knowing she wouldn't be able to sleep, she crept out of bed, slipped into her bathrobe, and made her way to her office, where she sent a quick message to her mother letting her know she needed to talk about something important. She logged on to Skype and waited, popping in her earbuds to keep the conversation from waking Javier.

She told her mother and grandmother the terrible news.

They spoke for most of an hour, sharing their tears and their fears for Klara, neither her mother nor her grandmother willing to surrender hope.

That was one reason she loved them so much. As long as she believed, they would believe with her, no matter how bad the odds of finding Klara might be.

"What are you doing awake already, *bella*?" Javier walked in behind her, still naked, apparently unaware she was online. He bent down and kissed her, giving her mother and grandmother an eyeful of grade-A Puerto Rican beefcake, complete with a manscaped package.

Her mother and grandmother stopped speaking and stared.

"You might want to step out of the line of the camera." Laura pointed to the screen and pulled out her earbuds.

Javier's eyes went wide, and he took a quick step sideways, hiding his bare, shaven man bits behind her chair.

"Javier, this is my mother, Birgitta, and Inga, my grandmother. This is Javier."

Her mother's and grandmother's faces were pressed as near to the computer screen as they could get, and both of them were smiling shamelessly.

Laura found herself fighting laughter.

"Good morning, Javier," her mother said, switching to English. "We—my mother and I—are very happy to meet you."

"It's good to meet you, too, ma'am. Laura has told me a lot about you."

Then her grandmother spoke, struggling with every word, her Swedish accent strong. "You are a very handsome man, more handsome even than Laura has told me."

"Uh . . . Thank you, ma'am."

"I am glad, Javier, that the two of you found each other again," her mother said. "I was so afraid Laura would be alone. I'm glad she has taken you to her bed."

"So am I. I mean . . ." Javier looked like he might choke.

Laura bit her lip to keep from laughing, chiding her mother in Swedish. "Mom, you're embarrassing him!"

"Oh, forgive me, Javier." Her mother smiled, still amused, her grandmother staring openly at Javier's bare chest. "We are so open about such things here. I sometimes forget that it is different there."

"No worries, ma'am."

Her mother frowned. "Laura tells me you were shot. I see you are bandaged. I hope you are not in pain."

He pressed a hand against the bandage on his side. "It was just a graze—nine stitches. No big deal."

"While I have you here, please let me thank you for all you've done to keep Laura safe. She is my only child, my mother's only grandchild." Birgitta's voice quavered. "We lost her once. We couldn't survive losing her again."

"I'm glad I was able to help. Laura means a lot to me, too. If you'll excuse me, I think I'll go . . . uh . . . put something on." He turned and walked away.

Laura watched her mother's and grandmother's gazes follow him, taking in the sight of his ass as he disappeared from view. When he was gone, Laura turned to face the screen again, laughing. "I can't believe the two of you!"

But they weren't listening.

"I think I just had a hot flash," her grandmother said. "Did you see his prick?"

"How could I miss it?" Her mother gave Laura a knowing smile. "You are a lucky woman to have a man like that."

LAURA AND JAVIER laughed together over breakfast.

"I don't think I've seen my grandmother that excited since she went on a date with that landscaper. She was seventy-one, and he was in his fifties. She is a very passionate woman. So is my mother."

"Like mother, like daughter." Javier grinned. "I'm glad they enjoyed the view. I don't think I've felt that embarrassed since I was a teenager and my mother walked in on me when I was jacking off."

Laura tried to imagine a teenage Javier caught in the act and couldn't help but smile. "That would be embarrassing, wouldn't it?"

"I can't believe how cool your old ladies were. All I know is that if I were talking to my mother and my *abuelita* and you walked into the room naked, the two of them would cry, *'¡Ay, Virgen Santa!'* Or something like that, and then rip my head off for taking advantage of you."

That seemed like an old-fashioned notion to Laura. What if she'd been the one taking advantage of Javier? "That's not what my mother and grandmother had to say."

"Tell me. What did they say?"

Laura leaned forward, brought her face within inches of his. "They both talked about how big your cock is."

"Yeah?" Javier grinned, not seeming to mind that at all.

JAVIER LET LAURA work in peace, knowing she had a deadline. McBride had asked him not to leave the building just in case there was anyone else out there who wanted to shoot him, so he went up to the rooftop of The Ironworks for his run, adding crunches, push-ups, and burpees to push himself. With the sun shining and the mountains off to the west, it was a pretty good place to work out.

Afterward, he showered, stuck a large adhesive bandage over his stitches, and went into the guest room to make a few important calls. He'd just finished his last call when his cell phone rang. "Hey, McBride."

"Agent Petras and I are about to head over. Looks like this Edwards might have been behind all of this. The pieces are definitely coming together."

"It's about fucking time."

"You can say that again. I also wanted to let you know that Tower has been moved out of ICU. He's off life support and more coherent. I'm stopping by the hospital this afternoon if you want to come. But this time—"

"Yeah, I know. Keep my mouth shut and let *you* ask the questions."

JAVIER TOOK ONE look at Petras's smug face and remembered why he couldn't stand the stupid *pendejo*. He walked in like he owned the place, not even bothering to say hello to Laura or to show her any concern or even to thank her when she took his coat and brought him a cup of coffee.

"How's Agent Killeen?" Laura asked him.

Petras frowned. "I have no idea how she is. I've been working this case."

"That's cold, bro, real cold." Javier couldn't imagine treating one of his teammates like that. "She's one of yours. She was wounded in the line of duty, and you haven't taken the time to find out how she's doing?"

Petras ignored him and sat in the middle of the sofa. "As you know, the bureau investigated the bombing. We tracked down the components used to make the bomb. The dynamite was stolen from a construction site with no surveillance, so that was no good to us. Everything was purchased with cash, so there was no credit card trail to follow. But using witness descriptions from the various hobby shops and hardware stores where the remaining components were purchased, we had an artist create a sketch of the perpetrator."

He snapped open a black leather briefcase and took out a drawing, which he placed on the coffee table.

There was no doubt about it.

Laura glanced at the sketch. "Sean Michael Edwards."

Javier nodded. "That's him."

"We were able to ID him yesterday—at which time we learned he'd already been shot dead by you, Mr. Corbray." Petras looked over at Javier. "I understand that shooting is still under investigation."

Javier opened his mouth to tell Petras how to unfuck himself.

McBride interrupted him. "It was self-defense. I viewed the surveillance footage myself. The man came out of nowhere and tried to shoot Corbray in the back. The DA won't be filing charges."

That was good to know.

Petras went on. "We located Edwards's residence and did a thorough sweep of the place. We found residue from the explosives as well as leftover materials, which we've already analyzed in the Denver lab. The materials are a match for those used to make the bomb that exploded outside the newspaper. There's absolutely no doubt that the bombs were constructed in Edwards's home."

"Does he have any roommates or a partner who might have been aware of what he was doing or perhaps even participated?" Laura asked.

McBride shook his head. "According to his landlord, he lived alone and was unemployed, surviving off his disability check. The only prints we found on any of the materials were his. We found an open box of 7.62 NATO AP with military headstamps that match those of the casings we found at the shooting scene. What's more, two of the weapons we sent to ballistic popped—a Smith and Wesson M&P twenty-two and the M110."

Petras nodded. "There's no doubt that Edwards is our doer. He wanted revenge on you for exposing him in Iraq. He bought the components for the bomb. He constructed the device in his home. He no doubt took advantage of flames fanned by Al-Nassar to manipulate Ali Al Zahrani into helping him, then shot Al Zahrani in the head to tie up loose ends. When the bomb didn't work, he went after you with a sniper rifle. Mr. Corbray foiled that plan, so he went after Mr. Corbray. We've got motive, means, opportunity—more than enough conclusive evidence to wrap this case."

Javier looked over to see Laura's eyes close, tension leaving her body in a slow exhale. She opened her eyes and looked at McBride. "So . . . it's over?"

McBride nodded. "You're cleared to go back to work at the paper. We'll be pulling our protection detail tonight once I've finished my final report."

She buried her face in her hands for a moment, and then her head snapped up. "How can you know for certain Ali Al Zahrani cooperated with him? I have evidence that Ali was framed. I haven't seen anything that has convinced me—"

Petras cut her off. "Ali Al Zahrani remains a person of interest in this case. There are some loose ends regarding his role in the bombing, but I suspect we'll have those tied up in a matter of days."

Laura frowned. "You said the only prints you found on the bombing materials were Edwards's. He bought the supplies. He built the bombs. We know Ali couldn't have done those Internet searches because he was at work when they took place. And let's not forget that he died with a bullet in his brain from Edwards's gun."

"It's far more likely that someone—his uncle or his mother—

is lying to cover up his complicity than it is that Edwards sneaked into the Al Zahrani home every day for two months to incriminate the kid."

"Not every day—just Monday through Thursday," Laura quipped.

But Petras didn't find that funny. "That brings up another matter. The bureau is still trying to decide whether to demand from you the source of the classified files you somehow obtained."

"The *bureau* can demand whatever it wants, but you'd be wasting your time. I've been subpoenaed before." There was a note of steel in Laura's voice. "If it didn't work for the Pentagon, it won't work for you. I don't reveal my sources."

God, Javier loved her.

Laura looked from Petras to McBride. "What about Derek Tower? Are we any closer to understanding what he was doing at the parking garage?"

Petras shook his head. "That's another unanswered question, but I understand that the marshals and Denver police will be meeting with him shortly, so hopefully they'll have that pieced together soon."

Javier looked over at McBride. "I've heard the evidence. It's pretty convincing. But I have such a hard time believing that the man who shot me was capable of any of this. He seemed . . . off somehow. If he was such a great shot with a sniper rifle, why didn't he just take up position somewhere high and out of sight and kill me with the M110? Why get close enough to me to put himself at risk?"

McBride seemed to consider this. "He was given a medical discharge due to a traumatic brain injury. It's possible that some of the lapses we've seen—what we've been calling his uneven skill set—are the result of that brain injury."

Javier thought about that for a moment, the whole thing seeming somehow strange to him. "I guess that's the closest thing to an answer we're going to get."

Petras looked at his watch, then up at McBride. "I need to go. I'm going to be late for the press conference."

"Press conference?" Laura asked.

Petras stood. "We're letting the public know that the bureau has solved this case so that people can feel safe again."

* * *

DEREK KNEW THE next couple of hours were going to suck when he opened his eyes to see McBride, Hunter, Darcangelo, and Laura's SEAL lover—Derek thought his name was Corbray—standing next to his hospital bed. "How thoughtful of you to stop by."

"Sorry we didn't think to bring flowers," Darcangelo said.

Derek knew what they wanted to know, but he doubted seriously they'd believe him, even if he told them the truth. "I think visiting hours are over."

"Yeah? Well, too fucking bad." Corbray glared at him. "You want us to leave, you got to answer a few questions."

"This isn't a social visit? I'm hurt." Derek said it just to fuck with them. He had every intention of answering their questions, if for no other reason than his friends at the Pentagon insisted he do so if he wanted to continue their association.

He simply had no choice.

Not that he had anything to hide, really. But secrecy was his nature. He didn't share information unless it served his purposes.

McBride set a small laptop on Derek's table and booted it up. "I've got footage from surveillance cameras that shows you—"

"No need to go to that trouble. I know what the footage shows." He reached for his blue plastic pitcher and took a drink through the straw, morphine leaving his mouth dry. "I went to the parking garage because I was pretty sure that whoever had made Laura a target would try to take her out before or after the interview. The TV station was doing everything it could to publicize her appearance. I was certain this would draw the bastard out, and I wanted to stop him."

It was as simple as that.

The four men stared at him.

"Why did you choose the parking garage?" McBride asked.

Derek shrugged. "I knew you had things under control on the ground. Our perp would know that, too. There are a lot of tall buildings around the station. It was pretty clear to me that the person who wanted her dead had a military background. If I'd wanted to kill her myself, I'd have taken up position on one of the rooftops and shot her as she made her way in or out of the station. The top floor of the parking garage gave me a view of every rooftop in the area—and gave me an excuse to park my car."

Hunter, the sniper of the group, glared at him. "Why didn't you contact police and share your hunch?"

"I don't play well with others."

McBride spoke up. "You want us to believe that you went to the parking garage on a hunch because you wanted to protect Ms. Nilsson."

"I can see why you're a chief deputy. You're real smart." Derek tapped his temple with his finger. "Yes, that's what I want you to believe."

"Or maybe it's like this," Corbray said. "Maybe you decided you didn't need her after all. You hired someone to kill her, then showed up to get rid of loose ends. Only the loose end got wise to you and almost got rid of *you* instead."

He'd known that was what they'd think.

Hell, if he were in their shoes, that was what he'd think.

"Did you see who shot you?" Hunter asked. "Did you get a look at him at all?"

"No."

McBride handed him a head shot of a man who was obviously dead. "Do you know this man? Have you seen him before?"

Derek shook his head.

"Is the name Sean Michael Edwards familiar to you at all?" Hunter asked.

Derek shook his head again. "Sorry. Can't help you. Who is he?"

"The man we believe shot you," Darcangelo answered.

Derek wasn't used to being in this position, and it was more than a little humiliating, not only because he'd let some fucker get the drop on him, but also because he was used to being the one asking the questions.

"Look. I need Ms. Nilsson alive. She's the only person who can clear my company of negligence in the matter of her abduction."

McBride frowned. "You want to blame her for what happened to her."

"My sources in Islamabad say that Al-Nassar's men were

tipped off by an American man who'd said she'd told him where she was going to be. She says she never broke my company's safety protocols, but clearly she did. Maybe she let some guy fuck the information out of her."

The anger on Corbray's face made Derek suddenly grateful that the other men were there. He had no doubt he'd end up in ICU again if he and Corbray were alone.

McBride put a restraining hand on Corbray's shoulder. "Your sources told you Ms. Nilsson was handed over to Al-Nassar by an American?"

Derek nodded. "If I can prove that's true, I'll be able to clear my company and get back to work. So you see—I need her alive."

JAVIER WALKED WITH McBride, Hunter, and Darcangelo out to the parking lot. "I know Laura, and I know she would never do anything to compromise anyone's safety, including her own. We met in Dubai two months before her abduction, and she was plenty good at keeping secrets. There's no way she leaked information about her whereabouts to anyone."

McBride held up the folder that held Sean Michael Edwards's photo. "Are you all thinking what I'm thinking?"

Hunter nodded. "This might not be the first time Sean Michael Edwards has tried to get revenge on Laura for her investigation against him."

That thought had crossed Javier's mind, too, but some part of him still had trouble believing that the man who had blundered after him down the sidewalk could be behind the attacks on Laura, much less the one who'd orchestrated her abduction.

"You got an extra copy of that surveillance footage from the parking garage?"

"Yeah," McBride answered. "Why?"

"I'd like to take a look at it again."

CHAPTER 28

LAURA GOT UP early the next morning, showered, and fixed breakfast while Javier made coffee. They fed each other bites of omelet, last night fresh in Laura's mind. These past few days with him had been the happiest she'd known since before her abduction. She felt like herself again, only better because now she was in love. Although she was still desperately afraid for her daughter—she had called Erik this morning, and he'd had nothing new to tell her—she no longer had to face that fear alone.

It was almost painful to think that Javier would be leaving for Coronado in a matter of days. He had no idea when he might be deployed again, how long he'd be gone, or even whether he'd come home alive. He couldn't even guess.

The last time they'd said good-bye to one another . . .

Don't think about that now.

Javier helped her clear the dishes from the table. "Mind if I spend some time on your computer while you're at work? I want to look into Edwards a bit more."

She'd heard what Derek Tower had told them yesterday and had a pretty good idea what Javier was after. "You think Edwards was behind my abduction."

Javier shrugged. "Tower thinks your location was given to Al-Nassar by an American. It's worth checking out."

"What he thinks doesn't matter much to me. He also believes I leaked the information myself."

"Hey, you know I don't buy that. If anyone was capable of

fucking secrets out of you, it would have been me, and you didn't tell me a thing."

Laura laughed despite herself, but she wished Javier would leave it alone. "Edwards is dead. What does it matter?"

"It matters."

"You can use my computer—on one condition. Send me some naughty e-mails. I'm going to miss you."

"You sure someone at the paper doesn't cache and read those?"

She smiled. "All the more reason to write something really shocking. Give them something to talk about."

He grinned. "You got it."

She grabbed her leather tote and checked to make sure she had everything she needed. Car keys. VA files. Banana. Cell phone. Debit card. Her handgun.

He walked her to the door, took her into his arms, and kissed her. "How about I meet you at the paper around noon and we head out for a little something?"

"A little *something*?"

"I have a big appetite."

Yes, he did. So did she.

"I'm feeling hungry already."

They kissed again, and then Laura had to go.

What had once been her normal routine felt strange— leaving home without a protection detail, driving her own car, making her way through the streets of Denver without a U.S. Marshal escort.

She arrived at the paper to find dozens of reporters standing out front, cameras and mics ready. She'd issued a statement through her attorney yesterday afternoon after the FBI press conference, but apparently that hadn't been enough. She walked through the crowd, taking the opportunity to thank the Marshal Service, the FBI, and the Denver police, mentioning Zach, Janet, and even Agent Petras by name.

She found her desk festooned with balloons, a bouquet of calla lilies in the center.

Sophie gave her a hug. "Welcome back!"

"Thanks." Laura sniffed the lilies. "These are beautiful."

Alex made his way past her to his desk, his black eye beginning to yellow. "Oh, look, it's our celebrity."

Laura ignored him, getting settled in at her desk.

"Hey, Laura, good to see you." Matt walked up to her in a pair of black trousers and a wrinkled blue dress shirt, a big grin on his boyish face, sunglasses propped on top of his short red hair. "Glad that's all behind you. I guess it wasn't Al-Nassar after all. That's good news."

"Yes, it is—and thanks."

She checked her voice mail, deleting a message from Gary in which he apologized once more—and asked her to come in for another interview tonight. He even offered to send a limo. But she wanted nothing to do with him. Next, she answered her e-mails, including one from Javier suggesting she pick up a spray can of whipped cream on the way home.

"For dessert," he'd written.

"My favorite," she answered.

She hadn't had time to read through the paper this morning, so she quickly perused it. She was glad to see that Alex had asked Petras about Edwards's ties to Ali Al Zahrani. Petras had declined to comment. She couldn't be a hundred percent sure her hunch about Ali was correct, but it seemed to her that Petras wasn't really interested in finding the truth. She might have called Zach and asked him to look deeper into the case against Ali, but she knew there was little he could do. The Marshal Service had coordinated her protection detail and the task force, but the bombing investigation had been left to the FBI.

She wished she could write an article challenging the bureau to reexamine the evidence against Ali, but she had promised Janet that she wouldn't reveal the contents of the file. Laura didn't break promises. But she didn't give up either. Maybe there was a way to get it in the paper *without* breaking her promise.

She would have to think about that.

Tom was in an unusually bright mood, probably because he'd just learned that several I-Team stories had won prizes in this year's Investigative Editors and Reporters Awards. "We're glad to have you back, Nilsson. Harker, what's going on with the city?"

Matt was working on a follow-up piece about Candy's Emporium. When the property had been vacated, one of the employees had apparently left behind a little black book of clients that included several leading city officials—and a state senator.

Sophie hoped to head into the mountains with a naturalist to see how the areas burned in last summer's catastrophic wildfires had recovered. "It ought to make for a really fantastic photo spread if you're up for it, Joaquin."

He grinned. "You know it."

Alex hoped to put to bed the first story in his series about prison gangs, this installment focusing on how gang members in prison, even those in D-seg—disciplinary segregation—managed to communicate with gang members on the outside. "I wore a camera for some of the interviews, so I've got video for the website."

"Nilsson, how's the VA story coming together?"

"I'm good to go. I'll finish it today."

Syd turned to Joaquin. "Photos?"

"They're all turned in except for the shot of Ted Hollis. When I called, he thought I was part of some government conspiracy or something. He freaked out and told me Laura had never said anything about photos. He sounded really out of it."

"Sorry, Joaquin. I told him I needed a shot of him and said he could expect a call from you. I guess he forgot. I'll call him."

JAVIER SLID THE CD of the surveillance footage into Laura's computer and played it, watching as the shooter with his strange glowing ball of a head scoped out his shot and waited. He fast-forwarded, then watched again as the guy set up the M110, got into position, and opened fire. He watched closely as the sniper spotted Tower and reacted, squeezing off two near-fatal rounds before getting in the vehicle and making his getaway.

There was no way the man in this footage could be Edwards. The sniper moved smoothly, efficiently, demonstrating a kind of dexterity that came from practice and experience. Edwards had moved slowly with an almost shuffling gait.

Javier stopped the playback, picked up his cell phone, and dialed a buddy of his in Coronado. He and Miles had gone

through BUD/S together. Miles had been a SEAL until he'd
lost both legs to a land mine in Afghanistan. Once he recovered, he'd found a new way to serve and now worked in naval
intelligence. "Hey, you got a second?"

"Yeah. What's up?"

"I need a favor."

"This wouldn't have to do with a sexy reporter, would it?"

"Yeah, and keep that to yourself." He explained the situation to Miles. "I just don't buy that this guy is the same one
who shot me. Can you run this footage and get a height and
weight off the shooter?"

"Sure thing—but it's going to cost you a steak dinner."

"You got it, bro."

"When do you need this?"

"Now."

Miles laughed. "Make that a steak dinner—and a bottle of
Glenfiddich."

"Deal."

"I'm creating a shared folder. Give me an e-mail address
where I can send the password and the URL for the folder.
Once you log in, upload the footage. I'll get to work on it as
soon as it's here."

"Roger that."

LAURA SAT AT her desk, listening with no small degree of
satisfaction to the shouting coming from Tom's office. She'd
told Tom how Alex had behaved when he'd come over for
lunch and demanded to know if Tom thought Alex's actions
were consistent with good journalistic ethics. It hadn't been a
rhetorical question. She'd been genuinely interested to hear
Tom's answer. She knew he was an aggressive journalist, but
she'd always considered him to be an ethical one.

She'd been pleased when he'd apologized for Alex's actions—
and then shouted, "Carmichael, get in here!"

He'd made Alex apologize.

She'd walked out with a smile on her face.

She'd been working on her VA story since then, hoping to
wrap it up well before deadline. She'd called and left a message
on Ted Hollis's cell phone about Joaquin and the photo situa-

tion, but Hollis hadn't called back yet. She read through what she'd written so far and made a few tweaks to the nut graph, summarizing the findings that would be in the article. She was about to go get another cup of coffee when her phone rang.

"Hi, Laura." It was Ted Hollis. "I'm sorry I acted that way. I guess I should have trusted the photographer, but I thought you'd be coming and . . . I just don't like dealing with strangers."

She tried to reason with him. "I'm a stranger, and you trusted me."

"I guess you don't feel like a stranger. I feel like I know you."

"I can understand that." People often thought they knew people they saw on TV or read about in the newspapers. "Joaquin is a friend of mine. He's very good at his job. I know you'll like him once you meet him. Can I send him out?"

"Oh . . . I don't . . . I don't know about that. Let me think about it."

Under most circumstances, Laura would simply cut the photograph from the story package. But she knew readers would want a face to connect with his story.

She looked at her clock and saw it was already ten thirty. Javier would be here at noon, and then Laura would be otherwise occupied—for a little while. That would leave her only a couple of hours of writing time before deadline, but she'd already made solid progress. If she could find Joaquin and meet him at Hollis's place, she could get the photo squared away and be back in time to meet Javier.

"If it makes you feel better, I'll meet Joaquin there. Would that work?"

"Oh, well, I guess that's better."

She reached for a pen and pad of paper. "What's your address?"

He gave her his street number.

"Would eleven be good? That's a half hour from now."

"That's fine. I don't have anything else to do."

Laura called Joaquin, who said he thought he could just fit it in before heading up into the mountains with Sophie. She offered to text him the directions she'd downloaded, but he said he didn't need them.

"I'll punch them into my GPS."

"Perfect. See you in thirty."

Laura e-mailed the directions to her smartphone and headed out.

JAVIER WAITED IMPATIENTLY on the line while Miles worked.

"Infrared LEDs—this could be a problem. I don't know if the program can extrapolate a height or weight when it can't get a lock on the top of his head. Oh, look, he brought an M110. Nice weapon." More clicking. "Okay, got a great shot of him. Hang on."

Javier paced the short length of Laura's office, the uneasy feeling that had been building inside him growing stronger. The FBI believed it had closed this case, and if it hadn't been for the fact that he'd seen Edwards in action, Javier would have bought it. But he *had* seen Edwards, and the lumbering image in his mind was nothing like the shooter in the footage.

"Yeah . . . This isn't going to work. The software doesn't know what to make of his head. I'm getting nothing but an error message. Sorry, man."

¡Que mierda!

"No problem. I understand. You'll still get that steak dinner. And the Glenfiddich."

"Happy to help. Sorry I couldn't do more. Interesting to watch a left-handed sniper, though. You don't see too many of those."

Left-handed sniper.

Javier's stomach dropped to the floor, his heart giving a hard kick.

Why hadn't he noticed that before?

¡Puñeta!

"I think you just gave me what I need. Thanks, man." Without explaining, he disconnected the call and dialed McBride, hurrying for his gear.

"Hey, Corbray, what's up?"

"It wasn't Edwards. The sniper wasn't Edwards. The shooter was left-handed. Edwards fired at me using his right."

"Are you sure?"

"Look at the footage. Also, I ruled out the possibility of

Edwards being behind Laura's abduction. He was lying in the hospital in a coma at the time."

"There went that theory. I'll pass this along to the police. I'm on my way to the cop shop now anyway. Hunter called to say that Edwards's social worker showed up insisting that Edwards couldn't have done any of the things the FBI claims he did. She says he had trouble tying his shoes and struggled to live independently."

How had Petras and his crew not ascertained that key fact?

Javier knew why.

They'd found exactly what they'd expected to find at Edwards's apartment and hadn't bothered to look deeper. Just as they'd done with Ali Al Zahrani.

Javier held the phone to his ear with his shoulder, loading a spare magazine with anti-personnel rounds. "Edwards may have been involved in this, but the man we're looking for is able-bodied and fit. It can't be a coincidence that Edwards had a beef against Laura. That has to mean something. Are we sure the alibis for his two surviving buddies are airtight?"

"I'll get on the phone with Miami and Detroit now."

"I'm catching a cab to the newspaper. I'll stay with Laura until we can figure this shit out. Whoever he is, he's still out there, and that means she's still in danger."

Javier ended the call, then dialed Laura's cell.

No answer.

He left a message. "Laura, stay at the newspaper. Don't go anywhere. Stay away from the windows. The man in the footage is not Edwards. I say again, stay at the paper. I'm on my way."

He checked his Walther PPS and secured it in his shoulder holster. The fit wasn't perfect, but since he didn't have his SIG, it was going to have to do. Then he grabbed the spare key that Laura had left him, picked up the CD, and headed down to the street.

LAURA LET THE call go to voice mail, the traffic on I-25 demanding her full attention. Holly had a theory that Denver's infamous Mousetrap was actually a psychology experiment gone awry, and this morning, Laura thought Holly might be right. There certainly seemed to be enough road rage going around.

"Hey!" She braked to avoid colliding with a car that had just cut across three lanes of traffic, heading for the I-70 exit. "Idiot."

Twenty minutes later, she found herself staring at an expanse of undeveloped land. Surrounded by a barbed-wire fence, it had probably once been pastureland. Now it was simply vacant, its scant cover of grass dry and brown. Realizing she must have made a wrong turn, she read through the directions once again, only to find that she'd followed them precisely. Well, it wouldn't be the first time that her browser's maps app had been incorrect.

She stopped the car and saw that the call she'd missed had come from Javier, who had left a voice mail. Afraid she was going to be late to her meeting with Mr. Hollis, she dialed Joaquin first, hoping he'd had better luck with his GPS. His phone had just begun to ring when she heard the sound of an approaching engine. Thinking it might be him, she looked up—and saw a black van hurtling directly toward her.

There was no time to react, no time to be afraid. The van hit her head-on with bone-crunching force, knocking the breath from her lungs, as something hit her hard in the face— the air bag.

Stunned, she struggled to regain her breath, reaching for her cell phone, which had flown out of her hand and lay on the passenger-side floor along with the contents of her purse, including her loaded SIG.

Then a man jumped from the van.

In his hand was a rifle.

CHAPTER 29

Javier reached the newspaper to find that Laura wasn't there. With a knot of dread in his chest, he tried to reach her on her cell again.

No answer.

He looked out across a busy newsroom. "I need to know where Laura is."

No one seemed to be sure.

Sophie looked over at him, still typing. "She left about a half hour ago. I think she went to meet Joaquin for a photo shoot with one of the soldiers for her VA story. Try reaching her on her cell."

He felt his teeth grind with the effort not to shout. "I need to find Laura *now*. Her life is in danger, and she's not answering her cell."

That had their attention.

Javier was used to giving orders and having them obeyed. He instinctively fell back on that. "Sophie, call Joaquin. Find out whether Laura is with him and where they were supposed to meet."

Sophie nodded.

Javier walked over to the desk he assumed was Laura's—the one with balloons—and looked for a notepad that might have an address or phone number. There were several manila folders, pages of transcribed interviews, handwritten notes and spreadsheets, but no address. He roused her computer

from sleep and found what he was looking for—a maps appli-
cation showing an address and directions. "Is this hooked up
to a printer?"

"It should come out there." A red-haired man pointed to a
bank of laser printers on the other side of the room.

Javier clicked Print and retrieved the page from the printer,
half-listening to Sophie, who was speaking with Joaquin now.

A big man with curly gray hair stepped out from behind a
closed office door labeled "Editor." Laura's boss.

"What's going on out—"

Javier met his gaze, held up a finger for silence, then looked
over at Sophie, who'd just ended the call. "Sophie?"

"Joaquin says she went to meet with a veteran named Ted
Hollis, but he can't find the address she gave him. His GPS
says it doesn't exist. He admitted he hasn't updated for a while.
He's tried calling Laura, too. No answer."

Javier didn't like this.

Wherever she was, Laura was alone.

He needed to get to her now. "I need to borrow a vehicle."

"Someone want to tell me what the hell is going on?" the
editor asked.

Sophie answered, her face pale. "Laura may be missing."

Alex stood, tossed Javier a set of keys. "Take mine. It's a
black Chevy Tahoe. I gassed up this morning. There's body
armor and an AR-15 and two loaded thirty-round mags in the
back."

Javier wasn't even going to ask why Alex carried all that
shit. An asshole like him probably needed it for self-defense.
He caught the keys. "Thanks."

He was on his way downstairs when McBride called.

"You with Laura?"

"No. She's not here. She left a half hour ago, and she's not
answering her cell."

"Son of a bitch!" McBride brought him quickly up to date—
and the news wasn't good. "I pulled up the files on the other
men involved in the shakedown scheme and called our Miami
and Detroit offices. While I was on the phone, Edwards's social
worker caught sight of the files and pointed to one of the men—
Theodore Kimball."

"He's the one who was declared dead."

"Right, but his remains were never recovered. The social worker swears she saw him at Edwards's place a few weeks back. He said he was Edwards's old army buddy. She says he introduced himself as Ted, but didn't give a last name."

¡Puñeta! Fuck!

Javier's heart gave a single hard knock, fear flooding his veins like adrenaline. "The man Laura was supposed to meet is named Ted Hollis. I'll bet my ass that's him. I've got the address, and I'm on my way there now in a borrowed vehicle."

Javier gave McBride the address and directions.

"That's north of Denver in an undeveloped area of Adams County," McBride said. "Hang for a minute, and I'll pick you up in my car."

"I can't wait. If he's got her, Laura doesn't have much time."

As he ended the call, the thought jabbed at him, a splinter in his mind.

She might already be dead.

"Wake up, Laura. Rise and shine. It's time to die."

At first, Laura thought she was dreaming, but dreams didn't come with throbbing headaches. She struggled to open her eyes, panic threading sluggishly through her veins. The voice was familiar. But something wasn't right.

Someone pulled her hair, forced her head up, and gave her head a little shake, pain making her scalp tingle and temples throb. "Open your eyes."

A man's blurred face swam into view, blue sky and steel beams above him.

Where was she?

She'd been on her way to meet Joaquin. She'd gotten lost. There had been open fields and then . . .

The black van.

It had struck her car, and a man with a rifle had come for her. Ether. He'd drugged her and dragged her away.

She'd been abducted again.

Blind terror surged through her, her heart slamming painfully in her chest, her eyes coming open. But she must still have been drugged. Nothing she saw made sense.

She was sitting tied to a chair in a room that had no ceiling, a building without a roof, nothing above her but steel girders and sky. In front of her was a partial wall with openings in the shapes of a wide door and windows that looked out onto a lake.

Was it some kind of partially constructed building?

A hand slapped her cheek, the pain sharp.

"There you are. Come on. Snap out of it."

Ted Hollis.

She recognized his voice now.

He loomed over her dressed in olive-colored workman's coveralls, blue nitrile gloves on his hands, and a baseball hat on his head with little lights sewn into the bill.

Infrared LEDs. The sniper.

Ted Hollis was the sniper.

Her pulse thrummed against her eardrums, fear making her sick to her stomach. Or maybe that was another side effect of the drug.

He reached for her face. "I guess I can take this off. There's no one out here to hear you scream anyway, except for me, of course, and I enjoy that."

He tore something from her mouth, pain making her gasp.

A piece of duct tape.

She swallowed, her mouth dry, whether from the ether or terror, she didn't know. "Wh-where have you taken me?"

He smiled. "Don't you recognize me, Laura?"

"Mr. Holl—"

"No, that's just an alias." He smiled, clearly satisfied with himself. "I'm Theodore Kimball, one of the soldiers whose lives you destroyed."

Her mind raced, trying to put the pieces together. Wasn't one of Edwards's coconspirators named Theodore Kimball?

Yes.

So Ted Hollis was Theodore Kimball.

She fought her fear. She'd been through this before, and this time she was not going to let it break her. If this was her last hour on earth, she would live it as much on her own terms as she was able, no matter what he did to her. He wanted the satisfaction of seeing her afraid, the control of hearing her plead for her life, the thrill of seeing her buckle under his cruelty. Well, she wouldn't give it to him.

And with that decision, she felt herself relax, her mind clearing.

"I understand now why you didn't want Joaquin to take your photo." It was perfectly clear in hindsight. "You were afraid I'd recognize you. There was no reason to worry. You have a forgettable face."

"You may have forgotten my face, but I haven't forgotten yours." He took her chin roughly in his hand. "All these years of living off the grid, pretending to be dead—I thought about you every day."

She jerked her chin away. "It's a good thing you've had so much practice being dead, because by tonight you'll be dead for real."

He backhanded her, the blow leaving her dazed, the taste of blood filling her mouth. "Don't threaten me, Laura. I've been a dozen steps ahead of the cops this entire time. They still haven't figured out half the shit I've done to cover my tracks."

"Like framing poor Ali Al Zahrani?" The startled look on his face told her she'd been right about that. "They know. They just haven't made it public yet."

He glared at her. "You're lying."

"I was the one who figured it out. Those searches all took place when Ali was at work. He couldn't have been responsible for them."

There was a spark of alarm in Kimball's eyes, but he quickly hid it behind a grin. "We're getting ahead of ourselves. I haven't yet told you what I plan to do with you. Aren't you curious?"

Another attempt on his part to regain control.

"Let me guess. You want to kill me. Is that supposed to be a surprise? You've been trying—and failing—for weeks now."

"Oh, much longer than that."

A shiver slid down her spine at the tone of his voice.

"You and I are going to have a little conversation. After that, I'm going to kill you and set this house on fire. All of this is wired to blow at a touch of a button." He held up a device with a gray button in its center and gestured toward gasoline cans she hadn't noticed before. There were dozens of them, including one on each side of her chair. "Out the windows behind you, I have an unobstructed view of the only road into this development, so if the cops *do* show up, I'll have to push the button early and let you burn alive. Either way, by the time help arrives, you'll be incinerated."

The thought of burning alive revived her fear, left her fighting panic. "You really need to listen to me and leave here while you can."

"Did you give Al-Nassar a hard time, too? I doubt it." Kimball leaned down and caught Laura's face between his palms, forcing her to look straight into his eyes. "I'm the one who handed you over to him. It was me, Laura. Every time he raped you, every time he beat you, every time he humiliated you, that was *me*.

"*I* did those things to you."

And Laura realized she was staring into the soulless eyes of a sociopath.

JAVIER CAME AROUND the corner and saw Laura's car just ahead.

¡Madre de Dios!

The front end was crumpled, the driver's-side door wide open.

He glanced around, saw nothing and no one, just open fields. He drew his Walther and stepped out of the SUV, moving in on Laura's vehicle. He knew he'd find one of two things—Laura's dead body or nothing at all.

Keeping his distance—her car might be rigged to blow— he circled the vehicle. It was years of working as a special operator that kept steel in his spine, kept his stride deliberate and even. The SEAL part of him responded tactically, even while the man inside him wanted to shout for her, to tear the world down in a mad rush to find her.

She wasn't there.

The breath left his lungs in a gust.

There was still a chance she was alive.

Hang on, bella.

He moved closer to the car, looking for blood or any sign of explosives. McBride had called him to fill him in on the details of Kimball's service record. It seemed the bastard had tried and failed twice to make it into Army Special Forces before Laura's investigation had ruined any chance he'd had of getting beyond regular enlisted ranks. Javier was willing to bet Kimball considered himself quite the operator—a strategist, a badass, a cold-blooded warrior. He did have some skills. He'd managed to fake his own death, to disappear and stay hidden for almost seven years. But he lacked experience and discipline—something Javier could use to his advantage.

Javier spotted Laura's handbag on the passenger-side floor, her cell phone and .22 SIG beside it. And his hope that they'd be able to use her cell phone to locate her vanished.

¡Coño! Damn it!

He noticed something on the dashboard—a wad of gauze. He reached for it, raised it to his nose, and caught the faint scent of . . . *ether.*

He called McBride. "I found her car at the address I gave you, but she's gone. Her car is totaled. Her cell phone is here and her firearm, too. It looks like someone struck her head-on, then drugged her with ether. I see traces of black paint on her hood and front bumper. There's no blood. I'm guessing he snatched her and ran."

"Son of a bitch! I've already contacted the Adams County sheriff and put a BOLO out on Kimball. I'll have units there in twenty minutes."

"Does that social worker have any idea where he might be staying?"

"No, but we've been contacting every lodge, hotel, and no-tell motel in the Denver area in search of anyone fitting his description. So far we've found nothing."

And then it struck Javier.

"You said this location is in Adams County. Where have I heard Adams County mentioned before?" Before McBride could answer, Javier remembered. "The dynamite. It was stolen from a construction site in Adams County, wasn't it?"

"Yeah, I think you're right."

"How far is that construction site from where I'm standing?"

"It's going to take me a minute to dig that up."

"Call me back when you find it. Send me that address as well as some kind of overhead view of the area."

He ended the call and walked back to Carmichael's SUV. In the rear storage compartment, he found a halfway decent Kevlar vest, an AR with seriously fucked optics, two loaded magazines, and about fifty spare rounds of 5.56. He carried them to the front seat of the vehicle, removed his shoulder holster, and strapped into the Kevlar. He'd just adjusted the shoulder holster and fastened it in place when his cell rang.

"Yeah."

"The site is about a mile north of you, and, Corbray, I think you're right. I diverted an Adams County traffic helo to do a distant flyby, and they spotted what looks like a black minivan parked between two of the houses."

Laura was there. Javier knew it.

If she was still alive, she needed him now. If she wasn't . . .

He couldn't even consider the possibility.

Javier fought to stay on top of his own adrenaline, his own fear, checking the firearms. "I need to know more about that site."

"The development is an old gravel mine that's being converted into a lakefront community with luxury homes. The mine pit itself has already filled with groundwater. The houses aren't completed yet. I'm sending you a satellite image now."

Javier looked to the north. "I can see the lake from here. Its southern end is about three hundred yards north of my position."

He set the AR aside and studied the image McBride had sent. The lake was roughly kidney shaped with houses in various stages of construction scattered along the far bank. There was one road in and out. No trees, outcroppings, or shrubs to hide behind. No ravines in the artificially created landscape. Near the mouth of the development, large excavation equipment sat idle beside a trailer that was probably used as an office. To the north and east was open pastureland.

"Where was the van parked?"

"They said they spotted it between the two houses at the northernmost tip of the lake—the two that are more fully built."

Javier assessed the situation. He could take the road, but

Kimball would see him coming almost immediately. That might provoke him into killing Laura, if he hadn't already. Or Javier could take a route that Kimball wouldn't expect.

"SWAT is already on its way. I'll be at your position in about ten minutes. SWAT should arrive in fifteen to twenty."

"I'll have her by then. I'm going to swim underwater across the lake and come up behind those two houses. There's a concrete pipe that spills from the lake into a nearby irrigation ditch off the road to my left here. It was probably built to carry away overflow. I can enter the lake that way so that he won't spot me climbing over that embankment."

"Corbray, listen to me. You're taking a big risk. It's March, and this isn't San Diego. The water in that lake won't be much over forty degrees, if that, and it looks to me like you'll have a least a half mile to cross."

"Hey, this is my job, remember?"

It *was* risky. The water temperature would begin to affect him immediately. Swimming underwater meant going for several respiration cycles at a time without fresh oxygen. The combination wasn't a good one. It wasn't unheard of for a SEAL to suffer shallow water blackout and drown even under better circumstances.

But Javier had more experience than most SEALs, and he had powerful motivation. If he failed, the woman he loved would die.

"I'm telling you to wait, Corbray. We'll be there in ten minutes."

But Javier's gut told him Laura didn't have ten minutes.

He disconnected the call, stripped off his coat, clipped the AR to a harness on the Kevlar—and set off for the concrete pipe at a run.

EGO.

That was the key to buying herself time. Kimball was a true narcissist. Some part of him wanted her to appreciate how hard he'd worked to kill her. Some part of him wanted her to be impressed.

Laura fought to hold herself together, fought to see beyond the loathing in Kimball's eyes, the joy he so obviously felt to know she'd suffered. "I'm supposed to believe you were behind my abduction just because you say so?"

He told her the story. How he'd bolted in the middle of the ambush that had pinned down his platoon in Fallujah, angry and humiliated by the sentence he'd received. How he'd gone into hiding, made his way to Pakistan. How he'd seen her one night as she entered her hotel. And how the idea had come to him.

"I realized I could get back at you. I was going to be a Green Beret, and you ruined that for me."

"You ruined that for yourself. You broke U.S. law, shamed your uniform, stole from innocent people. I did my job. I expose the truth."

He struck her again, the blow leaving her dizzy.

"You should have sided with us—with your own country-men. Instead, you stood up for the enemy. *You* are the traitor."

Don't argue with him.

She didn't want him angry. She wanted him to talk about himself.

She struggled to clear her head. "H-how did you know where I was going to be?"

"I followed you every day for weeks. I ate in the same din-ing room, stayed in the same hotel, drank at the same bar. You even said hello to me once when you bumped into me getting out of the elevator. But finding out your plans—that was the real trick." He leaned down and grinned at her. "I did a favor for someone, who hacked your phone and turned it into a rov-ing bug."

Laura had heard about that kind of technology, knew fed-eral law enforcement sometimes used it, transforming the mic in someone's cell phone into a listening device that operated even when the phone was off. "You heard every word we said."

He stood upright, still smiling. "I picked the time and place and made contact with some of Al-Nassar's men. They took it from there."

So Derek Tower had been right—in a manner of speaking. She had been betrayed to Al-Nassar by a fellow American who'd gotten her location straight from her. But it hadn't been her fault. Not that there was any comfort in knowing that now.

"I thought you were dead. He'd claimed he'd killed you."

Kimball reached out and slid his fingers into Laura's hair. "But I guess he wanted to keep you for himself."

Laura shuddered. "It must have been a shock to find out I was alive."

"You were alive, but you weren't the same, were you, Laura?" He knelt down beside her, speaking in that same sad, sympathetic voice he'd used in her phone interviews with him. "I enjoyed hearing about all the things that had happened to you. Then you came back to the U.S. and started living a normal life again, while I was working my ass off doing black ops for hire."

"You decided you had to kill me."

"Exactly. Took me a while to get here. I had to sneak into the country, get a fake ID, pull some cash together. Sean remembered me, helped me out, gave me a place to stay, a place to work."

"He helped you."

Kimball laughed and got to his feet. "He barely knows his own name. I drove him from place to place, gave him money, sent him in to buy supplies for me. He thought we were making fireworks. We talked about old times, but he couldn't remember much. I got him some replica firearms that fire pellets. We played with those indoors. Then his damned social worker came around, and I knew I had to get rid of him."

Understanding hit Laura, making her sick. "You set him up. You sent him after Javier knowing Javier would kill him."

"I painted the tip of my handgun orange, loaded it. I knew your SEAL boyfriend went for a run every morning. I watched, and when he set out, I went after Sean. We meant to catch him on his way back but he went a different route. I followed, dropped Sean off at the store. Sean thought we were still playing. 'See him?' I said. 'He wants to play, too. Just walk up to him and shoot. Score one for the team.'"

Laura felt sick for both Edwards and Javier. "You *used* Javier to kill Sean."

"Your boyfriend is good at killing. He got rid of a loose end for me. Oh, don't look so horrified. That's what a good Special Forces operative does. We work behind enemy lines, move in the shadows, turn one person against another, kill when we must. I would have made a great Green Beret."

She glared up at him, her stomach churning, rage, disgust, and terror coiled so tightly inside her she couldn't tell them apart. "A *real* Green Beret wouldn't screw up making ANFO. Or murder an innocent teenager to hide his own tracks. Or use a wounded friend the way you used Edwards. You're nothing but a loser, a psychopath who blames everyone around him for his own mistakes!"

This time when he struck her, she saw stars.

CHAPTER 30

JAVIER SURFACED, EXHALED, inhaled, his lungs aching, his body chilled to the core. He had about sixty meters to go. He took another breath, then propelled himself beneath the surface once more, willing his body to relax, his mind focused on swimming swiftly and smoothly through the murky water. He couldn't be sure how deep the lake would be on the other side. It wasn't much deeper than five feet here. At some point it would be too shallow to conceal him. He would have to be ready to bring it from that point on.

He'd gone maybe thirty or forty seconds when his fingers and feet brushed the bottom. Carefully holding his position, he lifted his head above the water and took a breath, watching, listening. He heard a man's voice coming from the house slightly to his left. The structure had plywood walls on the ground-floor level, but no windows and no doors, just openings that stared out at the lake. If he'd had some overhead support, he might have known where Kimball had her, what kind of weapons Kimball had, which direction Kimball was facing, but he didn't. He'd have to take his chances and be prepared for anything.

Realizing there was no background noise to mask the sounds of his movements, he army-crawled quickly and quietly to the shore, dragging his body through cold mud, his bones aching, his muscles stiff and sluggish. The water had been colder than he'd expected it would be. But then water was *always* colder than he expected.

A woman's voice.

"You set your bogus interview to coincide with the explosion."

Laura.

She was still alive.

Thank God!

"I wanted to hear you die. I listened to you scream when the bomb went off, just as I listened to you scream when Al-Nassar's men dragged you away."

¡Me cago en su madre! Motherfucker!

Javier locked down his anger, tried to channel it toward action. He unclipped and dewatered the AR-15, his gaze fixed on the house as he watched for movement, for shadows, for any sign of Kimball's location. It sounded to him like they were just on the other side of this thin plywood wall—which meant they would hear him unless he was very careful.

"You managed to startle me, but that was all. You killed that poor kid for nothing. Know what that makes you? A murderer and a coward." Laura was doing her best to act calm, but Javier could hear the fear in her voice.

There came the sharp sound of a hand hitting flesh.

Hang on, bella. *You're not alone.*

Javier set the AR carefully aside, then soundlessly drew the Walther PPS from his holster and made certain it, too, was drained.

"You'd better watch it, bitch. I have your life in my hands!" Kimball was shouting now. "Why do you even give a shit about that kid?"

Javier took advantage of the increased noise level to click off the safety on the AR-15 and move, positioning himself against the wooden wall near what would have been a doorway. His response times were slower than they should be, and he knew he must be hypothermic. He'd have to plan for that.

"The whole country is going to care about him when the truth comes out. How do you sleep at night? Do you see the faces of the people you've murdered?" She was trying to keep him off guard, trying to keep him talking.

"You think you're so brave, but I know you're not. I'm going to prove it to you. See what I brought?" The bastard laughed. "I knew you'd appreciate it. You're afraid now, aren't you?"

"Y-yes, I'm afraid. I'm afraid you've made a very big mistake."

"The only reason you're still alive is that I can't decide how I want to kill you. Once you're actually dead, I won't get the chance to do this again. I want to do it right, to enjoy it. I can either listen to you scream while you burn to death, or I can watch your face as I cut off your head. But I can't do both."

"How frustrating that must be for you."

Javier closed his mind to what he was hearing and crept into position, peering around the corner, taking in the scene at a glance.

Kimball stood with his back toward Javier, a large serrated bread knife in his hand. Laura was bound by duct tape to a chair in front of him. A half dozen gas canisters were placed strategically around the room, two of them flanking Laura.

Did they contain fuel or ANFO? Were they rigged to blow?

Javier had no idea. He drew back, working the plan through in his mind, visualizing each step of it, taking his own sluggishness into account.

"I know you were terrified by the thought of Al-Nassar cutting your head off like this. But isn't it better to die this way than to burn to death? What do you think?"

"I-I think . . . you should run . . . while you can."

Listen to her, pendejo.

Javier made his decision, his muscles tensing.

It was time to bring the pain.

LAURA COULDN'T STOP herself from shaking, fear stealing her breath, making her pulse race. She'd run out of time, and she knew it.

They weren't going to find her. Javier probably knew she was missing by now. One way or another he would find her car—either by tracing her cell phone or by getting the address from Joaquin. He'd call Zach, Marc, Julian—but they would be too late. They would only learn what had happened to her after firefighters reported discovering a charred body in the ashes of this house and the ME identified her remains.

A wave of despair washed through her, the hope that had held her together unraveling thread by thread.

Kimball moved to stand behind her. He fisted his hands in her hair and forced her head back, pressing the rough edge of the blade against her trachea and carotid artery. "If I cut your throat here, you'll suffocate, bleed out, die fast. But if I start here," he said, tilting her head to the side, moving the blade to press against the muscles at the back of her neck, "you might last a little longer."

Laura's mind raced as Kimball tormented her with his words, thoughts chasing one another through her mind.

An image of her mother's and grandmother's faces. They would never recover from this. Losing her the first time had devastated them.

I'm sorry, Mom. I'm so sorry.

She hoped her mother would keep up the fight to reclaim Klara.

Forgive me, Klara. I wish I'd at least gotten to see you, to hold you.

And Javier . . .

They hadn't been together long enough, not nearly long enough, but she was grateful for every moment she'd had with him. He'd brought her back to herself, made her feel alive again. Because of him, she wouldn't die the broken woman Al-Nassar had left behind. She would die as herself.

Somehow, that mattered so much in this moment.

I love you, Javi. Be happy. Be safe.

As hard as she fought to hide her fear, a tear slipped from the corner of her eye.

Kimball noticed, wiped it roughly away with his thumb. "You're not so tough after all, are you?"

And then she saw him.

Javier!

Wet and covered with mud, he appeared out of nowhere, rifle aimed at Kimball. "Hey, *pendejo*, who's afraid now?"

Kimball jumped, the knife blade falling to the floor. "What—"

Click.

The rifle didn't fire.

"Carajo!"

Javier quickly sidestepped, cleared the misfire, and aimed again.

"Put the weapon down, or I'll blow this place to pieces!"

Laura looked over her shoulder and saw Kimball backing slowly away, something clutched in his hand.

The detonator.

"I said put it down, or she's dead!" Kimball's voice was slick with fear.

Barely able to breathe, Laura looked up at Javier, whose gaze was fixed on Kimball, pure loathing on his face, his dark eyes cold.

BAM! BAM! BAM!

Javier fired quick three shots, making Laura gasp.

"No, motherfucker, *you're* dead." Javier walked over to where Kimball lay still and bleeding on the floor, pried the detonator from his hand, and set it aside.

And then he was there, kneeling beside her and peeling off the duct tape that bound her to the chair.

Relief soared through her, leaving her light-headed. "I can't believe you're here. I can't believe you found me. How—"

"Let's get you out of here in case this place really is set to blow." He tore off the tape that bound her ankles, scooped her into his arms, and carried her away from Kimball's body and out what would have been the back door.

Laura wrapped her arms around him and tucked her face against his neck, some part of her still struggling to comprehend that it was over, that she was safe.

He carried her past one partially built house and another, finally stopping when they reached a concrete foundation a few houses down. He set her down and knelt beside her, his hands searching her body for injuries. "Are you okay?"

"I'm fine now." In truth, she was still shaking like a leaf.

He caught her face between his cold palms and traced his thumb over her bruised cheek, his gaze going soft when it met hers. "God, *bella*, I was afraid I'd lost you."

"I was afraid I'd lost me, too." She reached up and ran her fingertips over his jaw.

In the next heartbeat, they were kissing, the rushing of her pulse all but drowning out the approaching sound of police sirens. Or was that helicopters?

Laura didn't know, didn't care. All that mattered to her in that moment was the man in her arms, the man who'd just saved her life, the man she loved.

They were still kissing when an unmarked SUV, a big SWAT van, and two Adams County sheriff's vehicles pulled up beside them, sirens blaring.

Laura heard Zach's voice.

He stood off to the side. "I want two ambulances—one for whatever is left of Kimball and one for those two."

Javier ended the kiss. "Kimball is three houses down. Be careful. He had a detonator, and there are fuel cans all over the place."

"I sure am glad to see you in one piece, Laura." Zach got on his radio and called for an EOD unit. He took a good look at Javier. "You're hypothermic."

"That's all you have to say, McBride? Not, 'You did it, Corbray,' or 'Way to kick ass, Corbray,' or 'You were right, Corbray.'"

"I don't need to feed your ego when you're so good at doing it yourself." Zach grinned and gestured toward his SUV with a jerk of his head. "Come on—both of you. Wait in my vehicle out of the wind. I'll grab a space blanket out of the trunk."

It suddenly occurred to Laura to wonder *why* Javier was wet.

She glanced to her left and felt a hitch behind her breastbone when she realized what he'd done. "You swam across the lake."

The water must have been ice cold, deathly cold.

"It was the fastest way to reach you."

He didn't have to finish the thought. Laura understood.

If he hadn't done it, she would be dead.

THE NEXT FEW hours passed in a blur of medical checks and debriefing. The two of them were treated by paramedics on-site and released. Zach drove them back to the Adams County Sheriff's Office, where they each offered a written statement and then answered questions separately. The U.S. Marshal Service, the Adams County sheriffs, the Denver police, and the FBI—everyone seemed to have questions for them, especially for Laura.

It was dark by the time they found themselves in Zach's SUV once again as he drove them back to Denver, filling them in on what had happened this afternoon when they'd been busy.

Laura's car was totaled and now sitting in the marshals' impound yard, where she could get whatever she needed from it in the next few days.

A deputy had already returned Carmichael's vehicle to him at the newspaper.

A forensic team had been sent back to Sean Michael Edwards's apartment to see whether they could gather any additional evidence that might help them understand what had transpired there.

Zach had paid a personal visit to the Al Zahrani home to bring the kid's parents up to date. "I made sure to tell them that you were the one who first suspected their son had been framed."

"Thank you, Zach." It was clear from Laura's face that this meant a lot to her. "Now they'll finally be able to mourn him in peace."

Javier leaned in and kissed her temple, careful to avoid her bruised and swollen cheek. "Your compassion is one of the most beautiful things about you, *bella*. Have I told you that?"

Her lips curved in a tired smile, and she rested her head on his shoulder.

Javier knew she must be exhausted, but she insisted they stop by the paper.

"They're going to need to interview me. You can head back to the loft if you want. If you're in the newsroom, they'll ask you questions."

"Don't worry about me. I think I can handle a few reporters." He'd almost lost her today. He didn't want to let her out of his sight.

"Your name is in the police report. It's going to wind up in the media again."

Javier nodded. "I know."

He'd already called the Boss to tell him what had happened. He'd expected the lieutenant to rip his head off and stuff shit down his neck.

Instead, O'Connell had congratulated him. "It's not in human DNA to think of water as an avenue of attack. That's why it always works so well for us. Way to go. I'll pass the news along to the men. See you in a few days."

A few days. A few precious days with Laura.

And then Javier would have some big decisions to make.

SEX WAS THE furthest thing from Laura's mind when they finally got back to the loft. All she wanted was a hot shower, something to eat that she didn't have to cook, and the feel of Javier's arms around her.

They ended up taking a shower together, Laura washing lake water and mud from Javier's body, Javier washing the scent of horror from Laura's. But as they smoothed soap over soft skin, Laura felt a need for Javier that was so much more than sexual. Touching turned to kissing until at last Javier backed her against the tile wall, wrapped one of her legs around his waist, and slid inside her.

They made love face-to-face, eyes open, both of them knowing how lucky they were to be alive—and together. It felt to Laura like a celebration of love and life, and when she came, pleasure shimmering through in liquid waves, she couldn't stop tears from spilling down her cheeks.

Afterward, Laura called her mother and grandmother, waking them to tell them what had happened. They listened, their faces showing Swedish stoicism until she finished. Then her mother insisted on speaking with Javier.

"Thank you once more for saving my daughter," she said, tears in her eyes.

Laura and Javier made a supper of eggs and bacon together, then snuggled on the sofa, Laura still in her bathrobe, Javier in his flannel pajama bottoms and a Navy sweatshirt, the gas fire burning.

"I feel sick when I think of all the people who died because of *him*." Laura couldn't say his name. "Drew, my cameraman. Nico, Cody, and Tim, my security team. Sabira Mukhari, the safe house director. Ali Al Zahrani. Sean Michael Edwards. They all died because he wanted to kill *me*, to get back at me for doing my job."

"Believe it or not, *bella*, the person he hated most was himself. He wanted to believe he was Special Forces material, when some part of him knew you were right—he was just a loser."

"I don't think I've ever met a true sociopath until today. I should have known from that first interview that something was wrong with him. He got so . . . *personal.*"

"Nah, how could you? You genuinely care about people. He was a manipulator. Hell, that *mamabicho* used me to commit murder. I thought it was strange that Edwards was laughing, but I never would have thought . . ." Javier's eyes closed for a moment, and Laura knew he felt remorse. "I wish I'd kicked the shit out of the poor guy instead of pulling the trigger and killing him."

The conversation drifted, and soon Laura found herself telling him about those last terrifying minutes when she thought she was going to die.

"Random thoughts started running through my mind. How bad I felt for my mother and grandmother that they would have to go through this again. How I hoped they would keep up the fight to free Klara. How much I wished . . ." Laura's throat went tight. She swallowed. "How much I wished I'd gotten to hold my little girl."

Javier stroked Laura's hair. "One day, you will."

Oh, she hoped so.

"It wasn't all regrets. I felt so grateful for every moment that I've spent with you. It might sound strange, but I was glad I was going to die as myself and not as Al-Nassar's victim."

"It makes sense to me." Javier held her closer. "Strength of the spirit is harder to build than physical strength, and you fought a battle of spirit today. I heard what you said to him. You kept your fear under control. You were a warrior."

"How did you know where I was?"

"A hunch."

She listened as he told her how he'd remembered that the dynamite had been stolen from a construction site in Adams County. When Zach had told him the construction site was just to the north of him, he'd decided it couldn't be a coincidence. Kimball hadn't had much time to plan and was falling back on something familiar.

"Your hunch was right. Lucky for me."

"Lucky for us both. When I saw your car . . . *Ay dios mio.*"

He swore softly in Spanish. "I haven't felt that way since the State Department declared you dead. It hit me in the gut so hard that I . . . All I knew was that I had to get to you. I can't imagine my life without you."

He'd never told her he loved her, but Laura knew it all the same. Those words were proof to her. She wrapped her heart around them, held on to them.

"You'll be leaving on Sunday. I'm going to finish the VA story tomorrow morning, and then I'm taking the rest of the day and Friday off. I don't care what Tom has to say about it. I want to spend that time with you."

Javier kissed her temple. "I'd like that."

LAURA WENT INTO the paper the next morning and rewrote the VA article, pulling out the bogus interview that Kimball had given her, and left the paper early, telling Tom not to expect her till Monday.

Tom wasn't happy. "You *do* plan on returning to work full-time at your full-time job at some point in the near future."

"Yes, starting Monday."

"And when Carmichael needs to interview you for a follow-up piece on your abduction and all this shit with Al Zahrani and Edwards—"

"He can call me at home."

She arrived at the loft to find a surprise waiting for her.

Derek Tower.

The only thing more astonishing than the sight of him sitting on her sofa was the fact that Javier hadn't thrown him out.

"I didn't call because I knew you'd say no," he said. "I came to apologize. I was hired to keep you safe, and I failed. I've read the report. I know how Kimball turned your cell into a roving bug. I'd heard of that technology, but never imagined anyone outside federal law enforcement or military intelligence could get their hands on it. I wish I'd taken it more seriously. I've already issued a statement to the press retracting my allegations against you and taking responsibility for Tower Global's failure to protect you. Bottom line, Ms. Nilsson, I owe you, and I'm a man who pays his debts."

He handed her his card. "Call if you need me."
Laura was left speechless.

LAURA AND JAVIER had just come back from dinner at the
Wynkoop Brewing Company, the restaurant they'd have gone
to if the paper hadn't been car-bombed, when Zach and Petras
called and asked to come by.

Zach went first. "Over the past twenty-four hours, we've
been following Ted Hollis's trail—that's Theodore Hollis
Kimball—and we've been able to piece together a good picture of his activities using his cell phone records, a laptop we
found in his motel room, and the information he gave you,
Laura. Fill them in if you will, Petras."

"Kimball has been hiring himself out as a mercenary in
the Middle East for some time, using a series of aliases and
falsified documents. But after you came back to the U.S., Ms.
Nilsson, he began working his way back here. He arrived in
Denver roughly four months ago and began planning to kill
you. He probably followed you, observed your routine. We
know he studied the location of city surveillance cameras."

Petras told them how Kimball had gotten reacquainted
with his old war buddy Sean Michael Edwards, taking advantage of the man's cognitive disabilities to use him to buy
materials for the bomb. Always careful to wear gloves, he'd
mixed the ANFO and assembled the detonator at Edwards's
house.

He'd found Ali Al Zahrani's name on a list of members of
the Middle Eastern Connection, a student club, and had followed Ali and learned his daily routine. After that, he began
visiting the Al Zahranis' home when no one was home to plant
evidence for investigators. He wanted to make the bombing
seem like an act of terrorism.

"On the morning of the bombing, he shot and killed the boy
when he was on his way to class, stuffing him into his own car,
packing it full of ANFO, and rigging it to explode. Careful to
avoid streets with surveillance cameras, he drove it to the
newspaper, parked, and walked a few blocks away to a coffee
shop, which is where he was when he detonated the bomb."

A cold chill ran down Laura's spine. "He told me he wanted to hear me die."

"He didn't get that chance, did he?" Javier said.

"When the car bomb didn't work, Kimball waited for another crack at you," Zach said. "That opportunity came when he heard about your appearance on Channel Twelve."

"A very ill-advised television appearance, I might add," Petras said.

Zach ignored him. "We'll probably never know exactly what went on with Edwards. We believe Kimball tried to get Edwards to hate you—which may explain the photos of you on his wall. Most came from old articles about the investigation that exposed them. It could be that he hoped to use Edwards as a weapon against you, Laura, but that didn't work. Then Kimball decided to use Edwards in another way. If he could convince police they'd found their killer, your security detail would be called off, and he'd have another chance at you. All the evidence was in place—the traces of explosives at Edwards's apartment, the firearms Kimball stored there. All he had to do was put Edwards in an incriminating position—and make sure he couldn't talk."

Javier finished the thought. "So he groomed Edwards to commit suicide by SEAL, playing games with those replica pellet guns, and then handing him the loaded M1911 with the painted muzzle."

Laura squeezed Javier's hand. She knew how much he regretted causing Edwards's death.

"That's it exactly," Zach said. "And it almost worked. You played a key role at a critical moment, Corbray. You both played key roles in this. Laura, your insights into what had really happened with Ali Al Zahrani were vital."

Petras took over again. "From what we can tell, he planned to go into hiding for a while, but then you called and offered to come to him. He didn't have much time, so he bought gas—we found receipts for a half dozen gas stations—and used what was actually a garage door opener to convince you he had a detonator."

"A garage door opener?" Laura was astonished. She looked over at Javier. "Did you know it wasn't a detonator? Is that why you just went ahead and shot him?"

Javier shook his head. "Stupid *cabrón* had it clutched tight in his hand. I couldn't see what it was."

"Thank God it's all over." Laura didn't want to think about it any longer.

"Being on a terrorist kill list is a lifetime commitment," Petras said.

What did he mean by that?

Javier glared at him. "A month ago you gave her shit for wanting you to take the threats against her seriously, and now you're telling her she faces a lifetime of this?"

"I don't know that it's that grave." Zach glared at Petras, too. "In the wake of the bombing, various federal agencies that monitor suspected terrorist sympathizers found an uptick in interest in you, Laura. As a result, we've upgraded our threat assessment. There's no immediate danger, but you should continue to take precautions. You have my word that we will stay on top of it."

Laura refused to let this news shake her. "Thank you, Zach. Thank you both."

LAURA AND JAVIER ignored the world for the next two days. No news. No Internet. No e-mail. Javier played his guitar and sang love songs for Laura in Spanish. They talked and laughed and made love with the same abandon they'd known in Dubai. Except that this wasn't a fling between two people determined to maintain their independence. It was love between a man and a woman who knew how easy it was to lose *everything*.

AS MUCH AS Laura tried to ignore it, Sunday came, dawning far too early. She made Javier's breakfast while he packed, checked in with his flight, and printed his boarding pass. They ate together, Laura doing her best to be cheerful when inside she felt like she was breaking.

She'd vowed to herself she wouldn't cry. He was returning to his job, a job for which he'd spent his life training, a job few men could do, one that was vital to the security of the nation. How selfish it would be of her to try to hold him back or make him feel worse about leaving by forcing him to deal with her tears. He was a special operator, a SEAL, and loving him meant accepting the fact that he would be gone—and in danger—much of the time.

She drove him to the airport, where Nate was waiting to say good-bye. Javier checked in his duffel bag and guitar case, and the three of them stood talking, the minutes seeming to race by until it was time for Javier to go.

He and Nate embraced, slapping each other on the back.

"Thanks, bro. You're the best friend a man could have. Do me a favor and watch over Laura, okay?"

"You got it. She's welcome at the ranch any time." They shook hands. "Happy hunting, Corbray. Damn, it was good to see you."

"I'll be back."

Nate glanced over at Laura, raised an eyebrow. "I'm sure you will be."

And then it was time for Laura to say good-bye.

She sank into Javier's embrace and held him tight, savoring the precious feel of his arms around her. She turned her face up to his and kissed him, unable to hold back her tears. "Promise me you'll do everything you can to stay safe. I love you, Javier Corbray. My world wouldn't be whole without you in it."

"I promise." He wiped the tears from her cheeks with his thumbs. "I don't know when I'll be in touch again, but you've got my numbers. I'll answer e-mails when I can and call you whenever I get the chance. If you need anything, call Nate or McBride."

She nodded, sniffed, tried to smile.

He ducked down, kissed her. "I love you. Remember that, okay? No matter what, *bella*, you remember that."

Laura nodded, then watched, her heart aching, as he turned and walked away.

CHAPTER 31

Two months later

JAVIER CROUCHED DOWN, his suppressed HK416 raised
and ready, NVGs giving him a clear view of the darkened
street beyond. He watched for motion, for any sign that they'd
been noticed, covering for Ross as he placed an explosive
charge on the locked front gate. They took cover.

BAM!

A dog across the street barked, roused by the blast.

The gate swung open.

They moved swiftly and silently toward the front door, the
men lining up on either side, staying out of the line of fire.

Javier tested the handle, found it unlocked. He nudged it
open and caught a glimpse of an empty hallway.

He entered, Desprez and the rest of the team following him
in a tight line. They cleared room after room, finding mostly
sleeping women and children, Javier making a mental inven-
tory of people old enough to offer resistance—men, women,
older boys.

They found him in a room upstairs. He lay asleep on the
floor on a bed of cushions, an AK propped against the wall
near his head, a young woman sleeping beside him—one of
his wives. Javier confiscated the AK and handed it to Reeves,
who was watching his six with Tower, the rest of the team
downstairs to cover their exfil route.

Javier moved in on the bastard and jabbed him in the head with the tip of his suppressor. "Wake up, motherfucker."

Salman Al-Nassar's eyes opened, and he sat bolt upright, staring wide-eyed at Javier, reaching for the missing AK and muttering something in Arabic.

"Look at him," Javier said to Tower. "It's a nightmare—and it's real."

Tower barked something at the bastard in Arabic.

Javier stuck with English. "I know you understand me, so listen very carefully. We don't want to hurt any of the women or children here, but if you fuck with us, we'll take this place apart—starting with you. Have I got your attention?"

Salman nodded, sweat beading on his forehead. "Yes."

"You know why we're here?"

The man nodded again. "You came for the girl."

"Wake the woman. Tell her to be quiet. Send her to get the girl."

The man shook the woman beside him and woke her, covering her mouth to keep her from screaming. She stared wide-eyed up at Javier as her husband spoke in rapid Arabic. She climbed out of bed and hurried past Javier and out the door, her long, dark hair hanging down her back, Tower following behind her.

Salman glared at Javier. "My brother is going to be a martyr."

"Your brother is a murdering, raping terrorist asshole. He's going to rot in hell. Keep talking, and I'll make sure you join him."

From somewhere nearby, he heard a woman cry out.

And then Tower was there, a sleeping toddler in his arms, dark hair spilling over the blanket, her little face so much like Laura's that Javier didn't need a DNA test to know this was Klara.

A woman appeared in the doorway, a distressed look on her face. She spoke in Arabic to the man, who hissed at her. She fell silent.

Javier walked over to her. "Safiya?"

Her eyes went wide.

He held his rifle against her chest and glared down into her face, letting the full force of the hatred he felt for her come through. He asked Tower to translate. "Tell her that this little girl was never hers to take or hold. Tell her that it is only for the sake of her children that I don't pull this trigger right now."

Tower translated, but the translation went on so long that Javier was pretty sure the man had added a few thoughts of his own.

Trembling, Safiya sank to the floor, terror on her face.

Javier turned back to Salman. "This ends here, dawg. You or any of your terrorist buddies try to harm Laura Nilsson or her baby girl, and I will personally hunt you down and rip your balls off. Got that?"

Salman nodded.

Javier turned to Tower and Reeves. "Time to go."

LAURA BENT DOWN so that Karima Al Zahrani could kiss her cheeks.

"You have restored Ali's memory, Laura. Please know that you are always welcome in our home."

"Thank you." Laura forced the words past the lump in her throat. "It was the least I could do."

Laura had spent the past few weeks putting together a feature package about Ali—his life, his dreams, his accomplishments— her way of helping Denver face the murder of an innocent young man whom most had been only too hasty to condemn. The article, which Laura had felt deeply driven to write, had finally run in today's paper. She'd called Karima and Yusif to ask whether she could drop a copy of the edition by their house and had arrived to find their entire family gathered together. When they'd invited her to stay for dinner, she hadn't been able to refuse.

It was a balm to her heart to see smiles on their faces.

Yusif offered her his right hand. "Thank you, Laura. You are a woman of good heart. *Ma'salaam.*"

Farewell.

"Thank you. And farewell."

Then Hussein Al Zahrani, Ali's uncle, stood. A proud man and devout, he did not offer to shake her hand. Instead, he stood before her, a sheen of tears in his eyes. "As Ali was my nephew, so you are my niece, Laura. If there is anything you need, call upon me. I will help you if I can. *Inshallah*."

God willing.

"Thank you. You are very gracious. *Ma'salaam*."

Under the watchful gazes of Ali's father and uncle, she walked to her car. The night was warm, the sky bright with stars, the air scented with lilacs. Winter had finally given way to spring. She made the drive back to The Ironworks through quiet streets, her mind turning to Javier as it always did.

God, she missed him.

Two months had gone by since he'd left for Coronado. She'd gotten a few e-mails, and he'd called twice. He hadn't been able to tell her where he was or what he was doing, but it had been wonderful to hear his voice. She'd been certain the last time they'd spoken that he was out of the country. It might have been the bad connection that had given it away. Or it might have been the goat bleating in the background.

That had been two weeks ago.

She'd been watching reports on the newswire since then, looking for international news that might indicate where U.S. SEAL teams might be deployed, but that had proven to be about as effective as consulting a crystal ball. She could do nothing for him but pray, and so she did, just as she'd done every night since her rescue. Only now she didn't have to pray for "the tall SEAL," because he had a name.

About Klara she'd heard nothing—not a single call from Erik in weeks.

She let herself into her loft, checked her e-mail for messages from Javier, then settled in for the night, fighting a growing sense of melancholy. She sank into a tub of hot lavender-scented water and tried to let her worries float away.

Four years ago, a day like today would have felt like a great success. She'd put together a feature story she was proud of, a story that had made a difference in someone's life. And although it *did* mean a lot to her, there was a loneliness to her daily routine that she couldn't ignore, an emptiness that stole the shine off even the most positive moments.

It wasn't that she lacked friends. The ordeal with Kimball had brought her closer to her colleagues and opened the door to deep friendships with Sophie, Megan, and Janet. Laura was grateful to have them in her life, but friends couldn't make up for the loved ones who were absent—Klara and Javier.

She'd always been comfortable in her solitude, but without Javier the loft now seemed empty. She missed his voice, the music he played on his guitar, the sound of his laughter. And sex. Yes, she missed that, too. Having the evenings and week-ends free to do whatever she wanted—something she had once cherished about being single—wasn't nearly as satisfying as doing those things with Javier.

But that's what it meant to love a military man. Other women managed to cope with the long separations and periods of silence. So would Laura.

She closed her eyes, inhaled the soft scent of lavender, let her mind drift.

But rather than relaxing, she found herself wondering what it would be like to work and live in San Diego. She could get a journalism job pretty much anywhere in the world provided there was an opening. She liked the ocean, liked sunshine and palm trees. But was she willing to leave the paper, sell the loft, and move across the country just to be closer to a man?

As soon as she asked the question, she knew the answer.

Yes, she was. Oh, yes, she was—as long as that man was Javier.

But how would he feel about that? He'd never talked about living together or getting married. Then again, neither had she.

She soaked until the water was lukewarm, then dried off with a fluffy towel and slipped into her bathrobe. Out in the living room, she set her iPod to play the mix Javier made for her—a mix of the songs that he'd played for her and songs that they'd danced to. She hugged her arms around herself to ease the ache and, without realizing it, began to dance in slow circles where they had danced together that special night.

Her phone rang.

She jumped, startled, and ran to get it from her handbag. "This is Laura."

"Erik here. Please don't ask questions. Catch the next flight to Stockholm. E-mail me your itinerary, and I'll send a car for you."

Laura's pulse raced. "Erik?"

Had they found Klara?

"I'll see you when you get here."

LAURA LEFT A message for Tom, telling him she had to fly to Sweden for a family emergency, then called Janet to cancel their visit this weekend. She was sorry to do that because Janet, who'd been much more seriously injured than anyone had told Laura, was still adjusting to her new life and needed both help and company.

Janet took it with good spirits. "Have a safe trip. I hope everything is okay."

Laura managed to catch a late flight to New York, then flew standby to Reykjavik, Iceland. From there, she caught another flight to Sweden, arriving at Stockholm Arlanda Airport twenty hours after getting Erik's call. As he'd promised, a car was waiting for her at the airport, even though it was only seven in the morning.

Sitting in the backseat, she called her mother, whose surprised squeal almost split Laura's right eardrum. "I'm not sure why I'm here. He just told me to catch a flight, and so I came."

"This must have to do with Klara. Do you think she's here?"

Laura couldn't fathom how that could be possible. "The last I heard from him, the Pakistani government had no idea where she'd been taken. Even if they'd found her again, it would take months to win custody of her."

Still Laura dared to hope.

Was it possible that Klara would be flying home with her? The thought made her pulse trip.

"Ring us as soon as you know."

"I will."

Pumped up on caffeine and adrenaline, she looked out the window, the familiar streets of Stockholm seeming strange to her, the city awash in the grays of clouds, sea, and rain. It was only when they passed Rosenbad, the street that was home to the foreign ministry, that she realized he wasn't taking her to Erik's office. He headed into Östermalm, passing Humlegården and the Royal Library before turning into a gate that led to a private courtyard of a three-story residence.

The car drew to a stop. "The minister is expecting you, Miss Nilsson."

Laura thanked the driver and stepped out, the air chilly. She made her way to the black double doors and rang the bell, too tense to stand still.

If the Swedish government had somehow won Klara's freedom, why couldn't Erik simply tell her so over the phone? Why was it so essential that she come to Stockholm at once? Was it possible that something terrible had happened, that they'd discovered Klara had been killed or . . . ?

Laura's stomach turned, even as her logical mind told her Erik wouldn't have made her fly halfway around the world to get bad news. She drew a deep breath, tried to rein in her imagination.

The door opened.

Erik gave her a tired smile, lines of stress on his face, his blond hair looking like he hadn't combed it since getting up. "Come in. Did you have a good flight?"

"Yes. All the connections went smoothly." Laura stepped inside and wiped her feet, wishing Erik would skip the small talk and tell her why she was here.

"Let's step into my office." He motioned toward a closed door to her right.

She followed him inside—and froze. *"Javier?"*

He stood by Erik's desk wearing jeans and a black T-shirt, a smile on his handsome face. "Hey, *bella*."

JAVIER WAS IN deep shit, but the moment he saw Laura, that no longer mattered. He couldn't keep the stupid grin off his face. "God, it's good to see you."

She rushed into his arms and held him tight, as if she thought he might disappear. "What are you doing here?"

Had it been only two months since he'd seen her? It felt like an eternity.

"That's a long story."

Erik's voice cut in. "Mr. Corbray is under house arrest. He claims he acted alone, but I find that rather hard to believe. He showed up on my doorstep early yesterday morning with Klara in his arms—"

"Klara is *here*?" Laura looked from Erik to Javier, eyes wide.

Javier nodded, unable to keep from smiling. "She's a beautiful little girl, Laura. She has your face and the sweetest blue eyes—"

Erik interrupted. "Mr. Corbray took Klara by force and entered Sweden illegally. I should report him to police, but instead I've confined him to my home and am doing my best to keep this secret. On the one hand, I don't want it to become an international incident. On the other, I don't want to break the law. But if I follow official procedure, I would have to hand Klara over to the Pakistani delegation. That is the dilemma Mr. Corbray brought to my door."

Laura's eyes were still wide, and it was clear to Javier that she wasn't picking up anything Erik was saying. "M-my daughter . . . is *here*?"

"Yes, she is." Erik went on. "I have been working round the clock with a few individuals in the Swedish government to ensure that Klara can remain in the country. We'll give her Swedish citizenship, give her a Swedish passport, but this is all very irregular. If the parties in Pakistan come forward—"

"I've already told you. Al-Nassar's brother is not going to talk." But Laura didn't need to hear any of this. Javier cupped her face in his palms. "Klara has already been seen by a doctor, and she's okay. They took DNA, and it checks out. She's your little girl. There's no doubt."

"But how—"

Erik glowered at Javier. "Let's hear that story again, because I don't think you've told me the truth yet."

Javier hadn't told the truth, but he wasn't going to incriminate any of the guys who'd helped him out, not even Tower. He told Laura the basics, not mentioning that he'd been part of a team of five. If anyone was going to hang over this, it would be him. "I went in after dark armed to the teeth and demanded they turn her over to me."

Laura looked up at him. "I can't believe the navy sent you by yourself."

Javier cleared his throat. "They didn't send me, *bella*. When I went to Coronado, it was to resign from NSW. I was given an honorable discharge from the Teams and set this up on my own."

"Oh, my God, Javi." Laura gaped at him. "You gave up the Teams?"

In the end, it hadn't been a hard decision.

"I couldn't let them keep her from you any longer." Javier knew Laura's mind must be reeling from all of this.

Her blond brows came together in a look of worry. "Did Klara cry when you took her away? She must have been terrified."

"I sedated her."

Laura blinked. "You . . . You drugged her?"

"I got a dose of sedatives from a pediatrician before I left the U.S. She slept in my arms the entire trip." He'd watched her sleep, tiny eyelashes on her cheeks, one little hand tucked beneath her chin, and had fallen hard for the sweet little thing.

Like mother, like daughter. They both steal your heart, cabrón.

"Can I see her? I want to see her."

Javier was surprised she'd held out this long.

Erik seemed to relax, anger fading from his face. He smiled. "Yes, of course. She's upstairs having breakfast with my wife and the girls. I'm sorry to go on like this. I wanted you to understand the gravity of the situation."

She took Erik's hand and gave it a squeeze. "Thank you, Erik, for all you've done."

Erik led the way up the stairs toward a kitchen, the sound of little girls' voices and a woman's echoing down the hall.

Javier held Laura's hand, an unreadable expression on her pretty face. He couldn't imagine what she was feeling. The whole thing was more than a little overwhelming for him, and Klara wasn't his daughter.

Though he hoped maybe one day she would be.

He watched Laura's face as they entered the kitchen. Her gaze fell on Klara and went soft, tears shimmering in her eyes, a tremulous smile curving her lips.

Klara sat on a booster chair, her dark brown hair in neat pigtails, a look of distress on her tiny face, little tears on her cheeks.

Heidi, Erik's wife, hurried over to Laura and hugged her, speaking in English for Javier's benefit. "It's so good to meet you at last, Laura. Klara is such a darling, such a sweet little girl, but she won't eat. She won't touch anything but her bottle."

Then Klara looked over at Laura, mother and child making eye contact for the first time. And Javier's vision went strangely blurry.

CHAPTER 32

LAURA LOOKED AT the daughter she'd never seen, taking in the sight of her from her long brown hair to her bright blue eyes to her sweet face, her features so like Laura's that they reminded Laura of baby pictures she'd seen of herself. She felt a visceral need to hold Klara, her throat suddenly so tight she couldn't speak. And although Laura didn't know much about babies or children, she knew that Klara was desperately unhappy.

She looked up at Laura, tears on her cheeks, her lower lip sticking out, a bottle sitting on the table before her.

Laura went to her at once, kneeling down beside her and speaking in Arabic. "Are you hungry, sweet one?"

Klara clearly understood her, her gaze now fixed on Laura.

Laura looked at the food on the table. Hard-boiled eggs. Cod roe. Cucumber. *Knäckebröd*. Corn flakes. "Heidi, do you have any French bread, maybe some yogurt or jam or a banana? I don't think she recognizes any of this as food."

"Of course." Heidi bustled around the kitchen, then set a half-eaten loaf of French bread on the table with a jar of strawberry jam and a ripe banana, her four-year-old twins Stella and Anette watching with wide eyes, their red hair in little braids.

"She hasn't eaten food like this before," Laura explained to the girls in Swedish.

She sat in a chair beside Klara, tore a small piece of bread off the loaf, and put a dab of strawberry jam on it, then held it out for Klara.

Klara took it, stuck it in her tiny mouth, and reached for another.

"More," she said in Arabic, her tiny voice like bells.

It was the first word Laura had heard her speak.

"You want more?" Laura tore another piece off, dabbed it with jam, and held it out for her, unable to keep herself from smiling. "You're such a sweet girl."

"Mama?" Klara glanced around, fear in her eyes, her little lip quavering again.

Laura knew she was looking for Safiya.

She couldn't imagine what Klara was feeling—being taken from the only world she knew, falling asleep, and waking up in a scary new place surrounded by strangers, everyone speaking a language that made no sense. Though it was good for Klara that she was no longer living in a hive of terrorists, Laura would have done anything to make this easier on her, to minimize the disruption in her life.

She stroked her little girl's cheek. "You're going to have a new mama, and a new name, a new home. I know it won't be easy at first, but you're safe now, Klara."

Laura tore several more small pieces of bread off the loaf and set them on the plate in front of her daughter, then did the same with the banana, watching in absolute fascination as Klara picked them up with her chubby little hand and put them in her mouth one by one. It stunned Laura to think this little person had come from inside her. Klara was so sweet, so perfect, so completely innocent.

Laura looked over at Javier, tears of happiness spilling down her cheeks. "Isn't she beautiful, Javi? Isn't she beautiful?"

He smiled, his voice strained when he answered. "Just like her mother."

LAURA CALLED HER mother and grandmother to share the news. Erik sent a car to pick them up, and Laura felt like she was lost in a dream as she watched her mother and grandmother meet and hold Klara for the first time.

"She reminds me so much of you, except for the color of her hair, of course," her mother said. "Oh, she's adorable, Laura!"

While Javier faced the consequences of his actions alone, answering questions in Erik's office, the three of them spent the morning with Klara, holding her when she seemed to want to be held, guiding her as she shyly explored her new surroundings, watching as the twins found ways to draw her into a kind of play that needed no language, doting on her like big sisters. When Stella gave Klara a kiss with a stuffed puppy, Klara laughed, the sound magical to Laura's ears.

"Mommy, I made her laugh!" Stella beamed.

As the girls played, Heidi and Laura's mother got into a conversation about raising daughters—and about the challenges Laura would face.

"We don't know if she's gotten any of her vaccines," Heidi said. "We don't know what illnesses she's had. We don't know if they'd started potty-training her at all. But it will all sort itself out in the end."

"How did Javier do this?" Laura's mother finally asked.

Laura shared what Javier had told her. "I still can't believe it. He gave up his career with the Teams for this."

"He loves you," her mother said. "Love makes us strong."

"I sure hope they don't plan on doing what he did and coming after her," Heidi said. "One reason Erik is keeping this so quiet is to prevent Al-Nassar's people from knowing where Klara is. We always have security because of his position with the government, but I wonder if he should increase it."

The thought of Al-Nassar's family trying to take Klara from her again made Laura's stomach knot.

"It will be much harder to keep her out of the public eye in the States," her mother told Heidi. "The American press has followed Laura like jackals since her rescue."

Heidi turned to Laura. "How are you going to avoid the media?"

Laura hadn't figured any of that out yet. "This was all so sudden. I haven't had time to think about it."

Her mother rubbed a hand on her back and gave a laugh. "You'd better start thinking about it soon, *älskling*."

And Laura realized there were a lot of things she needed to consider.

JAVIER MET WITH one government official after the next—some military, some civilian. He couldn't keep their names or titles straight. It was his second day of interrogation—very polite interrogation. They spoke with Erik in Swedish, then looked sternly at him and asked questions in English.

And Javier answered.

No, this operation was not approved by the U.S. No, it hadn't been authorized by the navy or NSW either. Yes, it was true that Javier had left the SEALs. Yes, he'd gone to Pakistan alone. No, he hadn't killed anyone. No, he couldn't tell them how he'd gotten in and out of Pakistan or how he'd known where to find Klara.

No one asked him *why* he'd done it. They all understood the brutality and injustice of what had been done to Laura. They knew it was better for Klara to grow up with her mother and not among terrorists. So, although they threatened Javier with arrest and incarceration more than once, it became clear to him that they were going to let him go—but not without a few stern lectures.

They finally finished with him around lunchtime. Javier made his way upstairs, where he met Birgitta, Laura's mother, and Inga, her grandmother, in person.

Birgitta shook his hand, hugged him, kissed his cheek. "I could never find the words to thank you for all you've done for my daughter. You love her, I know, and she loves you. I'm so happy for both of you."

Inga smiled. "You are very handsome man—very brave, too, I think."

That's when Javier remembered they'd seen him buck naked and shaved bare. He felt heat rush into his face and hoped to fuck he wasn't blushing. "Thank you, ma'am."

He joined the family upstairs for lunch, watching as Laura prepared a plate of food for Klara—leftover roasted chicken, some kind of pea salad, and more banana.

Birgitta sat beside him and leaned close, laying her hand

atop his. "I know what you sacrificed to free Klara. If there's ever anything I can do, please let me know."

He looked over at Klara, who was smiling up at her mother. "Seeing them together makes it all worth it."

Hell, yeah, it had been worth it. And yet . . .

If you're not a special operator, Corbray, what are you?

It was time for him to figure that out.

LAURA'S MOTHER AND grandmother went home before supper, not wishing to impose on Erik and Heidi, whose lives and routines had been turned upside down by Javier's unexpected arrival. Laura spent every moment of the day caring for Klara—playing with her, reading to her, changing her diaper. She gave her a bath after supper, entranced to see her daughter laughing and splashing in the water. And then it was bedtime.

Laura settled herself in a rocking chair, gave Klara her bottle, and began to rock her to sleep. She looked down at the sweet girl in her arms, her heart so filled with love that it seemed to swell. Some part of her had been afraid this moment would never come, that she would never touch or set eyes on her daughter. But here Klara was, a little miracle, her smile enough to light Laura's world, her laughter pure joy.

From the hallway beyond, Laura heard Erik and Javier speaking.

"Heidi asked me to bring on more security, but I told her she had no reason to worry. They have no idea Klara is here. Only when Laura appears in public with Klara will they know for certain where she is."

"I'm hoping they know better than to come after her. I tried to explain to them how dangerous it would be for them to try."

"Danger means little to a terrorist who finds glory in death."

Laura's heart raced to hear them talk like this. She'd always thought that freeing Klara would be the end of the nightmare, not a new beginning. Al-Nassar's threats from the courtroom came back to her.

I am in chains, but I shall be free in Paradise, while you *will always live in fear. You will never be safe, nor will anyone you love.*

She looked down at her daughter, held her tighter, the feel of her precious in her arms. Klara was almost asleep now, dark eyelashes resting on her cheeks, her little body limp, an expression of complete peace on her face. So small and helpless, she didn't know how cruel the world could be, didn't know she was the daughter of a man who had killed hundreds, didn't know that the world would be titillated by her very existence. She was just a tiny child.

And it was Laura's job to give her the best, safest life she could.

Laura set her carefully in the crib, taking the bottle from her hands and tucking a warm blanket beneath her chin.

"Sleep well, Klara. Dream of angels."

She had a few precious minutes alone with Javier, several of which were spent kissing on the sofa. "What are they going to do with you?"

"I'm under unofficial house arrest until we leave."

Relieved for him, she rested her head against his chest, still stunned to think he'd left the Teams for her, gone all the way to Pakistan, and come away with Klara. "When we get home, I want the whole story."

"What makes you think I haven't told you the whole story?"

She couldn't help but laugh. "Call it reporter's intuition."

Soon it was time to go. Erik summoned a car for her, and Laura found herself under her mother's roof in the bed where she'd slept so well and so deeply as a teenager. She'd had such big dreams in those days, her future overflowing with possibility.

But tonight she didn't sleep, and she didn't dream, Al-Nassar's threat echoing in her mind.

JAVIER KNEW SOMETHING was wrong the moment he saw Laura's face the next morning. She looked like she hadn't slept, her eyes red from crying. She spent a few minutes with Klara and then asked to speak with Erik and Javier somewhere private. Erik led them to his office and shut the door.

Laura looked at neither of them but sat up straight, her face expressionless apart from the despair he saw in her eyes. "I have done a great deal of thinking and soul-searching, and I have decided to . . ." Her voice quavered. "I have decided to give Klara up for adoption to a Swedish family."

Javier couldn't believe what he'd heard. He found himself on his feet. "What the hell? You can't be serious."

"I think she is." Erik motioned for Javier to sit down. "Laura, why don't you tell us what has led you to this?"

"There are two reasons." She cleared her throat. "The first and most important is safety. There is no way to know that Al-Nassar's family or his followers won't strike out at me or try to take Klara from me again. You heard Petras. 'Being on a terrorist kill list is a lifetime commitment.' The threat hasn't gone away. What's to stop them from coming after her and taking her the way you did, Javier?"

"*I'll* stop them."

She gave him a soft smile. "I know you would do everything possible, even give your life for her if it came to it, but I don't want you in harm's way either. If Klara were adopted in secrecy here in Sweden, they'd never know what became of her."

"We can hire security, get a team of guys—"

"Javier, please listen." Laura closed her eyes for a moment, as if fighting to control her emotions. "There's also the fact that her father is a convicted terrorist. If Klara grows up with me, she will learn the truth sooner rather than later. Someone will tell her, or she'll read an article about me on the Internet. She will have to spend most of her life knowing that her father was a murderer and that she was born as the result of rape while her mother was in captivity. I want to spare her that."

Javier felt like he'd been kicked in the chest, his rage so dark and thick that he could scarcely put it into words. "After all I did to get her for you, you're just going to give her away?"

Laura met his gaze, tears in her eyes. "I'm so sorry, Javier. But what you did—it wasn't for nothing. Don't you see? You freed her. You got her away from a group of killers who would have given her a terrible life. I can't change the choice you made, but your choice saved her. Now, it's up to me to do what's best for her."

"I love her. I love that little girl. I held her in my arms all the way here."

And Javier realized that this was at the heart of his rage.

He loved little Klara. The thought of losing her . . .

"I love her, too, and that's *why* I have to give her up. I won't put her at risk or compromise her happiness for the sake of my own." Laura looked pleadingly at Javier as if begging him to understand. "I want her to grow up knowing only that she is safe and cherished. I don't want the ugliness of my captivity with her biological father to be the first page in the story of her life. I don't want her to grow up looking over her shoulder and knowing she's the daughter of a mass murderer."

Laura's words began to pierce his anger and grief. He reached over and took her hand. "You know I'd do anything and everything to keep your little girl safe."

She nodded. "You've already done more than any other man could."

Erik's face was grave. "Are you absolutely certain, Laura?"

She nodded. "Yes, I am. I would like to find a family that would be willing to send me photographs and let my mother and grandmother visit her from time to time—if it is safe."

"Do Birgitta and Inga know about your decision?"

"I told them this morning. They are very upset, of course, but they understand."

"If you are certain, then might I suggest an adoptive family, one that meets the criteria you listed?" Erik asked. "Heidi and I would love to adopt your little girl."

IT WAS SETTLED very quietly and very efficiently.

Over the course of the next week, Klara was given Swedish citizenship. Adoption papers were drawn up and signed. Laura taught Heidi some basic Arabic words to help her communicate with Klara until Klara learned Swedish. Erik and Heidi held a private christening ceremony at the nearby Lutheran church where Laura stood as godmother to her own child, Javier and her mother and grandmother standing beside her.

"What is the child's name?" the priest asked.

Erik and Heidi gave Laura the honor of making that announcement.

Laura felt a moment of triumph speaking her daughter's true name. "Her name is Klara Marie."

Laura spent her last morning in Stockholm feeding Klara breakfast, playing with her, reading to her, doing her best to memorize the sound of her little voice, the sweet scent of her skin, the feel of her in her arms. When it was time for Klara's nap, Laura settled her in her crib, stroking her downy hair until she fell asleep.

"I am so sorry, Klara. I'm sorry you came into the world in such a rough way. I'm sorry these past several days have been so scary for you. And I'm so sorry I have to leave you now. But it's best for you this way. Heidi and Erik will love you. Stella and Anette will be your big sisters. You will have a family to love and cherish you. I will see you again one day. I love you with everything I am, Klara, and I always will, no matter how far apart we are. Sleep, my girl. Dream of angels."

She felt Javier behind her.

"The car is here, *bella*. Our luggage is loaded. It's time to go."

Laura nodded, bent down, and pressed a kiss to Klara's cheek.

Somehow, she managed to walk away from the crib without crying, something inside her screaming that Klara was hers. *Her* daughter. *Her* child. Taking one wooden step after another, she followed Erik and Heidi as they and their twins walked her and Javier to the waiting car.

"We will take care of her, Laura." Heidi hugged her tightly, tears in her eyes. "Thank you for the beautiful gift you have given us."

"We'll be in touch every week." Erik gave Laura a hug. "You are a very courageous woman. I promise you that Klara will learn the truth when she is ready, and she will be proud to be your daughter."

"Thank you—for everything," Laura said.

Javier helped her into the backseat, then sat beside her. And the car began to move—out the gate, down the street, around the corner.

And Laura broke.

With a cry, she sank against Javier, her grief spilling out in broken sobs.

Feeling helpless, Javier held Laura tight all the way to the airport. He held her on the twelve-hour flight to New York. He held her on the connecting flight to Denver. He held her on the cab ride from Denver International Airport to her loft. He held her as she cried herself to sleep.

He held her because there was nothing else he could do—and because some part of his heart had broken, too.

CHAPTER 33

LAURA AWOKE TO find herself still nestled in Javier's arms, his head on her pillow. But she wasn't ready to face the day—or the rawness of her own emotions. She snuggled against his chest and let herself doze, the steady beating of his heart against her cheek.

It was almost noon when her stomach woke her.

Javier brushed a strand of hair from her face. "Hey."

"Hey."

"Hungry?"

"Starving."

They brushed their teeth, and Laura couldn't help but laugh when she saw how puffy her eyes were. "I look terrible."

He kissed her. "You look beautiful."

They made breakfast together as they'd done during the weeks he'd stayed with her, Javier making the coffee, Laura putting together omelets and toast, the joy she felt at being with him helping her to keep her grief at bay. After two months of living by herself, it felt good to have him here again, something about his presence making the loft feel more like a home. Wanting fresh air and sunshine, they carried their plates outdoors and sat at the little table on Laura's balcony, the streets of LoDo alive with lunch-hour traffic and busy pedestrians.

Laura sipped her coffee, the familiar taste almost making her sigh. "Mmm. I've missed this."

He grinned at her over the rim of his coffee cup, his gaze warm. "So have I."

She knew he wasn't talking about coffee.

But it was time.

"Are you going to tell me what really happened?"

He set his cup down. "This can't go beyond us. You can't even tell your mother and grandmother."

"I understand, and I promise."

Laura listened as he told her the whole story. How he'd begun planning for the trip to Pakistan before he left Denver. How he'd contacted a few guys from his platoon he knew he could trust, putting together a volunteer black-ops team that included Tower.

"He feel he owes you—and he does. Turns out that he's not just an asshole. He's damned good at his job. He speaks as many languages as you do, has connections everywhere. He got quick intel on Klara for us, handled our supplies and transportation. The man blends in with the locals, just disappears in a crowd. He was a vital member of the team, that's for damned sure."

He told her what had happened once they'd gotten inside the house, what he'd said to Al-Nassar's brother and Safiya. Perhaps his threats of violence against them should have shocked her, but they didn't.

Instead, they felt like a tiny step toward justice.

"Once I was airborne with Klara, the others flew back to the States on separate flights. Tower took my combat gear with him so I didn't have to hassle with that. When I got to Stockholm, I called Erik, told him who I was and who was with me. He sent a car to the airport."

"How did you find him or know to go there?"

"You mentioned him—and I searched your e-mail in-box. I turned his name over to Tower, who did the rest."

She stared at him. "You searched my e-mail?"

He shrugged. "Hey, it worked, didn't it? You can't argue with success."

She glared at him. "Oh, I can argue all right. Don't tempt me."

"You're not seriously ticked, are you?"

"No, not really. You could have asked, though."

He shook his head, took her hand. "I didn't want you to

know anything about this. I didn't want any of the blame to fall on you if the op went sideways—and I sure as hell didn't want you to spend every day for the next two months worrying."

"I don't know how to feel about the fact that Derek Tower and a handful of your team buddies know about Klara now."

"They all wanted to help, *bella*. They feel a kind of connection to you. They saw how it was there. They know what you went through. They didn't want to leave your little girl there. And not one of them will breathe a word of it."

"Will you or the others get in any trouble for this?"

Javier shook his head. "We pulled it off. No one was killed. If NSW hears about it, they'll probably look the other way."

The enormity of what Javier had done hit Laura.

"Do you realize that yours were the first caring hands to hold her?" She laced her fingers through his, brought his hand to her mouth, and kissed it. "I still can't believe what you did for me, for her. You gave up your spot on the Teams. You risked your life, your freedom."

His lips curved in a soft smile. "I guess I found something that matters more to me."

"What you did—it was so incredibly selfless."

He gave a slow shake of his head, his eyes looking into hers. "Nah, *bella*. What you did for that sweet baby girl—*that* was selfless. You love her so much that you gave her up, even though it tore you apart."

And the grief Laura had been fighting so hard to keep at bay welled up inside her, the ache behind her breastbone growing sharp. "I was only her mother for a handful of days, but in that time, I was a pretty good mother, wasn't I?"

"You were the best." A muscle clenched in Javier's jaw, and he gave her hand a squeeze, a fierce light in his eyes, his voice rough. "Hold on to that in your heart and never forget it."

Laura fought tears. She didn't want to cry again. "I only spent nine days with her, but, God, I miss her."

"So do I."

AFTER BREAKFAST, LAURA found an e-mail with photographs of Klara. In one, Erik was holding Klara up so that she could pet a pony at Anette and Stella's riding lesson, a look of wonder and delight on her little face. In another, Klara sat in her booster chair in a pretty blue dress with cake all over her hands and face—part of an adoption party they'd thrown to celebrate with family and close friends.

Javier looked at the photos with Laura, happy just to see the smile on Klara's face—and the relief on Laura's. "She's going to be fine, *bella*. See that?"

He gave Laura some privacy so that she could write a reply, taking time to check in with the men to tell them what had happened in Stockholm. Speaking in code, he told them that Laura hadn't brought her daughter home—and that no one could ever hear about his little side trip to Sweden. To a man, they got choked up when they heard what Laura had done for her little girl, Tower most of all.

A half hour after Javier called him, he showed up at Laura's door. "We need to set you up with VPN, Ms. Nilsson. If you're going to be sending regular e-mails to Sweden, you're going to want your communications to be secure."

"Please, call me Laura." She walked over to him, stood on her tiptoes, and kissed his cheek. "Thank you for helping to save my daughter."

"I'm glad I was there." He smiled at Laura, the look in his eyes setting off Javier's radar. "I just want to tell you that I respect you to the core. What you did must have been hard as hell."

"Thank you. And yes—it was."

"She's an incredible woman," Tower said to Javier later when they were alone. "If you ever decide to move on—"

"Not a chance, dawg. Don't even go there, or it's back to me thinking you're just an asshole, got it?"

If Laura would have him, Javier was here to stay.

LAURA SPENT THE late afternoon unpacking and doing laundry—hers and Javier's—while he and Derek set up her VPN. It felt good to do something mindless. The simple act of folding clothes and putting things in their place made her feel like she was restoring some kind of order to her world.

Tomorrow she would return to her daily routine. She would head to the paper, catch up with Sophie and the others, and pick up the investigation she'd dropped when Erik called. And everything would be the way it had been before.

No. No, that wasn't true.

Everything was different now.

The realization dawned slowly, settling behind Laura's breastbone, the truth of it sending ripples through her.

Two weeks ago, Klara had been a captive, living with terrorists. But now she was free and settled out of harm's way. Two weeks ago, Laura hadn't known when she would see Javier again. But now, he was here with her. What's more, he had *chosen* to be here with her. And he loved her.

Her world had changed so quickly that she hadn't fully comprehended it, hadn't yet come to appreciate it, her grief over Klara making it hard to see anything else. No, things hadn't turned out exactly the way she'd hoped they would. Still, the pieces of her life were finally falling into place, so many of her fears swept away.

Klara was seeing and doing things she'd never done before. She had a mother and father who loved her, who would give her a safe home, and two big sisters who adored her. She would go to school, learn to read, and grow up to make her own choices about how to dress, how to live, whom to marry. It was everything Laura had ever wanted for her and more.

And Javier.

He'd left the Teams and was free to start a new life for himself. He hadn't said much about what he wanted to do next or how long he planned to stay in Denver. But she knew he loved her. Whatever he wanted to do, wherever he wanted to live, she would make it work for both of them.

She'd had a lot of time to think during those long weeks after he'd left, and she knew what mattered most to her. Yes, her career was important, but life was too short and uncertain to spend focused on a job. When Kimball had held that knife to her throat, she hadn't been sorry about time she wouldn't spend in the newsroom and articles she wouldn't get to write. She'd regretted not having had more time with Javier.

Her gaze fell on the laundry basket, his socks and boxer briefs mixed with her panties, their jeans tangled. She hadn't been looking for a man, hadn't been looking to fall in love.

But somehow, in the midst of her pain and fear and grief, life had seen fit to give her this precious gift.

And from far away she heard her grandmother's words.

Allt kommer att bli bättre med tiden.

Everything will get better with time.

AFTER SUPPER, THEY went for a walk along the river to help work off the jet lag, the evening air cool and fresh, golden light spilling over the mountains. The Platte was running high and fast, swallows dipping down for water, cottonwood trees standing on the far bank, their leaves shivering in the breeze.

Javier held Laura's hand, savoring the moment as they talked about everything and nothing in particular. It felt good just to be with her like this—nothing to do, nowhere to be. Then she asked a question that caught him by surprise.

"If you went back to Coronado and told NSW you'd made a mistake, do you think they'd take you back?"

Did she want him to go?

"Probably." He'd had more than one friend who'd turned in his Trident only to show up a few months later in uniform again. "Why do you ask?"

"You loved being a SEAL. I hate to see you walk away from something that means so much to you. I don't want you to regret that later."

So she was still feeling guilty that he'd left his career behind.

"Come on." He led her off the path and walked toward the riverbank, where they could talk without cyclists whizzing by. He sat on a rounded boulder and drew her down beside him, her hand still in his.

"I didn't resign just because I was about to go off and break international law, *bella*. I gave the Teams fourteen good years, and I realized it was time for me to go."

"But three months ago you were so determined to get back to active duty."

Yeah, he had been. But that had changed.

"You were right about me—you and Nate. Part of the reason I joined the Teams was to prove to myself and my family that I wasn't a loser. I guess I thought I could somehow make up for what happened with Yadiel if I was just good enough. I realized that nothing I did—no amount of medals or successful missions—could bring him back or change who I am. I realized that if I wanted to build a life for myself outside the navy, I needed to start now. I'm thirty-eight and not getting any younger."

"What are you thinking of doing?"

He was glad she asked. He'd been meaning to bring this up. "Not sure yet. McBride said he might have a place for me on his team as a deputy U.S. Marshal on the state's fugitive task force. Tower wants the two of us to form our own security company now that Tower Global is gone. I need to think about it."

"So . . . would that mean staying in Denver?" She spoke the words with a deliberate casualness that made him smile.

He tucked a strand of hair behind her ear. "I walked away from you in Dubai, *bella*. I won't make that mistake again."

"Is that your not-so-subtle way of suggesting we drop the 'no strings attached' clause from our relationship?"

"I want strings, Laura."

She arched a blond eyebrow. "What kind of strings?"

"Nothing too crazy. I was thinking maybe I could have a couple of drawers for socks and underwear, maybe a rack in your closet, some space in the bathroom, my own parking place. Maybe I could even be your steady guy."

She was smiling now. "You want to move into the loft and *go steady* with me?"

He raised his hands to her face, cupped her cheeks, told her what was really in his heart. "Or you could marry me instead."

Her eyes went wide, her pupils dilating.

Adrenaline?

"I know it's a big step from no strings to rings, *bella*, but I fell in love with you that first night in Dubai. It just took me a while to realize it. I thought there'd be time. I thought I'd find you, but then you were gone. This love we feel for each other, it's special, and I want to take hold of it with both hands."

Laura looked into Javier's eyes, the intensity she saw there making her pulse race. He'd just asked her to marry him. She hadn't expected this. Not yet, anyway.

She had to swallow the lump in her throat before she could

speak. "Are . . . are you sure? I'm on a terrorist kill list. Do you really want to live your whole life—"

"Looking over my shoulder?" His gaze traveled over her face. "Yeah, I do. In case you haven't noticed, bad guys don't scare me. What scares me is the idea of not being here when you need me."

There was one other thing.

"You come from a big family with lots of brothers and sisters. Are you sure you won't regret not being a father?"

He looked as if he might laugh. "I want to marry *you*, not your uterus. If I want to spend time with kids, I've got a dozen nieces and nephews. But there's also a sweet little girl in Stockholm who means a lot to me. I didn't have a thing to do with bringing her into this world, and I won't raise her. But I held her life in my hands for a few priceless hours, and there's a part of me that considers her *ours*. I want us to watch her grow up together."

Tears blurred Laura's vision, his words touching the most tender part of her, the tightness in her throat making it hard to speak.

He frowned and wiped a tear from her cheek, apparently misunderstanding. "If it's too soon, I understand. I didn't mean—"

"Yes." She answered without the slightest hesitation or the tiniest shred of doubt.

"Yes?" He seemed confused. "You said *yes*."

She laughed. "What did you think I was going to say?"

"Well, I . . ."

And she understood. "You didn't plan this, did you?"

Like everything about him, it was spontaneous, sincere, straight from his heart.

"I wanted to ask you one day when the time seemed right, but we started talking and . . . Hell, I don't even have a ring." He looked into her eyes, his knuckles caressing her cheek. "I'm naked here, *bella*, just laying myself out for you, telling you how I feel."

Something inside Laura melted to see this big, strong man so completely vulnerable. "What you've done for me . . . I never thought I'd feel this whole again. You helped me put the pieces of myself back together. But if my whole world fell apart again tomorrow, the piece I couldn't live without is *you*. Your love has been my salvation, and I don't want to live an hour of my life without you."

He ducked down, kissed her slow and deep, then drew back, a look of astonishment on his handsome face. "*¡Anda pal carajo!* I'm going to marry you. Who'd have thought that a woman as classy and beautiful as you would end up with a *Boricua* kid from the South Bronx?"

Before Laura could say a word, he scooped her up in his arms and swung her in a circle, shouting for the world to hear. "*¡Wepa!*"

She shrieked, laughed, then found herself on her feet again, held tight in his arms.

"You won't regret this, *bella*."

She smiled, kissed him. "I know."

They turned toward home, walking hand in hand.

For someone who'd never wanted to get married, Laura suddenly couldn't wait. "We could get a license tomorrow and get married on Saturday."

"Nah, that won't do. Mamá Andreína would kick my ass. If my *abuelita* is not at the wedding, we're not married."

"So what you're telling me is that this is going to be a case of 'My Big Fat Puerto Rican Wedding'?"

He chuckled. "See what you got yourself into?"

But Laura wouldn't change it for the world.

EPILOGUE

Seven months later
Private island of El Conquistador Resort
Off the eastern tip of Puerto Rico

LAURA WALKED HAND in hand with Javier toward a pair of waiting beach chairs, the sea breeze catching her hair, sand warm against the soles of her bare feet. She looked up and down the beach for Erik, Heidi, and the girls. "Do you see them?"

"They're probably eating lunch."

She'd forgotten it was almost noon. "I guess we slept late."

"Sleep had nothing to do with it." Javier grinned.

Grandma Inga and Mamá Andreína sat side by side beneath a beach umbrella of palm fronds. Javier's two sisters, Ana and Nayelis, were having an animated conversation while sunning themselves on beach towels. Sophie, Megan, Kat, Tessa, and Kara sat in the sunshine closer to the water, talking and watching their kids play together in the sand. Marc, Nate, Julian, and Kara's husband, Reece, had taken on some of Javier's former Team buddies in a game of beach volleyball—John LeBlanc, Brian Desprez, Chris Ross, and Steve Zimmerman.

"If you're going to call it, Hunter, at least hit the damned ball."

"If your foot hadn't tripped me, Dickangelo, I would have."

"You guys do know how to play this game, right?" Reece asked.

"They probably learned the rules by watching women in bikinis play," Nate said.

John ended the bickering. "You ladies going to talk or play volleyball?"

Meanwhile, Holly sat in her bikini in the shade near the bar holding court with three of Javier's male cousins—while sneaking covert glances at the shirtless SEALs in the volleyball pitch.

Natalie and Zach were nowhere to be seen. She had a good idea where they were. Having been married for almost two years now, they wanted a baby.

Laura glanced out over the waves, saw someone dangling a hundred feet in the air from a parasail that was being towed by a boat. "Oh, God! Is that Gabe up there?"

Javier glanced up. "Looks fun, doesn't it?"

"*Suicidal* is more the word I was looking for."

They settled into their beach chairs. Laura peeled off the short dress she'd worn as a cover-up, the sun warm on her skin, her body feeling languid from a morning of sleeping in, room service, and sex. She pulled a tube of sunscreen out of her beach tote, rubbed it into her exposed skin.

"Sure you don't need help?" Javier watched her, his eyes hidden by sunglasses. "You've got a lot of skin, and I've got two big hands."

"Can you put it on my back?" She turned away from him, drew her hair aside.

"You got it." He took the tube from her, planting a kiss on her neck before he began to rub the cream into her shoulders.

They had arrived in Puerto Rico three days ago amid a whirlwind of nightlong parties and wedding preparations, men from Cobra International Solutions, Javier and Derek's security company, having come to the island two days earlier to make certain the place was secure. Laura had left most of the planning to the resort—one of the best decisions she'd made in this entire process. She'd been able to join in the parties and get to know Javier's parents, siblings, aunts and uncles, cousins, and nieces and nephews, rather than worrying about arrangements. And she'd been able to spend a little bit of each day with Klara, who had just turned three in December.

Many of their friends had flown in for the ceremony, and although some had already returned home, most saw this as their chance to have an all-expenses-paid vacation. True, Laura and Javier had spent a fortune, but it had been important to them to have the ceremony they wanted, one that brought together their far-flung families and friends for a once-in-a-lifetime celebration. They didn't face the future expense of children—no strollers, no braces, no prom, no cars, no college to pay for—so why not make the most of their special day?

And it had been perfect.

The ceremony had been held amid palm trees and tropical flowers atop a cliff overlooking the ocean, far from the prying eyes of the media. Laura had felt at peace, a gentle breeze tugging on her veil as she and Javier had spoken their vows. She would never forget the look in his eyes as he'd slipped the wedding band on her finger—happiness, desire, and enough love to last a lifetime.

The reception had gone on through the night, with music, dancing, drinking, and singing. Laura and Javier had passed out *capias*—little tokens of the wedding that included the date and their names and were an old Puerto Rican tradition—and then sneaked away for a private celebration of their own.

Laura couldn't have asked for a more wonderful wedding—or wedding night.

"You're all greased." Javier finished, handing Laura the sunscreen, and leaned back in his chair.

Laura tucked the tube back in her bag and settled in beside him.

Nearby, Grandma Inga and Mamá Andreína erupted into peals of laughter. They'd been inseparable since the wedding—a true odd couple. Laura's grandmother was tall and spoke not a word of Spanish, and Mamá Andreína was petite and spoke no Swedish. The only thing they had in common was white hair and a tiny bit of conversational English—and the fact that their grandchildren had just gotten married.

"What do you think the two of them are talking about?"

"No clue. Can they even understand each other?"

"Have they been drinking again?"

"Your grandma is a bad influence on mine."

Laura gave a laugh. "It's the other way around. Look at the bottle they've tucked between their chairs. Isn't that Mamá Andreína's *licor de chinas*?"

Javier craned his neck. "What's she doing with that? That shit is illegal, man."

A homemade brew of rum and oranges, it was one of the most delicious liqueurs Laura had ever tasted, but it was strong.

And then Laura saw them.

Stella and Anette appeared first, bounding on foal-like legs across the sand, both wearing their red hair pulled back in ponytails. Klara ran after them on little legs that couldn't quite keep up, the sight of her putting a bittersweet ache in Laura's chest. She wore a little pink tankini, her dark hair drawn back in a long ponytail, a pink sun hat on her head, green plastic sunglasses covering her eyes. She was adorable.

Heidi called to the twins in Swedish, her hands full of beach toys. "Stella! Anette! Wait for your little sister!"

"She's grown so much already."

Javier rested his hand on Laura's. "She's going to be tall like her mother."

Laura watched as the twins turned back for Klara, each of them taking her by one hand and leading her toward the water, Heidi behind them.

"Aw." Javier grinned. "Now that was cute.

"Those girls really do love her."

Javier chuckled. "Look at that poor bastard."

Clearly the family's beast of burden, Erik had appeared dragging a rolling cooler while carrying two beach bags and five folding beach chairs, two for adults and three little ones for the girls. Wearing a blue tropical shirt that he hadn't bothered to button over a green pair of swim trunks, and a pair of loafers on his feet, he reminded Laura of every Swedish father she'd ever seen on the beach—indulgent of his family and not very fashionable.

Laura looked back toward the girls playing in the sand. Klara sat, legs splayed, digging with a plastic shovel and making dubious contributions to a sand castle that her two older sisters had begun. Heidi knelt beside them, a happy smile on her face. She looked up, saw Laura watching, and motioned for her to join them. "Would you girls like your aunt Laura to play with us?"

"Yes!" the twins answered, Stella looking over at Laura and waving.

"You go spend time with that sweet baby girl of yours." Javier sat up, kissed Laura's cheek, then called to Erik. "You look like a man who needs a hand."

"Oh!" Erik laughed, two of the little beach chairs slipping from his fingers. "I suppose I do."

Laura walked across the sand, her pulse picking up as she sat down beside Klara. "What are you all building?"

"A sand castle," the twins answered.

Klara looked up at Laura with guileless blue eyes. Speaking in Swedish, she parroted Anette and Stella. "Sand castle."

Laura met the gaze of the wonderful woman who was raising her child. "Thank you, Heidi, for letting me join in. Thank you for everything."

Nineteen years later
Los Angeles, California

JAVIER STOOD AT the side of the stage, watching as Laura gave the commencement address at Klara's college graduation at USC Annenberg's School of Journalism. Earpiece discreetly in place, he listened as his men checked in with one another. Tower was directing this operation, but Javier had come strapped anyway, body armor and a concealed 9mm beneath his suit jacket. Although it was unlikely that anything would happen today, he wasn't taking chances.

College officials had let slip that Laura would be addressing her goddaughter's graduating class, and the media had picked up on that. One paper had even run a photograph of Klara. Though almost twenty years had gone by since Javier had carried Klara out of Pakistan, there was a possibility, however remote, that someone would put the pieces together. He, Tower, and a team from CIS were there to make sure no one got near her.

And then there was Laura's safety to consider.

Her very presence here had caused a stir. As the face of the nation's top prime-time news program—the network had fired Gary Chapin and brought her on board the moment they'd heard she was interested in returning to broadcast journalism—she was more of a celebrity than she'd ever been, her ordeal a matter of public knowledge. Although there hadn't been a credible threat against her in a decade, the public nature of the event would give anyone who wanted to harm her an opportunity.

But so far, all had been quiet.

"It is true that reporters see both the best and the worst that human beings have to offer. Over time, it gets hard not to be cynical. It will take a lot of integrity on your part to keep your mind and heart open, to see beyond the brokenness and dysfunction of the people you meet, to be that voice for the voiceless."

Javier knew Laura's speech by heart. She'd been nervous about it and had asked him to listen as she'd read it a half dozen times. Javier knew the cause of her nerves wasn't a lack of confidence in her own abilities, but the fact that Klara was in the audience. Their little angel was graduating summa cum laude with a degree in journalism. She'd been inspired by her aunt Laura, whom she looked up to and loved, and despite Laura's suggestion that she follow a new and exciting path that was all her own, Klara had been determined. She wanted to become a reporter.

Journalism was clearly in the girl's DNA. She had already lined up an internship with the *L.A. Times-Sentinel*, and she'd done it without Laura's help. Her excitement for the job reminded him so much of Laura that it scared the shit out of him. So far she hadn't talked about going overseas to work, and for that he was grateful.

He loved the girl, loved her like she was his own daughter.

"Remember that life is not just your career. A career is what you do. It's not who you are. This was a lesson I had to learn the hard way. You'd be surprised how fast your priorities rearrange themselves when there's a knife being held to your throat."

Laura's speech was almost done. Javier could see that her audience was transfixed. He knew what they saw when they looked up at her, because it was what he saw every day—a beautiful woman with a big heart, a courageous survivor, a person who'd been through the worst and had come out stronger and more determined to make a difference in her world.

They saw a hero.

"When you leave this ceremony today, you walk in the footsteps of a dozen generations of American journalists whose job it has been to shine a light into the darkness. They made their mark on the history of our nation. Stand strong, think with your heart, and you will make yours. Congratulations, graduates of the class of 2033."

The audience of students and parents rose as one to its feet, the applause deafening. Onstage, Laura shook the university president's hand and those of several professors, a smile on her face. She took her seat, while the president asked the students to stand, invited them to move their tassels, and pronounced them graduates.

Cheers. Flying beach balls. Mortarboards in the air.

Laura came down the steps, the question in her eyes.

He answered before she could ask. "You nailed it. That was fantastic."

"You think so?"

"Did you miss that standing ovation?"

She smiled. "I didn't want to disappoint Klara."

He saw Klara making her way toward them, a bright smile on her sweet face. "I don't think you did."

"Aunt Laura!" Klara ran up, dressed in her black robe, and threw her arms around Laura. "That was beautiful. I got tears in my eyes."

"Congratulations, sweetheart! I'm so proud of you. We're both so proud of you."

Klara hugged Javier and gave him a kiss on his cheek. "You look so handsome, Uncle Javi. I'm not used to seeing you in a suit. But what's this?"

She punched his body armor lightly, teasing him. She knew what he did for a living, had seen him in body armor more than once.

"That's my toned and muscular body." Javier flexed his bicep. "You think your beautiful aunt would hang around with just any guy?"

Klara laughed, her smile making her look even more like her mother. "Are you coming to dinner with us?"

"Of course!" Laura glanced at her watch. "I want to head back to the hotel and change, but we'll meet you in the hotel lobby in an hour and go together."

"Perfect!" Klara danced off through the crowd, beaming, her long, dark hair spilling down her back.

LAURA STRETCHED OUT beside Javier, bliss still singing through her. Sex was the best way she knew to release stress. "We may be old, but we've still got it."

"Who's old?" He drew her closer, kissed her cheek. "You're a hot and sexy fifty-two, and I'm a badass fifty-eight. Fifty is the new twenty. You think any of those kids at today's graduation has a sex life that comes anywhere near to ours? We're just getting started, *bella*."

Someone knocked on the door. "Aunt Laura? It's Klara."

"Carajo!"

Fighting not to laugh, Laura jumped up, grabbed her bathrobe, and slipped into it, while Javier grabbed his clothes and disappeared into the bathroom. She called toward the door. "Wait just a moment."

When Javier was safely in the bathroom, Laura unlocked and opened the door. She could tell immediately that something was wrong.

"Come in, Klara. What is it?" She instinctively switched to Swedish, but Klara, who was very proud of her fluency, continued in English.

"You did a wonderful job today."

"Thank you." Laura tucked a dark curl behind Klara's ear. "Are you okay?"

Klara nodded, her gaze averted, her expression clearly troubled. She paced the length of the room. "I had a long talk with my parents just now."

"Oh, I see." Laura knew that Erik and Heidi wanted Klara to come home to Sweden rather than staying in the U.S. "Is this about the internship?"

Klara shook her head, her fingers fidgeting with her rings. "I made them promise that when I finished college they would tell me who my real parents were."

Laura felt blood rush from her head, her heart pounding so

deafeningly she didn't know Javier had stepped out of the bathroom until she felt his hand against the small of her back. "What did they say?"

Klara met Laura's gaze, tears in her eyes. "They told me *you* are my mother."

The words sent a jolt through Laura, making it hard to breathe.

"Let's all go sit down." Javier guided her to one of the chairs on the other side of the hotel room. "You need anything—water, coffee, tea?"

Laura shook her head, her gaze fixed on the young woman who sat across from her—her daughter.

So the day had come.

She wished Erik and Heidi had warned her. Despite the self-ish side of her that would have loved Klara to know, she hadn't wanted her girl to be burdened with this. She didn't know what to feel, happiness, worry, and grief tangling inside her.

"Yes, Klara. It's true." Laura reached out, took Klara's hand in hers. "I am your biological mother. What else did they tell you?"

"Everything, I think." Klara shared what Erik and Heidi had told her, and it *was* everything. "They said you gave me up for adoption because you were afraid that bastard Al-Nassar's relatives might come to steal me back."

"There was more to my decision than that." Laura gave Klara's hand a squeeze, fought not to give in to tears. "You were so precious and innocent. I didn't want you to grow up knowing how you'd come into the world. I knew that if I returned to the U.S. with you, the media would figure it out. Not only would Al-Nassar's family know where to find you, but you would grow up with that knowledge in your heart. I didn't want that for you. I can't imagine how painful it has been for you to hear all this now."

Klara's blue eyes were clouded with emotion. "I've hated that man since the day I found out what he'd done to you. It's hard to imagine that he's actually my father."

"Ever since Javier rescued you, you have been surrounded by love. Erik and Heidi loved you so much that the moment I realized I couldn't keep you, they offered to adopt you. Stella and Anette adore you. My mother, your aunt Birgitta, loves you, and although you might not remember much about her, my grandmother loved you, too."

"I remember her." Klara smiled. "She was fun. And Aunt Birgitta is really my grandmother. Wow."

Then a look of realization came over Klara's face. "I always thought all of the security we had when you came to visit was because of what had happened to you. I never understood that part of it was for me. It was, wasn't it?"

Laura nodded. "We all worked as hard as we could to keep your relationship with me and your location secret all these years."

"That's why you have to keep this to yourself." Javier explained the risks to Klara, told her what she could and couldn't do, her eyes wide by the time he finished.

"How do you feel?" Laura asked her.

"I've always loved you and admired you. I went into journalism because of you." Klara's chin quivered. "I'm proud to be your daughter."

She stood, reached for Laura.

And Laura took her daughter into her arms, unable to hold back her tears. "Oh, Klara, *min älskling.*"

Years of fear, grief, heartache seemed to pass through Laura at the pure joy of this moment. She felt Javier behind them, felt his strong hand on her shoulder as he did his best to support them both.

Klara gave a little sniff. "I hate knowing how much you suffered, and that I was a part of that."

Laura drew back, wiped Klara's tears away. "You were never to blame. You were a victim of it the same as I was. From the first moment I saw you for the first time at your parents' house, you've been nothing but a joy for me."

"I'm glad I know." Klara smiled. "I've always wondered why my mother left me. Mom and Dad always said she had given me up because she wanted what was best for me. I always wondered why she didn't try harder to overcome her problems or whether there was something about me she just didn't like. But now I understand. You never really wanted to give me up, did you?"

"No, I didn't." Laura wiped her eyes with a tissue. "But Erik and Heidi have been such wonderful parents. They love you deeply. They let me be a part of your life. They are your true mother and father. I am so grateful to them."

Klara wrinkled her nose. "I hate Al-Nassar even more now."

"He died long ago in a prison cell, alone and broken," Javier said. "Forget him."

Klara looked shyly up at Javier. "When I heard Laura was my mother, I'd hoped you were my father."

Javier drew Klara into his arms and hugged her. "I held you all the way to Stockholm. I'd never seen anything as precious or sweet as you in my life. I've watched you sleep, watched you play, watched you grow up. If you want to believe I'm your bio-dad, hey, that's fine with me."

For a moment there was silence.

Klara looked at both of them, clearly uncertain what to do next. Her world had just shifted on its axis. "I should go back. Mom and Dad will be wondering."

Laura tried to reassure her with a smile. "This must have been very hard for them. Go to them. We'll meet you in the lobby in ten minutes."

Klara turned to go, then looked over her shoulder at them. "I want you both to know I love you."

"We love you, too."

Then she was gone.

Laura took a step, then sank onto the bed, a riot of emotion inside her. "Well . . . that was unexpected."

"I'd say it went well." Javier sat beside her, held her. "Everything turned out just fine in the end. My guess is that it only gets better from here."

Laura looked up at the man she loved, the man who'd been her husband for nineteen wonderful years. "I couldn't have gotten through any of this without you. Through all of it, you've been my support, my anchor. I don't know how one man's shoulders can possibly be so strong."

He kissed her hair. "What is it your mother likes to say?"

"*Kärleken gör oss starka*. Love makes us strong."

He tilted her face up to his. "With the love I feel for you, *bella*, I could lift up the world."